William Venator

is a writer and philosopher living in the UK

To Chris & Derek

All the best

Alex

Wither this Land

William Venator

Published by WritersPrintshop

First published in Great Britain 2003 by Writers Printshop

ISBN 190462300X

Designed by
Rob Oldfield Design Associates

Wither this Land

*is dedicated to all those who are presently
struggling to maintain their freedom, privacy,
dignity, intelligence, creativity and enthusiasm for life
against political incompetence, bureaucratic inanity,
the reverence and arrogance of ignorance,
and the horrors of inverted moralites.*

www.william-venator.com

Contents

"There is no greater cruelty than to take away

a man's liberty"

A British Train Journey

The direction that a man's life takes depends on the ideas he lives by. Some ideas, such as those he daily entertains in his mind, he will own and enjoy as much as if they were old companions leading him along life's curious trails. Others he will encounter and draw into his circle as philosophical foils that may at times remind him of his path's greatness. But sometimes he will encounter ideas that change him, that radically charge him to reconsider his old friends and ways; and in embracing the new company he will make his departure on a surer foot.

But what befalls a man who has no ideas?

Flood brushed an errant long hair from his face. The thought was slowly germinating in his mind; it came unbidden - dimly connected with the faint strands of the week's thinking. He pursued an image: the man without ideas floats; he must be disconnected from the world, which means that he is attracted to those closest to him. Perhaps, another insight fluttered, in the battles that take place for the minds of men, the thoughtless mimic the loudest - they fall in with the crowd and flow with the current, whichever way it flows. They do not really care which direction their lives take.

The thoughts spun in and out of Flood's mind, weaving a web of barely integrated notions as the train rocked its way through the northern countryside. The black windows on his left reflected the carriage's sharp internal details in a grey yellow light. He could tell from the manner in which people alighted that the wind was getting up.

A group of lads had got off two stations before and Flood had observed them, listening to them joke, swear, call their girlfriends, receive text messages, and swig from cans of lager. They had been to a match, he surmised from their tribal colours and general rowdiness. He had held a passing interest in them, as there was not much else to occupy his mind while negotiating a cup of turbulent hot tea. But his thoughts had returned to them when the young men had been replaced by another set at the last station - they too were apparently bound for the pubs of the next town, and they also joked and swore, swigged from cans, wore the same aftershave, received text messages and had been to a game. What were their thoughts? What motivated their existence? he wondered, finishing off the dregs of his cooling tea. He watched and followed their reflections as they stood and paraded in designer clothes. It was early evening, yet the group was drunk and rowdy and ready for a Saturday evening's boisterous bravado. Their behaviour bordered on a slight belligerence that left some passengers disconcerted. But they were so similar to the previous group. So much the same. Did they realise it? If you put them together in a room would they laugh at themselves or be shocked? Did they have any ideas?

Flood was attracted to ideas. He was beginning an acquaintance with some. Not many, and, as he rode the train north, he was increasingly aware of an intellectual deficiency. He felt guilty for not knowing the things he was now reading about, and he knew that he faced a lifetime of learning to catch up. To what level, or by whose standard, he did not know; he just knew he had to catch up.

An older lady sat to his right engrossed in a paper to avoid attracting any unwelcome attention from the noious youths. She was sipping tea and reading in a nonchalantly contrived manner. Flood glanced at her and caught a connection with a world now gone; her short, curly greying hair, and thick woollen cardigan over a pale blue blouse were an echo from decades before his birth. Her attention to dress reflected a bygone era of ... something. He was not sure. Stodginess? Or was it the war again? He had seen many older folk whose clothing was reminiscent of the war and post-war austerity. He wondered if he would look as if he were from an ancient era when he retired. The incomplete description teased his mind. What was it? His inability to arrest the word riled his young mind. She turned and smiled at him, her face wrinkling into lines of confident kindness. Her unfaltering smile represented an etiquette that was out of place in his world - a relic of a lost ethic. He nodded an embarrassed acknowledgement. What was it? He shrugged inwardly and returned to his book.

Answers flowed from the page; new ideas were extolling their Truths with upper-case letters; here insights and the application of abstract ideas were unfolding mysteries, uncovering conspiracies, laying before his mind a clear path to truth and righteousness. The last word flittered from neuron to neuron, prompting its usual self-satisfying glow to the apprentice of enlightenment. Freedom is earned through the Truth, he reasoned, contented with his own intellectualising. And here are Truths setting me free.

Flood's book, given to him by Jez, was about environmental disasters, extinctions, global warming, but especially about animal cruelty and the vicious lies told by governments and media; it extolled the noble campaigns of liberationists and their daring exploits against big business and murderous scientists. It made sense.

"It makes sense," Jez had said. "Just read it. You don't have to read anything else."

But Flood was not the type to read and be satisfied with one book. In his quest to catch up with an imaginary horde of more knowledgeable people all around him, he could not rest with one book. He was too addicted to reading and gathering knowledge to terminate his thoughts with the conclusions of one author.

After absorbing facts and horrific stories for a while, he put away his political reading and fished out his required literature reading for last week. He had taken it to his parents for the weekend but failed to pick it up. The spine's stiffness and the book's new smell shamed him for not having opened it. He thumbed the pages and for a moment enjoyed the irony of his love of environmentalism and his love of the page. Should he atone for the death of the tree? He smiled at the paradox as he descended into Hard Times.

The train stopped again and the two seats opposite him were taken up by a man and woman. They seemed slightly older than Flood but not by much. They had caught the carriage's attention as they got on. Flood heard some insulting phrases mumbled by the youths but could not make out what was said. He looked up as they sat down and then understood. Both were wearing thick woollen green hunting jackets with white stocks. They were waving goodbye through the window at some indiscernible person blurred by the internal lights as the train pulled off.

Flood felt a wave of nervousness pump through his veins. In front of him sat his enemy: the barbaric relic of a savage and brutal past. The enemy of his propaganda personified: hunters. He should confront them. Attack them. Stand up and vilify them and embarrass them with all the Truths that he had learned from Jez and the literature he had been ravenously devouring. The two figures presented the grand vicious abstract that so many hated and lampooned - the cause of animal misery. Killers. Murderers. He watched them arrange themselves and saw them as ignorant medieval peasants whose lack of concern with anything and everything removed any right they could have to live in civilisation.

Except they were a handsome couple. He surreptitiously surveyed the woman. She was very pretty; tight blonde curls framed strikingly sharp features of high cheekbones and high eyebrows. She possessed intense green eyes and a pleasing figure that Flood could tell was extremely fit. He was dark-haired, blue-eyed and athletically built. Flood noted that he was very handsome indeed - the kind of man that women fawn over. The faces of both were red with a recent flush of exertion and fresh air. They had brought the sharp smell of the winter countryside into the carriage momentarily dispersing the carriage's strong diesel odours.

They sat down and both smiled at Flood. He instinctively replied with a brief acknowledgement and turned to his book, criticising himself inwardly for reacting so politely. As he berated himself for not standing on the table and denouncing them to the civilised multitudes, they started conversing and Flood was drawn in to listen. She spoke in soft Edinburgh tones and he betrayed a Midland dialect. They were discussing their friends who had been out hunting with them. Flood tried to return to his book but his awareness was divided.

"We certainly needed our energy to get up those hills," she was saying.

He laughed. "You did today, that's for sure. I covered about a quarter of what you did. You were up and down. Then you disappeared for ages with the followers. You must have covered a lot of mileage. Sugar?"

"Thanks. Puss kept coming my way. Your turn next week."

"I didn't mind where I was, I must say. I had some fabulous views of the hunting."

"She came your way a few times."

"Yeah," he laughed. "Caught me out the once. I'd come down the slope, right to the bottom, thinking the hounds would turn as they had before. But no, they came right past me and headed up the hill. Man, I was scrambling like the clappers to get ahead. I was sure they would head for the road."

"But she turned."

"Quite a relief actually. Did you see Talisman though?"

"When the hounds hit the brush?"

"Yes, silly hound was sniffing around the brook and was a good quarter of mile behind before he caught up."

She was laughing. "Aye - I saw you fall into the ditch! PT saw that too. Oh, we had a laugh. He's a good dog, though; he'll mature well."

"Unless we have to put them down," the man said suddenly with a bitterness that altered his demeanour. Flood looked up for a second from pretending to read. The man had clenched his fist and tightened his lips. He stared at the table.

"We won't. Those bastards in the Commons haven't gone through with it yet. There's still time. And there's still the European Human Rights laws. Or something. Anyway, we'll see the Scottish Act go down first. It's such a shoddy piece of legislation." Flood felt her tension and saw her scowl at the black windows. Should he feel triumphant at their potential demise? No, he didn't - he felt guilty.

"Hmph. I enjoyed your description, Sarah. What did you call them? The National Socialist Parliament of Scotland. Quite right too. Silly buggers know nothing of their own history."

"Or of rights. William Wallace would turn in his grave if he knew a bunch of lowland toffs had sold his nation out once more. It's a bloody history of betrayals up there, but to have a go at hunters, for heaven's sake. Worse than the Sassenachs. No offence, mind."

"None taken. I blame the Normans actually, not the Saxons. Perhaps they wouldn't have attacked them if the Master and Whips wore blue coats instead of red. Anyway, let's cheer up. Talisman turned out to have been in the right place, for when that scent had gone, PT brought him back and, whoosh! The hare bolted, not ten feet away."

She laughed. "Hard day," she sighed stretching her back. "Must get the physio to check that knee of mine again."

"You seemed alright running."

"For the most part. I caught a couple of rabbit holes near a hedge and twisted the knee. I've a brace on it now."

"I wondered where those two hares had gone."

"Bad joke," she rolled her eyes. "Don't start."

They sat quietly for a few moments and he asked, "Do you think we'll need another march?"

"Why? Last time the numbers broke all records. What was the establishment's reaction - pretend it never occurred. The BBC quickly switched stories and gave proportionately more time to three people who turned up to protest than the four hundred thousand that came from all over the land. You can see where its allegiance lies."

"So what direction do we take now?"

Flood wanted to hear her reply. "I'd fight," was all she said. He nodded. They returned to non-political matters and Flood tried to return to reading. Perhaps if he could focus on the story he could ignore the conversation. But their relaxed laughter drew him once more out of his book.

" ... then he said, if you lie down when she's coming towards you, and kick your legs up, she'll go on her hind legs and dance around you!"

Her shoulders convulsed with mirth. "Has he tried it?" she laughed.

"No, course not. He's worried what the Master would say!"

Flood found their laughter at an animal's suffering politically annoying. But his curiosity drew him into it. Again he automatically smiled at the couple who, for a moment, pulled him into their laughter; her green eyes met his and a connection was made into the secret world of hunting. He inwardly flinched, for his innate and driving curiosity demanded to know more. But all his new political knowledge objected. His stomach turned from his mental confusion. The couple continued their chatter and gossip, and Flood sat gazing out at imagined shapes that flittered past the windows.

Ideas, he cogitated ... there must be more ideas that can defend me against ... against my enemies. The term "enemy" sat awkwardly. They were such pleasant people. But how could hunters be pleasant? He grimaced at the rising contradictions and decided to put such thoughts aside till he had read more.

The train was slowing down and the youths were becoming agitated. Some started complaining that they would be late for the clubs and have to wait in line. The old lady turned a page but looked concerned. The train's speed decreased to a gentle amble and their frustration increased.

"See, the Ministry's buggered the trains up as usual," said the hunter. "I guess they couldn't just let the company alone." His companion smiled but she also looked anxious as the youths got louder. Flood watched them. A tension was forming in the air. The youths were becoming increasingly rowdy and Flood wondered why a ticket conductor or some authority figure did not come and calm them down. He wished the train would speed up.

The train stopped.

The carriage fell silent for a few moments. Then the youths began swearing profusely. Flood tried to hide himself in his book. The hunters opposite remained calm but quiet. No one in the carriage spoke except the youths, whose boisterousness now rested on the edge of intimidation and violence.

As always in such situations a spark was all that was needed to transform their anger into physical violence. A tall angry youth of eighteen with a number one haircut, dressed in jeans and an expensive shirt but with no jacket for the cold wintry air, pushed his friend backward, into the hunter. This man, bald, younger and smaller and in a collarless shirt and black jeans fell back and swore at his friend.

The hunter merely said, "Hey, steady," but that got the taller youth's attention and he suddenly became the focal point for his friends. They smiled, relieved that their leader's attention had been directed away from them.

"Who the fuck are you to talk to us like that?" he said vehemently, pulling his smaller companion out of the way and pushing his scowling face into that of the hunter's.

"All I said was that you should be careful," said the hunter staring back at him.

"And what the hell are you?" demanded the man touching his coat. "Fancy dress party, is it? And is this your gay friend going with you?"

"Just leave us alone," said the woman.

"Fuck you. I wasn't talking to you, bitch. Well, answer me! Who the pissing hell are you?" he insisted. His face contorted with streaks of hatred and violence and ignorant disgust. It occurred to Flood that the aggressive man was also frightened and that if he had been alone, he would not have done anything. But the seven or eight friends behind him gave him strength. It was a revelation to Flood but not one to ponder in his present situation. He raised the book to hide him further. The youth was persisting with his questions for the benefit of his snickering friends.

"So why the hell are you dressed up all like this?"

"These are our hunting clothes, something you obviously know nothing about. Now would you please leave us alone?" the man said.

"Hunting fucking clothes? What? You fox hunters or something? Do you kill for pleasure? How would you like it if you were chased by hundreds of toffs like yourself? You're spastics, that's what you are. I hope you die. Die in a ditch with dogs at your throat. That's what you deserve. If I saw you hunting foxes, I'd fucking kill you. You don't deserve to live. Look at you, all posh. Fucking wankers, that's what you are. Fucking wankers. I'll tell you what I'd like to do to you," the youth said, taking a grip on the man's lapel, pushing his face up to his, spitting as he spoke. Flood sat dead still. His heart pounded and his stomach churned. Is this what he himself was supposed to do - confront his enemies and berate them? Flood was embarrassed for the hunters. The fight was not supposed to be like this; it was supposed to be abstract, fought in books and films.

The yob was screaming, "I'll tell you what I'd fucking like to do to you ... "

He did not finish his sentence. From somewhere a stick rapped his head causing him to blink stupidly for a minute. The old woman was standing just behind Flood, her stick poised in the air. The youth swirled and snarled at the woman squealing a string of obscenities at her as he rubbed his head. Flood caught sight of a couple of his friends standing behind the bemused yob. They stood open-mouthed, paling at the woman's audacity and at its implications.

She spoke calmly and with an authority that caught the man's attention. "Any more language like that, young man, and you'll receive another smack."

The yob recoiled, aware of his situation. "What the fuck?" he screamed at the woman and prepared to lunge a fist at her. She promptly flicked the stick sharply, catching the side of his head causing him to lose his balance. He retreated as a quick second blow smashed the other side of his head. He paused and was shaking his head to regain his balance when a deftly aimed thrust smacked into the middle of his forehead, knocking him back into his friends. Flood watched her amazed. She possessed a certain heftiness and strength, but her moves were finely tuned and delicate. Flood wondered if she knew t'ai chi or some martial art. Kendo perhaps. He sat frozen to the seat, wishing he was not there, knowing that he could never have the temerity to stand up to such yobs himself. He watched the woman in admiration but also in fear that she would be over-whelmed by the youths, whose bewilderment was turning into vehement anger.

"I have never heard such foul language, and I will never let any such as you treat anybody like that. Now sit down," she commanded the whole group. All of them momentarily fell back into their seats. She held the stick ahead of her with one hand like a fencer. A younger, smaller youth with a short blond-dyed Mohican attempted to grab it, but she twisted it from his reach and, drawing a blurred arc, brought the wood back down onto his wrist with a dull crack. The youth shouted in pain. "And I won't have any language like that from you," she said tapping his head hard. He fell back into his seat, tears welling in his eyes.

The leader meanwhile had regained some composure and angrily thrusting away a friend's helping hand raised his hands to protect his head. With blood trickling down one side of his face, he began his next assault. It was stopped short by three sharp blows to his head and arms.

"I told you to sit down, you spineless, moronic, warthog, and pathetic excuse for an Englishman," the woman said calmly, emphasising her words. Then she changed her voice from that of a commanding headmistress to the voice of a lecturer slowly explicating her reasons. She raised her voice to catch everybody's attention. "We all know that if you were alone that you'd not have caused this trouble." She spoke into his angry wide eyes. "We all know that deep down you are a coward. You are a pathetic man, who has no sense of decency, no values, only a flimsy reputation to sustain in front of an anaemic gang of empty minds. How brave! Well, one step further and you'll lose that silly reputation forever, for your so-called friends will see you disarmed and beaten by a lady three times your age. How will you live that down, young man?" Flood could not believe that she was actually taunting the youth. Her voice remained factual, but each word hit home harder than her stick, for they sank into the yob's very being, and she knew what she was doing. His face reddened, his mind realising the truth in some of the things she said.

"You are scum," she added, "you're not fit to live or die for your country. I've seen more courage and bravery than you could ever imagine. You," she emphasised, "are a nothing, an embarrassment to this country and to all we've fought for."

It was too much: the man lunged. His reputation screamed out into the carriage. On he came - a flailing, drunken bull tossing his head, spitting fury at his enemy, heels digging into the floor to maintain a statuesque heroism in front of his gang, thrusting his hands out in an uncoordinated plan to strangle the woman. Her next move surprised Flood, who expected her stick to dance all over his head, leaving him to sit back in a cartoon-faced stupor, seeing stars. Instead, she twisted around and smoothly sat back into a seat as the youth flew past her, his momentum taking him past Flood's table. He tripped over the outstretched hunter's foot and fell on his face. The woman stood back up again and turning to the youth's friends rapped a couple nearest to her on the head causing them to sit. As she turned back to face her immediate threat the hunter had arisen.

"Keep your eye on them, I'll look after this one," he said. The youth had caught his balance on the armrest next to Flood. Flood had remained immobile watching the entire scene with a sense of unreality. He had been hit two or three times in his life, but had never had the moral strength to hit back or even to defend himself. The fear those situations had produced over-whelmed him now; the embarrassment of not standing up for himself underpinned his anxiety and fear. He had remained seated as the woman had stood up to accost the youths, and he remained seated now as the hunter stood up to deal with the isolated leader. A swift left jab to the nose stopped the bungling youth from getting up and a right hook floored him. The yob fell back next to Flood's seat, unsuccessfully reaching out for the arm rest as he fell. He lay there motionless, his body and reputation floored.

"Well done," said the old lady guarding the pack.

"Well, thank you," said the hunter. "Liam Johnson," he offered his hand. "I wasn't really in a position to defend myself before."

"No, these kind of idiots don't let you," she said, sharply rapping a pockmarked teenager on the head. "Pleased to meet you, I'm an avid hunter, you know. Beatrice Major. And you are?" She shook hands with Liam's companion who introduced herself as Sarah Campbell. Then she turned back to the youths. "Sit down, you ungrateful brutes. Gosh, don't your parents teach you manners? No. This is what becomes of a nation that pampers its people with a diet of welfare and ignorance. How's the idiot you knocked out?"

Flood surveyed the man. "He's awake. But I don't think he wants to get up," he reported. Blood trickled from his nose and from a head wound. His eyes were open and Flood saw tears begin to ooze from the corners. The hunter's companion had also stood up and was sitting on the table, her back to Flood, keeping an eye on the others. She had pulled out a whip from her jacket and held it calmly. For a moment, Flood caught a glimpse of an old Scottish warrior's tenacity in the face of danger. The woman appeared relaxed but her eyes, scanning the sitting yobs, expressed the experience and sharpness of battle.

The older woman laughed. "Yes, these unruly pups certainly need a couple of whippers-in!"

One stood up and began swearing and pointing at the three defenders as if he were on the terraces taunting the referee. "You're fucking out of order, you lot are. We know our rights - we'll have you. We'll fucking have you!" Sarah suddenly unleashed her arm and the tip of her whip caught the man on the cheek, leaving a thick red line as blood rushed to the surface. "Fucking cretin! You could have had my eye out!" he squealed and tried to clamber over the table to grab the retreating whip. Beatrice Major swung the stick onto his collarbone, causing him to miss his balance and to fall awkwardly onto his mate; Sarah sent the whip's tip at his right ear and drew blood.

"We'll have no more bad language," said Beatrice Major tapping her cane into her left hand like a prison warden. "I cannot abide swearing."

The youths sat sulkily, a few of them rubbing their smarting heads and open cuts. The two women oversaw them. The leader lay crying quietly to himself, oblivious of his gang and of their discomfort. His flattened position had unleashed a strange sense of relief, which, intermingled with the pain, had breached his aggression and rendered him helpless. He was aware of being guarded, but he had no intention of rising. The dirt and rubbery smell of the carriage floor cushioned him and gave him a solid comfort that he could not provide himself. He lay immobile and without will.

Flood sat taking in the scene, motionless and almost without will himself.

"Well, boys," said Beatrice Major addressing them all. "I suggest that you now get off the train."

"What the fuck? No fucking way. We're in the middle of nowhere," said one to her right.

"You should have thought about that before you began picking fights. Do we have to put up with your behaviour? Should we get off because you are louts? Next time you'll reconsider, I'm sure. Now, I'll give you five seconds to move yourselves to the nearest exit. You know that." The youths slowly rose and made their way grumbling to the doors. Their leader lay guarded by Liam. The first youth hesitated, glanced back at his floored mate, but a sharp comment from the old lady ushered them all out. She watched the last one out. The strong gust closed the door on them. "Now you," she said turning to their leader. "You can get out the other side. Come on, up you get, and no funny business."

He rose with difficulty, his drunkenness or concussion now apparent. "Off you go, to the right," she said, following him to the doors. He jumped out and fell, yelling with pain, into the dark. "Mm, probably an embankment. Twisted ankle hope-fully. Never mind. He'll learn to look before he jumps next time." She shut the door and returned to the carriage. A couple of other passengers stood up and congratulated her but expressed concern that she might get into trouble with the police.

"The police? Would they have done anything if we had reported their harassing behaviour?" She was astonished. "No, never mind. Anyway, these boys won't be going to the police. Too embarrassing for their little reputations." She returned to her seat as the train began moving and chatted to the two hunters, who had joined her.

Flood tried to get into his book to remove himself from the extraordinary situation he had witnessed, but he could not read a single word. No conductor had come along the carriage, and when the train finally pulled into the busy Northchester station, there were no police sirens or flashing lights to greet them. He got off, buttoned his coat up and, bracing himself against the howling winds, walked to his hall of residence, confused and shaken.

Laurenten

Lord Douglas Laurenten, laird of the forty-thousand-acre estate of Inverlochty in the northwest Highlands, sauntered up from the stream, his black-coated retriever, Wellesley, scampering ahead of him. He breathed in the cool air and savoured the moist, slightly saline, westerly wind. Throughout his life he had lived by the ideals of virtuous stoicism. He saw life as an unending series of challenges to overcome but also to enjoy. His philosophy was that nothing was beyond his ability, and that retirement was something to enjoy when dead. An absence of challenges would be the absence of life, he had always thought. He paused and scanned the hillside. But this impending legal challenge and the battle's utter pointlessness exhaused him. It was so thoroughly unnecessary and downright immoral to his mind. He was a man of tradition as much as of adventure, but the obstacles that politicians constantly put in his way were beginning to frustrate him. He had considered selling the ancestral lands and moving to America. He twisted his mouth to restrain the curse words that sat ready upon his tongue. One option remained though. It had grown in his mind for several years. Perhaps now was the opportune moment.

"We'll get them back, Doug," said his puffing companion, breaking the silence as he caught up. "They've taken lands from us before and we've always got them back." He referred to the Expropriation Proclamation passing through the Scottish Parliament that proposed to redistribute land from the large landowners to croft farmers and non-profitable, EU and government sponsored agencies.

"Aye," said Laurenten returning to the present problems. "But it will take a heck of a lot more this time."

"But the appeal process?"

"What? Appeal the state's processes through the state's judiciary? Bah! They'll just rubberstamp what that Parliament passes to give themselves and their friends credence. Most lawyers believe that Parliament creates the law and they can prohibit whatever takes their fancy. Just you wait, they'll demand state funding for their parties next. Worthless parasites."

"We'll challenge the Abolition of Hunting Act in Rome."

Laurenten laughed. "You mean The Hague? But a poignant slip, my friend. It does look like history's repeating itself. But I hold nothing for Europe. Just a bigger version of the Scottish Parliament - more corruption, more waste, and more power."

"Aye, but challenge it wherever they'll listen."

"Authorities don't listen any more, John, because they don't have any standard by which to judge anything. They are pragmatists - and that means they are dangerous. That's the nature of our so-called democracy. No limits on mob rule, which means lobby rule. Meanwhile the bureaucracies increase their power. It's a sham," he said, almost spitting the last words out.

"So another's march is out?"

"The last one symbolised a people's belief in tolerance and liberty. It reminded Westminster that there are those in the land who do not wish to live by its dictates. There won't be another one like that."

"Aye, but the bloody opinion polls have not shifted much, Doug."

"If you ask people whether they thought share options should be prohibited they'd agree.

Stewart shook his head. "I don't know about that, Doug. People would say they don't know enough about them."

"So why can't they be similarly honest when it comes to fox-hunting? They see some trumped up photos published by hunt saboteurs and think they know everything they need to know about hunting. The arrogance of people's ignorance is astounding, these days. It should be called the Age of Ignorance."

The two men pushed their way up the gentle muddy slope, through the dying bracken and stumps of heather: Laurenten, five foot eight, with dark thinning hair atop a square face with hardened blue eyes and a thin, straight mouth that rarely parted for breath as he moved; his heavy woollen jacket barely disguised his fifty-five-year-old sturdy frame as his thighs pumped and his right hand powered his long staff forward like a piston, propelling him up the slope. His older companion was seventy-eight-year-old John Stewart, the owner of substantial lands to the north; he had been Laurenten's mentor in all matters of farming, fishing, stalking, hunting, and, of course, politics. Thin and long in face, he sported a long scar on one cheek, from "Burma", as he said with an air of finality that permitted no further questioning. He had kept his thick hair but its red had faded to white, and his sparkling blue eyes, framed by bushy eyebrows, had softened to grey with the years. He fell back slightly as Laurenten thrust up the slope without pause. At the top Laurenten paused for his friend to catch up. They stopped and regarded the winding river gurgling alongside the forest edge below the otherwise stark and craggy hillside. The autumnal frosty breeze raked their skin.

"But what if nobody will listen, John?"

"I'm an old man, an old fool, my wife says. But I'll be with you. In whatever capacity," he added smirking. "It may be time to convene the Assembly."

"That would stir up the land. It has occurred to me, John. Come, let's get some warmth into these bones, Cosima was expecting us back before now."

They trudged on through failing light back to the grey stone manse. The two men were caught in their own thoughts. Stewart was often taciturn, but it was rare to see Laurenten frowning. His scowl reflected a disdain for how the land had turned, but it also represented an uncommon intensity of thought that preceded a momentous choice.

Wellesley ran on as they approached the house and was greeted by the family's old border collie who gently ambled out to greet the company.

"Ah, Wallace, what would your ancestor say to all this nonsense?" said Stewart bending down to give the dog a ruffle.

"Fight them, of course," said Laurenten, softening his expression at the dog's approach. "There are limits to a man's patience."

"Any fighting, include me in," said the young woman emerging from the high-gabled porch to greet her father. She smiled broadly from a soft white face framed by long black curls caught in a ponytail that fell over the lapel of a long equestrian wax jacket. Her thick cream Arran sweater was covered in dark dog hairs and her long coat opened in the wind as she bent down to stroke Wellesley.

"Aye. Just like your great-great grandmother Elisa," Laurenten kissed his daughter.

"Elizabeth knew her rights, father, and was prepared to take a stand. I'm ready, as you know. I'm half sick of shadows," she smiled coyly.

"Been reading poetry again," noted Laurenten as an aside to his friend. Stewart nodded sagely. The three entered the house as the dogs played in the garden.

"Time, my love, time," Laurenten was saying as he strode over to his favourite chair, took out his pipe, and settled himself. For a long while he remained silently frowning at the world, while Stewart and Cosima discussed the impending land redistribution. The loss of income would affect the family, and several jobs on the estate would perish, but the sense of betrayal overrode the monetary considerations. The men would be found other employment, at least temporarily. Some would have to move south though. Stewart breathed sharply whenever he mentioned MSPs. Cosima retorted if that was the way they wanted it, then they shouldn't be surprised when the talented and rich left the land for the south, or for America.

"Bloody irony, that would be," hissed Stewart. "The socialists have often whimpered and whinged about the highland clearances. But all their bloody communal property is poorly managed, of course. Poachers and pollution, that's all it's good for. We've sunk thousands into our lands, and look what they've done, 'such a bunch of rogues.' 'We will drain our dearest veins, but we shall be free!'" he mused, mixing up his Burns poems as was his wont. "It's not as if they'll be richer for it though. Poorer. Poorer in spirit and in purse."

"It's happening south of the border too, Mr Stewart," said Cosima, pouring them each a glass of sherry. "For the past few years the government has been mapping the land to give freedom to roam to any Tom, Dick, or Harry. Our property in Northchestershire shall be mapped soon, so I hear. I have arranged to make it difficult for them," she smiled.

"Cuch?" The name of their favourite Irish wolfhound brought Laurenten from his sombre thoughts.

"Yes," she laughed, passing the sherry. "And other pleasantries. I'm thinking of arranging a pheasant shoot on the appointed day, with a few cursing celebrities who are also similarly affected."

"I heard what you did when English Heritage came around, missy," Stewart glinted.

"They'll be back though. But my God, to have your house photographed and loaded onto the web! The terms 'privacy' and 'landowners' rights' have certainly been eroded."

"Destroyed, my dear," said Laurenten. "Violated and negated as if they did not mean anything."

"Aye, but what hurts is that most people don't give a damn," said Stewart.

"That's only because they don't know. Or don't realise," countered Cosima sitting down. "Analogies don't often work though," she added leaning back into the wide, soft chair. "Townies live on top of each other. Privacy doesn't mean much to them. So they think photographing a country house is no big deal. Or having access to our paddocks and fields should be a town-dweller's right. They enjoy peering into others' lives. Look at their television programmes. Privacy is not a value amongst the urban proletariat. They enjoy displaying themselves and exposing their neighbours to mockery and mischief. It's probably also because their houses are all the same," she concluded, chuckling at her own cultural audacity.

"She's off," said her father shaking his head. "You do generalise, Cosi. There are people who live around here who think they should have a right to traipse wherever they will, and I do know many city folk who are disgusted with the government's rural proposals."

"But it feels like it's us-versus-them," countered Cosima folding her arms.

"That's because you're idealistic, young girl. Life's more complex than that. Life's battle-lines are rarely Manichean, especially when it comes to political issues."

"Too right," added Stewart in agreement. "But this is no time for philosophising. We've lost too much in the past few years."

"At such times, philosophy becomes more important, John. Anyway, the problems have been around for a long time." Laurenten finally got his pipe lit. He enjoyed several puffs before continuing. "Since the farming community was given subsidies and special protection, it was only time before our freedoms were whittled away and lost. Money from the state is always followed by chains. Always is. I'm just surprised it's taken this long in coming." He shook his head. "Such a loss though, I still cannot fathom it. Who would've thought that having got through the forties and fifties they'd still want to take our lands and rights?"

"You'll get the land back," said Stewart rising from his chair. "I must be going. You will get the land back."

"At what cost?" inquired his friend from the comfort of his chair.

"Should fighting for liberty have a cost?" asked Cosima.

"Cosima, everything has a cost," said her father sharply, partly in response to some of his own thoughts and their grave ramifications. "But you are right to remind us of the context."

"Aye, Wallace would have agreed," added Stewart.

"Looks like Wallace wants to come in," said Laurenten getting up.

"Come on, boy," Cosima called opening the door to a bouncing Wellesley and plodding Wallace.

"A grand pair they would have been too," said Stewart fussing both dogs. "Do you think they'd have been friends?"

"Two great generals will always be cantankerous friends," said Laurenten. "They'll never agree on anything but that the enemy is to be defeated. Mind how you go, John, there are bloody socialists and bureaucrats everywhere. They'll be banning haggis and bagpipes next!" Laurenten called after him.

As Stewart drove off, Cosima turned to her father. "You're thinking about it, aren't you?"

"It's high time we all did. Perhaps we should have done something earlier."

She frowned. "The timing is never right or wrong, father, only created."

"You're sounding like your mother now, my girl," he laughed and squeezing her to his side. "Well, she's right, and you're right. Ah, I do miss her. Come, let us talk some more. I have much to arrange over the next few days."

Hickling

Earlier, Peter Hickling spotted four hunt protestors outside the Palace of Westminster and headed in their direction. He knew the area well from business trips but this was his first political trip. He paused momentarily, the soft rain dampening his face as he examined Big Ben. The clock took on a different symbolic meaning, he thought. No longer was it simply a convenient timepiece - now it represented an impending oppression. At thirty-five, for the first time he felt properly focused. He was good at his job and well remunerated, but it paled in comparison with this political protest. Lately, he had come to see himself as a cog in a machine, an interesting machine certainly, and a cog with much latitude, but still as a cog working for the benefit of others. But joining a protest kindled, or rekindled, a latent desire to connect more to life. A phrase he had read somewhere flittered through his mind. Only connect. He took in a deep breath. In many respects he hoped that the protests would continue, and that he would get more involved in the campaign.

He crossed over to the protestors. "Hello!" he said cheerily. They held makeshift banners announcing their allegiance to the cause. "Is this it?" His sincere face disarmed their fears of possible rudeness.

"Thus far," said one woman, seemed more like a librarian than a hunter. "We were told that people would be arriving around eleven."

It was ten-thirty. Peter read the signs: HANDS-OFF HUNTING!! and WHAT ABOUT OUR HOUNDS? The protestors were complaining that the Rural Alliance had underplayed the importance of the day's indicative vote on hunting. Peter suddenly felt demoralised. He had driven seven hours from northern Lindthorpeshire for this. He was a hunt follower of only recent standing, but had become so addicted to the thrill of the chase that he spent much of his spare time following the hounds. His girlfriend, Liz, had joined in not long after and both of their lives had been turned around. From watching the local football team sink down the league, spending evenings in front of the television watching incessant repeats and increasingly banal and humourless comedies, and the drudgery of a fifty to sixty hour week in offices and commuting, both of them had turned to embrace the exhilaration of cantering across the wide fens in pursuit of the fox. The television went, as did the football season tickets. They now spoke of opening up their own public relations and consultancy partnership. The hunt's exhilaration had awakened Peter's mind to a sense of his own reality and the superficiality of modern life in a generic new housing estate appended to a small town. The hunt had woken both of them to the thrill of risk as well as introducing them to the most interesting company they had ever met.

Neither had travelled to the previous marches, though these had, they noticed, created a strong bond among their hunting friends they had promised to go on the next one. Peter had left Liz at three in the morning; her company had insisted she travel to Leeds for a marketing meeting that day.

Liz had made him coffee as he showered. "Give them hell," she said as he left. "I don't want my Saturdays criminalised." He had smiled. They were both quiet and, up till then, unassuming but capable, upwardly mobile middle-Englanders, whose only passion in life had been Lindthorpe City scoring goals.

"Many more expected?" Peter inquired looking around for hopeful signs of hordes of placards. The rain dripped off his flat cap onto his jacket.

A bearded man next to him spoke of his disappointment with the Rural Alliance, saying how at a local meeting they had requested people not to go. "I mean," he said, "it's not as if those people will be out a job. I bloody well will be, though. And me. I used to be a Labour supporter. Who'd've thought they'd turn on their own supporters?"

"Who are you with?"

"Shooting club. I don't personally go fox-hunting. But we all know, we're next. We know. It's all we talk about at the club. Been shooting all me life, since I was a nipper. These idiots," he cast a thumb at the Gothic façade behind him, "don't even know 'ow to put on a pair a wellies, never mind the difference between cow and sheep."

"I'm new to hunting, but it's so addictive. It's become the cornerstone of our life," Peter related.

"You're not the only one," said the pale faced woman holding the other placard. "I used to be a primary school teacher. An old friend took me beagling, and it's cost me my job."

"They fired you because you hunt?" Peter asked.

"Not quite. I resigned. I used to read Horse and Hound and The Field in the staff room and challenge any of the idiots to come up with a reason why hounds shouldn't hunt. They couldn't. But I was overlooked for a couple of promotions, cold-shouldered, generally ignored by the thoroughly PC head-mistress, who wouldn't allow spontaneous games or teaching without forms in triplicate. So I handed in my notice, and now I'm happily working for myself teaching children privately. All my pupils have been beagling too - I take them out on a Saturday for a couple of hours to see what it's like. Some parents join in and love it. Now, this bunch of idiots - met their type before in the staff room. Typical lefties, oh, sorry, no offence," she said to the bearded man.

"None taken, miss, I've left that party. I won't ever be voting for them turncoats."

Peter excused himself to fetch a coffee and returned to find that the numbers had increased substantially. A hundred or more people were shunted by the police across to Parliament Square. Others were steadily coming up from the Westminster tube station and from along Whitehall. Some slowly shuffled across the road advertising their banners to bewildered motorists. Peter spoke to the whipper-in of a fell pack, and his girlfriend who had skipped a day off school to protest. Her teachers had complained, but the girl insisted that her livelihood was at stake and that the teachers knew nothing of her way of life. They chatted for a while, drinking coffee and munching home-made sandwiches, when a noise interrupted their conversation. It was a rasping, metallic, rhythmic yelling.

"Antis," someone said.

Peter peered over to the other side of the square. There were twenty or so black-clad people, holding up placards, yelling and screaming. Some were blowing whistles while one woman screamed unintelligibly into a megaphone. It reminded Peter of film footage of the Nazis tramping through the streets of Germany or of Mosley's blackshirts. He commented so to an older man standing next to him.

"Indeed," replied the man, "it's the same mentality. Same empty souls that would join any protest against something they don't understand. Rather than sort their own miserable lives out. They'd join the Communists or the Nazis - any extremist group really, because they can't understand life or the need to let others live and let live."

Peter nodded. "Do you farm?"

"Yes. I'm from a farming family. Midland-based. We've farmed the same lands for six hundred years or so, and hunted over them. Those people don't understand that we need to practise conservation in order to have a healthy farmland, which involves game keeping, hunting, fishing, and the cutting down of diseased or overgrown timber. What do you do?"

Peter explained that he hunted in northern Lindthorpeshire and that he had only been hunting for a year.

"No matter. What's important is that you are here. Thank you for coming."

"Do you think they'll ban hunting?"

"Can't say. But we in the county will not put up with it. My family's descended from the medieval Kingmakers, the Nevilles, and before that from William the Conqueror. Tradition's important to us. So, we're not likely to give up rights that we've held for centuries. Anyway, we're ready to break the law. I don't believe the Commons knows what hatred and frustration it's stirring up in the countryside. Will you be with us?"

"My girlfriend and I have talked about it a lot. We'll help where we can. We'll continue to hunt."

"Good man. We need the numbers. Problem is," said the man, "rumour has it that the government will charge the farmers with the responsibility for what happens on their lands. So, if we hunt, they will pay. And you know what they've been through recently. Talk about kicking a downed man," he added bitterly. "Bastards."

"If only there was a way that we could hold politicians responsible for the bloody mess they make of our land," said Peter.

The older man turned to him. "Oh, there is, my dear man. There is."

The rain came down harder. Several put up umbrellas and turned up their collars.

"Well, this'll keep the antis away," Peter observed. "This is more our kind of weather!"

His comment caught a few ears and people laughed. "True, true," said a woman behind him. "Look - there are some antis already fleeing for shelter."

Another man carrying a placard that said Laisser-faire, laisser-chasser, which Peter liked, suddenly pointed out. "Look at those idiots over there. Dressed up for a children's party!"

Three people wearing animal suits skipped across the road: a badger, a fox, and something indiscernible. They waved to the antis and met up with an MP for a photo-shoot.

"That's Thomas Waterside," someone said spotting the most virulently anti-hunting MP. "He's in the pay of animal rights organisations. We've written many times, inviting him to come out with us, but he can't be arsed. It would damage his reputation with the eco-left."

"And his pay-packet," said someone else bitterly.

The photo-shoot prompted protesters' horns, whistles and hunting calls. "Tally-ho! Hoick! Hoick! At 'em Valiant!" shouted one man, producing a good laugh from the protestors. The police manning the barriers stood nervously scanning the crowd, but since the protestors remained where they were, respecting the flimsy barrier of the law, they soon relaxed. Some enjoyed the jokes made at the MP's expense. The jeering got louder as the MP tried to make a speech.

"Why don't you come and hunt with us instead of watching cartoons?" shouted one woman next to Peter.

"You fascist bastard!" shouted another in a red boiler suit. "Cromwell!!" shouted another, followed by "Hitler!!"

The crowd had moved slightly and Peter found himself standing next to a new companion. "Why Hitler?" Peter inquired. She was a pretty, slim, young woman with curly red hair falling underneath a green and blue tartan hat with an upturned brim; she was equipped with thick brown corduroys and walking boots, a Barnborough woollen jacket, and a scarf wrapped around her neck. She held a large umbrella and politely extended it over Peter's head. "Thanks," he said.

"Hitler banned hunting with packs of dogs," she explained.

"You're kidding!"

"No. He hated the aristocracy. What we need is a few posters in London explaining that. A picture of Hitler with a banner: 'This man banned hunting with hounds.' That's all it'd take. But the Rural Alliance is too timid, I guess."

"Shame! That would certainly turn a lot of people from supporting the antis, I'd imagine. My God! Hitler banned hunting. Extraordinary. Yes, they should use that information. The impact would be shocking but effective."

"I agree," she said. "We tried it on our campus a few weeks back and the posters were torn down overnight. I guess the antis don't want to be reminded of their bed-fellows."

"Peter Hickling," he extended a hand.

"Gemma Lawrence."

"What are you studying?"

"I'm reading philosophy at Northchester."

"I studied economics there! Which college are you in?" They chatted for a while, exchanging stories about the drab architecture and legends concerning undergraduates eating ducks.

"How do they take to you at Northchester?"

"You mean my views on hunting? Well, I used to keep them close to my chest, but since they're thinking of banning it, I've come out the closet, as it were. I've found I enjoy winding up students in tutorials."

He laughed. "I used to do the same over privatising anything that moved."

"Sound," she replied. "Should the universities go private too?"

"Most certainly! Hardly a week goes by without some politician getting involved in Oxford's application procedures. With their name and funding they could just go it alone. And they should." They chatted about the state of education and of liberalisation. Until the hunting issue had come up, Peter had almost forgotten that he had been a radical at Northchester, but had calmed down a lot once he had begun work. His old ideas and the corresponding youthful energy were rushing back to him.

Gemma saw an old hunting friend and bade Peter a good day.

The crowd moved again and Peter made his way over to a familiar face. "Peter!" she said sidling up to him. The rain was coming down heavily. Patricia Forbes, the bottle-blonde ex-show jumper, who mingled with the rich and famous of three continents, and who, along with having had four incredibly wealthy husbands, controlled one of the largest race horse stud farms in Lindthorpeshire. She was also treasurer of Peter's local hunt. She took his arm in hers. "Peter, darling, glad you could make it. Not many of our bunch could get down today. Still, we're here. Now, the word is that at two, we storm the barricades and stop the traffic. Jolly exciting."

"Really?" Peter's mind whirred. This would be it, the first act of civil disobedience. And he would be a part of it.

"Really. The old folk want us to amble across the road slowly and obey the law like good little children, but most of us will stop in the road, that's for sure. We'll annoy the traffic for a while."

"Is this the beginning then?"

"We haven't started yet, dear boy. This will be a mere warning. The word's going round the counties. Beacons on the hills, more great marches. By then our campaigns should have worn down the government. It could get nasty, but what the hell, we're talking about our lives and rights."

"Liz and I are fully behind you. Count us in."

"It could get problematic, you know," Patricia added.

"We're ready. We know how complacent this nation has become. I mean, we're standing under Churchill's statue. This is not the time for pussyfooting around." Peter was still tapping into that old vein of undergraduate righteousness. The energy of opposition and the delight of argument surged again; fourteen years of paying the mortgage, watching the local team, commitment to the bank, steadily on the path to a safe and quiet retirement - all had held his politics in check. He scrutinised the crowd. The people appeared very law-abiding, he thought, but their faces indicated an incipient willingness to fight for their rights.

"This is what life is about!" he muttered.

"Glad you agree. Very glad. We'll be needing all the help we can get."

"Patricia, it's been a long time!" It was the man Peter had talked to earlier.

She let go of Peter's arm to plant a quick kiss on the man's cheek. "Do you know Peter?" she asked.

"We spoke a few minutes ago," said Peter.

"Ah, well let me introduce the two of you. Peter Hickling this is Colonel Arthur Stowington. Colonel, Peter Hickling."

The two men shook hands and the three chatted about the prospect of the Commons rejecting the anti-hunt bill. Periodically the protestors cheered or jeered various notables entering the Palace. The crowd laughed when one recent Cabinet resigné tripped on a loose paving stone. Peter watched the clock slowly move towards two. At the appointed moment the protestors, howled, shouted, jeered, whistled and tooted horns. Two, then three, then four and more pushed down the barricades and the police rushed in to stop them.

"Don't let the police arrest them!" Peter shouted. "Keep moving," he urged the people around him. "Keep moving! The more of us there are, the less chance they have of arresting anybody! Come on! This is a lawful protest!" He surprised himself with his audacity, but it worked. More and more joined those who had pushed through and who were now sitting down in front of the traffic. The police gave up and withdrew to observe. Peter saw a policeman filming them. He waved as the camera panned around, "Hey! We're on camera. What is this - a police state?" Caught up in the initial rush he felt the power of the crowd's determined stance. The traffic remained at a standstill and began to back up. "Imagine what we could do with a couple of combine harvesters!" he said to no one in particular, but Patricia Forbes replied.

"Oh dear boy, no, what we really want is a couple of muck-spreaders to remind London of its rural roots."

Then a familiar voice to his right caught his attention. "Giving them hell, I see." He turned and saw Liz reaching out for his hand. "I couldn't not come, I was ... " He stopped her with a kiss.

Cosima

Cosima and her father talked for several hours after Mr Stewart had left. She watched her father intently as he spoke. He was slowly but definitely beginning to bear a greater weight on his shoulders, and while her youthful energy spurred him on, she watched him with a concern for his health. He had once retired from the forays and skirmishes of political life, but it was increasingly obvious that he would have to play a new role in the land's politics.

She made strong coffee and put out some cheese and biscuits. As they sat in the kitchen eating, drinking, and discussing matters, she allowed him to use her as a sounding board. It was his usual way of mulling over important decisions. Ever since her mother had died when she was eight, she had listened to her father's musings. As a child, she knew that it did not matter whether she understood him or not, but she knew that he needed her as a sounding board whenever he was working on a major decision.

During Cosima's childhood, Laurenten had been active in local and then national politics after his army service, but he had retired from politics ten years back, to spend time with his growing children and to manage the family properties. Although independently wealthy since birth, he knew that the properties and lands had to be managed otherwise they would quickly slip from his ownership. The failure of many British landowners to adapt to the times had left them impecunious, especially after the First and then the Second World War had taken their toll on tax rates. From childhood, he had been trained to work with his inheritance, just as Cosima and her brother, Jeremy, the elder of the two, had been educated in the family concerns from an early age. They had also been made to work with their hands, as labourers or tractor drivers, whatever the task needed. But they had also received an excellent education from home tutors, their father's friends, and from a vast family library. They grew up without the airs normally associated with a privileged background. Their father had drilled into them that the privilege of wealth or power was never permanent, and while the former had to be managed well or it was soon lost, power rested on reputation, and that came, he argued, not only from managing their resources but also from ensuring they were never dishonest or surrendered their principles. He had left Parliament because it required him to bend his principles to avoid the whip's displeasure.

"Avoid the displeasure of the whips!" he was often heard mumbling to himself around the house for months after resigning. "The Laurentens work for themselves," he said to those closer to him. "A man must always work for himself, or he loses his identity. I certainly cannot be losing my identity when it's a fine rare thing to have. But they don't understand that."

He said the same again to Cosima now. She had heard them often enough, but only now were their graver implications beginning to unfold.

"It's not just my identity." He was thinking aloud as he poured another cup from the cafétière. "It's this whole country's future that's at stake."

Cosima sat back into the chair, pulling her feet up to the rung. She sipped on her coffee watching her father intently. As she had grown older she knew she was expected to listen and to contribute as she began to understand more of the things he spoke of. He in turn came to appreciate her input, especially when Jeremy left for Oxford. On graduating, Jeremy had worked for a year in investments before using his experience in the family enterprises and properties, permitting his father to relax more. With Jeremy away, Cosima had to shoulder her father's process of decision-making. Today's ruminations and their implications were revolutionary. She offered sympathetic comments but what her father was thinking of invoking needed a wider audience.

"I know what you're thinking, young girl. You wish your brother were here too. Don't worry, he's had his fair share of this over the phone. He's fully apprised of all this, up till now anyway."

"So you are decided then?"

"No. Well, not quite. Jeremy's assessing support from various parties, let's say. He keeps me abreast of the Cabinet's intentions as well as the Rural Alliance's and other countryside associations. Useful connections he has. More than I had when I was his age."

"It's more in his nature, Dad. Not really mine, I must say."

"No. We all have our talents, but I know you could do what he does, if you had too. But I'm not sure he could play or write as well as you do."

"True, the boy's got no rhythm. But he writes well. I've read a couple of his opinions in the financial sections of the Scotsman and the FT."

"Didn't tell me about those," said Laurenten rising from the table. "I need to nip to the privy. Coffee irritates my bladder."

"Daddy!"

"Ah, girl. Just bodily functions. Now, why don't you put some of that salmon on some bread and butter and bring it through to the living room. We can relax there."

She put together some strips of oak smoked salmon on thickly cut white bread with a thin layer of butter and a smear of Russian mustard, poured a couple of Laphroaigs and found her father sitting back in his chair, his feet up on the foot stool. He was thumbing through a book on salmon fishing.

"Appropriate," she said spreading the snack out over the coffee table.

"Mmm? Oh yes. One can always learn something from old authors, you know. I'd forgotten I'd got this one. Well, now, where were we?"

That was something, Cosima thought picking up her own plate and sitting down on the sofa. Usually he would say, "Where was I?"

"I do agree with you, my dear, that most people are too non-plussed to care. Too ill-educated perhaps."

"A century of socialised education is bound to affect how people perceive their own freedoms. It was inevitable that they could not comprehend what freedom entailed if they were spoon-fed from the cradle to the grave."

"True, true. You know your political philosophy well. But surely, I am not wrong in thinking that freedom cannot have lost all of its meaning to the people of our countries?" He put his book down.

"Complacency, then," she rejoined, chewing on her salmon. "Too many good things. If people are warm, clothed, fed well, have a reasonably satisfying range of entertainments, what more could they wish for? Why fight for freedom when all is provided - yes, sufficiently by the market place, but what a turn out. The system that requires freedom to flourish has done its job so successfully in feeding and housing most people, that they can now relax into thinking they don't need it."

"Well. There is that aspect, I agree. But it's more. And it's the more that I need to consider. If the state's power rests on habitual obedience, what will it take for them to remove that obedience and to strike a new contract as it were? I can't see people manning the barricades for freedom these days. They're too bothered about how well Rangers or United does, but those kinds of people were always with us, I guess, and always will be."

"Slaves."

He knew where her comment came from - the many in-depth conversations she and Jeremy had had over the kitchen table with their father, their great-uncle Toby MacIntyre and John Stewart.

"Slaves - in attitude, yes." It was his usual response. She was more critical than him of people who worked themselves to the bone or into depression for others. He agreed with the sentiment but his experience suggested that the issue was more complex. "After all," he would conclude against his Uncle Toby, "we all work for others in some respect or another - you for your whisky customers, and me for my tenants and sportsman who wish to shoot and hunt on my lands." The argument at that point would often turn to the question of whom Toby MacIntyre was working for. Toby insisted that he distilled his whisky for himself. "But others buy it!" Laurenten would retort. "Only because I choose to sell it to them! I don't give it away you know!" Toby would reply. And so the debate continued. Neither gave way and in turn Jeremy took up his father's point of view and Cosima her Great-Uncle Toby's. His was more interesting, she thought.

"But slaves, or complacent voters I should say, will follow strong leaders," she added.

"Yes. Or rather, they will follow strong ideals."

"Dad, they don't care about ideals. It's not their way. The masses are swayed by the latest pop idol and not much more. They'd get on, get drunk, have children, and die, whatever the system will be."

"You're shifting your ground there, Cosi."

"No I'm not. Well, maybe I am. I've been in the schools again recently and I'm not impressed by the potential or lack of it. There's just no moral fibre in most kids. They don't look for ideals or morals. Religion's a non-starter for them. Thinking requires too much effort. They get by. That's it. But offer them a strong leader and then they will follow. They won't care what they're following, just that they have someone to look up to."

"My goodness, you've become a little Hobbesian recently."

She laughed. "Too much time with teenagers I guess."

"Yes, that would do it. I agree with you. Mostly I do. Not fully. Don't forget that the pupils you see are there by law; you'd act in a similar manner if you were forced into a government school for your formative years. You'd rebel in your own way - theirs just happens to be by shutting their intelligence off. But, there's still that irksome area I'm not sure about. If we go ahead with reconvening the old republican Assembly, we'll eventually need the majority's support."

"You need the support of the majority of the shakers and movers. Once you've got those, the rest will follow. I've learned that from the history books, dad, and you must have learned it from experience."

"Yes." He sat up and reached over for his whisky. "Laphroaig. Ah. Good. None of that MacIntyre stuff for me, heh, heh. Too sharp for my tongue."

He wanted to lighten the mood slightly, but his idealistic daughter continued to pursue the threads of the argument. "So how many shakers and movers do you have on your side? Is that what Jeremy's working on?"

"Aye, he is. As well as others. We should have a good majority who'd support us on hunting and land rights, but as for re-establishing the entire commonweal, well, we're not sure."

"The country's going downhill though. It's becoming increasingly obvious every day."

She was impatient for change, he noted. But is the rest of the kingdom? "It's been in worse positions. I mean, consider what happened in the '50s and the '70s."

"But then the rule of law was still respected by most folk. Today, because of the state's encroachments the law's not respected. I read in the paper today of an Asian businessman who was beaten up by sixteen-year-olds. He'd warned the police many times about being targeted, and even arrested a couple himself. But have the police helped? No. Did they arrest the thugs, even though they'd been caught on his security cameras? No. Completely useless."

"Cosi, lawlessness doesn't entail a desire to re-establish a commonwealth."

"Dad!" she fired at him exasperatedly. "The riots and law-lessness are symptoms of malaise. People are rioting. We've had race riots. Then there are the fuel protests. And the number of strikes are increasing, even the police have been out."

"Race riots are minor issues. They soon clear up."

"Symptomatic of a general break down in the law though. And trust between people."

"Mmm. Perhaps. And the fuel protests are rather low key these days."

"But the Rural Alliance marches have not been. Three hundred thousand last year in London. A hundred thousand in Edinburgh. There's a protest today outside of Westminster. Now there's a movement! You even know Harrison - get on his back! He only needs a prodding and he'd be with you. What have they got to lose but the chains imposed on them by the politicians?"

"True. True." He scrutinised his daughter. She was certainly idealistic, as most well-educated young people were. He saw himself in Cosima, and her mother; then he saw a family tradition of rebellion and smiled. "I'm growing old though, Cosi. I've seen action, you know that. As we grow old we don't wish to put our children through what we went through, but I'm aware that your grandfather, who fought in the last War, felt the same, as did your great-grandfather. They did their bit, saw things they couldn't speak about, shut their mouths, and got on with life. In reflective old age, we look back and realise that those things did not have to be - the suffering and deaths. We want a peaceful world for our children, but of course, our children are what we were once like. My father explained that to me before we did the Northern Ireland tour. It was his way of saying he loved me. Hah. Presbyterian through and through."

Cosima relaxed into the sofa. She did not wish to stop her father from these thoughts. She could tell he was making his decision to set the Assembly into motion, but she was also fascinated by the opening up of thoughts he had not touched on in her presence before.

He sipped his whisky. "I remember his face. We were out shooting over the glen. He fired and then lowered his gun as Nelson ran to get the pheasant. He turned and said those words to me. He never looked at me. Except at the end. We stood for moment, silent. Nelson pounding his way back to us with the bird in his mouth. Then he looked me in the eye and said, "Just don't do anything rash, my boy. You've got too much of me in you." That was it. The father-son talk. Hah. I miss the old goat, but what a dour man he was. Hah, hah! I told your mother what he'd said and we hooted for ages. God, I'm glad he never told me about sex. But he was right. Still is. Hmm." He sipped again coughing slightly as the fire water felt its way down. "Where were we? Ah, yes. You're where I should be. Young, fiery, strong headed. Impetuous, yes that's the word. Idealistic. Ready to fight. I'm old. Retired. Semi-expired. Hah. But then again, I've fought for other people to gain freedom for their sons and daughters. Now it's the time I need to fight for my own. Well, Cosi, the night's not getting earlier.

Time for bed." His face lightened and the creases fell from his forehead. He got up and stretched.

"Dad. Have you made your mind up then?"

"I need more information. I'm not alone in this decision, you know that. Don't rush me. I'm not sure. Look, you have your concert Friday, we'll put this matter to rest for the moment. We can't make any kind of decision without more information."

Cosima watched him get up. He rose with a determination that settled her thoughts somewhat. He has chosen, she thought to herself, he just needs confirmation.

She got up, kissed him goodnight and retired to her own room. She jotted down a few notes in her diary about her father's musings and, going over several of their past meetings, noted that he was certainly on the verge of recalling the Assembly. His mind had been slowly moving in that direction for six months. At least that was when he first mentioned the word in conversation with Jeremy and herself.

She opened up her laptop and finished a brief a defence of hunting for a horse magazine, proofread it and emailed it off to the editor as the landing clock struck one. She showered and jumped into bed with her score. Within minutes and with only a few bars read her eyes closed.

Flood

Flood meandered into town.

In the cool autumnal gloaming, crowds of hovering youthful faces queued for the clubs in expectation of hedonism and escape. He gazed at passing faces and scantily clad bodies shivering outside of renovated warehouses. He wondered what kind of life such people led and whether they had good conversations, whether they knew a good conversation or not, whether they just got drunk and got laid because that was all they knew, or whether they were the ones living life properly while he was some outcast. Was he strange for feeling no attraction to the drumming electronic beat that his peer group succumbed to.

For weeks his mind had whirred with questions, and he was dimly aware of becoming more self-critical, especially after the incident on the train.

He paused for a few moments, listening to a busker play the harmonica. The man was always there, day and evening. He sat in a wheelchair, one-legged, cap in front of him, playing tunes from television series and other popular ditties to Northchester. For a moment, Flood did not realise that he was staring at the man. The music had caught his attention and he had turned to listen, but now he realised he held the awkward status of the busker's audience, and without anyone else around he felt obliged to contribute. He fished around in a pocket and pulled out some loose change. He dropped it in the man's box.

"Thanks," said the busker, pausing before the next refrain.

"No problem," replied Flood and shuffled away, embarrassed.

He crossed the square reflecting on the persistent notion that ideas make a man. The notion had swum around in his head for weeks. He could apply it to characters in a novel, to understand and analyse their actions, but he found it hard applying the same analysis to himself. His ideas were a complicated jungle of third-hand, confused and contradictory values that had surrounded his life. Although he was not sure he could put it into such words, he was increasingly aware of how superficial or inconsistent some of his beliefs were.

He stopped to peer into a music store. To his mind, everything was disconnected: periodically world events struck home political realities, but his scrambling mind could not make sense of such horrors as September 11th, the perennial violence and suicide attacks in the Middle East, impending war in the Gulf, the growing discontent, or was it apathy, in his own nation, or even the fight he had witnessed on the train. He felt overwhelmed by what he needed to know and understand. He was constantly attempting to resolve what he knew of life into ideas, patterns, and comprehensible structures.

He perused the intricate mechanism of a saxophone resting behind a music stand. He knew he was different from his fellow student friends and from his parents. His parents were neither here nor there, neither atheists nor religious, neither ambitious nor indolent, neither bright nor unintelligent. They were half there in the way many people were today, he thought, turning to glimpse a girl who was spilling both over and from under her halter top, a metallic pin glinting in her navel. Flood was not a great one for style but then, nor were his peers. As a teenager he had followed the majority, except in the upper sixth, where he had picked up a more radical set of friends who wore black and ex-army clothes, and who introduced him to bewailing the cruelties of man. He was in all respects a product of his generation - of the thoughtful or sensitive element anyway, which in turn was a product of the previous generation. His generation, he was slowly realising, provided little innovation or enterprise. It was not a rebellious generation X, for it had no values to grasp, or to deny, that it did not learn from the media or from a watered down education. It was not a lost generation either, for it had never had a place from which it could be lost. His peers were nihilistic but, unlike the highly charged minds of the inter-war years who embraced nihilism, they did not know it. The media, which hammered the young minds into amorphous shapes, was now full of the previous generation's sons and daughters, whose sense of humour and taste were mired in spouting inanities and sardonic, flattening comments to gain a reciprocal sarcastic smile or deadening laugh. He had come to realise that his generation learned from celebrities, news campaigns, adverts, and pop groups, who were merely parroting the previous generation's ideas and relying on well-worn phrases, intermingled with ejaculatory, breathy exclamations and swear words, to shock.

The underlying pathetic sense of his generation frustrated Flood. It was this growing sense of frustration that teased him with questions. He had always imagined that there must be more to life. He sometimes allowed the feeling of unease to seep over him leaving him disconnected with his friends and their culture. He did not need a job at university, for his parents supported him well, and he felt that middle-class guilt that many in his position have felt when they watch others work for a living. Campus guilt drew him, as it did with many others, into socialist politics, and rather than get a job to "see what work was like", he and those of his friends who read books preferred to pontificate about the coming ecologically sound revolution that would abolish work and pollution, and thereby - although it was unspoken - alleviate their guilt.

He strolled past smooth, metallic café-bars in which late workers and students sat smoking and drinking. Northchester, which he had come to two years before, offered a pleasant and intricate city to explore, and a society at the university offered rambles in the countryside. He had joined the Conservation Society, where he found a similar group of people to those of his sixth form days, who were cultivating revolution and reform in the environment and in animal rights by digging ditches, mending fences, and devising publicity leaflets. He enjoyed the work, yet the membership's nature nagged him. One weekend he helped secure barbed wire around a local farm, and he was not sure whether that could be called conservation. What was more irksome was that none of the others considered what they were doing. They followed their orders eager to "'do something'" for the environment in what he suspected was an expiation of their middle-class angst.

Through connections in both societies he fell in with the secretive Animal Rights Society on the campus and thereby met Jez. Flood was tall, dark-haired, brown-eyed and possessed a strong jaw with a goatee beard and high cheekbones that made him very attractive to women of all ages. Yet he had not felt comfortable dating the girls he had grown up with. Although he was often approached by interested women, he was too shy to follow through. Jez would not let him go, though: she almost took him by the scruff to ply him with her whims and enjoy him.

Jez was a hard-core activist. She possessed no qualms either about social mores or personal ethics. She spoke her mind, but her mind possessed little subtlety or intelligence. It exhausted its potential in her first year, for she often parroted the theories and sound bites of others, sometimes, Flood had noted, passing them off as her own. At first Flood believed that he had met an intellectual giant, then he demoted her to an intellectual equal. Now, the more he listened, he realised that she was not as bright as she tried to make herself out to be. But she slept with him and he enjoyed that - to some extent.

He caught his image in the window and saw himself drifting along with his generation, unattached to anything useful or good, like flotsam in a harbour, protected by the great walls of traditions, but so unconnected with anything real that should it leave its harbour it would find itself in fearful danger. He watched several people amble by in the window's reflection and spotted a CCTV camera positioned near a pub; he smiled laconically at whoever was watching him. He continued his odyssey.

The rebels he had fallen in with impressed him with their direction and purpose. At least they could espouse truths and had the moral momentum for a truly revolutionary crusade. They sought Eden, they disclosed cruelty, they acted on their thoughts, they wrote, argued, debated, marched, shouted, and sabotaged hunts.

The small caucus that Jez drew him into was even more committed. He found people who were the society's prime movers, and their energy was infectious. He had met a few of them before at the society committees that dragged on until the less committed disappeared or were too drunk and incoherent to take part except to raise hands. Jez kept Flood there, and he listened, contributed a little, and generally imbibed the atmosphere of the revolutionary vanguard over cigarettes and wine, but avoided the drugs.

He was eagerly anticipating some informal conversation with the academic activist, Dr Bernard Peterson. However, despite some excitement, his doubts remained. They exuded activism and a revolutionary energy to turn the world upside down. Yet he was not convinced about something. They were like Jez - a bit flighty, permissive, unattached to anything except their cause; perhaps the cause was just a fleeting outburst for some of them before they faded away or moved onto something more fashionable or expected. Something was telling him that this was not wholesome. But there was nothing in his culture to fall back on, no rock to cling to.

Jez had waltzed into his life, taken him by the hand, showed him her body, waltzed out, then come back, and again and again. There was a pattern to her meandering he knew, but he himself had nothing of value to reject her with, no ground from which to assert his own personality. He let things be and let her slip into his life when she needed him. He floated with the flotsam too but he was getting nauseated.

For a few weeks Jez had been urging him to join in a proper sab. "The time's coming," she had said, "we're almost there, we need to get more people on our side, need more people like you." And so she droned on until he agreed. He had protested against various companies' animal policies, and he had manned the society's booth both on campus and in town, seeking new recruits. Several had signed up the last time he had promoted the society in town, but again he had a persistent nagging sense of unease concerning their characters.

His mobile rang with a text message from Jez, telling him to meet her near the bus depot. He was on his way and did not have to change his direction. It was not far from Dr Peterson's house.

From a distance he spotted her standing near a shelter, smoking a cigarette. She was short, wide-faced, had cropped, coloured hair, dark eye shadow surrounding narrow eyes, and wore a fake leather jacket over a thin T-shirt, short skirt and high boots comforting thick stocky thighs. She was not the image of a student that Flood had carried with him in his sixth form days, but then again, nor were most students at the university. They struck him as too much like cast-offs from some soap opera rather than maladjusted geniuses forever bent over books, murmuring about deontology or post-modernism. Campus conversations were low-level for the most part, not dissimilar to the generic conversation to be heard in any pub, home, or football ground.

He took a deep breath as he approached Jez, preparing for anything she might say.

"Hi gorgeous," she said dissolving any lingering concerns with

a long kiss to his lips.

"Hiya," he replied, momentarily freeing himself from his doubts to once more flow with Jez into her world.

"Ready for the meet?"

"Sure, you lead the way."

She did. "How were your parents?"

"Fine. Usual. There was a fight on the train."

"Oh. Peterson's got something up his sleeve about tonight, you know," she said.

The students had already gathered in Bernard Peterson's flat and had settled down to their cigarettes and booze. The low distant thumping of the nearby nightclub beat a persistent rhythm into the room, soon superseded by an indescribable noise put on by a baseball-capped youth. Peterson was coming out of the kitchen when Jez and Flood entered. He always reminded Flood of a hobbit, with his receding but overgrown curly brown hair on a head that was slightly too large for his weak shoulders. His hair was manic, as were his clothes, which, although from an earlier decade, fitted in strangely well with the cocktail of the students' styles. He bent his head forward at all times in the traditional academic pose. Bad posture, Flood had also thought; and he was decidedly too pale. He smiled often at people, but Flood could not work out whether that was from short-sightedness or genuine benevolence, for his small eyes topped by bushy eyebrows were set back and he often squinted.

"Hi, Jez," shouted the youth over the thumping music, adjusting his baseball cap to see her.

"Andy, turn it down a bit!" said Peterson, offering a six-pack of beer to a group of seated students. They were dressed in an assortment of green army surplus gear, miscellaneous black attire, had a variety of coloured hairstyles, and had machine-gunned any loose skin with studs and rings. One of them mumbled thanks and split the cans between his uncommunicative colleagues.

A sharp-eyed girl with shoulder-length streaked blonde and brown hair came from the kitchen carrying two recently delivered pizzas on plates. "Get stuck in," she was saying, "one's tofu veggie with chillies, the other's tofu without." The taciturn committee, swigging their lager, simultaneously dived their hands into the pizzas. She went over to Jez. "Hi, Jez. Is this your squeeze?"

"Yeah, call him Flood."

"Cool, hi Flood. I'm Kylie, or Kite, as in the bird, not the toy. Why Flood?"

Jez giggled and grabbed his hips, "Oh, 'cos he starts weeping any time he sees an animal hurt on the telly. So sweet!" She gave Flood a tight squeeze around the waist. He was taller than her and skinnier; Jez was not slim, but not yet plump, though on her way to a permanent chubbiness that no end of aerobics or diets would abolish.

"Sweet," echoed Kite.

"Yeah, he's such a softy, aren't you, Flood?" said Jez giving him a hug that caused him to cough. He shrugged sheepishly.

"He's kinda cute," said Kite, her light green eyes measuring him up over her short, sharp nose. Jez darkened slightly. "How long's he been a member?"

"Not long. He joined a few months back at the Club Mart. S'when we met too. I was on the stand and offered to take him out for a beer." And then she quietly added into Kite's ear, "Yeah, got him laid that night." They both giggled and Kite feasted her eyes on Flood's groin. Flood's face reddened perceptibly. Nobody looked over except Peterson, who came over to say hello, told Flood to help himself to beer, and took the bag of three six-packs that Flood and Jez had bought.

"Is he ready for a sab?" asked Kite.

"Sure he is. Anyone who cries at Lassie Come Home is up for it," Jez laughed. "Nah, he's ready, alright. He gets so annoyed and frustrated at the bastards - farmers, hunters, fisherman, he hates the lot. Should hear him swear and shout at the telly. Hey, Andy, turn that down a bit, we're talking."

"No problem, Jez," came the reply, "I didn't think it was that loud." The unkempt and bedraggled youth got up from the floor next to the speakers. "Is this the main lay?"

"Yeah, Flood, this is Andy, or Rat, as he likes to be known," said Jez.

Flood presented a hand, but withdrew it, noticing Rat had turned away to grab a remaining piece of pizza. Rat's mobile phone went off and he entertained himself with replying to a text message.

Peterson reappeared from the kitchen carrying a bowl of crisps and a couple of bottles of cheap whisky. "Here you are. Help yourself." One of the sitting students grabbed a bottle and unscrewed off the cap, discarding it on the floor. "Cheers, mate," she said. At least Flood believed it was a she, though a second and longer glance made him sceptical.

Rat let out a shout. He had finished messaging and had picked up a paper and was reading the middle pages. "Bastards! Bloody bastards. Did you see that lab got more funding. Bloody tossers. We'll get them. Look who it is, the Morley Bank. There's one next to HMV. I'll take a shit outside the door on the way home tonight."

"We'll discuss that one later," said Peterson munching on some crisps. "More beer anyone? Jez has brought a few more six-packs. Good stuff too, Heineken." A long-haired man with the physique of a runner bean nodded approval and got up to help himself. Rat farted loudly, causing a couple of the females sitting on the couch to giggle. "Flood, you want a beer?" Peterson asked.

Jez was talking on her mobile. "Maggie, hi. You coming up or not? Peterson says he's got someone coming over later for us to meet ... You gotta be here ... Aw c'mon. Forget exams, you can revise in the morning ... Deff it, you'll do well ... Yeah, and bring some booze." She switched off and turned to Flood, "Brown Owl's coming. Bernie," she asked, "who's this you got coming over?"

"A surprise, my dear," replied Peterson.

Peterson had been a political science lecturer at the university for a decade and had entertained many students in his flat. He was proud of his left-wing credentials and often related stories to bored politics students of picketing with the miners or of being caught up in a riot, "Yeah, bloody good days. Pigs got such a battering. All part of the class struggle." Talk of class and of the Thatcher years had not garnered him much sympathy in the last few years' batches of students who had hung around him in the university bars. The rights of animals had superseded the rights of the proletariat, and the class struggle had become the species' struggle. He understood that a new proletariat had evolved and he slipped into his teachings that the new environmentalist movement was just another phase of capitalism's inevitable downfall. "The green nail in the gold coffin," he quipped, but none understood the reference.

Sometimes, and only to a select group of half-understanding students and after several pints, Peterson had intimated that he had seen the writing on the wall for old socialism and had been quick to sort out new followers in the student body amongst the greens, something about the critical point in the dialectic between various voices in societies, something to do with money and business, inclusion and revolution. Peterson would explain how he had adapted to the new language and how he had set up a course at the university on "Marginality and the New Politics", which gave him the flexibility to push his students to read Marx whilst superficially appeasing the greens and feminists, chatting a few of them up, or at least those who had not gone the "full hog", as he put it, and become political lesbians and general misanthropes cropping their hair and assuming the aesthetics and demeanour of cornered warthogs.

"Maggie's coming?" asked Flood seeking inclusion into the group.

"Yeah, she's coming. She's got some bloody test tomorrow she's studying for. Such a prissy. She'll end up mortgaged with children in three years the way she's going."

"Didn't know she had a boyfriend," replied Flood.

"She don't. But you know, she's that mumsy type."

Rat had wandered closer and interjected, "Yeah, that's right, fucking kids. Western society's doomed. Nike's brainwashing them anyway. Overpopulation and global warming - too many eating McDonalds. People have gotta stop having kids. Everyone knows we need to ... you know ... we need to ... "

"Reduce the population?" finished Jez.

"Yeah," said Rat getting animated again. "Destroys the bloody environment dunnit?" A couple of dreadlocks fell into his eyes, causing him to blink exaggeratedly as he spoke. "Live in harmony. We'd be much better off," he belched, "ooh, that was good. John Lennon eat your heart out." He sat down again and picked up another paper that lay on the floor. "Fuck, look at this toff." He showed Flood and Jez a picture of a business-man. "I'd like to smash his stupid face. Look at him! Arggghhhh!" he screamed, shoving his face into the photo-graph. "Cretin. Look, says this wanker here gave the bloody Tories millions. Scum. You're scum!" he shouted at the photograph. The man smiled back, unperturbed by the verbal abuse. "What a fascist!"

"Who's that, Andy?" asked Peterson attempting to calm the agitated youth. through some discourse.

"John ... Cart-hill," Rat replied, pronouncing the name with an endeavour worthy of the Elephant Man. "Says he made his fortune himself. Yeah right, exploiting the poor and bloody polluting the environment, you wanker." He punched the paper down onto the floor in disgust. Flood's eye caught the headlines. Fuel-strikers had disrupted the depots again and

- 48 -

further petrol shortages were expected following OPEC's oil embargo on the USA. He picked it up and read the article as Peterson attempted to explain things to Rat.

"Carthill? He's the man who sold his chain of butcher shops off to Sainsburys in the mid '80s." Peterson's reference to the decade would have normally gone unnoticed except he mentioned the word "butcher", which caused an animated conversation among the people on the chairs and couches about when they became vegans and how much hassle they had all experienced with their parents. "An old London Eastender, I think," continued Peterson to Jez and Flood who were the only ones paying attention to him.

"Yeah, I set the tape," said Jez to Kite.

"Butchers are all bastards," continued Rat, on his own path again. "I'd like to butcher him. How'd he like it? Tosser. Hung upside down and your throat cut, half-electrocuted and half dead, half hanging there. Pull his eyes out and rip his heart out. God, it makes you mad, dunnit?"

"Well, the recent foot-and-mouth epidemic may be a mixed blessing, with people not eating meat and stuff," said Kite.

"Yeah, but the bastards murdered like six million cattle," replied the runner bean. "That's a form of genocide, like. You know?"

"One day, there'll be no enslavement," said a voice from the couch.

Jez nodded swiftly and turned to Flood. "Get me a lager, would you?"

Flood put the paper down and stepped over some out-stretched legs to the kitchen. He opened the fridge door. Not much in there except his Heinekens and some cheeses. "You're not a vegan?" he asked Peterson who had followed him in to grab himself a beer.

"No, my doctor said I need the calcium. What do you expect if you're the product of thousands of years of class oppression when the starving masses were forced to eat from the beasts of the earth and their products? It will take a few generations to relieve us of the dependency that victimises some of us. The history of all hitherto existing society is the history of species exploitation, of dog eat dog, and man eat beef, and it'll take a revolution to put the proletariat, I mean animals on their rightful podium of rights and moral status."

"I don't mind a bit of cheese every now and again," replied Flood quietly. Peterson's quips confused him, so he thought he would keep to what he could understand.

"Help yourself, but eat it in here. The others - those on the couch - are full vegans and are likely to subject you to a lecture for a couple of hours."

Flood smiled and broke off a piece of cheese. "Thanks."

"No need to thank," replied Peterson, "thanks is an ingratiating symbol of obedience to the patriarchs and capitalists. Just enjoy. Everything will be free, come the revolution. Then thanks will disappear along with all other bourgeois polities and pleasantries. No more 'one slice of ham, please, Mr Butcher,'" he laughed to himself.

"What do you think about the petrol protests?"

"All part of the inevitable death throes of capitalism, and its ecologically unsound management of the world's resources. I hope it spreads and stops people getting to their cosy offices, so they will have to work at home or in their small community instead. Any protest is good by definition."

"What about the Rural Alliance protests?"

"Uh? Oh, those don't count."

Flood frowned at the contradiction but considered it wiser to return to environmentally sound topics. "Do you believe economising on petrol will lead to better methods of farming?"

"Uh? Oh, yeah, because farmers will have to revert to selling local produce to local people."

Flood saw an image of horses and carts but then considered that most animal rights activists would demean man's exploitation of horses. He pictured African women carrying pots on their heads to markets several miles from their homes. He smiled at the potential incongruity with modern life and mumbled that he had to take Jez her beer. He found Jez messing around with the jingles on her mobile phone and talking to Kite again.

"He seems nice," Kite was saying.

"Yeah, got him well trained, 'aven't I? Such a puppy."

"Is he coming out with us next time?"

"Yeah. We'll have to get him sorted with stuff though. He's got a balaclava but that's about it so far. I'll see what Bernie can lend him."

"Here you go," said Flood passing a can. Jez pulled the tab back and took a swig.

"Are you up for sabbing?" Kite gazed up into Flood's eyes with a broad smile as Jez was gulping her lager down.

"Course I am. It's about time all barbaric practices were ended."

"Course," replied Jez letting out a gaseous belch towards Flood. "You should hear him. He says he wants to get right in the middle of a bunch of fascist hunters and," she started to giggle, "then he'll," more laughter, "moon them!" She bursts out into giggles. "And on his bum, he'll 'ave written 'F' on one cheek and 'FF' on the other. So when he bends down," she crumpled up in laughter, "it'll spell F-OFF!" Her laughter had drawn the attention of the parked students who joined in with low-intensity giggles. "F-OFF! Brilliant. Bloody ace. Hahhh," she crumpled up again. "The bloody ace of spades - good job he ain't queer!!" Some enjoyed the joke but a couple of the sexually ambivalent frowned at the apparent shift to political incorrectness. "Hey, Bernie," Jez shouted to change the topic, "do you have any stuff for Flood?"

"Uh, not really. Maybe a whistle and a scarf. Not much else. We're low on funds for capital expenses at the moment. Still, things may change tonight."

"Who are you expecting?" Jez asked.

"Someone," Peterson replied sitting down in between some legs to feast on the crisps.

"Why doesn't he write 'Fuck off' on his arse?" asked Rat as the remaining giggles evaporated.

"Oh, Andy," said Jez, "'cos that's what it means. F-OFF, geddit? His anus, oh, I give up."

"Human life is so crap," said a student suddenly causing one or two heads to look towards the hitherto unconsidered body on the sofa.

"Yeah, complete shit," replied the pathetically sombre genderless entity. "I mean, I wish I were not here, I mean, you know, I would take up less space, you know, and I mean, I would not harm anything, like. I may be harming some carpet bugs right now, I hate that, like." It did not move at all but merely stated the opinion before belching.

Rat joined in. "You two ready to really fuck some people up then? We could all take a dump outside the bank tonight. Hah! Hah! Hah!"

Neal, whom Flood knew from the literary theory class, scowled. "What about some real action though? I mean, when are we going to really get someone and do them in good?"

"We will, just wait and see," said Rat. "Things may be happening as we speak," he added laughing and baring his teeth like his pseudonym.

"Andy, I mean Rat, has already got a record for positive action against speciesism. Be patient and he'll show you the ropes." Peterson looked up from scrutinising the undisclosed-gender entity. "Jez, did I hear Maggie's coming?"

"Yeah, she'll be here soon, her room's not far. Flood, we could do with some more beer by the looks of it, fancy going and getting some, there's a darl."

"Sure," replied Flood meekly. "I've got a tenner left. I won't be long."

Rural Alliance

Peter Hickling sat patiently thumbing through country mag-azines while Liz readied herself. He watched the clock knowing that she would cut it fine. "How are you doing, love?" he inquired gently. She could not find any black tights, a common problem. He made a mental note to buy a dozen pairs and place a couple in each car and the others with the First Aid box in the kitchen. "I'll get the car started, we'll pick some up from the supermarket." he added to gently push her on.

"I'll be down shortly."

Ten minutes, he calculated, leaving the house. He unlocked the Saab and saw a note stuck underneath his rear windscreen wiper. He unrolled it, thinking it was a flyer. It was a sheet of plain A4 folded into three and Peter paled as he read it. Hearing Liz shutting the door, he quickly shoved it into a jacket pocket.

"You look gorgeous!" he said giving her a peck on the cheek.

"Thank you. Handsome yourself, too. I've done well for time, haven't I? And I found an extra pair of black tights in my brief-case." She had put on a long black coat with a thin lapel of mink, which her mother had given to her but which she had not felt comfortable wearing. But a Rural Alliance fund-raising event was the perfect venue to wear it, she had said. Underneath Peter spotted a figure-hugging black velvet dress, accompanied by opaque tights and slight heels. Her soft, curly blonde hair was held up in a low bow at the back of her head and she had trailed several curls down either side of her face. Peter held the door open for her and enjoyed the sight of her pulling her shapely thighs into the car.

"May I ravish you later?"

"Promise?" she smiled up at him coquettishly.

"Promise!" He closed the door, whistling a low note of appreciation.

They set off, listening to classical music and then to the news. Violence in the Middle East was intensifying. The US was building up its naval forces in the Gulf. "What's new?"

mumbled Peter. More suicide bombers. Sacred Christian sites had become battlegrounds. "Hmm. Time for a new crusade." Petrol prices were going up by another five pence and the Chancellor was hinting at further tax increases.

"In the face of all those protests?" Liz asked. "Goodness, something will have to give there." Several UK casualties in Afghanistan. US action in Somalia and Iraq. Crime figures were reaching record rates in London and unemployment was beginning to rise. Strikes in the Post Office and on the railways. A cluster of deaths at a hospital, a national lack of teachers, and an increase in the national minimum wage to £5 an hour.

"This is depressing. To think we're part of the disaffected as well," said Liz searching through the glove compartment. She switched the news off and turned on a CD.

Mozart 21 eased the mood as Peter headed for the toll bridge across the Bore.

As he drove he considered the note. He would not mention it to Liz. It said, "We know you hunt. You bastard. We will hunt you. Murderer." No identifying group or individual. He would show it to the police tomorrow; nothing would come from it, he knew, but they could at least be made aware of the implied threat and perhaps others were receiving such notes. He would make subtle inquiries tonight. No point in worrying Liz.

"Something on your mind, love?"

God, she knows me well. "Yes. I'm worried about where this country's heading. I mean, so many people are acting beyond the law and the law is powerless." It wasn't a direct lie, because he knew he could never lie to Liz.

"Yes. I do worry. I'm glad we went on the last march. I know you've not been political since you left university, but this affects our life."

"It'll work out, I'm sure. The country will wake up to reality one of these days. Just recall how powerful this nation was; and it was not because we catered for criminals and were soft on the youth. And governments didn't take over fifty per cent of the national wealth."

"Why don't you stand for Parliament next time round? You'd make a good MP."

He laughed. "Me? Nah. I have my opinions, but I wouldn't like to join that club. Local council perhaps. But not Westminster."

"Don't sell yourself short, Pete. You never know."

He hit the bridge and paid the toll. As he drove over he imagined rising to make his debut speech in Parliament. "And what's more, the right honourable gentleman has never been hunting, and is thus not in any position to comment on it. Why, he could not tell a sheep from a cow nor say how many toes a pig has. In the name of tradition as well as rights, I urge this House to reject the bill completely." (Hear, hear!) Was it him though, he wondered as the bridge evened out.

"My god, it's black down there," said Liz peering out over the side.

"Hmm." (Order, order!) "Honourable member for Lindthorpe North again. "Thank you, Mr Speaker. The right honourable gentleman not only shows his ignorance of the countryside but he also expresses a bigotry and class hatred that is reminiscent of Nazism." (Uproar. Order! Order!) "For, if the right honourable gentleman knew his history, but we cannot expect that from him, after all he believes foxes are little people deserving Labour Party membership!" (Order! Order!) "If he knew his history, which the House is aware that he blatantly does not, he would know that a most famous politician of last century banned the hunting with packs of hounds, and having read the right honourable gentleman's comments in the newspapers, I am struck by the similarity of expression and tone of argument, I am struck, Mr Speaker, by the equivalence of moral position on this issue, and then, I am struck, Mr Speaker, by the ... oh, I have hit a raw nerve with some members of the Government!" (Order! Order!) "Perhaps, they do know their history after all, and perhaps, Mr Speaker, they have been running from the very point I am going to make. Well now, the game's up. I am struck by the similarity, Mr Speaker, of the totalitarian view point expressed by the right honourable gentleman in his desire to ban hunting and the view presented by none other than Adolf Hitler." (Uproar. Order! Order! Cheers from the Opposition benches. Grave embarrassment on the faces of the Cabinet.) "Isn't that why, Mr Speaker," (Peter shouting above the jeers and insults), "isn't that why, Mr Speaker, the Labour Government, a traditionally very socialist party, a party committed to social-ism on a national basis, isn't that why the national socialist party in Government," (Order! Order!) "wishes to ban hunting as did the Nazis in Germany?" (Uproar. Near riot. Radcliffe swings mace at Cramp.)

Yes, that would be fun, Peter mused as his fingers played out Mozart on the steering wheel.

"In a pleasant fantasy there?"

"Yes! House of Commons. I'm bringing down the govern-ment by exposing the similarity of its anti-hunting stance to that of Adolf Hitler."

"I thought I could see war in your eyes." She leaned over and kissed him.

They reached Northchester with an hour to spare so went for tea at Betina's Café. They sat listening to the pianist playing soft show tunes and watched the people of Northchester bustle past. They remarked on the students who ambled along the street.

"They don't change much. Look, still wearing black and dressing as if they lived on the street," Liz commented.

"Only the political science ones," Peter laughed. "The econ-omists are usually very well dressed."

"You weren't too much of a dresser back then from the photos I've seen."

"I was a radical."

"Yes. I see that," she laughed. "A colour-blind radical."

"I'm not colour-blind! I just didn't know what clothes went with what."

They laughed and watched a busker in a wheelchair pan for cash from passers-by. Few gave him anything. A tall student stopped for a few moments and listened to him play. He gave some change and then sheepishly moved on.

"That was nice. We should give him something too," said Liz.

"The busker? Of course. Here's our tea."

They ordered sumptuous cakes with their tea and talked more about Peter's university days in the city, of coming to Betina's for hot chocolate after spending hours in the second-hand book stores. He had met Liz after university. She had gone to Harrowby to study Psychology at the same time he had been at Northchester. Both had failed marriages behind them and they sometimes discussed what would have happened if they had met when they were undergraduates. "I wouldn't have liked you then," one would say, leading into a jocular attack on their discipline.

They finished their teas and headed over to the Georgian façade of the Assembly Rooms. A queue had formed but it moved swiftly through the large double doors into the reception. They found their seats at a long table and accepted sherry from the waitress. People soon sat down next to them and began conversations on the state of farming and the potential attack on fishing and shooting, which everyone around them agreed would be next on the antis' agenda.

"Time we revolted," said a farmer whose income had fallen to £3000 a year in the previous three years. "I've never known the community so disheartened and pig-sick of regulation and interference. Tell you the truth, I'm not sure that the Alliance is up to the task."

A woman next to him, who raised hunter horses, was more conciliatory. "We have to give the Alliance more time. We don't know what's happening behind the scenes. After all, we paid our membership and we must let those closest to the sources of power use their influence."

"Nonsense," said the farmer. "They've had enough time and this government has not budged an inch. Every time we've gone in to explain what hunting's about or how farmers are affected by draconian costs imposed on the whole industry by people who've never set foot in a farm, why, they carry on as if they heard nowt. We've given them enough time, and money, and it's high time that they came through with the goods, which they've failed to do, or gave up and allow some more forceful characters to do the work."

Peter agreed. "Appeasement has never worked. Think of Chamberlain. Will we look back in five years time and say that was why it all failed. It's obvious now. At the protest outside Parliament there were many who supported more direct action. Both Liz and I are up for it."

"Do you hunt then?" asked the farmer.

"Yes," said Liz. "But we've only been doing it for a year. We've put most of our savings into the sport. Quite addictive."

"Ay," said the farmer, "time wot's not spent 'unting."

"Is time that's wasted," three voices completed the sentence. They laughed, refilled their glasses and toasted Jorrocks.

The Master of Ceremonies ascended the stage, a man both Liz and Peter recognised as someone who had hunted with them a couple of times. He wore a dark suit over a slim, fit body, sported the Laurenten Hunt tie and held a few notes in his hand. He commanded the hall's attention.

"Lords, Ladies, and Gentleman. Or should I say, supporters of hunting?" Cheers. "For those who do not know me, my name is David Carlton, Master of the Laurenten Hunt in Northchestershire." He spoke for several minutes thanking the assembled supporters for thèir financial contribution to the evening, the funds from which were going to assist a campaign of national advertising and legal representation across Britain, as well as thanking the committee of the northern section of the Rural Alliance for its unfaltering media campaign to dispel the myths surrounding hunting, and to promote it in the face of criticism.

"We all are feeling frustrated at the moment," he added in a more sombre mood. The audience nodded its quiet assent. "This is a time when we are fighting for our rights as well as our livelihoods. I do not wish to make this a political rallying speech. That is not my purpose tonight. Mr Vincent Harrison from the Rural Alliance will be making a speech later in the evening. Those who know me, know how I feel about what's gone on, and know how I stand on what is to be done. I shall not cloud the proceedings with my thoughts. Now we have a wonderful evening of string music awaiting you. May I introduce to you the MacIntyre string quartet?" From his left entered four strikingly handsome and beautiful musicians arrayed in evening wear, each carrying their instruments to their seats.

"On first violin, Mr Dugald MacIntyre. On cello, Miss Cosima Laurenten. Second violin, Miss Amy Sutherland. And on the viola, Miss Cecily Gordon. The quartet won acclaim at last year's Edinburgh Festival and are embarking on recording their first album, called, I believe, 'Music of the Scottish Enlightenment.' Tonight they will be playing two great works of the romantic period. Schubert's 'Death and the Maiden' and Verdi's String Quartet. And of course, they all hunt!"

The hall cheered and clapped as the performers took their places and arranged their instruments. When the hall fell silent the lanky, curly red-haired Dugald nodded to the others and the four burst into a sharp flurry of bows and hands, their pace and precision catching the audience by surprise; they quietened as the tune mellowed for a few bars before heading off on a trotting pace, developing the layers of the main melodies. Each musician swayed gently to the first movement's undulating rhythm, and the entire assembly was riveted to the music. The sound of wine glasses and the odd murmur of approval were the only extraneous elements disturbing the listeners' avid attention. The movement's cascading melody and swirling complexity dissolved frowning faces and tired bodies and acted to unite the audience in a solid appreciation of accomplished musicians perfecting their skills. Periodically the crashing opening bar was repeated, played by the young musicians with a defiance that certainly caught the hall's underlying mood. The adagio, involving a background pizzicato while a softer melody danced over the top, drew the audience into a solemn reverie. Most sat reflecting on their animals' plight over the past decade, the horrors of BSE and FMD, the new government legislation that permitted the arbitrary killing of stock; others contemplated the horrors to come if the government's urban prejudices were to ban their pursuits.

The Schubert piece ended to enthusiastic applause. The quartet gave their bows and left for a break. Mr Carlton rose to introduce Vincent Harrison.

A youthful-looking man in his forties made his way to the podium. His dark hair was fighting the onset of greyness. He swept his hand nervously through it several times as he took the stand. He sipped some water and then began to speak. He started off with a survey of the Alliance's achievements over the previous two years, and thanking the Northern group's staff by name for their work in the locality. The hall sat politely listening to him, but as Peter took stock of the audience, he noticed that the faces were stolid, jaws pushed forward, mouths tight, some people with their hands over their mouths as if to stop themselves from disrupting his talk, others sitting back in their chairs arms crossed, signs of anger quite visible.

"And now to the future." Harrison stopped for another sip of water. This, Peter could tell, was not going to be an easy ride for him. "We have submitted reams of evidence to the government, explaining what hunting and country pursuits are all about. Many of you here have been part of that process. We have demonstrated with peaceful marches to back up the force of what we have had to say. But this is a democratic process and we must all submit to the rule of law in the land." Peter felt the silence in the room deepen. "We are entering, what we all hope to be, the final phase of negotiations ..."

Someone shouted out, "There's nowt to negotiate. We've been there before, Harrison."

"We must," Harrison continued, "we must maintain dialogue with the government."

"Or else what?" shouted another.

"We must," he flustered, "present our arguments to the ministry and work within the land's constitutional framework."

"They're threatening the use of the Parliament Act, Harrison," shouted a man sitting at the same table as Peter. "They're not playing by the rules, so why should we?"

The hall burst into an applause. "Hear! Hear!" most shouted. "Well, said!" The Parliament Act hung like the sword of Damocles over all their heads. Designed to assist parliamentary reform of the second chamber, it was never meant to be employed to push through moral or controversial legislation, but Jones and other colleagues had hinted that they may use the Act should the Lords once again reject any legislation on hunting.

"If I can have your attention, please," insisted Harrison, waving his arms down at the crowd for silence.

An older woman's voice called out. "You've had our attention for years. We've got nowhere. Time to change your stance, lad."

"If I can put forward our policies, please."

"Your policies!"

"The policies of the Rural Alliance. Please, ladies and gentle-man, if I may at least explain." The hall quietened down to hear him out. Harrison brushed his hair back again. His forehead shone with perspiration. "Thank you. I understand your frustration and pain. Look, I'm not shirking from any respon-sibility. We need to talk with the government. It is the only way forward. We at the Alliance listen very closely to your views, and I cannot hear them all tonight, but know that we are presenting them to the government's highest officials. We are fighting for your jobs and rights, and we will not let you down."

"You're beginning to sound like Cramp!" Peter shouted out referring to the Prime Minister. Liz gave him a warm smile as the audience burst into sympathetic applause. The calling out began once again - demands for action now, resign Harrison, no more negotiations, and time to go followed, one after the other. Harrison managed to quieten the hall down again.

"We shall be organising another march ... " The rest of his sentence was drowned out by cries demanding to know what good the last ones had done and why should people march to defend their rights against a deaf and tyrannical government.

"Look," Harrison managed to shout over the crowd, waving with his arms to be heard. They hushed. "We're working for you. Just give us time. We need time to co-ordinate our approach. Don't rush headlong into something that would only get the politicians' backs up and attract the population's wrath. We need the public's support. Give us time." Then he stopped, shaken and added, "I'll leave it at that. Thank you for your time."

Visibly upset, he made his way back to his table. Peter watched him make a few comments to his secretary or agent, a corpulent, moustachioed man in his fifties who reminded Peter of marketing types he knew at the office. Mr Carlton arose once more.

"Thank you for letting Mr Harrison finish his speech. He has a lot to consider, we all know that. We must remember, he is not the enemy and does require our support. But he also needs to know how we feel." he added giving Mr Harrison a sharp look. "Hear! Hear!" many said again. "But let us finish our evening off with music, the great unifier of all peoples and nations. The MacIntyre Quartet shall now play Verdi's String Quartet. It is, I gather from Cosima, an appropriate piece, politically speaking."

The quartet took their places. Peter saw Harrison rise with his secretary, obviously going to make his exit. "I'll be back shortly," he said to Liz quietly. The first bar began as Peter followed Harrison and his companion out of the hall into the reception area. They had picked up their pace as they vacated the hall, but Peter called out. "Mr Harrison, I'm sorry, may I have a quick word before you go? Peter Hickling. I hunt with the North Lindthorpe."

"I'm sorry, I must really go. I have to get back to London this evening."

"Look, I'm a paid-up member and like many of the people in there, I spend most of my earnings on country pursuits. I will probably never be able to talk to you again. It will only take a few moments."

"Okay, okay. Make it quick. Terry, you go and get the car and meet me outside."

His secretary left and Harrison turned to face Peter.

"Mr Harrison. You heard the reaction in there. They're not going to allow you to continue much longer. I've worked in and with big companies for a dozen years and I've seen what happens when the shareholders or the employees begin to get even slightly frustrated, never mind what you experienced in there. You don't have much time left."

"Thanks, that's just what I want to hear."

"Face the facts, Mr Harrison. You have to adapt soon and substantially, otherwise you'll be going nowhere fast. Consider the chairmen of large companies that begin to sound distant from the workforce, who begin singing a different tune from the rest of the company, who begin to feel that their position is owed to them by virtue of their status. I've seen this so often. I analyse companies for their investment potential. I work for a bank and liaise with some of the country's biggest companies. I've seen what happens all too often. The writing's on the wall, and my goodness, one could not hear it plainer and louder than you did tonight."

"Look, Mr Hinkling."

"Hickling."

"Mr Hickling. I know what I'm doing. I believe that I'll get us through this."

"No, you don't. That's the problem. It's what all the top dogs say just before we pull the loan facilities, or before the shareholders begin to revolt. 'Trust me, I know what I'm doing.' I've heard it so many times. It's usually the biggest indication that someone doesn't know what they're doing. But, Mr Harrison, and this is something I've tried to express to dozens of business leaders over the years, it's not a matter of you making the world better, as if you were the only one who could. You're not God, you know. You're a mortal man with the mortal limitations of one person. There are three hundred people in there who may not be able to wheel and deal like you, but their understanding of what you should be doing is changing. Now, you have to adapt or lose your job. It's simple."

"Well, I thank you for your advice, Mr Hickling, but I'm sure the Alliance will be able to work out a plan to get through this latest, and hopefully last, phase."

"It's too late for that. A company should never be in a position of not knowing what to do when the shit hits the fan. It should know about the shit's potential, examine its fan, prepare for impact, and then set out its contingency plans to come out looking squeaky clean as if the shit had never happened. Now, it looks as if you've been left high and dry and do not have a leg to stand on, if I can mix my metaphors. You must act now. Decisively. With confidence. And with the confidence of the side which is in the bloody right, for heaven's sake. Otherwise, you'll be gone and others, more strident and less patient with your political cronies, will take over. Have you not read your history? Decisiveness, man. Boldness. Dig the heels in, stiffen the sinews. You're hearing the blast of war in your ears and if you're not up to the challenge you should go. I was going to give you some thoughts on marketing experience, but the time for that has passed. From my experience of companies that suddenly stand naked and without direction while the customers are fleeing in droves and the workers sit disenchanted and worrying about their jobs, I would say you have days, not weeks. I'm not sure what your reception in other parts of the country will be like - maybe you could stretch it to a couple of weeks, but after that, no chance. Anyway, here's your man and car," said Peter showing a pliant Mr Harrison out to the car as he would a business client. He opened the door for Harrison before his secretary had reached it.

"Think about it, Mr Harrison," said Peter closing the door. He turned his back and heard the car slowly pull away as he entered the reception area. He stood listening to the quartet until the end of the first movement and then quickly rejoined Liz.

"Where were you?" she whispered.

"I talked to Harrison for a few minutes. Had to. Only chance. I'll tell you later."

After the Rural Affairs fund-raising concert most people went out into the piercing northern night. A brisk wind caught the leavers' cheeks. They pulled their collars up and tightened their scarves. Liz and Peter remained behind, mingling and swapping comments with various hunters, followers, and farmers, until they happened upon the musicians.

"Most enjoyable," said Liz extending a hand of introduction to the tall first violinist. Liz played violin in some amateur orchestras and Peter left them discussing teachers and the quality of recordings and classical radio. The cellist was closing her case and turned around as he approached. She stood up and smiled as he introduced himself.

"Peter Hickling. I believe I worked with your brother in London not long ago."

Cosima Laurenten shook hands. "Pleased to meet you. Yes, Jeremy mentioned you. Most impressed of your talents, he said." Peter expressed his delight in the playing as Cosima led him to the bar for refreshments. "Now, what did you say to Vincent? I saw you follow him out and when you sat down, you said something to your partner that, given her reaction, suggested you'd spoken to him."

"Goodness, you are observant. Well, let me bring Liz in on this as well, for I promised to tell her later." They made their way back through the tables and gently interrupted Liz and Dugald's conversation. The four sat down at a table.

"I told you he spoke to him," said Cosima to Dugald, taking a seat. The other two players came up and bade their goodnights.

Peter explained what he had said; the conversation had lingered in his mind and it was easy to recall. Liz sat back impressed.

Dugald laughed. "You're the kind of man we want on our side."

Cosima leant forward. "Peter. My brother said he had been impressed with your forthrightness. Dugald's right. You're the kind of man we may have much need of. I shall mention your name to my father. He may have need of your skills."

"I didn't do that much."

"To you, perhaps not. But to many people, including us, what you said needed saying, and it sounds as if you expressed it in the right tone. The message probably got through. Are you easy to get hold of?"

"Is this a job offer?" asked Liz. "I mean, we're both thinking of leaving our current posts and setting up on our own."

"And we work as a team," said Peter slipping his hand into Liz's.

"It will probably be an interesting job offer. I'll speak to my father. He's in need of people like you, and if you come as a team, so much the better."

"Any details?"

"None yet. You'll have to wait until he calls. It may come to nothing, so I would recommend carrying on as you were. Forget I said anything, but if he does call, then I'd seriously contemplate what he offers. Let's swap contact numbers and email, and I promise to speak to him tomorrow."

Peter and Liz left soon after, talking in earnest about what the offer could be but trying not to get too excited in case nothing came of it. They drove back chatting about a possible future outside of the corporate world, the nature of a job offer from Laurenten ("Sounds political," said Liz, "you'll probably like it") and about the music they had heard. Liz's mobile sent through a message and she picked up her phone to read it.

The atmosphere changed. "Something wrong?" He knew there was.

"Well, I've never received hate texts before." Her voice shook slightly but she said the words in an disinterested manner to hide a growing shame and anger.

"Hate texts? What do you mean?"

"Nothing, I guess, I don't know. Probably someone at work who doesn't like me hunting."

Peter pulled the car over to see. It read, "C HOW BTCH LIKES 2B HUNTED. WE KNOW WHRE U LIVE." Peter immediately pressed for the caller's details but none were displayed. "Shit." He reread the message several times, not knowing how exactly to proceed. He tried the operator but could not retrieve any more information.

"Who has your phone details?" he finally asked.

"Friends of ours. But we know they're all sound on hunting. The only possibility is that it's someone from work. The office computer staff perhaps." Then she shook her head. "My boss has it, but he's pro-hunt. Uh, Joe, Sandy, John, and Tony. They have it, but they are so apolitical it's not funny. But then it's on the office network, so that could mean anyone who knows I hunt and who wanted to scare me could get a hold of it. Petty mind, whoever it is," she said, smiling at Peter and raising a hand to smooth his frowning brow. "Don't worry, love," she said. "It's just a prank. A one-off."

"Not quite. Look, before we left, there was a note attached to the back of the car. I didn't want to tell you about it. I didn't want to worry you," he added as he pulled the note out and passed it to her. Her face fell.

"Then it's a neighbour. But none of them know the mobile number. Except Sally, but she's wholly trustworthy."

"Of course. Anyone else got your number except potentially hundreds at work?" He gave an exasperated laugh.

"Hmm. We can't do anything about it now. Let's just go home. It's probably nothing. Your note is something we can give to the police. We shouldn't worry," she added to calm her own anxieties.

They drove home in silence but turning into their road Peter again had the feeling something was not right. He pulled up to the house slowly and parked the car in front of the hedge before their driveway. He told Liz to stay in the car and cautiously went up the drive. The front door was open. He had half-expected it, but the realisation of his fear caused his stomach to churn and his heart to pump faster. As he approached the gaping black crack that had wrenched open their privacy, he knew that they had shut the door.

No lights on in the house. Quiet. He reached the door and focused his ears above the din of his thumping heart. No sound. The door had been forced. "Oh, Jesus." A strong smell reminiscent of turpentine hit his nose. Perhaps someone had gone through his tools under the stairs and knocked the turps over. He walked quietly back towards to the car in case someone rushed out.

"Liz. We've been broken into. Call the police on the mobile. I'm going in to check the place is all right. I don't hear anyone in the house."

"Oh my God, oh, God, no," she repeated fumbling for her phone but her hands shook too much to dial.

"Here, I'll call." Peter informed the police of their address and the problem and was told a car would be around in fifteen minutes and that he should not enter the house.

"Look, there's a light on at Sally's," he said, shutting the phone off. "Go and knock. She won't mind. I'll keep watch." Liz got out of the car, trembling, and headed to their neighbour's. Peter returned to his post, his mind racing through what the burglars could have taken. He heard Liz knock and a shocked Sally invite her in. Five minutes later they returned carrying hot tea.

"I thought you two'd stay in, just in case there was trouble."

"What and leave you here by yourself?" Liz took his arm and offered him a cup.

"What have they taken?" asked Sally, her cheeks red from falling asleep next to the coal fire.

"Not sure, I've not gone in yet. Police said to stay outside."

They stood talking and shivering for a quarter of an hour before calling the police again. "Another half hour," he said switching the phone off. "They've told us to go and get warm but not to enter. Sounds as if they've got a few break-ins in the area tonight."

Two hours later, with Liz falling asleep on Sally's couch, and Sally and Peter taking it in turn to watch the house, the police finally came. Peter hurried out the house.

"Evening," said the officer, a broad-shouldered man in his twenties, with short cropped hair and a generic officially polite attitude. "PC Robinson. This is PC Gough, my partner. Is it your property, sir?"

Peter introduced himself and explained what they had seen. "We've not entered since I noticed the door forced open. We also received a note that had been left on the car earlier." He proffered the note to the officer who pondered it for a moment.

"Right. We'll have a quick look around, sir. You stay here, we won't be too long."

His female companion, a short flat-faced woman with blonde hair caught in a tight ponytail which protruded from her cap followed him in.

Ten minutes passed before PC Robinson returned.

"Well sir, it seems you've been the subject of politically-motivated vandalism. You both hunt?"

"Yes," said Liz. "What's been taken?"

"Station again," said PC Gough coming over. "We have another one to go to after this," she said coolly. "Farm buildings up near the Bore."

"Well," said Robinson, striving to find the right words. "There have been a lot of attacks like this across the county. All on hunt supporters, we gather. The attacks were all between 8pm and 10pm, as far as we can tell. They've done some damage to your property."

"How much damage?" Liz wanted know.

"Painting slogans. Anti-hunt slogans, that sort of stuff. Similar to the other half a dozen houses we've seen tonight. We have colleagues visiting about twenty other properties around the county."

"Anybody hurt?" asked Sally.

"A couple of people knocked out and being treated, as far as we've heard."

"Sabs?"

"I'm sorry, sir?"

"Hunt saboteurs. Were the hunt saboteurs hurt?"

"Uh, no sir. The residents."

"Bastards. Well, what information do you need from the house before we can enter?"

"We've made a report, sir. There will be no sign of any fingerprints if that's what you mean. It's the same as the other houses. My colleague is going back in to take photographs. That will be sufficient evidence for the station. Unfortunately, we have another one to go to after this. It'll be a long night for us."

From what the policeman said, Peter realised that there would not be any comeback or justice. He waited while Robinson took notes and Gough entered into the house. After a couple of minutes she returned, which led Peter to believe that the damage was not too great. Robinson offered to go in with him, and requested that the women waited, but they would not be stayed.

Gough had switched on the lights and the first thing Peter noticed was the paint. Then the smell of what he had thought was turpentine hit his senses and his understanding simultaneously. Daubed on the walls were crudely painted red slogans expressing hatred towards all hunters and animal killers. The paint had been purposefully put on heavily - it ran down the walls like blood from a massacre and dripped onto the carpeting. But it wasn't just the hall walls that had been painted: the mahogany side table that acted as their phone table, the ornate gold leaf mirror in the hallway, the old oak doors they had restored and fitted to the living, dining, and kitchen rooms.

Peter went upstairs with the PC to verify nothing had been taken. Gough stayed with Liz and Sally. The two women moved slowly around the house expressing their dismay, disgust and anger at what they saw. Peter returned a few minutes later with the officer and on his way down noticed the phone stand and the phone book lying next to the phone. "That's where they got your number from, Liz. Liz received a nasty text message around eleven. We were on our way back from Northchester, from a charity do. We don't keep the book out - you'll probably need that for cross-checking mobile phone calls made during the hours you said, won't you?"

The policeman gave the sympathetic look of one who still thought idealistically about his role but one who was beginning to realise that it would do no good. "You'll have an inspector come round tomorrow. I'd leave it untouched until then."

"Can we clean this mess up, though?"

"I'd call your insurance people first. Get a quote," said Gough who had mellowed somewhat as she had gone from room to room with Liz and Sally, hearing their cries of horror. "They'll sort you out with the right kind of cleaning specialists too. I'm sorry about this. This is dreadful. I don't care about hunting personally, but this kind of act, I wouldn't wish upon anyone."

"What's the chance of catching the culprits?"

"Not much," noted Robinson shrugging. "No fingerprints have been left at the others. Probably wore latex gloves. Quick job. From what we can gather thus far, someone toots the horn a few times as if they are saying goodbye to a neighbour, at the same time as their colleagues force entry."

Sally confirmed she had heard a horn earlier. Robinson made a note. "Then they come in, make their mess. Car meanwhile has probably turned around, or a second car is ready, and the culprits make a quick get-away."

"Without anybody seeing them?" asked Peter.

"Not sure about that yet," said Gough. "That may come out when we make our inquiries in the neighbourhood. The inspectors are concentrating on the ones where GBH was committed tonight."

"Of course," said Liz worried. "Are we safe, though?"

"You should be," said Gough.

"Would you stay in your home after an attack like this?" Sally asked her.

Gough reflected for a moment. "To be honest, no. I wouldn't want to. Not until it had been cleaned up."

Sally offered her spare room and Peter and Liz gladly accepted. Emotionally drained, they both agreed they would have to call off work for the next day. They switched on their mobiles to call in and Liz nervously watched the logos come on as she waited for the signal. Her phone rang out its electronic melody. A text message arrived. "LIKE THE ART BTCH? NXT TIME UR BLOOD."

Sally took Liz's phone and read the text. She swore. "I'd not really thought about hunting, until you two told me you were doing it. But my God, I never thought you'd have to pay such a price for your Saturdays," she said adamantly. "Next time there's a march, count me in. Can't let bastards like that run the country. Were you sending the office a message? Do it quickly, and then get some sleep. Don't let those bastards get you down."

Warbler

Flood returned to the party ten minutes later with Maggie. "Bumped into her in the offie," he said as they came in.

"Hi Maggie, did we tear you away from your riveting books?" enquired Jez.

"Well, no, well, I'd almost finished," said Maggie, shifting her long fringe away from her glasses.

"Exams don't matter. It's the cause that matters," said Kite. "We're on the verge of getting all cruelty banned and we're needed more than ever. It's all for a good cause," she added looking at Maggie's face which had suddenly twitched with panic. "Don't worry, you'll do fine in the exams. You always do. Besides, Bernie says he's got someone special coming over tonight."

"Who you got?" asked Rat, who had been rummaging through a pile of CDs.

"You'll find out," replied Peterson who was gazing at the chest of the unidentifiable object sitting on his couch. Male or female? Mystery.

Maggie took her coat off. "Are we going out this week, then?"

"Yeah, and Flood's coming," said Jez. "He needs some stuff though - you know, the gear." She dug into the bag Flood had brought back. "Here you go, love, a can for you. Put the rest in the fridge." Flood obeyed.

"Shit!" cried Rat, "bloody Arsenal won again. They should bloody shoot that manager. Three-one to Rotherham. Bunch o'tossers." That began a heated discussion between several members of the floor fraternity on England's chances for the next European Cup.

The flat's door buzzer rasped and Peterson enthusiastically shouted, "Come in! Third floor, first on the left." He turned to the group. "Now, my surprise for the caucus. Professor Doug Warbler, who, as you know, is giving a lecture on campus next week, and I managed to get him for tonight." He rubbed his hands together smugly at this little coup.

"Doug Warbler?" inquired Jez. "Wow, isn't he the one whose article I photocopied last year. I didn't read it. Flood told me about it a couple of weeks back - 'Rights for Rats'."

"Yes," replied Peterson, "he also wrote The Expanding Heart, Man and Bacteria, Fish have Feelings Too and, oh yeah, Fighting for Jungle Rights: an activists guide to 'gorilla' warfare, a classic. We met several years back when I gave a paper on 'Marxism and the emerging animal proletariat'. Shared a few beers that night, hah. I send him my papers and updates on how the fight is going; he's really interested in the group."

"Cool," said Kite.

"Who's coming?" demanded Rat.

"Oh, Jeez. Professor Doug WARBLER!" shouted Maggie to Rat, who had stuck his ears into the woofer.

A swift knock at the door, left ajar by Flood and Maggie, preceded the professor's sudden entry. "Good evening," he said. "Nice of you to introduce me to the neighbours."

Peterson sprang over to shake Warbler's hand. "Glad you could make it. We've got the entire group here - one or two new ones who've just joined the inner circle. We're on the brink of banning hunting and fishing."

"Yes, I know, I've been following the news. Do you have a drink?"

"Oh, gosh, certainly, Andy, no, Maggie, can you get the professor a drink. Stiff one?"

"Please,"

"Oh, you're welcome," replied Peterson, leading the professor over to a table on which various articles, books, magazines were strewn. "Would you mind signing your latest book?"

"No problem," replied the professor. He wore a black turtle-neck sweater with khaki trousers and Oxford shoes. His thick lips matched a flattish nose but his wide cheeks hinted at Slavic descent. His short dark hair and dark eyes, magnified by thick spectacles, gave him a beatnik-look, though it also made his stare disconcerting.

"What you a professor of?" shouted Rat from deep inside the speaker.

WILLIAM VENATOR

"Andy!" cried Kite. "That's PROFESSOR DOUG WARBLER. Oh for God's sake, take your head out of the bloody speaker, you might hear! Better. Right, Professor Warbler; he's the one who wrote the books we read at school, you know: Butterflies and Butter: the New Economic Ethics and Trees, Timber, and Murder, and his best-seller, Man the Bastard. You know, I've showed you a picture several times." Rat frowned but smiled in what he thought was a polite manner but which came across to others as the height of ignorance. Kite sighed and turned back to the conversation.

The Professor signed the book and turned to accept the offered drink. "Single malt?" he sniffed the whisky.

"MacIntyre single malt - twelve year old," replied Peterson helpfully. "I keep it for special guests."

"Well, it was nice of you to invite me. Have you been publishing recently?"

"Oh, well, uh, a few book reviews. Two supportive ones for you. I prefer reading papers at conferences; much more sociable."

"Yes. Good for a great piss-up too," replied the Professor. Peterson laughed. "Is this your gathering? Twelve disciples by the looks of it."

"Thirteen including me," said Peterson.

"Yes." Warbler took a sip and gasped. "Fine stuff. Now who have we got here?"

"This is Maggie, or Owl, she's a final-year student. Very bright. Wants to do postgraduate research on feminism and vivisection in Victorian literature." Maggie smiled back. "That's Jezebel, quite an activist, very strong-minded and doesn't mind shouting at the hunters. That's her friend, Flood, who's just joined the caucus, a decent liberationist. He's coming out with us next time. That's Kite heading into the bathroom; she's a post-grad researching animal rights and marginal peoples under me. That one's Seaweed, or John Glynn, yep, the long-haired chap. Very quiet until you get him out, then he's a bit of a madman. That's Andy, also known as Rat, the normally loud one. He's our brute-force man - he's got a good heart and a lot of strength. He pushed over a hunter and horse a couple of

- 74 -

weeks back. He's got his own network of uh, well, shall we say, helpers? That's Slug, or Chris, uh, just joined last week - good credentials, according to Seaweed." He added an aside to Warbler, "No, I'm not sure either. Name doesn't help. Over there, sitting on the ground is Blossom, or Laura; she's brought a lot of money into the organisation. Her parents own a meat-processing factory down south - she's disowned them, but they still support her with about £200 a month pocket money and we get £50 of that. Then there's Hog, or Petra, a German student studying politics (also very rich - German war guilt still pays!). And some first years, er, Mole (Ben), Bean (Neal), Lynx (Samantha), and, uh, there that's Vicki or Vixen."

"Hello, Professor Warbler," said Vixen. She was prettier than the other women and insisted on flirting with all men within a range of ten yards. Up close the prettiness of her long chestnut hair over a soft sweater and ample bosom faded to a pockmarked face and eyes too close together for her rounded cheeks.

"Hello," replied Warbler, spotting her type and interests immediately and smiling back. "Call me Doug. That goes for everyone, the title's a title. What matters is the person behind the title."

"Hi Doug," said Rat finally standing up to shake the professor's hand. "Kite's told me all about you. You write books don't you? Which team do you support?"

"Uh, I follow the cricket actually."

"Ah," said Peterson laughing, "we shouldn't mention our performance recently - we can't bowl for toffee!"

"I agree," said Warbler. "Well, I must say, your group is getting quite a name for itself, you know. I read reports of what I can only assume to be your exploits mentioned in the Los Angeles Times a couple of weeks ago."

"Yes, that was following our very successful sit-down in Sainsburys, raising awareness of what household cleaners do to life's microcosms," said Vixen.

"Yes, I remember reading that one," replied Warbler, "but you're also getting a name through other channels. The dog theft, for example, and the letter bombs were your doing, I believe."

"Too right," said Rat, "bastards deserved losing their dogs. Poor things had been mistreated and cruelly oppressed into hunting and meat-eating."

"Quite," replied Warbler. "Who was in the photograph?"

"That was me!" shouted Rat gleefully as if he were posing for another shot. "My very own mug shot. Famous for five minutes!"

"Fifteen minutes, Andy," said Jez, coming over to shake Warbler's hand. "You'll have to excuse Rat; he gets excited easily."

"Yes, but nobody knows who you were," said Seaweed John raising his head from watching for carpet bugs.

"I do, and you do," replied Rat. "And at least I was in the paper."

"Who received the dogs?" asked Warbler.

"Twenty went to friends around the area," replied Jez, "and we cared for ten here."

"I took four to Mummy," said Laura in a polished home counties accent, "she never asks questions and we do have lots of land. I told the gardeners to feed them and walk them."

"And the other ten? I thought forty were stolen?" Warbler smiled at Laura.

"Yes," said Peterson, "we had to put seven down. They were much too aggressive, and we can't afford to be bitten and then have to go to hospital. Vixen was bitten on the ankle, but fortunately the teeth didn't sink too deeply. We had to draw a line somewhere. Besides, they'd ask questions if we went to the doctors, and I'm not sure all of us here," he added quietly, "could sustain an interrogation on the NHS. Some doctors are hunters. Capitalist hypocrites. If only," he raised his voice again, "if only we'd got the poor puppies younger, then we could have trained them out of their speciesism."

"You were bitten?" Warbler asked Vixen. "Not too badly?"

"No, well, it hurt at the time, look," she pulled up her trouser leg to show a half oval of teeth indentations.

"It looks as if it's healing nicely," he said, and bent down to touch the marks, "yes, no permanent damage done." His fingers rested for a second on the soft hairy leg.

"Yeah, I know. Good wounds, though," Vixen laughed with a slight levity in her voice. "Rat got the dog off my leg. Poor misguided creature, he didn't know any better."

"No, I guess not," replied Peterson, also enjoying the sight of a female calf in the late autumn when most had been hidden away behind longer trousers or thick woollen tights.

Jez reached out to replenish glasses. "Another drink?"

"Thanks, but who's got the other three?"

"Oh, the other three? Unfortunately, they ran off a few nights back," said Peterson, watching Vixen pull her socks up.

"We almost caught one last night," said Flood. "He was whimpering behind a car round the corner and Jez almost got her hands on him, but he ran off again."

"You won't get them back," said Warbler. "They'll run for days until they die of starvation, or the police pick them up and euthanaise them"

"Bloody pigs," said Rat presenting his wisdom to the conversation. "I hate the pigs. I was almost nicked last time we went sabbing."

"Really?"

"Yeah, I was caught sticking a banana up some toff's exhaust when they saw me. I had to leg it across two fields before I lost them. Kite said I should be called Fox," he laughed loudly.

"Well, do be careful. We don't want to lose any troops before the final victory. We're almost there," Warbler said taking another offering of whisky. "Phew! Strong stuff, I must say," he coughed. "You could start a revolution on those ethers. Well, you have a very decent group, and I wish you all the best. I cannot stay for much longer since I have a pressing engagement with other colleagues at the Fox and Hound. Quite appropriate really. Before I go, I want you to know that the Global Animal Federation, of which I am an executive member, is donating a couple of thousand to your group next month. I'll arrange the transactions with you later, Bernie; they have to be clandestine of course. My contacts hint that hunting will be banned in this parliament, so you must step up the demonstrations and publicity - I've brought some propaganda pictures for you to use as you see fit, posters around campus and to the local press." He passed a thick folder to Peterson. "The next goal is, of course, the seasonal murdering of pheasants. We have six MPs eager to push for legislation outlawing the shooting of wild animals and we are arguing that the impaling of animals with hooks, snares, traps, and so on can be sneaked into the shooting bill."

"Does that mean an end to fishing?" Seaweed John inquired.

"Yes, if it gets passed which it should do. My friends, some ex-students of mine, in the Society Against Cruelty to Animals are allotting sizeable funds for full-page ads on the cruelty of fishing, with the help of some Hollywood funds. But what we will be wanting of all the sab-groups in the forthcoming months is for you to step up the campaign. We're close, you know. The one poster in the pack shows a half-eaten fox that some brothers were able to rescue from a hunt pack a few weeks back. Below it is a fish lying helplessly on a dock, its lungs gasping and its eyes fading into death. The advert asks whether there is a difference? Another, which I kinda like, shows an apparently dead baby drowning in a lake whilst a fish drowns on land. It says, 'you wouldn't do this to your baby, so why do the same to an innocent fish?' It'll move people in the right direction."

"Oh, how sad," sobbed Laura.

"Piscecide," said Petra in her thick accent, then added, "diskusting." She sat cross-legged in her Birkenstocks and woollen socks, her colourful mid-calf trousers showing long darks hair that she was quite proud of. She poured the remnants of her lager into her mouth then belched.

"Quite. Our purpose is to confuse the minds of the gullible public into a systematic sentimentality that will dissemble any distinctions between fox-hunting, pheasant-shooting, and fishing. All forms of cruelty to the animal kingdom must be abolished if we are to reduce suffering, and that requires as much emotionally moving footage that you can get your hands on."

"What will we go for when we've banned hunting?" asked Mole.

"The enslavement of animals. Pets, ultimately. There can be no pets in a just world. Just as people were slaved by oppressive regimes, so too are animals. They are our silent brethren, the dumb victims of mass enslavement and programmes of forced sterilisation, genetic engineering, and euthanasia. For this, we shall be targeting turkey factories, chicken runs, cow and sheep barns; we'll be ripping down fences, burning barns, smashing mass production factories to free our friends; they will not be forgotten once we secured the freedoms of wild animals. Then we shall turn all domesticated and farmed animals back into the wild."

"What about the pets? When will we go for them?" asked Blossom.

"That will take time. We must first secure the conditions of freedom, which means securing their rightful place on the human rights codes, and once we've established that, no man may treat an animal with disrespect, no man may discriminate against any animal, no man may take away the life or property of an animal, no man may enslave an animal. Soon all artificially-bred poodles, Pekinese, collies, all the selectively bred Siamese cats and blues, and all the goldfish, tropical fish and birds will be set free from slavery and confinement. Free! Free! Free at last! They will bark, purr, cheep, squeak, bleat and moo their hymns to liberty."

"How will you know what they're saying?" asked Rat without any hint of sarcasm.

"A man does not have to know what a child says to know it is grateful; it will be in their eyes and in their movements. They will flee the terror man has brought them: the thousands of years of murder and slavery. They shall be free."

"Hurrah!" said Slug, whose voice did not betray its gender either.

"Go for it," said Jez.

"We will, or rather you will," said Warbler to Jez. "It's your destiny to be amongst the most highly regarded sabbing groups in the country. Groups in Australia and the United States are applauding you and endeavouring to emulate your successes. In fact," he laughed nervously, "we're not sure how you do it. Six untraceable letter-bombs a month in the past three, forty dogs liberated, five animal-testing centres daubed in paint, two of which suffered irreparable damage to their factories from well-placed small explosives. Of course, your methods are your own to follow and we know nothing. We take no responsibility either. Remember, especially if you're new to the group, I know you've all been vetted, but do not inculpate any of your fellow members or divisional heads. You work alone."

"We understand," said Peterson. "None of the members is here without proper vetting."

Flood wondered what that entailed - wondered for a moment whether it was sleeping with Jez - but felt honoured to have passed whatever tests he had been put through to get this far, into what was turning out to be a secretive radical organisation. But this was what he had been yearning for - a sense of belonging to something that could make a difference; and here he was listening to Professor Warbler, the most famous proponent of animal liberation in the world. He felt the power in the room and liked it. He looked around. The others had all been paying close attention to the professor, and they too were eager for action and power to change the world for the better.

"I've got copies of Howling Jackal's book," said Warbler. Peterson edged closer. "It's hard to get your hands on it, so I've had it privately printed. Make sure you pass it around to those who can stand it. It's the future, but most people can't handle the future of an animal liberated world, so we have to go slowly, warm them up to the idea." He opened his briefcase and pulled out several loosely bound laser-printed manuscripts.

Flood caught the title: "A Declaration of Total War: Killing People, Freeing Animals by Howling Jackal." He let out an audible low whistle. Peterson turned to him.

"Flood, in this game, we are fighting the real oppressors and we must consider all methods. Man has oppressed man, class has oppressed class for centuries, and now we are awakening to the fact that man has oppressed his fellow species on the planet. Now some here don't think much of man. I happen to, but I don't think much of those who would oppress others. I hate capitalists for exploiting the poor, and I hate the capitalist laboratories for exploiting linguistically challenged animals. The poor we can teach to have their own voice, but animals we can't teach, so more than ever direct action, really focused direct action, against the oppressors is needed. We must never lose sight of throwing off the yoke of capitalism, but we can lever it off quicker if we get to the roots of all oppression and exploitation, and that's the exploitation of animals."

Flood smiled his consent, but a worrying image of two sky-scrapers being rent apart by suicidal maniacs passed through his mind.

"Right!" said Warbler, "We liberators have come to the con-clusion that people will never make peace with animals. It's not in their natures or in the natures of the societies they have created. Ultimately, we believe that if you really want to save the animals, you must stop wasting time seeking to improve humanity, you must declare war against humans. This is the only logical, consistent, and morally correct conclusion, stemming from the true belief that animals should be free to live their lives unshackled from human exploitation. Human society and its laws are implicitly and irrevocably immoral. We liberators are people of conscience who feel, therefore, morally obligated to break those laws and revolt against this oppressive regime. And this revolution will not be like any other in the history of the world. Revolutions usually seek to gain privileges within society for a disenfranchised group of people - the kind of people Bernie has spoken up for. Poor, blacks, women, gays, transsexuals, Jews. Such movements were for inclusion in society, but it's different for animals and the animal liberation movement. The battle for animals' freedom has, up until now, been nothing more than an impotent whimper in the face of gross inhumanity. Now we feel this movement demands a different approach because human groups fight for inclusion. The movement to free animals must fight for exclusion. Oppressed people want to be accepted as equals into society. Oppressed animals want to be left alone by society. We must fight for animals' rights to be excluded from our oppression, whether it is in the form of domestication for cattle or for pets, for trapping in tanks or cages. Free the beasts, that's what I say! Well, troops," he said, closing his bag and smiling at the band, "I must be off to meet some colleagues. It was a pleasure to have met you and I wish you continued success." Peterson showed him to the door and, following a couple of exchanges, the professor departed.

"That was brilliant," said Kite.

"Yeah, he speaks so good too," said Jez.

"Looked like an old fogey to me," said Rat.

"He doesn't look that old," said Jez, "he just doesn't dress like you, Andy."

"I liked what he said," said Flood.

"Right, everyone," interjected Peterson removing cans and packets of half-eaten crisps and unfolding a map on the table. "We have victory in our grasp. Our brother animals will be soon liberated. But it's up to us. Pay attention. We shall be meeting at eleven o'clock in the vicinity of Wartnam Farm where the hunt will be meeting. Full country get-up camouflage is required and keep your hair tucked in Andy. You too, Slug," he added, hoping for some response to indicate the owner's gender. None came. The students gathered around to study the map. "For God's sake, keep the horns and whistles hidden at all times. We don't want to arouse suspicions until the attack team is ready. We will be dividing into teams. According to the OS maps, the hunt is likely to head off to the north-east,. So I want one group, the attack group, to head into the woods by Upper Bampton, the other to head down to the woods and hedgerows to the north-west, by this abandoned farm," he pointed. "I'll have copies of the map done for you in the department. Do not lose them and once the day's over, destroy them. Now, me, Jez and Brown Owl, I mean Owl, will be talking to hunters and their sick followers. We'll be a father and two daughters up from the South for the day and we will just happen upon them. We'll be undercover all day - at the end of the meet, we three will return and mingle once more. I don't want to raise any suspicions and I want to gain this particular bunch's confidence. We'll tell them stories of how we saw saboteurs in the woods. So, on no account should any of the rest of you identify us, wave to us, or acknowledge us. You don't know us - got it?"

The meeting wound down with various bodies leaving to hit the pubs.

Jez made an excuse to Flood that she had arranged to go clubbing with Kite. Peterson piped up, "What, seal clubbing?" but his joke fell flat.

"Fine," said Flood and he followed Maggie down the stairs, "You sure you didn't mind giving up your revision tonight?"

She answered uncertainly. "No, I'll finish it when I get back. I didn't have much more to do. It was nice though, meeting Professor Warbler."

"Yeah, he's brilliant, isn't he?"

"I guess. I mean, I'm not sure about all of his arguments. I believe it's good to save animals, but microbes and things, well, that's taking it too far, isn't it?"

"But ... but perhaps they have a right to exist too. After all, just because we've brains doesn't mean that we're intelligent. Most organisms have been around longer than we have, and we should respect that."

"Yeah, I guess so," said Maggie opening the bottom door to the street. "Are you going to buy your gear tomorrow?"

"Yeah, I should. I want to be ready for my first sabbing. Jez gave me a list of items, and I've seen what she wears when she goes off. I can't say I'm looking forward to changing into such a get-up though. It's so - so posh, you know."

"Yeah, mind you, the wool sweaters keep you warm. I some-times wear mine in my room when I'm studying. But don't tell Jez; she'll think I'm some hypocritical animal hater."

Flood laughed, "No problem. I'll see you tomorrow in lecture, right?"

Maggie smiled at him, "Yeah, maybe we could go for a coffee afterwards."

"Sure," he said, "see you later then."

"See you," she replied, still smiling, before turning to go.

Residence

Flood headed down the road under the orange lights, past the cramped, uniform terraced houses.

Some gardens had been ripped up and replaced with tarmac or paving stones, others left to grow wild. Television sets glowed from behind curtains, blasting out muffled voices and music. Another CCTV camera watched him as he crossed the road to the alley entrance that led to the campus. On the one side lay a decrepit churchyard. Rubbish had been thrown in amongst the graves, the roses had become overgrown and ivy crawled up the disused church's darkened sides. To his left his eyes alighted on the various student posters and graffiti adorning the wall. "Entifida on Capitalism". Hmm, he thought somewhere in the recesses of his mind, how does that connect to the New York attacks? Next poster advertised the "Battle of the Bands"; then came "Women are angry about Men". Then graffiti: "Fuck the System". Another poster: "Battle of the Bands: Semi Final". Then: "Total War". The last one prompted him to stop. He inspected the accompanying photograph of balaclavaed students advancing towards the camera, one with a fist raised in the air. No society claimed the poster, except that it said meet at The Red Lion next month on the tenth. Flood stood for a while. The poster disturbed him, he was not sure what the aims of this group were, though the poster suggested violence and revolution. But for what end? He continued on, his mind digesting the poster's possible meanings.

A group of fourteen-year-olds stood at the end of the path. Some were smoking, others were talking and messaging on their phones. "What you looking at?" one demanded of Flood. His heart jumped, but he ignored the universal declaration of a fight. He strode on with the air of purpose, ignoring a few insults thrown after him and his student demeanour.

He wondered about the sabbing he was going on and felt a slight nervousness and unease, which his active mind tempered with slogans to quash any lingering doubts. It was surely right to disrupt ignorant humans killing innocent animals. After all if he did not get involved who else would stand for their rights? Or if their rights were secured as Peterson hoped, how would he look back on his student days if he did not get involved. It was right, he concluded, right and dutiful. Then the incident on the train came back to him. He hoped that the campaign would not involve any violence. Then it would be right. Nonetheless, a host of quiet objections unsettled him.

Before going into his room, he popped into the convenience store and bought some nuts and milk. No organic, so he had to make do with ordinary. He felt a tinge of guilt, for he could hear Jez mocking his purchase, "What, buy milk exploited from a cow tied up to machinery all day? Why aren't you vegan yet?" Well, I do like my cereals, he countered, and purchased the pint.

The residence hummed as he approached. Some windows were open and students were listening to TV or to music. He checked his mail: one bill for residence fees, still unpaid. Never mind, he thought, I may not continue doing this. I'm going to be a soldier and fight for the freedom of animals everywhere. But a second later this thought was tinged with a guilt that told him he would be paying it next week.

He climbed the stairs to the second floor and entered his messy room. He tidied the pizza boxes into the rubbish bin, made a neat pile of his books, folded up student newspapers, and put his laundry into a bag. Pleased with his organising, he sat down in the armchair that he had bought. The hall of residence's chairs were decidedly uncomfortable - not for reading in at all, which he thought was rather ironic, since reading was the sine qua non of coming to university.

He put his kettle on and flicked through the broadsheet that his politically-minded neighbour shoved under his door periodically. A headline caught his attention on the second page. "Lords arrested." The kettle boiled and he dropped a herbal bag into the mug, poured in water and sat down to read.

"Four Scottish Lords were arrested yesterday in the House of Lords for refusing to obey the new Scottish Land

Redistribution Act. The Act requires that they sign property over to croftholders residing on their lands. The summons were announced on Monday, but since then the four Lords have remained at Westminster, trying to argue for their case during Parliamentary Questions. In an ironic twist on the attempted arrest of five MPs in the reign of King Charles I, the police were led into the Upper Chamber by a Commons MP, Mr Thomas Waterside, MP for Huntingthorpe.

"The arrested Lords complained that their rights to argue against any government proposals had been unconstitutionally removed by the New Parliament Act in the previous session and that they would be taking their case to the European Court. Mr Waterside, who has been earmarked by the Prime Minister as a candidate for the European Commission, claimed that the Lords had broken the law in refusing to sign over their land and that the police had in fact the right to arrest people in the chamber. Mr Waterside, an animal rights activist and committed Socialist, was pleased that the arrest had been made. 'Their property was stolen from the peasants and we're making sure it's given back,' he said on leaving the Commons.

"It is the first time in the history of the Lords that Peers have been arrested in the Chamber. MPs and Peers do not possess any sanctuary from the law at the Palace of Westminster, but some MPs expressed their misgivings that the police were led into the Chamber during a debate. One MP, who preferred to remain anonymous, said the action reeked of totalitarianism and warned the nation that the last time such a symbolic arrest was attempted, civil war broke out..."

Flood stopped reading and chuckled at the accompanying cartoon of the four Peers, dressed in wigs and gowns, being led out by Oliver Cromwell dressed as Charles I. He flicked over other headlines and pictures of growing traffic queues outside of petrol stations, of the falling pound, of rising taxes, of the FTSE 100 being below 3000, of pension problems, and onto more stories about teachers leaving the profession, more calls for a public inquiry into the massacre of seven million cattle, more scandals about larger donations to the government, and so on.

Having had enough of the world's problems he picked up a play, Eugène Ionesco's The Rhinoceros, whose first act had amused him earlier. He read slowly, enjoying the words, enjoying Ionesco's humorous vision of humanity. Then a low humming and drumming sound shook the floor. His neighbour below had returned from the pub. Flood reached over and turned on his own radio. Jez had shifted the dial to a commercial station, which blasted out music he could not concentrate to. Flood turned it back to the classical station. Barber's Adagio had just commenced. Good, he thought; this is perfect for reading to. The Adagio softened the thumping from below and allowed Flood to return to his reading. Then his neighbour turned the music up slightly; this time the low bass had been replaced by a fast, drilling monotonic bass beat, punctuated by what sounded like a ball bouncing against the walls. His floor shook. Shit, he thought, I can't concentrate. The music caused his heart to race and his mind to be distracted, he felt his pulse resound with a violence and aggression mimicking the techno-beat's drilling sounds. He banged twice on the ceiling. His neighbour turned the music up even more. His room shook, the tea in the cup rippled, a book fell off the shelf. "This is a bloody joke," he said, getting up. He went down the stairs and banged on the door.

It opened and a younger student, a first year, peered out. His eyes were glazed, his nose was pierced twice and his hair stood up in a fearful display of gel and spikes apparently caught as if he had been standing in a wind tunnel at a strange angle. It reminded Flood of kids' Pokemon characters and he laughed inwardly at the pathetic caricature he faced.

"Would you mind turning the music down? I'm reading upstairs."

"What you bloody reading for?" retorted the student aggressively.

"My course. I can't concentrate."

"So?"

"I need to concentrate. I have books to read. I'm a third year and I'm studying English. I need to read, in peace."

"So why don't you go to the library, where ever that is."

"Because it's shut, it's late, and that's my room, and I'm paying for it."

"Should get the government to pay for it, then shouldn't you? I do. I got everything for free, hah," he laughed, his eyes widening as he swigged beer from a can.

"You can't hear my music, can you?"

"No, and I wouldn't want to. You look like a ponce to me. Anyway, I like my music and I like it loud, any problem with that?"

A girl's voice came from the bed. "Paul, wassamatter? Turn the music down if he can hear it. We won't be that loud tonight," she giggled.

"Alright," said the student. "I'll turn it down." "Thanks," said Flood, turning to leave. As the door shut, he heard laughter and the music was turned up very loud. He turned to go back to the door, ready to punch the little shit in the nose, when it was turned down to a more reasonable level, if the machine-thumping rhythm of a drill could be considered reasonable. Still, when Flood was in his room, he could feel the floor vibrate and his tea rippled sympathetically. He returned to the play and enjoyed the irony of his surroundings and the play itself even more.

View From Westminster

Alan Jones MP, Minister of the newly created Department of Ecology, Food, and Rural Affairs sat staring through his office window at the Whitehall offices opposite. He rested his head against his office chair, crossed his hands on his soft belly, and closed his eyes. Five mornings running he had been woken up by hunt protestors blasting their horns outside his Westminster apartment. At night his colleague Thomas Waterside pestered him on the phone about his promise to use the Parliament Act to abolish hunting and reminded him of campaign funds. The man never gave up, even though Alan pointed out that he was aware of pressing local issues in Waterside's constituency. The lack of sleep was beginning to affect him. Earlier, his attention had waned, listening to his son on the phone chattering about school, and he had thereby upset his suspicious wife; he had sworn at a receptionist, bumped into office furniture thee times and twice spilled coffee on departmental files. He could not doze. His eyes fell upon a cartoon of himself and his assistant in the London paper - they had been christened Duckface and Platypus. He sniggered at it. He was supposed to be Duckface. He closed his eyes again. Just five minutes would cure the impending headache.

The phone rang. Another meeting in five minutes. His boss - Diane Taylor, head of the Department of Ecology, Food, and Rural Affairs; Professor Douglas Warbler, famous ethicist, popular philosophy writer, and friend of the PM's; and Mark McLaren, present head of ARUK, Animal Rights-UK, a well-funded pressure group started up by his mother, Lucy McLaren and some Hollywood friends.

"No, I hadn't forgotten, just hadn't realised the time." Alan put the phone down, swore, swigged back his cold coffee and stood up to do some stretches. The door opened just as he was touching his toes for the eighth time, his face flushed with the effort.

"Oh, sorry, Alan," came the voice of his assistant. He shot up, tucked his shirt in, and turned to deal with the interruption.

"Clarissa, I do wish you'd knock louder."

"Sorry, Alan," she smiled back. Soon, he thought, contemplating her form, soon. A recent masters graduate from Cardiff, she was dark-haired, demure, curvy, quite plain faced but attractive brown eyes, and he liked her smile. Another week, a couple of more lunches, yes, she'd be fun in bed. "I've brought you the agenda, in case you'd not read it yet," she said putting the papers on his desk. "You're looking awfully tired, you know. Why don't you get some sleep instead of doing exercises?" Her Powys accent emerged when she spoke more intimately.

He smiled and promised he would get an early night. She's lovely, he thought, watching the pleasant rhythm of her hips as she left his office. I don't get this kind of attention at home. The wife wouldn't say such things - she'd be nagging about Jonathan's latest misdeeds committed on his sister. I shouldn't have had children, he thought, sitting down again. Now, let's see. Warbler, not met him before, but I have to be on my best behaviour. McLaren; yes, the wife wants me to get into one of their parties, I'll see what I can do there. Diane will be here, though.

Alan was not fond of his boss. Very few people were, but they respected her connections with the unions and old Party supporters. She moved around the middle departments, had her input into the Cabinet, but was not really taken much notice of by the Prime Minister, Hugh Cramp - always referred to as Hugh by his associates and Cramp, Crap, or CraPM by the tabloids. Her comments had been contradicted a few times by Hugh, but she had swallowed her pride to keep her job. She wanted to avoid removal to some irrelevant department such as Overseas Aid. Alan was good at listening - he had spent years working with disgruntled, doped-up inner-city youths and knew how to listen - and Diane was often bending his ear about her latest plans for getting the party back on its proper track as she called it. And as long as he kept on her good side he would remain a well-paid minister, he surmised.

Always, after speaking with Diane, Alan felt that the whole hunting issue had been foisted upon him and that he was some pathetic decoy for grander policies. Another Gulf War, perhaps. But he needed to sustain his loyalty in return for whatever rewards might come after the next election. His orders were to buy time for the government. Hugh had voted against hunting, but it was well known that his support was only in order to give the back-benchers some hope for a total ban on fox-hunting. A month ago, the PM had actually said to Alan: "Personally, I'm not bothered; I mean, I have some old friends who hunt, but it's not really our policy not to support it though, is it? We have a lot of support in the constituencies for this. Have some important bills this session. Need support. You keep your head above water, and you'll come out well, I'm sure, but we need to get the timing right, six months more? Do you think that would be good? Okay, good ... you're doing a good job ... " and so the conversation had progressed. Alan's head had swum a little afterwards, but the PM's Press Secretary had popped around later to spell out the intended details and to provide him with his Commons statement.

Alan had not really considered the hunting debate before. He was anti-hunt, of course, but he was in the Labour Party and it was almost expected. So he'd gone along with party traditions. When he thought of the hunt, he saw images of aristocrats riding over Tolpuddle Martyrs and Wat Tyler standing up to huntsmen. To be anti-hunt was, by definition, what his party membership entailed, so he was surprised to be pulled aside by a few colleagues who believed differently, and who pointed out what the impact would be on jobs in the valleys, and did he know many ex-miners would be once again badly hit by the government? But the momentum came from London nowadays, not the land of Nye Bevan. The power came from smartly dressed suits with incessantly texting phones and sarcastic political science grads filling him in with what to say and how to present himself. Clarissa could help. He should take her out next time he went touring. It would be a good excuse.

A knock at the door and Clarissa poked her head around to make sure Alan was not compromising his dignity again. "Minister, your meeting is here," she said nervously and frowned to herself as she caught the awkward grammar of what she had said.

"Show them in," he said, rising from his desk.

Diane strode in with the air of ownership that always made Alan retreat a step. Dressed in her ubiquitous dark red suit, she passed Clarissa her long black coat and introduced Professor Warbler and Mark McLaren. Alan's background had not really prepared him for the etiquette of ministerial meetings. He felt his shoulders tighten and the impending headache loom nearer. He shook hands and motioned awkwardly to his guests to sit at his boardroom-sized table. Diane took command over placing the other two, leaving Alan wondering where he should sit. McLaren and Warbler sat next to one another. Diane was sitting opposite them. He would take the end. His mind was not fully aware of his choice but it turned out to be the right one. If he sat next to Diane, that would present a two-against-two confrontation, this way the conversation could be opened up more. Diane, nonetheless, shot him a look but he had committed himself to the chair and it was his office after all.

Clarissa was offering drinks. Alan, still in a reverie about her hips, caught her perfume as she leant over to place the cups on the table. He didn't want this right now, he wanted to curl up in her arms and fall asleep under that intoxicating smell. Diane began the proceedings. He transferred his attention back to the table and his guests. McLaren was a twenty-something, long black hair caught in a ponytail, a well-trimmed, goatee, and both of his ears with their fair share of piercing. His immediate bearing suggested poverty, but Alan had spent enough time with the poor to recognise highly expensive, tailor-made Gothic-style clothes. His nails were manicured too, Alan noticed. Warbler was young for a professor, he thought. Australian or Kiwi, not sure. Late forties perhaps, thick lips slurping from his coffee mug, held up by soft white hands; Alan wondered if he had been punched on the nose when he was young, for his nose was slightly offset in his wide face. Dark eyes peered through thick glasses at Diane, who continued with the preliminaries.

"So, we are left presently in limbo, but that's politics," she was saying with an exasperated edge to her voice.

"But we'll get the ban, won't we?" McLaren's intonation gave away a public-school accent that his affected cockney twang could not camouflage.

"Of course," said Alan, picking up his warm coffee. "The bill will get through without much fuss."

"The back-benchers deserve it," said Diane candidly. "Between us, the PM's really stretched their loyalty at times and they're waiting for their rewards. This will be it."

"About time, as well. But the timing has to be right, and I think we've got them now," added Alan.

"Your statement to the House acknowledged as much," said Warbler turning his attention to Alan. "We understand, in all the animal rights movements, that politics sometimes gets in the way. I enjoyed your statement. I thought it was well balanced. You threw the hunting lobby a bone of hope, but the intention was clear enough."

"But they're getting another season's hunting in," said McLaren petulantly. "Can't we just push ahead now?"

"Timing is crucial," explained Warbler. "Besides, our activists are enjoying another season of disrupting the hunts."

"True. We have a few surprises this month."

"Nothing illegal, I hope," said Alan. "We couldn't do with any last-minute upsets disturbing the polls."

"Some groups are impatient," said McLaren.

"Keep it to yourself, Mark," said Diane forcefully. He sat back slightly and crossed his arms. "We enjoyed one of the Rural Alliance's marches just last month. Bigger than any we were in. We had to work hard to minimise its impact. The Mayor and the BBC were of course sympathetic to us and obediently looked the other way, and we made sure we were all out of town. But some in the press supported them and we have to wait until the noise dies down to make our move. Hugh has his finger on the nation's pulse. He knows what to do."

"Okay. But once this is through, what are the chances for banning fishing?" Warbler demanded.

"I've got a lot of constituents who'd be pissed off," said Alan.

Diane spoke over him at the same time. "Shooting first. We've put the wheels in motion for the next bill. As for fishing, we'll have to rely on you," she nodded to Mark, "to do the info-campaign." She turned to Warbler. "Maybe a couple of years after shooting?"

"Not bad. And Europe?" Warbler asked. "I know Hugh's got influence there," he added, emphasising his personal connection.

"I've got a meeting next month with the Council of Ministers," Diane said nodding. "Our European Hunting Bill will be presented to the Council, but the Commissioner for Ecology and Animal Welfare, Karl Goebbels, is thrilled with our progress. He's keen to push for European-wide bans on hunting, bull-fighting and the human consumption of horse-meat and thrushes."

Warbler nodded. "I know Kurt - ex-student of mine. But how will the French respond?"

"The intellectuals are too concerned with anti-immigration riots in the south to notice, but the farmers are keen to get more money, whatever the finer details," Diane replied. "Karl hopes to push animal rights directives in conjunction with the new Farming Bill. Majority voting should get it past the French and Spanish and their vile bull-fighting."

"You mean, we buy off the hunting lobbies across Europe with the new eco-friendly CAP?" asked Mark.

"Exactly," said Diane.

"Quickest way to control someone is to give them taxpayers' money," added Warbler.

Alan frowned. He could not quite see why but nodded as if he should know.

"The Association's up for giving the party another million," said Mark. "But we want results soon, you know."

Diane's face brightened. The possibility of another large donation coming through her contacts and her department could only make her look good. She pushed some hair off her face. Alan caught a glimpse of her desire for promotion. He wasn't bothered too much himself - he had recently come through some quasi-scandals cooked up by the press and it had tamed his ambition. Now his ambition had turned to bedding Clarissa within a week. Much more fulfilling, he smiled; still, I've duties to the party, he thought, shifting away from fleshy fantasies.

"I have several meetings around the country over the next few days. I'll be getting feedback on rural feeling, although I'd prefer to be enjoying some Rural Affairs," he quipped and instantly regretted it. Diane's face suggested that she understood his implication. Mark nodded without understanding, but Warbler laughed.

"Yeah, me too. I do enjoy my visits to Blighty. So, things are looking up - they can only get better, as Hugh once said to me. Anyway, I've got a 12 o'clock appointment at the LSE, so you'll have to excuse me." Mark mumbled that he had something to do over at Bloomsbury Square but Alan couldn't catch what he said.

After they had left Diane returned to Mark's suggestion of another donation. "We'd have to do some reworking of its implications, of course," she was saying, "I mean, if we received another million from the anti-hunt lobby while we were pushing the Bill through, it wouldn't look too good, but then ... one million ... that would help the department's image." She pushed back her greying hair away from her prematurely wrinkled skin, dried from too many hours under sun lamps. "And bank balance," she murmured.

"Hugh'd be impressed," Alan noted thinking of her potential promotion to some other bigger department.

"Certainly, that'd be true. But also think of the back-benchers and the support they would give the department."

Alan knew she meant herself but went along with it. She inquired into how the consultation with the various lobbies was proceeding; and he read out a list of the various people he had recently met.

"Good. Keep it up Alan." Her voice changed to a more serious tone. He had been waiting for whatever it was she had been keeping to herself. It was her way and he had become accustomed to her strategy. "I couldn't say anything while Mark was here - he'd go blabbing to the press. He's an excellent link, of course, but too young to be trusted with much information. Timing is crucial, as you said, but Hugh is keen to push ahead with the hunting bill. You and I know that the consultation is mere playing for time. Keep your head above water for the next few days - keep a straight face and pretend to remain neutral. We've got full backing on this one.

"Why?"

"Hugh needs support for external policy from the back-benchers and he's willing to allow Waterside to table his private member's bill to ban all forms of hunting with hounds. He's promised us parliamentary time and the use of the Parliament Act if needs be."

"In return for acquiescence on the other issues?"

"Does it matter what his motives are?" Diane countered sharply. "Fact is, we've got the backing to change history in our little corner of politics. I've never had that chance before in any of the departments I've worked in, and I'm not going to turn my back on this opportunity." She sat forward and crossed her arms. "If we get this right, we'll be going down in the history books, but more importantly the road will be clearer for the rest of our rural policies."

"How long will we need before we can begin implementing the broader policies?"

"Alan, we're almost there!" She sat back, exasperated, but then returned to the provocative position so familiar to television viewers. Alan was used to the pose but still found it unnerving. "Once this troublesome bunch of individualists is silenced by unemployment, then we can proceed more quickly. Remember what Thatcher did with the unions and how she did it. Saw the off the enemy within, she claimed. Well, we're going to do the bloody same to the Tory bedrock in this land." She glanced at the ceiling reckoning a calculation on her fingers. "I believe three years. There will be a knock-on effect from banning hunting with hounds, as the Rural Alliance so often explains. Their data has been highly useful for planning the next phase, or so my secretaries tell me. In three years time the majority of stables will have converted for pleasure rides or shut down. The fox-hunting countries will have been annihilated and with them all the old aristocratic links and all bastions of traditions and old thinking and downright bloody-mindedness." Her eyes widened as she spouted her deeply held but rarely expressed inner opinions. "The new EU measures will have prompted more farm mergers, creating larger and larger units, which, in conjunction with the Right to Roam and the new Organic Standards Directives, will have decimated the smaller farms. Our government will be dealing with fewer and fewer representatives of a declining industry, which means the industry will be even easier to control than now. That'll mean protecting European farming from Eastern European and American farming interests will also be easier. Don't forget - free trade is easy to kill when you only have a few heads to chop. After the next election, which the pundits say we ought to win with a majority of fifty to eighty, we'll implement phase two - the gradual nationalisation of the land under my aegis."

"You mean the formation of 'UK Farming' we've spoken of?"

"Precisely. Then 'EU Farming', of course. Farmers will rent land off the government, which of course will earn us substantial rents, instead of them going into the hands of the Tory gentry and bourgeoisie, and we'll be setting the licensing standards for the farmers much more stringently than we can do now."

Alan nodded. "Yes, take away a man's land and he becomes more flexible."

"Politically pliant, Alan. Let's be frank. I'm interested in our party ruling for the next fifty years, and it won't be able to do whilst there's a bloody property-owning democracy. Most of the land of this country is set aside for farming, while our voters struggle to pay the high cost of city and suburban housing. Once we have control of the entire countryside, we could plan anything. Transport will love it - trains could go anywhere; Housing will love it - could build new towns wherever; and the Treasury would enjoy the rents now lost to the private sector," Diane smirked.

Alan was not sure whether she smirked because she was realising her idyllic ideological future or ensuring her political immortality. "Why can't we just go for phase two now and avoid the confrontation with the hunting lobbies? Surely, if we nationalised the land we could control hunting and fishing as we saw fit as a department, rather than needing Acts of Parliament to be haggled over and massaged into law?"

"I told Hugh that we didn't stand a chance while the hunting community was still active. The bloody Rural Alliance and their spin-offs are becoming increasingly annoying." Alan nodded and mentioned his lack of sleep because of the dawn chorus of hunting horns. Diane said that her country house had been plastered with pro-hunting stickers but had had the culprit arrested.

"I read about that. He was some rock star's son, I gather?"

"Yes. Second offence - he'd already tried his luck at Hugh's but couldn't get anywhere near it. Mine was a softer target I guess." Diane guzzled her coffee and continued the outline of her political strategy. "Three years from now, I said, we would be free of their interference. They'll be a forgotten force. Not many people in London know about their issues anyway, and that's only good for us. If we went to phase two right now, we'd lose the hunting bills and the land bills. All has to come at the right time. If you don't know your history, the country and its gentry have always formed the stumbling block to progressive legislation in this land. Too wealthy and too independently minded by far. Socialism will not recover while we still have such bulwarks of conservatism in the land. No, Alan, first things first - let's placate the hunting lobbies for the meanwhile, and then we'll hit them hard. Hugh's hinted that he'll allow time for Waterside's bill when the shit hits the fan over the Gulf and Africa. He needs the diversion. We need the policies. Blunderton's always got his five-a-day initiatives and we need something big to match him." She sat back and tapped her finger on the desk.

Alan put his hands behind his head. "So. I keep up the façade of listening and we'll get the ban anyway. Okay. Okay. I'll be patient." He hoped that he would enjoy some of the limelight for his performance and that Diane Taylor would not hog the nation's attention.

They discussed other departmental business for half an hour before drawing the meeting to a close. They were both expected in the Commons later for Prime Minister's Questions and had to go over some prepared research. Alan tried to avoid showing his face too much in the Commons these days. He did not like the obvious disdain and even hatred in some Tories' eyes as he passed them. One or two hunting back-benchers in his own Party also regularly reminded him of rural workers' rights and their unions, which gave him a headache. He turned to his memos and the day's order of business. He worked out the hours he would need to be in the House and what time he would be free to offer Clarissa dinner. He could do with some sympathetic company. She knocked on the door and slowly opened it.

"Vincent Harrison," she said with raised eyebrows. "He was passing and wondered if you had a couple of minutes."

Vincent Harrison, Chair of the Rural Alliance, nice man really, politically of the same background, but his calls were becoming a little too persistent recently. Every time any of Alan's juniors went out they were stalked by hunters, each time Clarissa opened his email account she was deluged with pro-hunt correspondence, wherever he turned he heard horns or saw large vans advertising massive posters demanding the countryside be left alone. His head pounded. "Show him in," Alan said.

"Alan, I noticed Mark McLaren and Professor Warbler leaving the building earlier. Been to see you?"

"None of your business, Harrison," Alan said, emphasising the surname as if it implied something less than salubrious.

"It is if it affects my members," Harrison replied, taking a seat unbidden. "Is McLaren offering you money again? What is your price?" He crossed his legs and looked at Alan.

"You know that we are not up for sale."

"Pull the other one. Any porn dealer can buy your party. So,what will be the Danegeld for the hunting lobby, Alan? A million? Two? A free holiday for the PM at an exclusive hunting estate in Rumania? It can be fixed you know. Would that buy our freedom? Because that's all we're after." Then he stopped and leant forward, placing his hands on his knees. "Freedom should not cost anything though, should it?"

Alan shuffled his papers to prepare his briefcase.

"Not quite the party's history, is it?" said Harrison rhetorically. "Don't forget I was once a member."

"New Labour's not for sale," quipped Alan.

"It won't be working soon, either," retorted Harrison playing on an old Tory campaign poster from 1979, but a sharpness to his voice unsettled Alan.

"Harrison, you know that we are in the middle of a consultation on all hunting matters. I have to look at all the evidence, from all sides. I'm not interested in an emotional barrage, I have to look at the facts."

"What good will that do my members? You've already got your opinion. You voted for an outright ban last time. Are you really the best person to be handling this? It's like asking the Inquisition to examine its own methods. 'oh, we'll look at the facts, and ah, yes, after looking at the facts, we are right,' it would say. Come on, be honest."

Harrison had never been so adamant or rude even. Alan cracked his fingers. "Vincent, I need facts not opinions. This is a serious consultation exercise."

"Given this government's past, that's rather rich. Besides, what are you going to do with the facts? Shall the truth suddenly jump out from them? No, mate, you've made up your mind and you're buying time. Not much more to it, but I can tell you things are beginning to feel tense outside of London. Did you know that only eight million people live in London? That leaves fifty-odd million that don't. I reckon your party has forgotten that simple fact. Anyway, my members are on my back all the time, and since I'm paid to represent them, I'll be on your back. Name the price for our freedom, Alan, go ahead - we'll make the donation," he added, impersonating Dirty Harry's famous movie line.

"I have to go to the Commons," Alan replied.

"Then I shall see you around. I gather you're visiting a few DEFRA buildings around the country. Expect the petitions. Oh yes, here's some to keep you company." Harrison opened his brief case and passed over a wad of handwritten letters. "I'm sure you'll read them all. Each one of them written by some person who just wants to get on with his life and be left alone by your party's bullying."

Harrison got up and made his own way out. Clarissa entered with some more email memos. "Some more pointers for the day's debates. The PM wants you to raise a question about British troops stationed in Bosnia and Rwanda before answering questions on the hunting debate. It's all here. You're still too pale, you know," she added softly, looking concerned. "Well, as soon as you're out of the House get yourself home and put your feet up. You work too hard, you know." Her soothing words struck home and wove a temporary intimacy between them that Alan knew he had to capitalise on. His next words flowed naturally.

"Would you mind coming over when you've finished? I would prefer not to eat alone, that is, I'd like to have dinner with you." He flustered and sought refuge in getting his coat on. "I've got lots in the fridge that should be eaten and I can cook well. No pressure, though, just fancy some company."

She smiled. "I'll bring some wine."

He gazed upon her with a sense of familiarity. Not much of an age difference, he noted. He was thirty-six, she twenty-four. Twelve years - but she stood as an equal before him. Not that the women MPs would see it like that, another part of his mind reminded him. He had power, he was the man, and he was by definition exploitative and a patriarch. His head ached and he frowned.

"Did it not go well with Harrison?" Clarissa inquired, helping him on with his coat.

"He's becoming more irritating," Alan replied. "But it won't be for much longer. A few months and he'll be history, along with his supporters."

"It's so barbaric, isn't it? I can't understand why people want to hunt. What wine should I bring? Red or white?"

"I was going to do a nice Welsh lamb dish, so how about red?"

"Red it is. Now you'd better be off. I'll put NewsFM on to listen to your question. I know you'll do well. Good luck," Clarissa added. Alan almost bent down to kiss her - it would have felt so natural. As he left he thought, this is how a marriage should be. Or a friendship at least. His heart had shifted from Clarissa's sex-appeal to Clarissa's spouse-appeal, and it felt right. His headache diminished and he picked up his pace as he made his way to the Commons. As he crossed Parliament Square he caught sight of the Hunt Vigil, which had been outside for several months now and he wondered if he could follow the tourists around to the left to avoid the usual heckling. His phone rang and he scrambled deep in his coat pocket for it. It was his wife. His headache returned as she pitched complaint after complaint at him, threw in a few of her usual mind games and added one on his son's behalf. Caught up in her barrage, his frown intensified and he slowed; he withdrew from the herd of tourists and the hunters spotted him.

As he took his seat in the Commons his head was pounding fiercely. He left soon after he had done his party duty and headed straight for the chemists next to the Westminster tube station.

Laurenten Decides

For Douglas Laurenten life had suddenly intensified. A few calls to friends and colleagues to gauge their opinion and he knew had to make the decision to call the Assembly. Now every minute passing seemed to count towards a vast something that his life careered towards. Each decision he made wrenched itself from his very being and stood aloof as something tangible and paramount that could later be held against him. Such were the decisions that the great men of history were later vilified or celebrated for, and such was the kind of decision that challenged Laurenten.

He could not know whether he would prove himself to future historians as the man of the hour, or whether his actions would remain part of the inexorable and forgettable tide of daily life.

Laurenten sat pensively in his office at Stanthorpe Manor in Northchestershire after driving down from Scotland the night before. The office overlooked the main drive to the house and the autumnal gloaming. The panelled room had been the butler's office, for it possessed a good position to notice any arrivals coming along the drive. Laurenten's father had taken it over for his study and enlarged the hitherto narrow lattice windows; Laurenten had it wired for his computer and satellite television. There were two floor levels. The lower level acting as a vestibule with two smaller doors, one leading out to the servant's passageway underneath the house and to the kitchen, the other into the Great Hall via a hidden door.

Laurenten's wide walnut desk was covered with recent papers and commentary magazines. He had spent much of the past few weeks reading the news and commentaries and re-reading aspects of British history he thought pertinent. In Scotland he had effectively made his decision: the Scots voted for the man rather than the party, and his reputation was strong enough to gain broad support across the Highlands and Lowlands outside of the cities. He knew he could carry a sufficient number of disenchanted and disillusioned Scots: within months of devolution their new chamber had shown its true self-seeking, aggrandising colours. It would not take much to direct the implicit anger of the nation at that bunch of rogues, as Stewart called them, into a consistent and unrelenting attack. Barracking MSPs was child's play. What was needed were the proper words to attract people over to freedom's cause. No, it would not take much to draw people's attention to the indelible inconsistency blotting out freedom in the northern lands.

For Wales, he had to defer to colleagues closer to the political centre. But he felt that the grievances fomenting there were not dissimilar to those in Scotland - the rural populations were being battered by cumbersome and invasive EU and UK legislation and by threats to hunting and traditional conservation practices from the urban elites.

England was more complex though. Its larger population held wider variations in opinion, but also a greater flexibility and intricacy than Scotland and Wales. Should he manage to call the Assembly to sit, he believed that the potential secession from the Westminster government would produce a very patchy political map. Nothing was certain here. The political centre of gravity could move swiftly and with such a momentum as to depart quickly from what may have seemed a forceful position.

As if to underline his thoughts the wind was getting up. A blustery gale whistled around the outside of the office. He stood up and looked out of the window and down onto the fading images of the drive and saw the taller trees shake off more of their summer foliage. He watched a car drive up to the manor - his housekeeper returning from an evening's shopping for the house. Mrs Arthurs, recently widowed, was now content to live at the house. 'To keep an eye on you, Douglas,' she said. She parked the car and fought the wind as she made her way to the entrance and Laurenten lost sight of her.

The heavy verdure landscape faded to greys and Laurenten turned to gaze upon the papers and books on his desk. Scattered across the desk were notes he had written over many months. Periodically, he had compiled them onto A4 sheets and then circled and connected concepts. He sat back down and fumbled through several sheets attempting to enforce some order. It was no good, he countered: the direction was obvious and the choice increasingly apparent. I could arrange and re-arrange these papers all night and I would draw the same conclusions.

Laurenten decided on a different tact: to clear his desk completely. He placed all the newspapers on one pile and his own writings on another, then put both piles on top of a filing cabinet. He sat back down and tried to study the desk's form and patterns. Disgruntled, he got up and left the office. He took the door to the Great Hall.

Standing underneath one of the heavy chandeliers, Laurenten surveyed remnants of his ancestors' exploits. Shields, stag heads, swords, muskets, armoury, hung silent on the walls. Despite its openness and high ceiling, the Great Hall felt claustrophobic. It was as if the walls could not contain the massiveness of his choice. He needed to get out. He quickly sought his long wax coat and boots and donning a broad rimmed bush hat exited into the gale.

The air enlivened his body and, as he had hoped, sharpened his thinking. The heavy rain fell sporadically in sheets rhythmically rushing along the ground. He could hardly see anything, but that helped him to focus his mind. He walked along the driveway for a hundred yards and then took a bridle path that circled the house and could, if he walked the entire path, take him on a five mile walk. It was easy to follow and as it cut through the woods, it partially sheltered him from the wind and the rain.

It was a good quarter of an hour before his body surged ahead automatically and his adrenaline freed and empowered his thinking. He began by summarising the case for calling the Assembly to sit. For over three hundred years its Members and Delegates had sat as guardians of liberty; its origins lay in the Civil Wars and it had never been called to sit; so why call it now? Surely its jurisdiction was antiquated and its political meaning would be lost on present generations? But he was the presiding chair of the Assembly. The Member on whose shoulders sat the responsibility for convening it. Not quite, he reminded himself. If two-thirds of the Members or two-thirds of the Delegates wished to call a convention, they could petition him to do so, and he would be bound by their vote.

The Assembly had almost been convened in recent years - five times, he noted, over the past century, when it looked like the land was about to lose its cherished liberties for good. They had made a mistake not to convene after the Second World War, he believed. But older Members had explained to him that the general population knew enough about freedom and liberty to ensure all would not be lost. Politically, the lands had moved towards a centrally controlling and intervening state, but culturally Britain had remained nobly committed to the liberal values. Even two decades ago, when the land was ripping apart along some of its seams, most Members thought that enough of the past's cultural momentum existed to sustain the great liberal heritage. But now. But now, he considered, things had changed.

Life - the freedom to live life - was slowly being strangled from the land. Generations grew up without a conception of freedom, and because of that, they knew nothing about responsibility. The latter was frequently attacked by the greater population, but few connected it to the dying embers of a free society. Regulation entailed the removal of responsibility; but so few saw that. People griped, but they rarely connected it all together. It was if they thought progress meant more regulation and more interference, more knowledge about every citizen held on record, and more prescriptions and policies from political bodies.

Laurenten stopped and turned around. The silent path evaporated into the dark and rain. The only sound, apart from the rain, was made by his breath and heart beat. Did where he had come from matter now? Was his history and the history of the country relevant at all? The path vanished into the bleak tunnel of trees. He turned to face the direction of his walk. It similarly disappeared from view after about twenty yards. The wood acted to frame his present, capturing him between history and future. He toyed with the temporal metaphor. A man is blind to much of what surrounds him, he philosophised. His past recedes behind him and he wonders what it was all for. His future is just as blank.

"And so too with the land," he said out loud.

He looked up at the cover and thought that if he climbed the trees he would perceive the direction better. Isn't that what I'm doing? he considered. Am I not standing on the treetops and observing where we're going, and isn't it so damn obvious that any would be blind to not know? But most people keep their noses to the floor and don't see where they're heading. Not their fault, he added: life's hard enough without having to pay attention to political decisions unknown people make.

But that was what was now happening. All across the West the machinery of government was expanding its influence and removing local power and individual decision making. He returned to his walking and let images and stories of recent interventions remind him of the growing evidence. It was not as if it were as blatantly visible and obvious as the Westminster government taking over a hitherto free city and declaring it now under its jurisdiction like the Russians taking over Grozny. The state's advance was more subtle; more cancerous. Caligula wished the Romans all had one neck, so he could chop off the head: that kind of tyranny, Laurenten reasoned, people could comprehend and react against. Or the malicious, invidious assassination of a political opponent by a paranoid incumbent made sense; even the conspirational machinations of intellectualising megalomaniacs could be comprehensible to the masses. But death by a thousand cuts: which one would kill you? That was what the land was suffering from.

Laurenten picked up pace as the path descended slightly. The evidence was certainly amassing. The discontent, albeit implicit or unguided, across the country was growing. The government's attack on hunting surfaced in his thinking. Cosima was right to emphasise how strong - or rather how numerous - the reaction had been. Were we watching the last historical echoes of rural freedom? he wondered. How ironic that the sport of kings should come to represent freedom's last stand. But few knew that, he reminded himself. They were to be told what it represented, and Vincent Harrison was particularly failing in that regard.

Halfway around the walk stood an old cemetery, and it was this that Laurenten now entered. He pulled away a few briers and opened the wrought iron gate put up by his Victorian great-grandfather. The private cemetery was overgrown in parts - the family preferred it that way. Cosima went there often in the summer to read novels and had requested as a child to permit some of the forest's intrusions to remain. He had worried at first that she was pining her mother in an unnatural fashion, and he had questioned her on her visits when she was twelve. She admitted to speaking to her mother's gravestone now and again, but emphasised strongly that it was like a den to her. Somewhere she could call her own and not be disturbed. He had nodded and as the years passed he was relieved to note that she did not exhibit any weird tendencies. Besides, on several evenings of the year he would come alone to the cemetery to commune with the dead and with his thoughts.

He approached his wife's grave and stroked the soaked lichen limestone and traced the letters of her name, Sylvia Laurenten. Although he could not see the words, below her name was Shakespeare's verse, "O Song, resound to Sylvia/to fair Sylvia's glory/long has she acquired every grace/that earth can bestow/bring her garlands/and the sound of strings." He knelt on the dwindling mound, kissed the stone and murmured his words of love. He stayed their for a long while wishing her tomb would open up and pull him in. It was an old desire that had faded only gradually over the years. He also knew that she would tell him to get up and get on with it. He could just about recall the intonation of her voice and the mirth she would bring to their arguments and stand-offs as he called them. He smiled now and patted the stone. "I know, I know. Time to move on, lass. I just wish you were here." He got up, a tear trickling down his damp face, and pulled away a vine that had made its way over to the grave.

The rain eased up and he decided to walk around the other stones. What for? asked a part of his mind. Inspiration, answered another. It was a strange place to look for it, he added to his thoughts. He wandered to the side and down to the rear of the small park of headstones and tombs passing several illustrious family members and nodding his acknowledgements as he had done since childhood. He wound his way to a tomb that he also knew intimately. Its shape and silhouette were very familiar to him from hours of studying and drawing it as a youth. The stone had been carved by the man in life; at the head lay an open book and on the book a skull. Crossing the book under the skull and extending out and along the stone were a short sword and a long plume-feather pen. At the foot of the sarcophagus, Laurenten traced the words of its creator.

In slavery wrought
Freedom I bought
Penmanship I sought
And for liberty I fought
Charles Jean Bodin -

Charles Bodin, an African slave, had moved to England from France during the hectic year of 1793. He was already a free man, but he sought to improve his virtues through employment in the Laurenten household. George Laurenten had met Charles on one of the family estates in the Loire region where he was working as a grape picker and labourer; the two young men had made an impression on each other and when Charles turned up at the English family home applying to work for the family he had been heartily welcomed in. Laurenten had read the man's diaries and had checked the veracity of the story with external sources - the family had given him employment and he had settled on the grounds; he lived in his own cottage and did not marry; and he had become a stone mason as the work was in great demand at the time. George had also insisted Charles learn to read and write, which he did with some flair.

Laurenten often had his misgivings about the relationship, for he sometimes believed George may have been acting as a patronising Pygmalion. Despite family assurances to the contrary, he returned often to the letters and diaries to seek evidence of paternalism. He could not find any. Charles's independent spirit shone through. He was a man who had gained control over his destiny and, from what he had written, he was not letting it go. Charles became a local celebrity whom the locals believed brought them good luck (a rumour probably circulated by George, Laurenten felt), but what struck Laurenten most was Charles's deeply held belief in himself. In one entry, which Laurenten had re-read many times, Charles had written: "I have walked alone. At times it has been a lonely path, but I am free, and how many of my brethren can say the same? I know my friends despise slavery and sincerely seek to overthrow the pernicious yoking of their fellow man, but will they recognise its guise in other forms? I have seen the horrors of war and of the violence reform brought; I knew it not then, but have learned why France revelled in bloodshed. I should not wish it upon any man. I took up arms to fight for liberté, and I put them down once the war was no longer for freedom. Many fought on; but the many soon lost themselves to the war - they no longer knew what they fought for. They had become slaves."

Laurenten reflected on Charles's words as he stood next to his tomb. The many were losing themselves to regulation and hence to slavery. Charles would have understood. He thanked the skull and, after bidding his wife's grave a good night, he hurried back to the house via one of the shortcuts.

Back in his office he opened his address book, took out a clean sheet of notepaper and wrote down several names and their numbers. The key players - the movers and shakers as Cosima had called them. The time had come to raise the sword and fight for freedom.

Country Store

Flood awoke, dressed, and checked his text messages. One from Jez: Get stff 2dy cu 8am tmrrw < ;). And one from Maggie which said: cfee aftr lect urs 8>). His neighbour's drilling music had continued until three in the morning and he was tempted to make a lot of noise himself. He opted for dropping books heavily onto the floor, and after the third thump he could hear some shuffling and cursing below. Flood smiled, left the room, stomped down the stairs, and let the fire door slam.

The morning air was fresh and slight drizzle dampened his face. People sauntered past, their eyes avoiding any chance of contact; the individual's evasion was the done thing in cities, but sometimes, Flood thought, why not say hello, why not smile at passers-by? When he had tried it though, he had received glares or ignorant indifference, so he had stopped his crusade to brighten up urban etiquette.

Flood found the country clothing store away from the centre of town. The street was less crowded - patisseries, cafés, some second-hand book stores, a couple of smart clothing stores, and "William Jorrocks, Esq. - Country Clothes": a simple dark green sign with white lettering, a small shop front with a couple of torsos robed in checked shirts with ties, waistcoats and sports jackets. A pair of brown Oxfords festooned with ties and braces was laid out on the shelf and tweed hats and caps with feathers and insignia completed the display.

He entered. It was unusually quiet - normally there would be the omnipresent booming techno-beat of his generation. Here his feet creaked on lustrous wooden floors. Old timber eaves drooped with the centuries' burdens. Spotlights lit up dark oak shelves containing neatly folded plain sweaters and checked shirts. One section contained nothing but hats, the kind of hats he had seen in early twentieth-century books; there were even deerstalkers such as Sherlock Holmes wore. He smiled and gently placed one on his head, but his beard made him appear more like Professor Moriarty than Holmes. He laughed to

WILLIAM VENATOR

himself and was putting the cap down when a voice greeted him.

"Hello, sir. If I may help you with anything, please do not hesitate to ask."

Flood turned and saw a tall man, in his mid fifties, dressed immaculately in tan cotton trousers, well-polished Oxford shoes, and a starched white shirt with a yellow tie, He was smiling at Flood. Flood noticed the shoes and felt embarrassed about his own muddied and forlorn trainers, that had trodden the streets, attended lectures, driven cars, and generally festered in his room.

"Thanks," he mumbled, seeking the appropriate gravity and demeanour for the shop. The shop was overwhelming in both its simplicity and its prices. The colours bespoke of country life, the prices of lottery winners, Flood thought. Fifty-pound shirts. Hundred-pound shoes. He approached the coats: three hundred pounds. This had better be worth it, he said to himself, seeing another price tag of five hundred pounds on a long cashmere coat.

"Are you looking for anything in particular?".

"Uh, yeah. I need some country get-up. You know, wax jacket and stuff."

"Right sir, upstairs for the jackets. Let me help you with a size." The man led Flood up the stairs. The long room upstairs was divided between evening wear on the one side and wax jackets on the other. "Are you a student at the university?" the man asked as he fiddled through a selection of jackets that gave off unfamiliar odours.

"Uhuh."

"What are you reading?"

"Reading? Uh, The Rhinoceros at the moment, and Dickens's Hard Times."

"Ionesco? Oh, yes, I did enjoy that play. I first saw it performed in Paris."

"In Paris?"

"Yes. I used to have a store there - books and hunting clothes pour la societé Venérie. I left in the late 1970s to set up this

- 112 -

store. But what are you reading at the university - what subject are you taking?"

"Oh, English."

"Understandable. The best subject, don't you agree?" The man introduced himself as the proprietor, Mr Wakeman.

"Miles Thomson," mumbled Flood, shaking Wakeman's hand.

Wakeman took out a jacket and showed it to him. "How about a wax Barnborough, sir?"

"A Barnborough? How much are they?" Some lines were on offer, Wakeman explained and described how to take care of them.

"So why's this better than those bright rambling jackets you see in camping stores?"

"Those are really for city ramblers, who drive out to the countryside for an afternoon to enjoy the rural theme park before fleeing back to their neon domes."

"Their neon domes?"

"Yes, that's what I call cities, they look like domes of neon as you drive towards them."

"Do you live in the country then?"

"Oh yes, most privileged to. I grew up in the inner city of Brumthorpe, as far removed from the country as you could get, except perhaps for London. I moved to the country about ten years ago, after living in town for about fifteen years, and my goodness, what a joy it has been. Most pleasant. Most quiet."

"Do you hunt?" Flood ventured as he tried on another jacket and glanced at several hunting and shooting prints.

"Whenever I can, sir. Time wot's not spent 'unting, is time wasted," quoted Wakeman in a cockney accent.

"I'm sorry?"

"Ah, Mr Jorrocks. Who I named the store after, except I employed my first name too."

"Who's Mr Jorrocks?"

"One of the most hilarious hunting characters ever created. You've not heard of R.S. Surtees?" The man helped Flood into another wax jacket.

"Who?"

"But you're reading literature aren't you?"

"Yeah."

"Have you read any nineteenth-century literature?"

"You mean Dickens? Yeah, plenty of him. And a bunch of women authors I didn't care too much for. I enjoyed Eliot, though."

"It's Dickens's politics you know, not his writing, that keeps him popular. That's why they do not teach Surtees."

"What do you mean?"

"Oh, Dickens was always on about the oppressed and criticising the rich; his champagne socialism goes down well with the middle-classess bleeding hearts. Certainly he could create his memorable characters, but so could Surtees. Surtees, however, lies beyond the pale for modern academics. Now, let's have a look at you."

The coat fit well. Flood began playing with the buttons and zips and moving his arms about.

"Surtees" Wakeman was saying, "writes much better than Dickens, but his politics is wrong. He enjoys the countryside, relishes in it and especially the sports. And his descriptions of contemporary clothing cannot be beaten. One could almost work out the pattern. And Jorrocks's lectures on 'unting, as he calls it," Wakeman added, chortling, "well, they stand as some of the most meritorious and enthusiastic descriptions of the chase ever written. 'It's the sport of kings,'" he quoted, "'the image of war without the guilt and only five and twenty per cent its danger.'"

Flood's stomach turned. "He likes blood sports then?"

"Of course. My goodness, they don't teach you much, do they? Mind you, they never taught me any Surtees and I was lucky enough to go to a grammar school. I was forty, can you believe, before I found this treasure trove of writings, so much better and so much funnier than anything else I'd read from that century."

"Did you go to university?"

"Yes, here in town. Not long after it had been set up. After which I left for Paris to teach English, then I started my own business, which paid the bills sufficiently for me to enjoy a few days a week hunting and reading what I wanted to. A most enjoyable life."

Flood felt the jacket all over. The price was good, and he liked the way it felt on him. "Do you have any trousers and shirt to match?"

"Yes sir, we do. Are you after a full country outfit?"

"Yeah, my girlfriend likes rambling and she says these are the best kind of clothes to wear."

As they went back down to the other clothes, Flood got up the courage to ask Wakeman why he liked hunting.

"Goodness, it's like being asked why do I like being human? It is difficult to describe to anybody who hasn't been hunting. You don't hunt, do you? Have you ever fished?" inquired Wakeman.

Flood shook his head.

"Goodness. Even when I was young the city poor enjoyed fishing in the brooks and streams. We caught hardly anything, but it felt good to try. Why do I like hunting?"

"Is it the killing?"

"The kill is only part of it. That is the culmination of the hunt, if you're ever successful. Now, properly speaking, only the Huntsman hunts. The rest of us follow the hunt. The kill is an anti-climax and a climax; it shows the hunter's success and mastery over nature, and over himself; it shows that he's worked within nature, with the hounds, and with the horses. But if you're stalking, you've pitted yourself against the environment in a way that can never be expressed in our mortal language. That's why so many people get the wrong end of the stick and think it is cruel. They're too removed from nature."

Flood chose from a variety of proffered clothes. He had briefly seen an image of an advert upstairs that guided him in his choices. Each item was so unfamiliar that the picture was his only clue as to how it all fit together. He tried on Oxfords and brogues, caps and gloves, checked shirts, waistcoats and ties. Finally, when he was fully dressed he approached the mirror. He hardly recognised himself. The clothes transformed him tremendously; he felt obliged to stand straighter and to puff his chest out a little.

"Well, sir, you certainly do look the part now."

Flood wondered what part he was supposed to be playing. Deep down he felt that the clothes suited him. They reminded him of his smartly dressed grandfather, an ex-army officer who had profitably turned his hand to business. Flood also felt English - rural - different - it was a difference that did not annoy him but rather that settled deep within his conscience.

"I'll take them," said Flood smiling slightly at his own image.

"All of them?" the man was surprised. He gave Flood a discount and recommended Dunn's for walking-boots.

"Thank you," replied Flood. "Do you mind if I keep the clothes on?"

"No sir. Let me get you a bag for your things, and I shall remove the tags."

While the man added up the prices Flood ventured another question.

"Don't you think that humanity has got past killing animals, though?"

"You mean outgrown it, as if hunting were an immature or barbaric state?"

"Yes, I mean, do we need to hunt, or even to farm for that matter?"

"Goodness, they do teach you a lot of philosophy but no life at the universities. I heard that Professor Warbler was in town. Should be an interesting lecture, no doubt, but has he ever lived outside his air-conditioned apartment, surrounded by books written by people with whom he agrees?"

"I don't know. He has some good ideas, though."

"Yes, I've read most of his books. They are good, if you think good means logical; they do follow a nice logical pattern. But are his premises sound? Are his premises even real?"

"You sound like a philosophy teacher I had in my first year."

"That probably was Dr Morley."

"Yes, how do you know?"

"I attend some external lectures at the university, and Dr Morley comes in every now and again to buy some shirts. He has a passion for our waistcoats," he said pointing to a yellow waistcoat with fine blue and red grid lines.

"So you don't think Warbler's premises are right?"

"Premises cannot be right or wrong; they can be good or bad though."

"What do you mean?"

"Oh, something logicians probably would fail me for; we can create any argument from any premise, which means the important thing is to get good premises. For example, Warbler's premises ultimately involve a hatred of man; he probably hates himself really deep down, never mind the world he lives in. Now you can create a wonderful argument, even a philosophy and especially a religion, from that position, but you cannot say that his premises are good or tasteful. Good would imply that they reflect man's nature, and Warbler rejects the idea of human nature."

"Perhaps there's no such thing as human nature."

"Man has a nature, whatever that nature is, just as much as sheep have a nature, or fish, or bacteria have natures. And we are all part of the same natural world, with its laws. If man does not have a nature, that would surely be an awful plight for us - we are, after all, an eating, sleeping, pooping, yawning, lustful species," Wakeman laughed. "To say we do not have a nature strikes me as wrong, but I prefer to describe it as a bad premise, one that is displeasing to the mind, indeed to who we are."

"So why should we continue to hunt?" Flood caught himself saying "we". Did wearing the clothes change his thinking? Kleide machen die Leute? He left the thought to mingle with other tricky ones he was dealing with, as the man continued.

"It's such a strange question. As I say, it's like asking, why should we continue to be human or to have sex? We all hunt, even the antis. They employ hunting and warlike strategies, using camouflage even, never mind some terror tactics. I say, you're not an anti, are you?" Wakeman asked curiously.

"Uh, no." Was that pure deceit or was Flood's reaction truer than he could possibly say? He continued with the subterfuge.

"My girlfriend likes to go rambling. Her parents are country types as well, and, well, I want to impress them."

"Better to be yourself. The old Greek proverb: know thyself, which should be followed by 'be thyself'. Still, if she's a cracker, I'd do the same," Wakeman winked, passing the credit-card slip over to Flood to sign.

"I must say, if I were a fox I would surely wish to die having led a pack of hounds for miles rather than being run over by some speeding urbanite rushing from neon dome to neon dome along their neon corridors, or shot by a farmer with a .223 rifle from out of the blue. I'm genuinely surprised that most environmentalists do not understand hunting, but then again, they rarely understand environments," Wakeman laughed. "My goodness, the tales I could tell there. Have you ever seen the University Conservation Club trying to conserve the environment? Biggest mess-ups you could imagine. They're in for a few years, run around pretending to do some good, and often leave problems that will develop over decades to destroy habitats or flood fields. Last term I saw them putting up barbed wire, for heaven's sake. You wouldn't find a hunt doing that. They're the ones that keep the hedgerows maintained in the middle of nowhere. Have you seen the state of the lake recently? My goodness. They think they're in control of nature, which is another of those bad premises. Goodness! Anyway, I should let you go." He passed Flood his bag of old clothes. "I can tell that you're not sure about hunting. All I can say is that if you are ever invited to go out on a hunt, do take it up. Then you'll know what it's really about. Until then, although you're entitled to an opinion of course, you do not know what you are missing." Wakeman smiled graciously and led Flood to the door. "I hope I haven't bored you, it's just that hunting does get me excited. So thoroughly real. Takes you to the limits of life and there are few things that can do that today. Anyway, you have a good day, sir, and tell Mr Dunn I sent you round for some boots, and he'll put you right. Come round for a chat if you have any more questions. Good day to you."

"Uh, thanks, and goodbye," said Flood stepping back into the world he was used to. But now it seemed different. There were changes - to his gait, his mien, and his general deportment. A few people smiled at him and he instinctively and confidently grinned back.

He found Dunn's and entered to the smell of new camping gear, of memories of buying a tent when he was ten, and excitedly and fearfully camping out in the garden. A stocky, square-faced man with shorn hair greeted him at the counter. Flood mentioned that Mr Wakeman had sent him around for boots.

"Ah, Jorrocks suits him so much better. Not as plump, but he can certainly enthuse about hunting," said the jovial, slightly rotund sixty-something behind the counter. "So he wasn't hunting or shooting today, was he?"

"Uh, no. Although he certainly talked about it."

"It's his passion. I can see why, been out a few times myself. I prefer the beagling. That way I can stand still and enjoy the landscape and watch the hounds circle around me. I'm a bit plump around the waist to go chasing after 'em myself, as you can see," Dunn smiled, taking Flood over to the boots.

Flood sat down in a chair and gently removed his new shoes. Two hunters in two shops. Something was not right, he thought, or maybe this is what hunters do for a living. But then, weren't hunters supposed to be all lah-dee-dah and terribly, terribly posh, have no chins and horrendous accents from the previous century drilled into them, or be women who were born on the back of horses and grew up with an uncanny resemblance to their equine best friends? Mr Dunn was inspecting his shoes.

"Ah, yes, a nice shoe that you've bought. Good company, should last you a long time." He took Flood's size.

"Definitely need a half size bigger if you're rambling. Let me get Rachel to get the right size. Rachel!" A jimp girl of fifteen going on twenty appeared. "Do get the gentleman a size ten in these, please."

Rachel skipped over and grabbed the box and skipped back to the storeroom. Flood watched her hair bobbing up and down.

"Ma niece she be. Pretty little thing, but a bit too skinny. She's one of those vegetarians, you know, those funny half-people." Dunn scowled at her. "I keep on at her to eat some good Lindthorpeshire sausages but she won't have it. Talks about the brutality towards pigs and other such stuff she's pulled off a cereal box."

"Probably healthier for you in the long run," ventured Flood.

"Healthier? Look at her," Dunn said as she returned, "skinny as an anorexic or a concentration camp victim. Get some meat into you, Rachel," he said as she passed over the box.

She ran her eyes over Flood, "Well, maybe some meat's good for you," she smiled.

"Saucy minx, go and tidy the stock room." Mr Dunn scowled again at the retreating waif.

Flood blushed. "Well she certainly has guts!"

Mr Dunn chuckled. "Ah, guts, just like her mother, ma sister. Headstrong and certainly one for the boys. Goodness. Anyway, how's this boot for you?" It fit well. Rachel had sneaked back and was leaning over the counter and casting obvious glances at Flood. He smiled in her direction. "Rachel, come and sort this gentleman's boots out. You can thread the laces properly while I put them through the till. Now, if you keep your hands off my niece until she's eighteen, I'll give you a ten per cent discount."

Flood laughed appreciatively and thanked Mr Dunn. He left feeling much brighter. So few of those kinds of characters around, he thought, as he strode back to the town centre, but that was, he realised, because he did not normally go into anything but the generic fashion stores with Jez or the trendy second-hand shops with other students.

The crowd perceptibly changed as Flood entered the High Street's human flow. He watched groups of teenagers swarming around on scooters, sending text messages to gaggles of the opposite sex across the street, some enjoying underage smoking, others running in and out the CD stores and games shops. Nightmare for the security, Flood pondered, watching some particularly unpleasant cartoon-like youths dressed in Chicago gang-style clothing, hats pulled almost over their eyes, trousers falling down over their hips and flaring over their shoes, their hair spiked.

He bumped into a woman and apologised. She turned on him. "Better watch where you're going, you fucking toff," she spewed out through a cloud of cigarette smoke. He retreated into himself with great embarrassment. Never been called a toff before, he thought. He followed a clump of young women through the crowd. He followed their scent like a hound, for they left an invisible slick of cheap perfume in the air, mixed with the smell of stale cigarettes. He wondered if a fox were as easy to follow for hounds and whether humans could smell them. One of them, teetering on absurd heels, turned around. "Like what you see, mate?"

Flood reddened and ignored the ensuing giggles. Then he thought, no. He turned sharply right to enter a different stream of people and followed a couple of young girls pushing babies. They turned into W.H.Smith's with much effort; he held the doors open for them and was thanked by the second girl. They were both very attractive except for their pasty skin, but neither was more than sixteen. "You're welcome," he added as they thrust their way to the magazine racks with their pushchairs.

He checked his watch. Half an hour until the lecture. He increased his pace and dodged the scooters, the teen gangs, the young mums, and the toneless buskers. He realised that he would not have time to return to his residence room. He made the lecture with five minutes to spare. Maggie stood outside, reading Hard Times.

A Job Offer

Peter had lain awake for another hour or so before falling into a light sleep. Every sound woke him: the creaking of a tree in the wind, a cat's screeching, the scuffling of a badger or fox had his eyes fast open and his heart beating heavily. He slept deeply only after seven, but was awoken by Liz shortly afterwards, scrambling over him to go the bathroom.

"Sorry, love. I'll make sure the offices got our messages."

"Good thinking, Batwoman," he said, curling up into her space and falling into a deep sleep.

He felt her get back into bed and he knew nothing until she stirred again. "Wow, it's eleven o'clock."

"Hurmp?"

"Eleven."

"I thought it was eight."

"Not any more. We've slept in."

"Can say that again," he said turning to her and kissing her shoulder softly. "Is Sally out?"

"No, she's taken the day off to help us get the house sorted."

"Bugger," Peter said, sitting up. "I broke a promise last night and I was hoping to fulfil it."

"You two up, then?" came a voice from down the stairs. "Coffee? Strong?"

After breakfast the first task was to call the insurers. The day left Peter and Liz exhausted and after having got the lock fixed they accepted another offer from Sally to stay until the cleaners could put their house right. That evening they opened a bottle of wine after a take-out Chinese and were settling down to watch the nightly news when Peter's phone rang.

"Hello? Yes, this is Peter. Oh, yes, of course. No, not at all. Right. No, but just one minute, sir."

Peter muffled the phone and answered Liz's worried expression. "It's Lord Laurenten. Remember Cosima, the cellist? It's her father. He wants to discuss the offer Cosima mentioned. I'll take it in the kitchen if you don't mind." Liz hastily agreed and filled Sally in on the events of the previous evening. Peter was gone for one hour and two glasses of wine.

"I have just heard the most insanely attractive offer of my life."

"What? You've been headhunted?" Sally poured more wine. "I dream of being headhunted."

"Could say that. Laurenten's son had already mentioned me as a possible candidate, and it was fortunate that I was able to speak to his daughter. She filled him in with a few more details. He's offering me an interesting project."

"Doing what?" asked Liz impatiently.

Peter's mind buzzed. There were so many details and potential opportunities dancing in his mind that he did not know where to start. "Gosh, I mean ... to help him ... Well, it's a long story. It's not quite an office job. PR I guess. Political." He tried to formulate the words to get his thoughts across in some comprehensible manner.

Liz was sceptical. Sally sat on the edge of her seat. "Go on," said she, "start from the beginning."

"Lord Laurenten is formulating a plan, let's say, to defend hunting and other traditional rights."

"Like the Rural Alliance?" asked Liz.

"Not quite. I'm not sure of the full details, and he said to keep the plans he explained to me a strict secret. I'm only allowed to say a few things."

"Why?" Liz's concerns were deepening the furrows on her face.

"Because it deals with constitutional matters. The law, parliament. Our land."

"Sounds a bit wishy-washy," said Sally, leaning back. "What exactly is he offering? You know - money?" They often spoke about finances, so Peter had no compunction in telling Sally along with Liz.

"Well, the salary would be initially much less. A stipend more like. For the two of us." Peter could feel it coming. He was severely testing the women's incredulity, but what he had heard on the phone overrode his concerns. Getting that across to Liz and to their close friend was not going to be easy. He had never gone into a business meeting unprepared, and now he was stripped of any means to allay their fears.

"Much less? For the two of us? Can you be any more specific?"

"It's for the country. Oh, that's about as non-specific as I can get," Peter chuckled, nervously sipping wine. "But I'm really interested," he added, sitting up, and his eyes sparkling. "Laurenten is going to be heading, let's say, an assembly or a committee, and he wants us on board to assist in its formation and running. I told him we come as a team and he was happy with that. We get expenses, which should be adequate."

"What about the house, the bills, the mortgage, the savings?" Sally asked.

"He'll take care of them," said Peter, hoping that this might clinch Liz's assent. "Pay them off immediately. Then we'll have a stipend to live on. Hunt subscription thrown in too."

"He'll what?" Liz was not sure if she should be excited or displeased at Peter's vagueness. "Is that the package?"

"It's more, love. Much more. It's not just about the money. I mean, you and I are thinking of setting out alone and that would hit the finances hard for a couple of years anyway. This, in contrast, offers, well ... a say in this land's future."

"Why care about that?" asked Sally.

"Well, from a business perspective, when we do go it alone this contract would connect us to many of the nation's most powerful and wealthy people."

"Good point," said Sally. "Potential customers."

"I also care about where this land is going."

"So, what would I do?" asked Liz.

"We work together, I told him. I presume whatever work requires attending to we'll divvy the tasks."

"And we get a stipend and our bills paid?"

"Yep."

"Hmm," said Sally slightly sceptically. "When does it start?"

"Monday."

"Monday?!" Liz exclaimed. "What about our month's notice and ... what about ... what the heck are we doing?"

"Laurenten will clear everything with both of our offices. He knows people," said Peter excitedly. "This is an opportunity that cannot be missed. Neither of us can see what will come of it, but I know that this is not something to pass up. Trust me," he added. "This is big. From all accounts this will change the country's entire fabric - and we can be a part of it!"

Liz studied Peter intently. His face presented the picture of a young man still caught in the idealistic adrenaline rush of early manhood, but his eyes expressed a deep, and sure wisdom that she could not deny.

"I trust you," she said reaching out and squeezing his hand.

"Thanks. Now, Sally," he said turning his intensifying confidence to her. "Fancy a new job as well? I mentioned your credentials."

"Me? After hearing that, I'm game."

"Then I'll get back to him and say you're in with us."

A Free Lecture

"Hi Maggie."

Maggie squinted, pushed her hair from her eyes and gaped. "Goodness, Flood, you look, uh, rather different. Rather handsome." She blinked through her glasses.

"Uh, thanks. I didn't have time to change."

"Well, they suit you. Is this what you'll be wearing tomorrow?"

"Yeah, oh, and I've got some hiking boots from Dunn's." Flood showed her the bag.

"Cool. Oh, there's the professor. I haven't finished my reading yet, but then again most people haven't even picked up the book."

"I read The Rhinoceros last night instead of Hard Times. Dickens is so depressing."

"Yeah, I know, but it's so important for understanding the development of nineteenth-century humanitarianism, social progress and reform," Maggie reeled off.

"I guess. I sometimes wonder whether Dickens is having a go at all that though. Anyway, have you heard of Surtees?"

"Who?"

"Surtees. Wrote something about a character called Jorrocks - the country clothing shop is named after him."

"Oh, Jorrocks's? I know the shop, but I haven't heard of Surtees. Who is he?"

"Uh, the shopkeeper said something about he was better than Dickens. A mid-Victorian writer, I gather."

"Well, there's the professor. Ask her," said Maggie, pointing to Professor Whitman who was moving to the lecture-hall door.

Flood got up some courage. He felt as if he could approach the professor in the clothes he was wearing. Apart from Peterson, whose status he discounted heavily, he had not spoken to a professor outside of a tutorial before. The context made him nervous. Add to that the fact that she was particularly beautiful. "Professor Whitman," he stammered, "have you heard of Surtees?"

"Surtees? By Jove, yes! Where did you come across him?" Professor Whitman stopped and gave him her fullest attention.

"Uh, the, uh, Jorrocks country store in town, the owner..."

"Ah yes, Mr Wakeman, what a character! I suppose he kept you talking. Mentioned you were reading English literature? Surtees was one of the greatest writers of our period, and the most under-read by far. See me afterwards and I'll explain more. No, better still," she paused, "I'll add him to my lecture. Easily done, and a pleasure to have the opportunity. 'Keep the tambourine a roulin'," she added in a Geordie accent which bemused Flood.

"A strange phrase used by the Geordie huntsman, James Pigg in Handley Cross," she explained. "It will be a pleasure!" she added with a glint in her eye.

Flood thanked the professor and went to sit down next to Maggie. He watched the professor sort her notes. She was on the young side of forty and immaculately dressed in a long grey skirt and jacket, a delicate blue silk blouse and a coral-coloured scarf draped around her shoulders which she adjusted once before beginning her talk. She was slim, attractive, had long curly brown hair, and each time Flood attended her lectures, he fell in love with her, imagined winning her over with deep intellectual arguments, which, in his more private fantasies, were swiftly followed by a slow seduction under a full moon in a botanical garden. He thought of that now as he began head-lining his paper and wondered why it was always a botanical garden and why she kept her bra on. Probably something to do with poster adverts, he mused.

She lectured for forty minutes on Dickens before stopping for a pause. It was a gripping lecture. She left her notes unread on the podium and paced back and forth, svelte and graceful, spouting the intricacies and theories of Dickensian literature - of social criticism, Chartist and union movements, Pre-Raphaelites, Ruskin, Carlyle, Collins, Eliot, Queen Victoria, poisoners and opium addicts, and of all kinds of crime. Then she stopped her flow of connections to muse about Dickens's conception of rural England, and how his romanticisations were removed from the reality, as if he had only seen rural England through Constable's paintings; it was at that point she introduced Surtees, excusing her tangent but justifying it in light of present events and a question from a student. She smiled at Flood, who was at that moment engrossed with her thighs and blushed a complementary red to his yellow waist-coat.

"Now, compared to the rather pale, removed and almost tangential vision of rural England, that we read of in Dickens, R.S.Surtees presents a much more realistic picture of rural England at its peak: of the hunts; the 'swells' who are seen in the country but do not partake in country life; the men and women who hunt and who thoroughly enjoy all that mid-Victorian life has to offer. The return to Arcadia that the Pre-Raphaelites sought, but without the romantic idealism of idyllic medieval landscapes and damsels in distress. No, Surtees' stories find the apogee of life in mid-Victorian England and country pursuits. Surtees wrote for The Field. He wrote of fox-hunts, of Handley Cross and Jorrocks's adventures there, and of Mr Facey Romford's Hounds and the most stunning heroine huntress, Lucy Glitters. Now there's one for the feminists to examine! But will they heck! But to give Dickens his due, he wrote that 'there is a passion for hunting, something deeply implanted in the human breast.' That's from Oliver Twist, but Dickens is put in the shade when we turn to Surtees. He's not on the reading list - but he should be. However, claiming his rightful place in English Literature is most difficult with a profession that is more concerned with parading the latest pathetic, opiate lesbian, pedestrian mind who penned some less than mediocre lines." She paused expectantly, awaiting the challenge to her provocation. Silence.

"Surtees," she continued, "offered Victorian Britain a thoroughly enjoyable characterisation of rural life and country pursuits. Supposedly not the most politically correct literature to read, but to my mind any suggestion of political correctness is a less than subtle demand for censorship.

"Good Lord!" A hint of restrained exasperation leaked out. "A neighbouring so-called university censors students and faculty for using allegedly demeaning or abusive words such as 'history' and 'mad'," - she signed quotation marks in the air. "Well, I wonder what they would think of Surtees? Probably never have heard of him in their English department, since, to judge from the faculty members I've met, they're too concerned with deconstructing tertiary literature for its cultural signification. No originality as a result, never mind any expeditions into the dark recesses of country sports literature. Surtees! What a breath of fresh air. Just like the loveable rogue Jorrocks. Country life, supposedly adored by the Romanticists, yet how many of them truly lived it? Most were too weak-chinned to endure a night's camping in the back garden of their London terraces!" That got a laugh from those students who had been camping.

"Tales of fox-hunting! At its best!" she recommenced with vigour and enthusiasm. That received a few hisses and an uncomfortable shuffling around from some students. But Professor Whitman had warmed up and her eyes glinted with the enthusiasm of an evangelist, unknowingly mimicking her great-grandfather's steps as he had preached in Lindthorpeshire's rural churches. Flood could hear several students groaning and hissing at her topic; he heard whispered comments of "cruel" and "barbaric", but after another five minutes of her seamless connections interspersed with wit and political commentary the entire hall had fallen silent and sat listening intently to each word. It was traditional rhetoric that none of the students had been exposed to it at such a level before. Their minds were overwhelmed, finding it difficult to latch onto anything they disagreed with, for they agreed with everything she said. She had them mesmerised, and her energy flowed into them and when she finished and returned to the lectern to pack up her notes, no one moved or spoke.

"Not long ago, I heard some of you mention cruelty and barbarism. Yet do we not extinguish an animal's life to eat it? And if you exclaim, 'oh, no! I'm a vegetarian?' then as a supposed animal lover, would you wish to impose your chosen vegetarianism on carnivores - on hounds? No, you feed your dogs and cats meat, and it would be cruel if you did not. Now, take out the middle man of the tin can, which most anti-capitalists wish to do anyway, and you have dogs getting their food from nature. When the hounds hunt fox, mink, hare, and stags, they are seeking a meal, but men and women train them and keep them in order. But of course, you don't think about that. I know from marking hundreds of essays, few of you know how to think and many of you just don't think.

"If your ancestors could hear you extolling the moral sanctity of animals they would laugh at you and wonder how you think they survived in the past without killing predators and vermin? To kill a rat is acceptable, because it looks nasty. But to kill a hare, fox, mink, stag, or a seal, or a boar - that you cannot stomach because you are partial to them. Oh, how speciesist! Warbler should be ashamed of his diminutive excuse of a logical argument," Whitman observed, for the benefit of those attending his lecture at the university. "And you cannot stomach it because you've not had to deal with these animals first hand. I hunt. I am proud to say it and I defy anyone to come along with an open mind and say that they did not enjoy it. To hunt is to be human. It brings out elements of your nature that sitting listening to me you could never be aware of. You're denying your own nature if you believe hunting is somehow cruel.

"I have seen barbarism in real life. I've been to Bosnia. I taught there three summers ago when the people were coming to terms with man's barbarity in their own country. But we are also reminded of it every night on the TV: of suicide bombers, of thousands of fanatics demanding the death of political foes, of child soldiers, of parents who abuse their children, and I would add, of politicians who deign to control us. Barbarism is something we commit when we reject each other's dignity." Flood caught a word that he had been seeking for days: '-dignity!' That was it - the woman on the train - the country store owner - the clothes he wore now - but as Whitman continued the word slipped from Flood's awareness again.

"If we stopped thinking and stopped building shelters, making clothing, and protecting ourselves from the elements, we would soon feel nature's barbarism towards us. Think about it. I know that those who have been camping have had a taste of that vulnerability, as have any of you who have ever got lost in the woods, even momentarily. That moment, when you hear something you cannot define or cannot see, and your ancient instincts jar your mind into a fear for your life." Whitman paused and returned to the podium, holding onto its sides. "The appreciation of nature and of animals that we now cultivate is a luxurious pursuit. We have created the wealth to enjoy a drive in the countryside, a gap year in far-off places around the world, and the equipment to bring into our homes research on the lives of the world's creatures. But take the modern trappings away and we remain a vulnerable species.

"But back to Surtees and hunting literature. Even if your stomach is not up to the thought of hunting - my goodness, how did your ancestors survive?" she asked as an aside. "Then you should still read Surtees. After all, a pacifist would be doing himself a disfavour by not reading war literature, as would any of us who refuse to pick up any form of literature, because we may disagree with it. If you start becoming politically picky with regard to what you read, then there is no hope for your own intellectual development. Perhaps that is why our land is going to the dogs, instead of following the hounds," Whitman added, laughing.

"Thank you for listening," she said with a defiant but proud face, "it is so rare these days to be able to speak freely. This gives me hope for our future." She smiled warmly and exited calmly brimming with a pride Flood had not seen before in any of his teachers. And dignified - there, he recalled the word.

As they rose from their seats, Maggie turned to Flood. "Goodness, what do you think of that?"

"I rather enjoyed it," he replied hesitatingly. "It was so spontaneous. So, I don't know what - brilliant. In terms of its delivery," he quickly concluded,

"Yeah, I wish I could speak like that."

"Well, I guess if you know your stuff you could do. Wow, that was good, wasn't it?" he added.

"But she spoke of fox-hunting as if it were ... "

"A good thing? Yeah, I know," Flood said. "I guess she has a right to her views. But the literature sounds really interesting, I mean, the way she described Jorrocks. That made me laugh."

"I'm not sure what Professor Warbler or Dr Peterson would think of Surtees," said Maggie as they left the lecture hall and sought out the café.

"Who cares what they think? Who cares what anyone else thinks about what you read or hear. Whitman said to think for yourself. And this is literature. This is not politics. We should read about things we don't like as well as things we do. I think I'd enjoy reading Surtees." Flood pondered the words "think for yourself". He was told to think for himself, which seemed to be a paradox; but then, how else could it be put? If someone said to him, "think like me," or "think like Hitler," he would know where he stood, but being told to think for himself in such positive tones left him rather dazed. He wondered whether he had ever really thought for himself.

"But it's about killing animals," continued Maggie. "I mean, we are, you know, members of the Animal Rights Society. Well, I guess we read about that whenever someone eats meat, too," she said, digging into her pockets to count her change. "I have three pounds, enough for a sandwich and coffee. Shall we go to Lancolm College?"

"Sounds good. I've got a fiver." They crossed the bridge over the muddy and algae ridden lake. Ducks quacked and waddled along the bridge.

"They're so sweet," said Maggie, watching a couple of drakes.

Flood watched them keenly. Surely you could grab one after tempting it with some bread and snap its neck. It could feed a couple of people. "Yeah, they're sweet," he replied belatedly, but the image was of duck swimming in orange sauce on a bed of rice. He recalled Mr Wakeman's words about the state of the lake; it was rather dirty and in places it stank of stagnation.

They bought lunch and found a space in the café. They talked about Professor Whitman, Dickens and Surtees and politically correct and incorrect lecturers. The café was busy and smoke from the smoking area wafted to where they were sitting. He looked around the room and caught a glimpse of Jez. He felt guilty about having lunch with Maggie. Jez turned and caught his eye. However, rather than any jealous response he saw a flash of guilt cross her face; she turned back to the bar and he saw her say something to somebody. It was Dr Peterson. He turned around and waved a pleasant hello to Flood and Maggie.

"Who's that waving," said Maggie, cleaning her glasses and squinting in the direction of Flood's gaze.

"Oh, it's Jez and Dr Peterson, they're over at the bar."

"Oh yeah, hope they know I can't see them without my glasses," she said. "Are they coming over? Where are they? Oh, there, I see."

"Yes, they're coming over." Flood feigned nonchalance and then wondered why he should bother.

"Hi Flood," said Jez, bending down to give him a kiss. "Oh, hi, Brown Owl, you two discussing literature again?"

"Yeah," said Flood. "Dickens. We just listened to Professor Whitman and were talking about Dickens."

"Ah, Professor Whitman," said Dr Peterson coming up behind Jez with two almost finished pints. "She's very right-wing, an old Thatcherite Tory. We're trying to oust her in favour of more modern and progressive thinkers."

Flood recalled Whitman's lecture and inwardly shuddered at the contradiction his mind perceived. "Well," he ventured, "she gave quite a good lecture just now."

"Giving good lectures doesn't make you politically correct," replied Peterson. "Her kind want to bring in performance-related pay schemes and decentralise the universities from national control. Dangerous thinking. I even heard her argue once that several unis should be privatised. Jeez, can you imagine? 'Welcome to the University of Northchester, PLC, this is our present CEO,'" Peterson quipped sarcastically.

Jez guffawed and Maggie smiled. "Well, we were just discussing Professor Warbler's latest article in the national press. It's really good, all about how we can ban pig-farming in Lindthorpeshire," said Jez. Then she whispered, "Andy's friends will be attempting to free a few pigs this weekend. Breaking up fences at night. I may go, but then there's the fox-hunt sab. Anyway, I've got to run to class, I'll talk to you later, Flood." She turned and added, "see ya," to Dr Peterson before Flood could make any comment on her usual non-attendance of classes.

"Well, there she goes. So, you two coming out tomorrow then? Goodness, you've certainly got the gear right!" Peterson said to Flood. "Still got to do something about the hair though? Don't want to stand out. No offence, but it looks too studenty. We'll be meeting the rest of the troops at seven a.m. I have to get there early to make sure everyone knows what they're doing. Well, I have a class in Bede College to get to - see you tomorrow," he said, placing the beer glasses on their table.

Flood sat staring at the glasses for a moment.

"Flood," began Maggie.

"Hmm?"

"Uh, about your hair. I can cut it if you want. It'll save you a few pounds."

"Oh, really? Okay, that would be cool. Yeah, I spent a bit today," Flood said, rubbing his hands along his new cords.

"Pop round at five and I'll give you a cut, if you're free."

"Sure, that'd be great. Room 236, isn't it?"

"Yes. You know, I'm not sure about Peterson. I don't know, you know, he's kind of, well, rather stuck on ideology isn't he?"

"Yeah, I guess so. I suppose he has to be. Maybe that's how we should be. I don't know. It wouldn't be right for them to get rid of Whitman for her politics though, would it? I mean, what if the Tories were in power and wanted to get rid of Peterson and the socialist worker lecturers?"

"There wouldn't be many left, especially in the politics department!" laughed Maggie.

"No, and half the sociology department might suddenly have to find real work," added Flood, thinking about some of the lectures he had heard. "Whitman's right. Universities need their freedom and she has a right to her views regardless, even though we disagree with them."

"Yeah, I suppose I agree," replied Maggie, fumbling in her folders for her timetable. "I have Literary Theory in ten minutes; fancy coming along?"

"I would, but I've got to go and do some photocopying for next week's essay. I'll see you at five."

Maggie got up. Flood diligently picked up the trays and plates to return them. "See you later," she said.

"See you," replied Flood, seeking the returns trolley. He found it in the corner and made his way through the crowded room to the exit and fresh air. He breathed deeply and set off to the library.

He was conscious of many passing glances and of several cutting comments. An elderly English professor carrying several books and an old leather briefcase caught Flood's eye and smiled at him. A shabbily dressed entity, probably female, that looked as if it been through a wash cycle and hung out to dry in windy weather, whose trousers were too long and too baggy, and whose top was two sizes too small scowled through unkempt and knotted hair. An attractive girl in a long skirt, the hint of laced boots, a figure-hugging long coat, and ponytail of curly golden brown hair smiled as she passed. Flood cruised into her airstream and breathed the subtle fragrance of a lily-of-the-valley perfume. He entertained images of expensive restaurants, sleek Range Rovers, stables, thoroughbreds, and kisses on the back of her delicate neck as they surveyed their lands at sunset. Well, least I've got out of the botanic garden in this one, he thought, but the lack of nakedness now worried him.

Samson Agonising

Flood reached Maggie's room at five and knocked.

She invited him in, took his coat, and poured him a fresh coffee. The aroma filled the room drawing him into Maggie's atmosphere. He tuned his ears to the music - Pachebel's Canon with whale sounds added; if environmentalism could be embarrassing, here was the evidence. He sat down surveying her room and all of its corners and shelves.

Maggie talked about the practicalities of cutting his hair and of the tutorial she had attended while he gazed at her posters. Airbrushed mythical horses and lots of cats. The room, apart from the makeshift barber's chair and newspaper-covered floor, was immaculate. He drifted, enjoying her brushing his hair.

He heard a question. "Hmm?"

"How short do you want it?"

"Traditional cut, I guess. I mean, it needs tidying up, it gets in my eyes."

"Right. Hold on, this could take a while then," Maggie said, laughing. "Do you mind the music, or would you like me to put something else on?"

Something else. The whales were irritating. "No, this is fine." Pathetic, he rebuked himself. "Unless you've got any traditional classical music. I like classical. Well, I'm beginning to appreciate it."

"Uh, let me see. I have a compilation of new age classical, uh, what else, no, no classical. I'll put something else on. The whales are good to read to, but every now and again I feel as if I ought to go and rescue one." She changed the CD. "Hope you don't mind Frankie."

Frankie? A big band sound opened up and a clarinet took some notes up the scale to introduce Sinatra's voice. Maggie gently swayed her hips to the beat as she brushed Flood's hair.

"I can't live without Frankie," she said. "So romantic."

Flood closed his eyes and was transported to a dance floor, dancing with Maggie in a see-through muslin shirt and long flowing skirts, her large green eyes magnified through spectacles to cartoon proportions. ("It's the last dance," crooned Sinatra). Around them miniature blue whales drew their tails across a watery floor while dolphins pirouetted in rows behind them. Flood smirked at the image. Maggie joined in softly singing as she straightened his hair out, ("save me the first dance in your dreams, tonight ... ") He let his shoulders relax under her gentle, persistent brushing. Flood was now dancing with a dolphin and Maggie was partnered off with a white unicorn as she attempted to rescue a whale that was stranded on a bandstand.

As she cut his hair Flood enjoyed the closeness of her breasts to his face and his mind moved on to more erotic dreams of her white bosom, finally freed of a bra he noted, while getting a kick out of champagne with Frankie. Her figure undulated with the band's rhythms. He caught faint whiffs of her perfume and put them both in an Arabian Night special.

"There," Maggie finally said. "Have a look at yourself."

Flood stood up and examined his appearance. Shorn of scraggly ends, irritating fringe, unkempt sides, he did not recognise himself. "Jesus," was all he could say.

Maggie and Sinatra crooned about "the way you look tonight" and she laughed at his open-mouthed narcissism. "I look like I'm ten years old," Flood said.

"No you don't - you look dignified, especially wearing those clothes. Quite handsome," Maggie said, blushing slightly and quickly turning around to pick up the newspaper from the floor.

"Jeeze," Flood hissed. "Mum wouldn't recognise me. Well, I hope it's worth it."

"It is," said Maggie, "you have to fit in. What will Jez think of it?"

"Uh, oh, I don't know." Then he added, "I don't really care," followed quickly by, "well, I mean, she knows it's for a good cause." He paused for a moment staring into his own soul; it was difficult to hold, but he forced himself to hold it, looking at himself as an observer would. He caught something ineffable and too fleeting to be trapped again. "No, I don't really care," he replied, more emphatically, to himself rather than to Maggie.

"Is everything alright between you two?" ventured Maggie.

"Yeah, uh, no, uh, I don't know," then he turned to face Maggie. "Well, I don't think there's anything there. I mean, she comes round and that, but we've not really dated for months. I think she uses me, and I'm not bothered about, well, I don't know, I guess I am," he confessed.

Maggie replied matter-of-factly, "She does use you." She looked embarrassed. "Gosh, I mean, I don't mean to intrude, it's not really any of my business.".

"That's okay, you can say what you want. I'm not really, well, I don't know," he floundered. Flood sat on a chair and lifted his legs as Maggie vacuumed the floor. A wall between the two of them had been breached and he now felt freer to talk to her. She vacuumed up the remnants of his former potency, which now, as he reached back and played with its new, shorter length, seemed artificial.

"Happy?" Maggie switched the machine off. She was also aware that they had reached a new level of intimacy.

"No, well, she's, you know, well, uh. Well, she sees me when she's free I guess."

"For shags?"

"Yeah," Flood laughed and then inwardly died of embarrassment from uttering a conclusion that had hummed around in his mind, waiting for explication for a long time. "God! That's really pathetic isn't it?"

"You said it," said Maggie sharply. "Sorry," she added softly, "I mean, she does use you - I don't see any love between you two."

"Love? No. No love at all." Flood laughed sarcastically.

"Well, I don't know what love is, but I wouldn't sleep with someone just because I was lonely. Gosh, I didn't mean to offend you. It's just ... "

"No offence. And don't apologise. I need this. You're right. I feel a bit pathetic to tell you the truth. I met Jez a while back, and I was a virgin and felt pretty silly. I mean, most lads from school had, you know, years back. Jez, well, she ... " Flood was bathed in cathartic, confessional awkwardness.

"She knew that and took advantage of you."

Flood recoiled, thinking that only men could take advantage of women.

"Oh, she's the type to do that," Maggie explained, sitting at her desk, "to find some innocent lamb, cut its neck and drink its blood. Many girls are like that. Didn't you read The Robber Bride for A-level?"

"No. What do you mean?"

"Well, another way of putting it is guilt. She takes your cherry and you feel that she's somehow special and that you were meant to be with her or some such nonsense." (Sinatra had moved appropriately onto love and marriage.) "Jez likes to string men along, giving them enough of herself every now and again that they do not lose interest, but taking from them what she needs at the time. And," Maggie added, "I can tell you it's not sexual pleasure. She's an incredibly lonely and twisted woman, fearing her own self more than toying with many men's lives." She caught herself again, "Oh, I didn't mean to imply ... "

"That's okay," said Flood emphatically, becoming slightly annoyed at Maggie's excuses. He dimly recognised the game Maggie was playing but he was willing to go along. Maggie liked him, he knew that. He weighed up her conversation and sought the purposes it held. Wherever this conversation might end up, he felt glad to be having it, but then he wondered whether he was floating again. "You don't need to apologise. I suspected it. Say what you think. I'm just feeling really pathetic that I've let myself go along with her for so long."

"She's good at what she does. Very good. But it's up to you, whether you continue it or leave her." Maggie got up and made some more coffee. Both were content to talk of other matters while they took in what had been said.

They drank their coffee and the old conversation came back. They could both feel it in the air and for a while they were silent, waiting for the other to speak first. Then Flood ventured forth. "I don't particularly want to see her again. No, I mean, it's over," he said, enjoying making a firm decision and commitment. (Frankie sang that he had someone under his skin.) He saw an intensity in Maggie's eye that he could not fathom.

She poured more coffee. "What are you going to tell her?"

"Don't know. Well, something like, it's over, isn't that how it's done?"

"Did it really begin though, Flood?"

He paused. "Hmm, good question. No, I guess not."

"It's up to you, you're free, you know."

Flood boldly inquired, "Maggie, have you, uh, you know, slept with anyone?"

"Me, goodness, no. Not that I'm waiting for marriage or for anything like that. Just ... " Maggie blushed and looked at the dark pane of her window.

"The right man?" finished Flood.

"Yeah!" she laughed. "The 'right' man," she made quote marks in the air. "Goodness, sounds so old-fashioned. It's just that I've not met anyone who was interested in me. I've met many who've been interested in my breasts, or my bum, but not me."

Flood blushed, for not only did his recent fantasy of her immediately spring back, he had also often watched Maggie's bum and had particularly enjoyed seeingthe tight muscles pump forward. She had a very well-proportioned body, and as for her breasts, well, he had observed them too for a long time, fantasised, curious to what lay underneath the thick sweaters she normally wore, how round they were, how pert, how much they fell to the side when she lay down. A loud thumping knock at the door interrupted anything he could have said in her defence, or his own, he thought. Maggie opened it to find Rat, sweating and panting, his partial dreadlocks falling over his face and sticking out at awkward angles from under his cap.

"Great, found the two of you together. Brill. Got news. I need to get a hold of Jez too, any idea where she is?"

"No," said Maggie, not offering him entrance.

"Never mind, I'll go to Bernie's. She's often there, I mean, shit, I mean she had to go and get some notes from him earlier," said Rat, stepping from foot to foot in obvious agitation and embarrassment. "Listen, we've had to change the plans. Something weird happened on the news. Something about a fight involving hunters. They've begun to hit back or something. We had a good evening a couple of nights back, you see, and I think that's pushed them finally. You know? Anyway, we need a big meet tomorrow. Full protest. I just got word and have to tell everybody. That's what I'm doing. Telling everyone."

Maggie became irritated. "What? What are the plans now?"

"What, oh yeah. Fuck, what was it? Yeah, got it, we have to leave at three in morning, we're, uh, meeting up with some regular antis at eight somewhere then walking to the sab, you know."

"Where?" she asked.

"No fucking idea. Just know it'll take a while to get there and we have to sort ourselves out. Uh, no, yeah, I do, same place I think. Just know that we have to get on the bus at three in the morning. Just when I'm getting home, too. Well, must find Slug. I'll try his house. You know the score."

Rat turned and ran down the corridor to the toilet. His loud urination echoed along the corridor.

Maggie shut the door. "Three o'clock in the morning, that's rather early."

"Yeah, what time's it now?"

"Uh, six-thirty. Wonder what he was on about. Should we listen to the news?"

"Nah," Maggie replied. "He's probably just trying to excite us into action so we don't lie in tomorrow. Do you fancy something to eat? I've got some veggie sausages in the freezer - won't take me long to cook them. I'm expecting Gemma over later, but we could eat in the meantime." Gemma, Flood knew, had been Maggie's neighbour from her first hall of residence, and they went out together now and again.

Flood offered to get wine and set out for the nearest off-licence. The cool night air felt particularly cold against his shorn locks and especially around his jaw where his beard had been. He thought about Jez and how much of a fool he had been. Worse than prostitution, he caught himself thinking. His conscience bugged him about Maggie. She was nice and she liked him, that was obvious, and he liked her. Well, perhaps without the whale music and the unicorn posters, he laughed inwardly. No, she was a nice girl, and pretty, but something indefinable about her irritated him.

Flood entered 'The Wine Dungeon' off-licence. Overwhelmed by the bottles and boxes, he asked the attendant which wine he could recommend for veggie sausages.

An elderly man in a golfing sweater peered over his reading glasses. "Veggie what?"

"Uh, veggie sausages, you know veggie burgers, veggie nuggets." An incredulous face forced Flood to change tact. "We're having a vegetarian meal and were wondering what kind of wine would best accompany it."

"Vegetarian, eh?" replied the old man, coming out from behind the counter. "You don't look like a student. Never mind, follow me. I have just the thing. Not sure what veggie sausages are though, but I have a wine that goes well with vegetables. This is what you might call plonk," he said, lifting up a green bottle whose label prided itself on being "Fab with vegetables".

"£2.99 and tastes like it. Now, what's this girl like? I presume it would be a girl. You never know with folk these days. Do you wish to impress her? Looks as if you're dressed well enough to impress her." He picked up another. "Depends on what kind of evening you want. £2.99 or £7.99, gnat's pee or a reasonable wine, if I may put it bluntly. Now, if you want a really good wine ... "

"Uh, we're just friends. But I'll take the £7.99 bottle for after dinner, thanks, and I'll have the Fab With Vegetables bottle with the meal."

"Prudent move. You wouldn't believe how many of the 'Fab With Vegetables' I sell to the students. Sells like hotcakes. They've no money but what's really wrong is that they don't have any taste," the man said, ambling back to the counter to wrap the bottles up. He looked at the second bottle. "Now this will go well after dinner. Very smooth on the palate. Well," he returned to his topic, "students must all be vegetarian these days, no wonder the farming industry's collapsing in this country. In my day, there were four butchers along this road. And people made so many different meals with the meat they bought, even though we had none of that fancy Italian stuff or Indian curries. Mind you, I am partial to korma. Most tasty," he chuckled at his own hypocrisy. He rang up £10.98 and gave Flood with change. As Flood turned to go, the man inquired, "Tell me, what goes into these vegetarian sausages?"

"Don't know really, vegetables and flour I'd imagine."

"Who makes 'em ?"

"Uh, there's a few companies, but Lucy McClaren's the most popular."

"Lucy McClaren? You mean that woman who married John McClaren, the old actor? Didn't know she made food."

"Yeah, tons of it. She's a strict vegan."

"A what?"

"Somebody who doesn't eat any kind of animal products."

"Good God, what kind of person is that?" The man was genuinely curious. "I'll ask Ramesh down the road, my Indian shopkeeper friend. He'll probably know. Sounds an Indian sort of thing, you know - for their high castes. But how can you live life without tasting meat? Anyway, you enjoy your wine with your veggies, let me know if it went with the veggie 'sausages'. After all, I like to serve the market and if more are becoming emaciated eastern monks I should adapt to their needs," he laughed to himself.

"Thanks," said Flood, leaving feeling rather bemused.

Nolite Servire

Earlier that day, eight hundred people had gathered to await the arrival of the new Minister for Rural Affairs at a DEFRA office in a provincial market town. The press had been fully informed by the Rural Alliance, but none had bothered to turn up except for one local reporter, who was astonished to find himself in the usually enviable position of speaking to the top organisers. The town was just one in a thousand to the London-based staff of the Minister, but it had played crucial roles in the development of England's early history, a history that was lost on most people who drove by on the major roads, but not by the locals, who took the town's motto nolite servire to heart. For the Minister it was the third obligatory meeting in two weeks: another market town, another large crowd of protestors. The Minister would arrive, Vincent Harrison, head of the Rural Alliance would hand him petitions and letters, the Minister would visit for a couple of hours, horns would blow, the crowd would sing, whistle, yell; the Minister would make a quick retreat, and he'd get the hunting ban anyway.

The unsympathetic, balding, moustachioed reporter was interrogating Harrison in front of the DEFRA building. "Without the national papers here, what hope do you have of changing public opinion?" Harrison mumbled something about the protest being one of many that day and that the reporter should not discount the growing discontent and anger fomenting in the countryside. He anxiously contemplated the crowd: could he go through with the plan?

The crowd stood chatting to each other under the fine drizzle, the host of green jackets and coats forming a motley regiment. Large white umbrellas advertising their allegiances to country pursuits sheltered some protestors. The message was not getting through, he had realised. This army of supporters would not be around in five years. They would find work in call centres or indoor shopping malls. "Adapt or lose your job." The words of that insistent man had haunted him since Northchester. "Adapt."

Shakespeare prodded his memory. "Now will I imitate the sun."

"Yeah, but surely," the reporter was saying, "your time's up. Hunting's a thing of the past, as are those people's jobs. I mean, the miners had to face facts, and so must you." The reporter, sheltering under Harrison's umbrella while he berated his cause and following, could not be bothered to take notes. Harrison scowled; the man's mind was closed, and nothing he could say would change it. But, dutifully, Harrison went through the RA policy stance, explaining that the miners had lost their jobs because the Coal Board had artificially supported the British coal industry for decades, and while he recognised that farming ultimately had to become more self-reliant and less dependent on Whitehall, hunting was something that subscribers paid for, and that they hunted on the private lands of farmers at their behest to conserve both the land and the species they hunted. He pointed out that the reporter's analogy to the miners did not apply in this situation. This situation was a matter of liberty.

"What, you think you have the right to chase some poor fox across fields? I call that downright cruel."

The rain fell more heavily and more umbrellas shot up. The churlish reporter sneered, thinking he had trapped the leader of the Rural Alliance with this petty point, as if the little man had solved the entire issue by himself. Well, thought, Harrison, why don't you run for Prime Minister? I'm sure you'd enjoy the country you'd wish to impose on us all. "You have come to report this protest. You've not come an open mind. You're just like the Minister. He's got a thoroughly closed mind. Always has to check with his superiors that he can breathe and fart. He's pathetic. And so are you." The reporter flushed angrily, making a note to report Harrison's insolence. "Look around you. Here are decent, law-abiding folk who have had this government trample all over them. That's what I call cruelty. Now, I'm here to defend it, and I don't give a damn what you say about me. You are rude and ignorant." He took away his umbrella. "Now, I have work to do. Find your own umbrella." He stormed off into the crowd of supporters. Many had guessed what had transpired. A cheer went up that caused him to blush and drop his head in embarrassment as he crossed the road. Harrison was a quiet man who preferred committees and conversation over dinners to mass protests. He had never felt comfortable surrounded by large numbers of people, feeling partly overwhelmed by them but also insignificant among them. But the situation required him to do something. He hoped it would go as planned. The choice for today rested with him alone. It was still in his hands to effect or not.

His assistant sidled over with news from HQ. "I'll go and circulate for a while. I'll be back in quarter of an hour." Harrison mingled with the crowd, chatting to unknown faces about their prospects. He knew that their anxiety had given away to a determination in recent months.

"But what if this fails," one woman asked. "Do you think the government will listen to us? They haven't yet." Harrison acknowledged her concerns and made his usual policy reminders and moved further into the crowd and anonymity. He came across two men and a woman who had brought a brazier. They were warming themselves in the flames' crackling glow. The rain hissed and spitted on the metal cylinder but the fire burned brightly.

"Alright, mate? Come and warm yourself for a bit. God knows how long we have to wait. But it's worth it, isn't it?"

Harrison examined their faces. There was none of the usual recognition in their eyes. Perhaps they don't know me, he hoped, joining them.

"Where do you come from?" asked one.

"Oakingham, originally," Harrison replied.

"Ah, a lovely old town. Excellent school, I hear," said a woman. "So what do you think of our countryside around here then?"

"Difficult to assess. Most farmland I see these days is depressed."

"It's been a hard couple of years, what with the foot-and-mouth, and this nonsense. How's your livelihood?"

"The same as here, I'd imagine. Same fields, same bureaucracies to deal with, same labour issues no doubt.

Perhaps our land is wealthier, but we still face the same problems. We're all in this together, of course. United we must stand, and not show any division, or fear," he added.

A man leant forward and handed Harrison a tea. "Here you go, mate, this'll keep you warm."

The woman spoke up again. "It's all very good you saying we need to stand united and all that, but you'd probably prefer to be standing at Oakland water than standing here with us, eh? I mean, the quicker all this nonsense is over, the better off we'll all be."

"But what about this so-called leader of ours?" The younger man frowned at the fire. "I bet he wishes he were back in London or something. Cosying up to ministers over cappuccinos."

"No, I'm sure he wouldn't want to be anywhere else," Harrison replied.

The young man looked up at the skies. The heavy dreary clouds hung around but the rain reverted to a steady drizzle.

"Well, wherever he is right now," said the man gazing around at the dozens of bodies within proximity, "I wish he was with us, I'd give him some of my mind. God, if he put himself in our shoes, and had been through what we've been through with the farms recently, I know he'd do what would be right for us. But, he's probably married to his desk and fine dinners and posh clubs in London."

"Perhaps you know him better than anyone else," Harrison replied. "But it's good to speak your mind. He's here somewhere. I'm glad I'm here, though. This cause is just."

"I've given up thinking about what's just," the woman shrugged. "We're on the verge of losing our business, and none of them toffs from the Rural Alliance or the government gives a damn. Justice and fairness are words that mean nothing to us." She grimaced and stared into the fire, her face concealing years of economic frustration, of unbidden intrusions into her farm life, and of the devastation of hundreds of cattle, of two young children who had witnessed an unnecessary cull of their animals, and who were subjected to seeing the carcasses for days on end.

"I agree. Who cares about the justice of this fight, when all notions of decency and justice have been abandoned?" said the older man who looked like the brother of the younger man.

"True," said the woman. "But if we don't win, it will be a black day for the Alliance and for all of us. We've got too much to lose." Harrison saw her clench her fists and put them into her coat pockets. Her brow and lips tightened to hold back a tear.

"I bet he'll be negotiating our livelihoods away, that Harrison," said the younger man. "That's what they say. It will be a small sacrifice, he'll say. We had to give up coursing, or earth-stopping, or wearing red coats, or riding to the hounds like in Scotland, or blowing horns. But then the war's lost, isn't it? Once one form of hunting goes, the rest of it will follow as night follows day. Fishing, shooting, the lot."

"I heard that Harrison is not negotiating any more," replied Harrison.

"So he says to us all in his emails. So he says," said the woman. "But mark my words, politicians are all the same, they smile, promise, then stab you in the back. And we'd be going out week after week, protesting against DEFRA, and the hunt ban, and they'd be making their deals. We don't know a thing about what they're talking about."

"If that happens, I'll never trust his word again," said Harrison rubbing his hands over the brazier.

"More fool you!" said the older brother. "And not much good your optimism can do us all. You might as well say you trust the Prime Minister as say that. They're all the same. Just wish they'd leave us alone. We only want freedom."

"Your anger's misplaced," replied Harrison. "We're all in this together, aren't we? And we all have to accept the leadership and trust them. Who else can we rely on?"

"Nah, I disagree with you mate," said the younger brother. "We'll be waiting on politicians' words all our lives and you know nothing will come of them except taxes and regulations and death in their hospitals."

"We'll see," said the woman. "Harrison hasn't much time left. Writing's on the wall. This government's not listening to him, and everybody is up for something else. Strongly-worded graffiti's all over. Civil war, some want. But I'll make a bet with you that the Minister turns up, Harrison says a few cosy sound bites, and we all go home until the next week, when he'll say the same thing at a different place. Nothing will change."

"I'll lay a bet on that," said Harrison.

"Go on then, fifty pound," said the younger man. "Harrison will say the usual stuff and expect us to retreat quietly and mingle again next week."

Harrison weighed the bet. A bet was a serious challenge to him, having grown up in a betting family in which one did not offer odds unless one meant to follow through. "Done."

The woman crossed her arms "Serious? If you're serious, you're on."

"I'm serious."

The older brother was laughing. "Hang on, though, how will we find you later on? You're bound to lose this one, mate."

"You'll find me. The Alliance is setting up a platform over there near the corner of the car park. You'll find me there, and I dare say you'll owe me fifty pounds. I'll keep my side. Excuse me, though, I have to look for an old friend. Thanks for the tea." Harrison grinned at the three of them who'd helped his conviction.

"I'll find him," said the woman, "we'll treat ourselves later. But in the meantime, let's get closer to the front so we can heckle that bloody minister."

"We Band Of Brothers"

Cosima Laurenten moved amongst the protestors, seeking familiar faces, chatting for a few moments to those with whom she had hunted since she was child, offering encouraging smiles to those she had not met before.

A woman's voice caught her attention. "Cosima! Well! When was the last time I saw you?"

Cosima turned. "Beatrice! My goodness, I didn't think you'd be up her." Beatrice Major leant forward and gave Cosima an embrace that almost knocked the wind out of her.

"Gosh, you have grown! You must have been a young slip of a fourteen-year-old last time I saw you, and what a beautiful young woman you have turned into. Goodness, your mother would be proud!"

Cosima blushed. "What brings you this far north, though? I thought you were wedded to your southern counties and warmer climes?"

"Ah, well, your father has invited me up to Stanthorpe. Then I heard the Minister was in town and I was staying at Barrowgate seeing some old friends. I could not pass up an opportunity to heckle," she laughed.

"Did Father say what he wanted to discuss?"

Beatrice assessed Cosima. "I can't really disclose anything here, but let's just say it involves a duty that one cannot abstain from."

Cosima felt a flurry of excitement rush through her veins but it was not the place for further questions. "I understand," she nodded.

"Good, glad you do. Do you know what an awful time I had coming up? Met a bunch of dreadfully ill-mannered youths on the train."

"I'm sure you said something to them."

"Oh, more than that, my dear. I clobbered a few of them with my cane before I could restore order."

"Oh, Beatrice!" Cosima laughed. "I don't suppose you told them your qualifications?"

"Not at all. Why should I? Best keep such things a secret. They were picking on a couple of beaglers. Damn rude yobs. Still, between the three of us we calmed them down and put a few of them off the train in the middle of nowhere. Dreadful service though. Back and forth through rural sidings, one hour late before we rolled into Northchester."

"I presume you came out alright?"

"From the scrap? Of course, dear. Thirty years of training special forces does not fade quickly. Besides, I lead the local ladies' self-defence classes these days."

"Gosh! Anyone else would think you'd be arranging flowers or teaching embroidery."

Beatrice laughed. "Still, I did experience one more symptom of this nation's declining morality. Yobs on trains, I mean. Damned rude nuisance. So, how is your father?"

"Same as you last saw him, I'd imagine. He doesn't change."

"No, fathers don't from a daughter's perspective. He's a strong man, though. If he goes through with what I think he'll be doing, he'll need our strength as well."

"You're fully behind him?"

"Of course. We have, let's say, met in the past for similar reasons. Twenty-five years ago, for example, when General Bellers was on the cusp of you-know-what. It was close then. And I was also called in thirty-one years ago, when my father died and I took his place. Since then it's been sufficiently quiet, until now." Beatrice eyed the chatting, foot shuffling crowd. "I think we have good reason now, though."

"So do I," Cosima replied.

Harrison was making his way to the very back of the crowd to the Alliance's platform. The workers had almost finished raising the banners. Some were making last checks to the scaffolding. Many more protestors were still arriving, settling quietly to make a stand against the government's onslaught.

The pundits may as well lay the odds in the government's favour, he reasoned. After all, the government owns the powers of the courts, police, and army. He had recently reread his undergraduate texts by Friedrich Hayek - the obligatory and much-maligned pol sci reader, The Road to Serfdom; detested by the left because they did not understand freedom, he reflected. The context in which he now found himself had changed his opinion on the libertarian message. It now made more sense. The state could abuse its powers by taking away liberties, but that's not why they needed the state - they needed it precisely to protect our liberties. He had also revisited historical works on mass movements and rebellions, and, as he wandered, he entertained images of the Civil Wars. The English have not always lain down to allow the state to run over them. Let's change the odds now, he decided. These people's livelihoods rest on my shoulders. Am I of the calibre to follow through?

"Damn!" he swore inwardly, tightening his lips against the burden of choice. I cannot turn my back on the deprivation that this government has wrought, or on the attacks on these people's liberties. What has been the point of all those meals and meetings, Summer parties with aristocrats and royalty, the chauffeurs, secretaries, high connections and touring the land if all it has come to is a war of attrition on the government's part - demoralising the rural communities until they are too weak to stand up for themselves, as they have done in the past?

Now, this is an extraordinary crisis in which the ordinary statesmen is apt to fail - hmm, words from some undergraduate tutorial, he recollected. What worth is my title as leader if I do not lead? I have to secure their peace and liberty for these people. All comes to nothing if I cannot lead. Those three at the brazier can fight, but against the power of the law imposed from London, against the hundreds of ignorant politicians who have never trod in their shoes, or have no conception of liberty and what it truly means, these three and all the others amassed here have no defence. They don't possess the appropriate language - the appropriate ideas. The land has forgotten freedom.

A voice disturbed his philosophising. "Vincent! The local committee has been looking for you."

"Thank you, Terry, get them together at the stand. I'll meet you there." Harrison watched Gibbon head into the sea of green macs, coats, and tweed jackets. Now you shall need your strength, he thought, looking at the protestors. God, I hope their mettle does not fail them - today they'll need it. They have paid enough in blood and money, in sweat and toil, let's hope they do not give way now. He stiffened his back and approached the platform. He was greeted by several colleagues from his local and national team.

"Vincent, good to see you!" Beatrice greeted him with a strong handshake.

"Beatrice Major! I wouldn't have expected you up north. But I suppose I know where you are going," he added, regarding Cosima, who offered her hand. "I spoke with your father yesterday, Cosima. He had much to say that has, well, influenced my thinking." I'm still prevaricating, he noted.

"About time!" said Beatrice. "So you've been fully briefed? The choice rests with you. The rest of us are prepared. You make the decision, though." Cosima looked puzzled but the mischievous glint in Beatrice's eye told her something was up.

"Hmm, I know. I've been fully briefed. I know it's my decision. But, uhm, I have two more engagements this afternoon, then I'll speak to him again. After that, we'll see. I now know the errand we're on. We'll see." God, why me? Why me and why now? A voice from another book - or was it a film? - spoke, "Because no one else is in your position, mate."

"Vincent, we've heard they've spotted the Minister's car. Fifteen minutes or less," said his secretary.

Harrison paled for a moment and then remarked off-handily, "I'll be back in a few minutes." Terry Gibbon watched Harrison make his way through the crowd.

"Where's he off to now?" asked Beatrice. "Shouldn't he be addressing the crowd?"

"Perhaps he's checking the battlefield," Cosima replied.

"Hmm, no, he's coming back to the platform," said Gibbon. The noise of cars turned his attention to the road. "There're the police vans coming." Gibbon shrugged his shoulders and let out a long sigh. "What can we do against that lot? I mean, if the government don't get their way, all they have to do is bring their troops and police in and we're done for."

"Let's make this protest worth our while then," said Beatrice.

Harrison returned and took his position on the platform.

Beatrice turned to Cosima. "If only we had the thousands who've been on the London marches with us today. That would show them, wouldn't it?"

"What's that? Beatrice? Why do we need thousands more?" Harrison's microphone was on and it caught him by surprise, as it did Beatrice, who heard her name echo around the car park from several sets of speakers. Harrison paused for a moment, realising that he was live. Hundreds of faces before him turned and gazed up at him. He felt their eyes bore into him, some supportive and others highly critical. A few stared passively.

"No, Beatrice." He addressed the protestors, "Enough of us stand here to take on the government today. The fewer we are, the more the papers will recognise us, and the greater the honour will be for each of you standing here today. No, we needn't wish for any more." He watched the police form their line in front of the protestors. He looked up at the concrete-and-glass three-storey building. Some clerks were peering out at the array of rural frustration - a product of your work, but you don't even care, you're just following orders, he thought bitterly. Then he recalled his bet.

"I'm not in this for the money. None of us is. It is not money that drives us to protest but the threat to our liberty." Murmurs of assent rippled through the audience. "In the week I have to wear a suit in my dealings with the so-called government of this land, but those things do not matter. It does not matter what clothes we wear, such things don't matter when we stand together to fight for a common cause - freedom!" He shouted out the last word to great cheer. "No, we don't need any more with us today. I promise you that the rest of the kingdom will soon have cause to envy us. But if any now wish to leave the fight, do so now. It will turn nasty." Cheers from some quarters.

"Those who don't wish to take part in the fight we're now embarking on can cancel their subscriptions." Shouts of "no!" "The Rural Alliance can ask no more of you. I know that our tactics will shock and revolt some, who thought law-abiding people would lie back and think of England as the government's juggernaut rolled over them. No more. Consider this town's motto: nolite servire - we serve no one. How appropriate!" Loud cheers and horns blasting.

"I thank you all for having turned up. Your stand will not be vain. One day, you shall tell your farming and hunting children ... " Great cheers. "You will tell your farming and hunting children that you stood here today and took on the government. This day will become part of the great annals of British history, for we do not forget our cousins in Scotland." Cheers from a few people flying Saltires. "We stand united against the foe. And like all foes, they can be defeated by the truth and sincerity of belief. And the belief that we all share, is that liberty shall triumph over ignorance." Cheers throughout the crowd. "We few, as Shakespeare wrote, we happy few, we band of brothers!" More cheers. "We are all united in this just cause. Let us wake up this nation. Those who are not here shall regret their absence. For today, we will change the nation. Today we fight not just for rural Britain, but for everyman's freedom. Let us prepare for liberty or let us die fighting!"

The crowd roared, cheered, horns and whistles rent the air. Such words had not echoed in the land for generations, but they could still kindle a pride and patriotism that was sometimes needed to remind men of what was truly valuable.

Several men broke into a local hunting ballad. A Geordie voice was heard above the rest. "Keep the tambourine a roulin'!" he shouted to much laughter and applause.

Harrison descended. Gibbon spoke hurriedly. "The Minister will be here very shortly."

"Are all in place, as I requested?"

"Indeed, sir."

"Then I've decided. Let's go for it."

Gibbon nodded and gave a thumbs-up to a few helpers nearby.

Beatrice was following Harrison through the crowd. "Well done, Vincent. That is the kind of stuff we've been waiting for. You've decided, then?"

"Yes, although I'm bloody nervous. Do you believe that we need the numbers now?"

"After a speech like that? Good Lord, no!" she laughed.

"Beatrice, take Cosima and follow Terry. He'll fill both of you in as to what we're up to."

The two women followed the secretary as Harrison continued to make his way through the crowd, a multitude thanking him and cheering him on. A woman's hand shot out and placed a fifty-pound note in front of his eyes. He stopped and took in her face- the woman from the brazier. "There you go, mate. You deserve that."

"No, keep it. Unfair odds, really. You'll need it in the forthcoming weeks." His earnestness prompted her to slowly withdraw the note. "We'll have another wager some other day," said Harrison, smiling at her as he pressed on.

He reached the police line, showed his pass and was let through. Two colleagues stood near the office awaiting him. "Two minutes," one said.

A thin-faced, prematurely aging office manager came out and, remaining under the porch, addressed Harrison. "Mr Harrison, the Government wishes to know whether you are going to persist in your campaign."

"Who sent you?"

"The Minister for Rural Affairs."

"Did he now? And do you expect us to stand by when the so-called Minister's own campaign is to destroy rural affairs?" Harrison had raised his voice for the protestors. "Tell him from me that the Minister mocks every man, woman, and child standing over there. Tell him that his presumptuousness will not be accepted by these people whose livelihoods and liberty he wishes to destroy. Tell him that those who stand here today will not stand for him much longer. Our patience has been exhausted. Tell him that we are all hunters - all rural workers, all British citizens. We do not take his ignorance and arrogance lightly, and we are shall remind him so at every turn. Tell him that the rain that falls today is our kind of weather; this out-of-doors is our office ... " - cheers began from behind him - " ... and that the Minister should prepare for a reminder of what it is like to dumped on by the countryside. We," he said turning to the crowd, "shall not be trodden on, and we are sick of being political pawns." Cheers. "Tell the Minister that tonight he will go home with a reminder of rural life that he will not forget. He is not welcome today, nor any other day from now on." Cheers and whistles.

The manager slithered back into the office. Harrison nodded to Gibbon, who came immediately over. He whispered into Harrison's ear.

"Good decision. You've done well. May I give the signal at the appropriate moment? I believe the police will be watching you carefully."

"Do so," replied Harrison smiling. "Here comes the Minister. Let's see what we can make of this day."

Two black cars turned off the main road and onto the road to the DEFRA office. Following the normal protocol, Harrison was accompanied by a police officer to the pavement next to the entrance. He stood there with his two colleagues, Katherine Markham from the London office and Joanna Ribblesdale from the local office. Three other police officers stood nearby and fifty or so stood along the barricades. Two vans presumably with back-up officers, waited in the wings. Several hundred protestors began their whistling, jeering, and horn-blowing.

The cars stopped. The Minister's assistants, one woman and one man, got out first and gave Harrison the usual smarmy and patronising smiles that said, "we are in power, and you're not". Their dress code was that of the smart London set: the man, Harrison recognised, was Steven McDoherty on an outing from the party HQ; he was suitably equipped for the countryside with a broad pin-striped suit and Italian tie, a rouge-coloured shirt; she, the Minister's assistant, was a short, plump figure, with a well-sharpened hairstyle, wearing a thin wool pin-striped dress down to her knees, dark tights and black shoes, her shoulders covered by a pink and orange shawl. Both were particularly incongruous in this provincial environment, Harrison noted, as McDoherty opened the door for the Minister.

"Good morning, Alan," said Harrison as the Minister got out.

"Hmph. Same bunch of crap from your supporters?" retorted the Minister. The woman nervously scanned the crowd for a moment and tried to smile at the Minister's false confidence. She knew however, that he felt particularly out of his depth in this region, for the local Labour MP had refused to join him today, disgusted, as he said in an internal email, with the government's arrogance and illiberal stance on countryside sports and the rural workers' unions. The MP's absence would be noted by someone in the press, although the Prime Minister had sent the national reporters off on an errand to follow the Home Secretary into inner-city schools where a riot had taken place last week. The Minister's assistant surveyed the scene and felt intimidated and fearful. She looked protective and concerned for the Minister. Harrison smiled sympathetically. He had spoken to her several times at the London office. Clarissa something, he recalled. She had mentioned that she had not been beyond London's borders much since getting her job and her face now, he thought, was priceless.

Two local councillors and the neighbouring anti-hunt MP from the city constituency got out of the second car. Joanna had filled him in regarding their political leanings. Both councillors had been elected following the closure of a local factory; voters had assumed their politics could change international markets, but they had not expected they would support the banning of local traditions. All six now approached Harrison and the Minister reached out for the usual collection of letters and petitions.

"Not this day, Alan," said Harrison. He nodded to the officer standing next to him.

"Come with us, please," said the policeman to the six suits. The two other officers stepped forward and motioned to the Minister and his colleagues to come away from the building. The Minister obeyed instinctively but then began protesting as Joanna and Katherine blocked the DEFRA entrance and locked the door from the outside.

"What the bloody hell's going on?" demanded an over-weight, red-faced councillor.

"What are you doing, Harrison?" the Minister demanded.

"Just follow us," said the officer. The six became flustered and anxious. Things were not supposed to be altered like this without forewarning, Clarissa was complaining. After locking the door, Joanna and Katherine stepped over to shut the car doors. Two more policemen began running over and the Minister looked momentarily relieved. However, they reached the cars to inform the chauffeurs that they ought to get out too.

"What the fuck are you playing at, Harrison?"

"A taste, Alan, of what it's like to have your liberty taken away from you."

"What the fuck do you mean? Where's my phone? What are these police doing?" He scrambled around in his pockets for his mobile, realised that he had left it in his briefcase in the car and watched with astonishment as the numerous officers at the barricades took off their helmets and donned flat country caps. The crowd laughed, applauded and cheered and then quietened to watch the quickly unfolding events.

A hunting horn blew a short tune to their left. Gibbon's signal, Harrison noted, as he and the two women followed the escorting officers across the road. He heard the deep diesel rumbling of a couple of large tractors; from behind the office building he saw them trundling along with their large muck spreaders trailing behind.

The Minister stood aghast as the two vehicles quickly covered the hundred yards to the cars. The crowd guessed what was going to happen and blasted every horn and whistle. Loud hurrahs greeted the first spray of manure from the spreader as it landed on top of the Minister's car. More office workers had crowded the building's windows to watch the spectacle unfold. The six officials stood incredulous and shivering as their cars were drenched with manure. The tractors turned and came back for another spray.

"What's it feel to be shat on?" some were shouting at the Minister. The crowd was becoming boisterous. Harrison realised they wanted the Minister's blood, so he motioned to his officer. "Time to take them away. Don't want it to get horrendously nasty, do we?" The officer turned and called four assistants who escorted the six into a police van. They got in, too shaken and unnerved to react.

"Where are they going?" one woman asked.

"We'll dropping the councillors off at a local village where there is a reception committee of horse- breeders, Whips, earth-diggers, farmers, and ex-miners who enjoy their fishing, hunting and shooting, who want to have a proper talk with them. The Minister and his courtiers are going for a longer ride."

"What? Back to London?"

"Oh, no. You won't be hearing from him for a while. He'll be getting a taste of his own medicine at a secret location. We'll be imprisoning him, and any other minister that dares to trample on our freedoms." His last words were drowned out by cheers from the people standing nearby, cheers that rippled back through the crowd as the word was passed along.

Harrison ascended the platform. "Today," he shouted, "is the beginning of our contingency phase. We had hoped we would never have to resort to this level of action, but the government has given us no choice. Britons will never be slaves! And that means we will not suffer violations of our liberty! That means we will also fight for that liberty! The fight has begun!" The crowd cheered.

"The local police you see are on our side. Most fish, shoot, and some hunt. But all of them are sick of being pawns in bureaucratic games and want to be policemen again." Cheers from the police. "They have agreed, in this area at least, to support our cause. I told you from the platform that it could get nasty soon. It certainly will. We will keep you all informed of events and actions. In the meantime, keep your wits about you. There will be a backlash from the antis. Avoid confrontation if you can. We will be outlining our programme - our battle plans - shortly. Let this day be a warning to the government. The state is always only a minority of people. We have their minister, who, as it happens, is only one man! The government will rue the day it took on the countryside!"

The crowd cheered. Harrison motioned to Gibbon to get the muck spreaders out of the way. They complied. Joanna Ribblesdale, accompanied by several officers, went back over to the office door. She unlocked the door and the police moved in. Harrison ignored questions as he discussed other arrangements with the police. After several minutes workers filed out of the offices, carrying their belongings in plastic bags and briefcases. Some looked fearful. Harrison approached the man who had spoken to him earlier.

"Can I have your word that everybody is out of the building?"

"Yes, yes, they are. There are only twenty of us. I've counted them out. I want to know what's going on."

"Twenty out, sir," a policeman reported.

"Good, now I would recommend you all go home. Go to your cars," Harrison ordered them. Most obeyed without a second thought, glad to be out of what had become an extraordinary day. A few stood by the head clerk, refusing to go.

"We want to know what you're up to," said one.

"You'll see," said Harrison. "Now, get back over there." The police were urging the crowd further back. Several men in yellow boiler suits and builders' hats ran into the building, carrying boxes. When they returned one of them reported to Harrison that all was in place and the building thoroughly cleared.

"Good, then proceed when you're ready, gentlemen," said Harrison.

The crowd hushed. It had spread out as individuals sought to get a glimpse of the events. The police had ushered them to a new cordon. A vast empty space now stood between them and the building, marred only by the two small hillocks of manure under which sat the Minister's cars.

A dull wumph from somewhere inside the building was followed by several loud cracks from inside the building, like wood and metal smacking against each other. The building seemed to pull in air and then a searing glow could be seen through some of the windows. Black smoke began to wallow around the open windows before being dispersed by the gentle wind. White smoke billowed from the other side. As the heat intensified, the silent crowd heard glass shatter and from inside the building they could discern the roar of flames as they fired years of unwarranted and unnecessary files and records on the local farmers. No one spoke or moved. The crowd stood unbelieving and unsure of what to think or say.

As the flames died down and the building's charred carcass could be seen, Harrison stepped in front of the crowd. In silence they awaited his words. He knew that many would never condone what he had ordered.

"This action will be remembered," he began, "as what happens when a government becomes tyrannical. Such despotism will never be acceptable on this island of ours. We are not interested in hurting people, unlike the antis, but we will strike at government buildings and offices - endeavouring that none are hurt in the process. Unlike the government, who seeks the harm us all by its infringements of our liberties, we will merely remove its ability to file, record, document, licence, and therefore rule us. We were once a free people. We shall regain that freedom."

The crowd blew horns and whistles and cheered. Some older members were too shocked to cheer. They stood shaking their heads. But excited conversations erupted everywhere that persuaded the sceptical of the merits of Harrison's policy. His assistants and other helpers in the meantime began distributing a leaflet that the Alliance had prepared the day before, in case Harrison chose the contingency plan. Cosima and Beatrice returned.

"Well done, Vincent. A splendid job."

"Thank you, Beatrice, for your men. Very clean. I will be talking to your father later, Cosima. Are you heading to Stanthorpe with Beatrice?"

She shook her head. "I have to head back to our lodge for a few days. I may see you up there sometime." He shook hands and then, with Gibbon at his side, headed for his car, the crowds still cheering and hooting. Harrison noticed the local reporter photographing everything in sight - a definite scoop for the little rat, he thought, but still, someone had to have it.

The Philosopher King

In a concrete-bound anonymous London hotel off Hyde Park, Doug Warbler heard the sudden TV news of the burning of the DEFRA building and the kidnapping of the Rural Affairs Minister, Alan Jones. It cut short the passionate embrace he was caught up in; his awareness slowly shifted from the kisses which he was planting on Jerri's stomach to the newscaster's words and to the images they portrayed. He paused. Jerri's hands slid from his hair as she felt his attention drift away from her. He rolled over and sat up.

"Did I hear what I thought I heard?"

"I think so. Turn the sound up," said Jerri, indicating the remote next to the bed.

They listened to the report in silence. In fact, the news left Doug momentarily speechless and, what was more worrying, without answers. This kind of action was not supposed to happen: he knew the ideology of the left and knew the hard-line factions presently residing in the kingdom. As a professor of ethics he should not normally be involved with the extra-curricular activities of radical political groups, but through his research and own earlier political activism, Warbler had amassed connections with some of the most infamous names of the past three decades. He was kept informed of the general policies of most revolutionary environmentalist and animal rights groups across the English-speaking world. On first discerning the nature of the report, he considered it might be an advanced and complex action by some of Peterson's students; but as he listened, he had realised that such an action was beyond the capacity of even that group. And then the news reported that the act had been committed by members of the Rural Alliance, who were apparently abetted by members of the local constabulary. Warbler burst out laughing and clapped until Jerri insisted he stop.

"For Christ's sake, Doug, this is serious stuff. Can't you listen for a moment?" Jerri pulled the sheets over her exposed legs and sat up. After the report, Doug turned the TV off. He grinned and clicked his tongue.

"This is fucking great! Who'd've thought it of that bunch of rural yokels? Quite sophisticated too! Wow."

"Extremely bizarre," she replied.

"Bizarre! This could be the beginning of a massive counter-attack on the Rural Alliance. No, this is fucking crazy!" He whooped with joy and got out of the bed to open the fridge. "Man, we must celebrate this one. What a screwed-up organisation! Such disestablishmentarianism is the kind of thing our lot should be doing. Brilliant! Well, ARUK will look like a bunch of saints after this." He opened a couple of gin bottles from the mini-bar. "Here, love."

He got back onto the bed. Jerri ran her fingers down his back. "Come closer," she demanded. He complied and smothered her neck in kisses.

"I've not seen you so excited for years," she said, tilting her head back to swig some gin.

"Yeah, this makes life suddenly rather interesting," he said, leaning over and tenderly kissing her collar bone. "Think of the repercussions!" He fell back onto the bed and looked up at the ceiling. "Oh, the power that's coming our way."

"You're well placed," Jerry agreed, lying down next to him and resting her head on his chest. "You've got what you want."

"Almost. It's within reach. I can feel it." Warbler smirked and stroked her hair.

"The philosopher-king. It was always your goal. I wanted to be the best revolutionary, but I guess I got caught up in the humdrum of politics."

"Hey, don't knock it. You've got power. You're having an impact."

"Not like you, Doug. Remember Marx said to change the world. You've unleashed so much through your writings. Often, I feel that all I'm changing is my office. What good have I done?"

He felt her head become heavier and he hugged her tighter. "You are making a difference. More than most people. I guess we have different specialisations," he added softly.

She sighed deeply and twisted to look up at him. "Yeah, you're right. I'm up there too. But not like you," she said, not jealously, he thought, but sadly. With a free hand she pushed her hair away from her face. She smiled. "I'm sorry, I get rather lonely. Let's look at the bright side. Your books have changed modern ethics. You've set the tone for the new millennium. You're in demand and you're climbing higher and higher each year. You will be the UN's philosopher-king the way you're heading."

He coughed humbly. "I'd settle for Europe."

"Big head!" She was half-joking but again there was the hint of self-pity.

"Aw, Jerri, what would you have me go for? Adviser to the London mayor, planning tram systems and other such schemes? C'mon."

"I was joking," she said settling her head back on his chest and stroking his hairs.

"You could be there too, you know."

She paused for a moment and then continued. Then she pulled herself up and kissed his cheek. "Let's quit the politics - just for a while," she murmured. "Just love me, I need it. Let's talk politics later." Her hands continued to stroke his chest and his stomach; he soon lost himself in her massaging and, pulling her on top, entered her as she continued to massage his chest and shoulders.

An hour later, they slowly roused from their nap.

"What time do you have to go?" Jerri asked as they awoke.

"Soon. A couple of hours maybe."

"I wish you could stay longer. You know, the whole night. You used to."

"I know, love. But times change. We're older. We have much more to do."

"Can't you stay one night. I've missed you. It's been a couple of years since we really spoke."

Warbler relented a little. "Maybe." He and Jerri went back twenty years, to when they were both undergraduates in London. He was the chairman of the Philosophy Society and she the chair of the Debating Society. They had a lot in common, including a love of Marx, Sartre, French films, radical politics, and their own ambitions. Although they agreed that their relationships should be open and that they should be free to choose other partners, their friends had been surprised that they did not marry or form a life long relationship. Instead, they rejected what they derided as bourgeois notions and insisted on remaining true to the philosophical beliefs that they had gathered from Friedrich Engels at an impressionable age, hardened by readings of Plato and a host of nineteenth-century utopian thinkers. They lived by their ideas and as a result, both had flitted from relationship to relationship for several years, until Jerri had finally and rather unexpectedly got married. Warbler's philosophy had not prepared him for such a shock. He fell into a depression lasting several years; he took long sabbaticals, where his ire and frustration were worked out in increasingly radical political tomes on man's inhumanity towards the beasts, as well as in bedding his students. He had always assumed Jerri and he would be like Jean-Paul Sartre and Simone de Beauvoir. He had wondered what it had all been about - she had so often derided marriage! It seemed to him such a sell-out, such a betrayal of all that they had stood for. It had been a political marriage that augured well for her career at the time but there was no love in it. Nor children to keep her tied to the house. She had declared to Doug ten years before that she had regretted falling into the bourgeois institution for the sake of political advancement, but knew that she could not get out of it easily nor without losing the potential it offered. She had kept up her pact with Doug to meet whenever they could - she had no other liaisons except with him. He, on the other hand, had gone to pieces. He had felt jealous and angry; he could not reason it through, which had annoyed him even more. What kept him going had been the rise in activism in animal rights circles as a result of his books and lectures. Ex-students kept him in contact with their actions; he received invitations to give talks and press interviews; he saw many of his students climb Disraeli's greasy political pole to powerful and influential positions; then politicians were calling on him for advice. It all acted to boost his flagging interest in life; but then he had realised that he was attaining the power that he had read about in The Republic - the power of the philosopher-king. It had been his lifelong dream to influence politicians and the last ten years had propelled him into positions he had never thought existed. Committees, agencies, quangos, and commissions across the English speaking world. In his vainer moments he foresaw himself as Time's Man of the Year.

He gazed at Jerri lying next to him. She was curled up like a cat, which suited her feline mien. She hardly made an impression on the bed. Whereas Doug had wandered slightly at the midriff, she had sustained a skinny body through the years. She sat up to put on her bra; afterwards her breasts hung like small orbs from the straps. He ran his fingers down her bony spine. "You need to eat more," he said though he knew it was useless telling her. After reading books on Third World poverty as an undergraduate, she had cut her diet substantially, become a vegan for several years, and raised funds for the perennially starving of Ethiopia. She shrugged; he knew that she looked upon her visible ribs as a symbol of solidarity with the world's poor and that she could not give them up. He leant over and kissed the skin covering her scapula, and put his arm around her waist.

Jerri passed him a cigarette.

"What do you think the government should do about this?" she asked offering him a light. She half-closed her eyes as she inhaled; it was her habit before entering a serious discussion to light up, squint, exhale deeply and then twist the cigarette around her fingers as if it were a pencil.

"It's a fascinating issue," Warbler replied exhaling. He got out of the bed to find his clothes. He felt his demeanour change slightly, to that of the professor teaching a tutorial, but he caught himself and relaxed. After all, this was Jerri and not some wanton undergraduate he'd just screwed. "I think it offers a great opportunity to get some legislation passed. Hugh's just been landed with an enviable situation - a domestic outrage with potential repercussions. He's in a good position to pass the animal rights bills we're after. And that could enable him to commit the land to war in the Middle East." She scowled and stopped twisting the cigarette. "I know, you hate war, but victory could provide him with another term in office. Yes, I see that suits you better! Ah, Jerri, we're in a position to make the changes we dreamt of when we were young, so what if it means a war in some god-forsaken place?"

She took a long puff and then stubbed the cigarette out. "But we're both pacifists, Doug. I can't abide war. It's disgusting and evil and merely puts profits in the hands of arms manufacturers. How's that going to help the starving?"

"Politics requires, let's say … flexibility." He sat back down on the bed to put his socks on. He intended to leave shortly and his preparations certainly indicated that to Jerri. She got up, resigned to the short assignation they had enjoyed. He watched her walk over to the table on which she had left her bag. She was naked apart from her bra. Her short hair bobbed softly against the back of her neck. His eyes followed her spine down to her small buttocks and thin thighs. She began brushing her hair. She caught him looking at her in the mirror. She smiled wistfully and shrugged.

"Okay, let's make it a night," he said.

She turned and for a moment he saw her as she was when she was the twenty-year-old activist he had shared digs with. An energetic, lithesome girl with sparkling eyes had swirled to accept his offer. The relief on her face was patent. "Oh, thanks D," she said, her voice similarly retreating a couple of decades to a softer, higher pitch. "It does mean a lot to me. I'll get some food ordered for us." She threw on the hotel gown, efficiently and swiftly made up an order from the menu and called it down. "Now, we can relax, watch a film, just be together. I've missed you. It's not the same without you." They both saw the pathos in her statement but turned from possible implications.

After enjoying a dinner of fish and new potatoes, of which Jerri managed to eat more than her usual share, they returned to the political situation.

"Well, the land certainly faces a grave and growing problem. Parliament's moral and political supremacy is being challenged by a minority. That minority, has taken the law into its own hands and carried out what can only be described as an act of terrorism." Jerri listened attentively. Doug was on a roll and she knew to pull back and to let him go.

"Now, if that irksome but almost defunct Opposition makes light of the action, they needed to be reminded of when they were in office and were targeted by the IRA. This kind of terrorism cannot be condoned. Hugh needs to be tough on terrorism; that will free him up for our kind of legislation." He got off the bed to remove the trays.

"What he needs to do is argue vehemently that the country cannot be held to ransom by any form of terrorism, whether its source is foreign or domestic. That will undermine the Opposition's moral position, which will allow him to proceed with whatever he wants to do in the Middle East and the Gulf. And while the country prepares for a war abroad, Hugh's then left with a free run on changing the country. It's an old trick, love, and one that can only be used as the opportunity presents itself. It is presenting itself now. Goodness, the government could really go to town. Especially following the kidnapping of a minister. Blunderton's after his ID and DNA bill - that could easily be got through now. And of course hunting!" Doug laughed. "If he understands what's taken place, Waterside should be thrilled. This is brilliant! The hunting lobby walks straight into the jaws of the Behemoth! Oh, Hobbes would have been delighted. No, this is excellent. The timing's now perfect - created by the Rural Alliance itself. Hugh should go for a complete ban on all country sports! Who knows, as the bill passes through the chambers, we may actually get some blood-sports banned and pet slavery curtailed. In light of the Rural Alliance's inexcusable and indefensible acts against civilisa-tion, he could claim, it's now necessary to punish the Rural Alliance and its terrorist membership." Doug fell back onto the bed laughing. Jerri, still in her dressing gown, jumped on top of him to tickle his ribs. They both convulsed into laughter.

"I can feel the power!" he squealed. "This is fucking excellent." Her gown had come off her shoulders and exposed her encumbered breasts. "So too is this," he murmured, twisting her around and pinning her down onto the bed. He pushed her arms above her head and ran his tongue over her ribs and reached around to undo her bra.

"I'm glad you stayed," she whispered. "I miss you. Perhaps, you know, one of these days, we could make this a more permanent fixture in our lives?"

He stopped and looked at her. He witnessed the passing of the years in her voice and the lines in her face. For a moment he saw how pathetic the ideology was that had kept them apart as youngsters; it was, after all, only an ideology and a vehicle for advancement. He had realised that a long time ago, but he could not publicly confess that he did not believe in his publications - there was too much money and reputation in them. As if to accentuate the difference between the abstract world of his work and the real life he could have, she gently gyrated her hips against his chest. He kissed her stomach then raised his head.

"Why not?"

A flicker of intense love passed over her face that was marred only by the acknowledgement of her present situation and status. She grinned and then grimaced.

"While we're changing the world," he added, reaching up to stroke her lips with his thumb, "we could change our lives."

"Let's see," she said flatly. "Give it a year or two. You're on the verge of what you've always wanted. Let's not spoil it. Once you're there, then we could ... you know."

He nodded. They had created a new pact; he also knew that it would be hard for them to see each other for the foreseeable future, until he had attained his political apogee. Inwardly he damned his politics, and as he moved to kiss her protruding pelvic bones he dropped his head onto her abdomen and almost sobbed.

Gems Of Wisdom

Flood had returned to the hall of residence to find Maggie in the tiny kitchen, grilling her sausages and boiling some pasta while one girl tried to fry an egg in a half-inch of oil and another was digging into a large cardboard box, swearing that she couldn't find her pan and that the cleaner had no right to put it in there even if she hadn't washed it last time.

The girl stood up. Flood realised that the persistent tinny drumming was coming from her personal stereo. She had dressed herself in a tight pair of mid-calf trousers, heavy platform shoes, and a halter-top that squeezed out a rather pale and flabby belly. Two metal rings punctuated her navel. Flood thought it would be funny to tie her to a cattle market stall and auction her off. From between strands of dyed lifeless but greasy blonde hair parted in the middle, her voice squeaked if she could borrow a pan from Maggie.

"Help yourself," said Maggie pointing to her pile of dishes. "You will clean it?" The girl huffed rudely and said "of course" in a manner that Flood knew meant she would not.

The other girl poked her egg and asked Maggie if she knew whether it was cooked yet. Flood studied the broken yolk bubbling in the vegetable oil. His stomach turned. This girl, Kelly, who wore her hair in pigtails and painted a multitude of colours around her eyes, turned and giggled. "I've never cooked before," she said. "I thought an egg would be easy." Maggie spent some time explaining the rudiments of egg cookery and told her to borrow a recipe book from her later. Flood wondered why Maggie had not given her a lecture on eating chicken abortions.

Maggie and Flood went back to her room to eat. He opened the wine and she apologised for only having mugs. They sat down on the floor and began their meal.

"Good wine," said Maggie sipping from a mug with a large cartoon of a happy sheep running and bouncing over green fields.

"Thanks. Cheap plonk but it's recommended to go well with vegetables." Flood showed her the bottle label, which he had kept hidden. They both laughed at the base marketing. Kelly knocked as they were finishing and Maggie showed her a couple of recipe books, recommending her to read both to see how principles of cooking could be garnered from a comparison.

"I don't like to read," said Kelly, eyeing the books with fear and disdain in her eyes.

Flood started. "You don't like to read? You're at university, though. What are you studying?"

"Psychology. We don't have to read much really," said Kelly undeterred by Flood's shocked face. "You know, just the textbooks and stuff."

He was undaunted. "But surely, to be a good psychologist, you need to read a lot - you know, articles, how famous psychologists like Freud worked, and that sort of thing?"

"Er, I guess," said Kelly, "but I just want to get my degree, so I can be a counsellor."

"I see," said Flood, pouring some more wine. He did not want to sound judgemental but it came out as such. Kelly thanked Maggie for the book, promised to learn some recipes and left. They returned to their conversation and when Kelly was out of earshot they commented on their fellow students' illiteracy and how, even in the English classes, so few of them read widely.

Flood lay back onto Maggie's bed. A knock at the door startled him into a slightly more formal position as Maggie rose to open it. Nice thighs, he thought, as they passed his vision: definitely ones to bite hard into and to create masses of giggles.

Gemma entered. Flood was always reminded of Viking raiders whenever he saw Gemma's long, curly red hair. Her ancestors, he fancied, could be found in the Jorvik museum. She studied philosophy but rarely mixed with the students from her own department, preferring the English literature students, with whom, she said, she could have some decent arguments rather than pernickety pedantic point-picking over words' meanings. "At least they read books," she would say. She looked down at Flood.

"Hi Flood, got the message you were over. I've brought a couple of bottles - hope they're okay."

Gemma settled herself down on a large cushion from Maggie's bed, crossing her slim legs underneath herself and took the glass offered. Flood looked at her pale, freckled face and blue eyes, her small hooked nose and high cheekbones. Her broad shoulders were the genetic remnant of the men who rowed long boats for an occupation; he imagined ancient drinking parties before the ships sailed for the Western Isles, of her toasting the brave, bearded warriors, and the success of their pillaging missions.

Gemma wanted to know about Flood's new image. He made his excuses about meeting some friend's parents in the country.

"Looks as if you're part of the hunting set," Gemma remarked.

Maggie sat upright, ready to defend her beliefs. She said that she hoped hunting would be banned soon and that she had been a vegetarian since she was eight.

"I'm not, but I couldn't eat veal though," said Gemma, "I love little lambs so much, they're so cute and cuddly, aren't they?"

Flood caught Maggie's eye but they let it pass, although he was not sure whether Gemma was teasing them slightly. She had a gleam in her eye which suggested that she enjoyed playing with words and minds. Her comment, he noted, was laced with a sarcastic element that was perhaps directed at the two of them. "Besides," she added, "what's being a vegetarian got to do with banning hunting? You could be a vegetarian and still support the culling of vermin and predators."

Maggie chimed in that hunting was wrong, cruel and barbaric, and that she thought hunters were a bunch of toffs. Flood added facts about the disembowelling and tearing apart of foxes from what he had been reading in his magazines and the writings Jez had lent him about the brutality of hunting. Gemma sat patiently listening to them both fly their flags, but Maggie, he could tell, was warming up for a passionate argument. She was on a roll to educate their guest. "Fox-hunting is evil," said Maggie, her eyes emphasising the word. "It's an outdated pursuit. Just a bunch of bloodthirsty toffs indulging in their taste for blood and cruelty."

Gemma suddenly interjected, "Do I look like a toff?"

The other two started. They were not sure how to reply, but finally, after several cool moments and under Gemma's unrelenting stare, Maggie inquired whether she hunted or not.

"Of course I do, and I'll defend my right to hunt. I've hunted since I was eight."

Maggie obviously had no idea that her friend was a hunter. She sat back and squirmed uncomfortably. Flood also sat back, bemused at how many hunters he had met in such a short period of time. Again, he felt uncomfortable encountering the real version of the abstract enemy he had read about.

"I can't believe it, Gemma. I thought you were a nice person, not someone who gallops around the countryside setting packs of dogs onto innocent and defenceless foxes." Maggie swigged wine to calm her nerves. She looked around her room for guidance and security and briefly caught Flood's eye. He was not sure whether she wanted to explain that she was part of a hunt saboteurs' club or not. He arched his eyebrows and turned to Gemma. She had crossed her arms and was weighing Maggie up.

"Hounds," she said.

"I'm sorry?"

"Hounds. It is a pack of hounds. The pack comprises dogs and bitches, but the pack is a pack of hounds. Hounds hunt. If the government did ban hunting with dogs, we'd go out with the bitches," Gemma laughed sardonically. "Anyway, do you think I'm a toff?"

"No," Maggie replied hastily, her politeness overwhelming her political ideologies. "But ... "

"So not all hunters are toffs then? Since you've met at least one who isn't," replied Gemma, falling back on her first-year logic course.

"No, but ... "

"But even so," Gemma interposed, "even if all hunters were toffs, why should that be a good reason for prohibiting hunting? It's like saying, football should be banned because all supporters are moronic, tribalistic, Bruegels."

"Bruegels?" inquired Flood.

"Check the paintings of Pieter Bruegel the elder and you'll see the resemblances," Gemma answered. "So, why should my activity be criminalised?" Gemma raised her head slightly. Flood imagined a banner of a black raven on a red cloth and fiery red-haired pillagers preparing to invade what he hoped would be an impregnable defence of banning hunting.

"God, it's so obvious, Gemma," replied Maggie sharply. "You don't have a right to terrorise animals. It's cruel and barbaric and should be made illegal."

"Why? You've not given me any reasons."

"Well," said Maggie, her eyes everywhere except on her friend, "we have to consider the fox or deer's right to live unmolested. A long time ago we thought nothing of killing other humans, but we stopped that, even though some enjoyed it, like in the Roman amphitheatres, you know? Chasing and enslaving of animals is just like hunting and enslaving people. Except animals can't organise any defences against humanity's onslaught."

Flood recognised the last argument as a quotation from a pamphlet the society distributed, The Silent Oppressed.

"That's a bunch of nonsense," said Gemma. "If we didn't cull animals, we would be overrun with them and their diseases. We used to be hunted, and we still are if you think of all the parasites and viruses that attach themselves to us and which can kill us. But what made us special is that we learned to defend ourselves and to protect our interests by hunting. Now, you wish to see that banned. Why?" she inquired once again. Flood envisaged Gemma's ancestors terrorising settlements along the North Sea coastline before enjoying great feasts of roasted hog and peasant. She sat calmly but surely. She had uncrossed her arms and had taken up her glass.

"Because we're better than that," Maggie replied irately. "Just as we've advanced to protect all people by giving them rights, now it's our turn to protect animals. I mean, what right do we have to hunt and farm animals and slaughter them just for our taste-buds, when really we can live without meat, and even dairy products? Although," she declared quietly, "I'm not completely vegan yet; soya milk takes some getting used to. But I'm moving ethically in the right direction," she said. "And so should the rest of humanity."

"But why is humanity so different from the animal kingdom that foxes can kill rabbits with impunity but we can't kill foxes?" tested Gemma or, as Flood romanticised, the old warrior taunted her enemy with a blast on her horn to call forth battle. Here comes the Norsewoman's onslaught, he added to his unfolding storyline, enjoying his Viking analogies while avoiding the realisation that both he and Maggie were paraphrasing the propaganda too much.

"Well, we just are," said Maggie. Gemma smiled. "You know, animals can't reason, and uh, we can, so we need to treat them better, like they are children." This was an ambush, Flood thought. "It's not whether they can reason or talk," Maggie continued, now paraphrasing Jeremy Bentham, or probably in her case, Body Shop adverts from when she was younger, "but whether they can suffer. That's what counts and we should stop the suffering."

"What if you were suffering?" asked Gemma pulling her legs up. "Wouldn't you want to be cured if that meant experimenting on some animal?"

Into the ambush we venture - this should really be mead, Flood smirked, peering into his glass.

Maggie faltered, knowing deep down that she would put human life above an animal's, but tried to circumvent the instinctive reaction. "I'm sure there are other ways to cure us of our sicknesses," she reasoned, "without recourse to torturing animals."

"And what if there's not? Do you agree that experimenting on an animal is not as great an evil as experimenting on a human?"

"Yes, but ... " began Maggie struggling to find an answer from her memory.

"And if it were a dilemma between saving a human life through experimenting on another human and experimenting on an animal, would you not agree that it would be better to experiment on the animal?"

"No. The human should die," answered Maggie quickly.

"Really, Maggie? Think of your mother suffering. Wouldn't you prefer to save her life at the cost of one animal's life?"

Maggie relented. "If it were necessary."

First game Gemma, mused Flood. One village lost, a few more vulnerable towns left.

"Well, the next question is: do you really value human life and living over that of animals?" asked Gemma.

"No, we're all equal," ventured Flood into the battle, visions, through the wine, of heads rolling, arms flailing, and horses tumbling, as the Viking goddess - for she had now been promoted in his mind - swung her double-headed axe around her head, sending arguments crashing to their death. "All living things have an equal right to life. All life is sacred, and all life is equal."

"Are we? Are all humans equal? Is a murderer morally equal to a saint? But more relevantly, is a rat the moral equal of a man? Let me ask you, if it were between saving a rat and saving Maggie, how would you act?"

Flood was caught. He recognised that to reply that he would save the rat would be morally repellent, so he answered, "I'd save Maggie, of course." Maggie frowned and then smiled.

"Hence, when you say we're all equal you are conflating terms - drawing abstract ideas out of the air that really mean nothing. For instance, in thinking of animals, you are thinking of some animals that you like, or imagine that you would like. I mean, you probably are referring to pets - not the animals that actually live in the wild. For instance, you wouldn't mind sharing your relaxation time with a cute pussycat, but a black widow spider, or a mountain lion might be something different. Outside maths, the notion of equality is rather an empty one. In politics it is a vile and destructive concept. Regardless, of which," she added, taking a sip of her wine, "if you believe that other animals have a right to defend their values, such as the fox taking the chicken, why do you deny man's right to defend his interests?"

Maggie leaned forward and almost spat her argument out. "Gemma! Man's a destructive and evil species. Look at the damage he's done, look at all the species he's exterminated and the environments that he's uprooted and violated. We're killing this planet and we've got to stop. Global warming and ecological disasters! Hunting's one more symptom of man's arrogance and it has to be prohibited to return us to some form of symbiotic normality."

Flood recognised another set of terms lifted from a propaganda pamphlet, Globalisation and Animal Extinctions. He was troubled by Maggie's repetition of others' words. "Think for yourself," Professor Whitman had argued. He was trying to. He knew that the phrase held a philosophical key to life. Gemma's contentions clashed with his prejudices, but, he reasoned, prejudices were surely a bad thing; after all, isn't that what we animal rights activists are fighting against - man's prejudices against the animal kingdom?

"Maggie," said Gemma calmly, "why do you hate humanity?"

Maggie blinked. "I don't hate humanity," she retorted bitterly, but Flood noted how she was momentarily caught by the question and had responded without reflecting.

Flood considered Gemma's question as he leant over to refill their wine glasses. "You don't have to hate man to love animals," he ventured. He felt like a Saxon priest stepping forward to assuage a party of Norse raiders.

"So why do so many animal rights fascists terrorise hunters and scientists?"

"Because they're evil bastards, that's why," said Maggie quickly.

"Because they want to alleviate animal suffering and to stop people from being cruel," added Flood, holding Gemma's eye. "You say that you hunt," he continued, "surely then, you love your horse and would do anything to protect it from harm?"

Gemma smiled and her face relaxed. Flood was not sure whether it was because she was recollecting her fondness for her horse, or whether it because he had offered her a more intriguing question than Maggie had. His instinct told him the latter, for she paused, drank some wine and considered his question. "Of course, I would," she replied. "But if you know horses, you can't love all of them equally. Some are nasty and destructive ... "

"Because we've made them like that," interrupted Maggie.

Gemma ignored the comment. "Others possess the sweetest natures. But if it were between keeping my horse and paying for a vital operation for my mother, then I would sell the horse. Your question is interesting, Flood. But what you should consider is whether, firstly, you can actually love an abstract concept." He frowned, puzzled but interested, so she continued. "Some people say that they love all humanity. That's not possible. It's implausible. You love certain people - people you know and whose values you admire and respect. But you can't love 'everybody'. That denigrates your love for the people you actually do like. I mean, how absurd it would be to say to your wife, 'Darling, I love you,' and with the same emotion repeat it to some stranger walking down the street, 'Stranger, I love you.' Don't you think that would be silly?"

Flood considered the scenario and nodded.

"So to say that we should love all animals is just as nonsensical. Some possess greater value to us than others - hence we farm some, hunt some, and domesticate others."

Flood gazed at Gemma and wondered whether that Viking bellicosity had found its outlet in philosophical speculation and logical victories over unclear minds. His mind went back to the time on the train when he was thinking about ideas. Here was a woman who cut ideas open, sliced them, disembowelled them, if they possessed no logical rigour. But as the wine affected his head, the thought was rather lost and could not easily be retrieved, even though he believed that he was onto something in his own understanding of life - a secret, or mystery perhaps. He frowned and then sought to recall what he had just thought.

Maggie, meanwhile, had stood up and was collecting miscellaneous pamphlets into her hand.

"Read these," she said sitting back down and handing the colourful brochures to Gemma. "Then you'll understand."

"Thank you, I will," said Gemma patiently, politely putting the pamphlets to the side. "But Maggie, have you ever been hunting?"

"I've been to the meets," Maggie replied coyly.

Gemma caught the obfuscation and spread some pamphlets out with her fingers to read some titles. She drew in a breath and nodded gently to herself. "You've been sabbing, haven't you?"

Flood felt the tension rise in the room. Gemma flicked through a couple of pamphlets. Flood drank some wine. Maggie leant forward, her wine glass tilting almost to spilling point.

"Yes, I have," she said defensively. "In fact we're both going sabbing tomorrow."

Gemma glanced at Flood. "That's a shame," she said quietly and then added to the air, "I thought you were more intelligent than that."

Maggie flushed. Flood's mind reeled, but the dizzy alcoholic swiftness left him intellectually disarmed. He smiled sheepishly at Gemma.

"It's a just cause," said Maggie heatedly. "Hunting's cruel."

"Is it just to terrorise people, just because they ride horses to the hounds?"

"You're terrorising foxes, so we're just giving you some of your own medicine," Maggie retorted.

"You're interfering with something you know nothing about."

"What's there to know beyond the cruelty of dogs, or hounds, or whatever, chasing a poor fox over the countryside?"

"It's not cruel, Maggie. If you actually came on a hunt rather than interfered with it, if you came to see with your own eyes rather than read ignorant and malicious propaganda, then you'd see it was not cruel."

"I don't know how you can sit there and calmly say it's not cruel, when what you're doing is evil." Maggie's face was suffused with anger.

"I'm not just sitting here, I hunt and I am proud of it."

"How can you be proud of killing animals?" fumed Maggie.

"The fox doesn't have a predator, except us. He is a predator and kills wantonly, and his numbers have to be culled for the sake of other species as well as our own livestock. Maggie, I know what I'm talking about. I've lived on my uncle's farm for all of my summers. Foxes kill without compunction. Now, even your animal rights fascists have not produced anything to keep a fox out of their glorious Edenic sanctuaries of freed battery hens. I read the other day that at one idealistic centre they had lost over half their chickens to foxes!" She stretched her leg out and rested her back on the desk drawers.

Flood captured her image and paid further homage to it and a fleeting glimpse of her lying stretched back and naked, with an axe lying safely apart from her. She had power, a power that was too sexy for him to grasp. He focused his mind and considered that he should run to Maggie's defence, but Maggie was taking Gemma on by herself.

"That's all rubbish. Foxes only kill livestock because we domesticate animals, and that itself is an evil that should be abolished. One day all animals will be free. There will be no pets or cattle in a just world. Just as people were slaved by oppressive regimes, so too are animals. They are our silent brethren, the dumb victims of mass enslavement and programmes of forced sterilisation, genetic engineering, and euthanasia. We will first secure the conditions of freedom, and once we've established that, no man may treat an animal with disrespect, no man may discriminate against any animal, no man may take away the life or property of an animal, no man may enslave an animal." She finished off her wine. "Hunting will be pointless," she added.

Flood glared at Maggie. She was parroting Warbler's words. Gemma caught the revelation on Flood's face, but she had already learned to recognise the altered tone of Maggie's voice when she spoke another's argument.

"Maggie, you're spouting crap. You're not thinking about what you're saying. Where did you get that claptrap from?"

Maggie's eyes bulged from behind her glasses. "It's, er, it's ... It's the truth."

Gemma's face relaxed sympathetically. "Don't believe all you read, Maggie. Why don't you come out with us tomorrow? I'm going hunting with some friends. Come and see for yourself what really goes on and how and why we hunt."

"That's like an SS officer asking a Jew to come and really see what happens at Auschwitz and how good it really is," said Maggie defiantly.

"That's a rather strange analogy," replied Gemma.

"It's a good one. The Nazis culled people and you cull animals, what's the difference?" Maggie challenged sarcastically.

"There is a world of differences, Maggie. Can't you tell the difference between people and animals?"

"We're animals too," Flood added. He had wanted to bring the argument back to a reasonable level, but he realised that his rhetorical flash would not go far.

"Yes, we are an animal species," said Gemma. "Which means that if you believe that each species has a right to follow its own nature, then you'd accept man's right to hunt just as much as you'd accept a lion's right to hunt. But we are a special species - we can reason. That sets us apart and above other animals."

"But that's speciesist, which is as vile as racism," barked Maggie. She had raised her pitch and her words shot out dogmatically.

"What? Fighting for blacks' rights is equivalent to fighting for animals' rights? That's rather denigrating of your fellow human beings," said Gemma.

"Shit, that's complete shit," replied Maggie vehemently.

"Okay, so if you've got a rat and a Bangladeshi applying for the same job - not that rats can apply for jobs, but you'd give them an equal opportunity? What's that say about your view of man? Now that is something I call evil."

Maggie, Flood noted, had not really heard the argument. He had and in his inebriated state tried to integrate it into the animal rights literature he had read. He frowned and was unsure of how to proceed.

"Of course, rats don't go for job interviews," countered Maggie, reverting to childish "told-you-so" tones. "And you're misrepresenting our position. We're fighting for animals' exclusion from human life, not their inclusion. We want to set them free from man's evil ways and violence."

"Yes, as it says in this leaflet," said Gemma turning a leaf over. "Hmm, Community: Inclusion and Exclusion - the new codes of animal citizenship by Ronald Crabtree. So you wish to impose an artificial apartheid on humanity, keeping us completely separate from animals?"

"Yes, that's the ideal," said Maggie condescendingly.

"Where do you draw the line? How will you enforce this separation? Tell the rats that they're not welcome in our homes? Put up air-defence systems to stop birds from violating our pure animal-free sanctuary? Mandate against viral invasions?" Gemma laughed pitifully at Maggie, Flood thought. She looked briefly at Flood and an understanding passed between them; it was as if she considered him more on her side than Maggie's.

"It's not a laughing matter. We're an evil species and our oppression of animals needs to be expunged."

"Expunged? Hmm, yes, here's the quotation, I saw a couple of seconds ago. 'Man is a belligerent and evil species, whose very existence endangers species that have existed long before man arrived on the scene. Our lack of respect for other animals is something we must challenge. Our oppression of our fellow species must be expunged.'"

"It's true. If you read all of these, like I have, and read the works of Warbler and Green, you'd know that it's right. You're just blind to your ignorance, Gemma," \Maggie added. She suddenly leant forward, pulled her blouse up and sharply slapped her own side. Flood turned to her startled. Gemma raised her eyebrows, curious as to what Maggie was up to.

Maggie looked down. A crumpled, twisted, contorted three-inch house spider fell down dead to the floor.

"Agh," said Maggie shuddering and standing swiftly up. " I hate spiders. Ugh, Flood, could you get rid of it for me?" She gingerly stepped backwards scanning the floor for more.

He picked the carcass up and tossed it into her bin.

"Inadvertent hunting?" inquired Gemma smiling.

"I hate spiders, okay?!"

"A lesson there," murmured Gemma catching Flood's eye. "It's getting late and I have to be up early tomorrow. I have an early class. Nine a.m. or something ungodly for philosophers. I can never think well before evening. Then I have to prepare for the meet." She stood up and bade them good night. Maggie thanked her for coming. She was too polite to allow a guest to leave on a bad note. Flood rose too.

"You made me think," Flood confessed. "But I need time to think about some of the things you said. Except I'm a bit too drunk to think clearly right now."

"Thinking is always good - come out on a hunt one of these days," Gemma replied and left the room.

Flood stared at Maggie and her dishevelled hair, which she had messed by frequently running her hands through it during the argument. Her eyes were still scouring the floor for more intruders.

"Goodness, it's ten-thirty and we have to be up at three." He stretched his arms up and almost fell over. "Phew, I'm rather, er, drunk. Haven't been like this for a while. Shit, I'm still wearing this get-up. What are we doing? Uh, never mind. Well, I'd better be making my way back if we're to get up on time."

"Why don't you kip here for a bit? I mean - I have cushions for the floor. Then you don't have to go home." She had returned to the land of commonsense. Her face had relaxed and she began picking up the glasses and bottles.

Flood considered it for a moment and agreed. "Okay, if you don't mind."

"It's not a come-on," she said, "just practical."

"No problem," said Flood laughing.

Maggie passed him a throw and some cushions which, with some difficulty, he managed to set into the shape of a bed. He threw his socks and shoes off and took his shirt off, but kept his trousers on. Maggie threw a huge white sheet over her head and dropped her clothes to the floor, or so it seemed to Flood's spinning mind. "Funny girl's trick," he murmured.

She jumped into her bed and they talked for a while about Gemma's arguments. They both agreed that they were too drunk to reason properly. Maggie wished that she had argued better, and Flood noted that Maggie retained the anger he had earlier witnessed, so he began doing impressions of their lecturers and other students to calm her down. Maggie eventually giggled, and as the wine sloshed around her head she doubled up in laughter. That prompted Flood to do his favourite animal impressions - owl calls, bear growls, doves cooing, a lion roaring. Someone banged on the wall, and in a fit of hysterics, he promised not to do any more. They tired around midnight.

"I've set the alarm for two-forty, which should give us enough time to grab a coffee and freshen up," said Maggie.

"Thanks," said Flood sleepily, then he fell into a dream of riding unicorns over the sea, whilst Maggie was a siren calling him from the great cliffs of Dover, but a siren who was plugged into to something, a jukebox, in a circus run by a Norse goddess who demanded animal sacrifices, men's blood, and constant sex.

He awoke slightly to feel Maggie's arm dangling next to him. In the dark he could make out her form and the pale glow of her exposed skin peeking out from her nightdress sleeve. He stroked her arm and she murmured an appreciative sigh.

Saboteurs

Flood and Maggie groggily strolled down to a silent campus to find the mini-bus purring its fumes out into the cold air. On boarding Flood saw that Jez was seated next to Rat; she had thrown a sweater around her neck and was rigged out in a purple, politically correct T-shirt with Bambi eating grass next to a smiling Thumper. They were giggling in a drunken manner. Rat was tickling her ribs. She spotted Flood and offered him a place in the neighbouring seats, but he declined and continued past a few seats before showing Maggie to the window seat. They sat down and the bus trundled out of the campus.

Peterson stood up and announced to the bus that it would be a long journey - about four hours; they had to pick up some other saboteurs and they were meeting up with regular troops who were convening in the Penkingrath hills in the Laurenten fox-hunting country. "I'm sure you all heard the news yesterday about the kidnapping of the Minister for Rural Affairs and the burning down of the DEFRA building," he said. Flood and Maggie shot upright. "Nothing else," Peterson continued, "has been reported yet, except that Scotland Yard think some local police were also involved. The locals are not responding well to questions, from what I heard on the radio last night. Some office workers said it was the Rural Alliance who instigated it all. Well, well, they're beginning to use our tactics!" The bus laughed.

Flood looked at Maggie. She shrugged.

"Anyway," Peterson continued, "what this means is that there is an urgency in our action today. Because of yesterday's events, we want to keep our protest non-violent. At least for now," he added looking at Rat. "We want public opinion solidly behind us, so no nasty tricks. That will put the hunters' violence into relief and the public will be right behind us. Got that?" The bus nodded its dozy agreement.

"Wish we had put that radio on, now. Anyway, who are the regular troops?" Flood asked Maggie when Peterson had sat down and the coach had began its journey.

"They're the paid extras. You know, the people you normally see on the telly, running around and causing as much mayhem as they please. They turn up in great numbers if they're told there's a pay cheque or free coat. Most are new-age travellers, students, the homeless, vagrants and drug addicts." As she spoke, Flood could see that she was dealing with an uncomfortable facet of the campaign, and he was not sure whether it was because the regulars included groups of people she did not care for, or whether they were paid. He pressed the financial aspect.

"They get paid for turning up?" he asked incredulously.

"Of course, and we do. We get about a hundred pounds; they usually get fifty or seventy."

"Goodness," said Flood letting out a low whistle. "Where do they get the funds from?"

"Some film and music stars, vegetarian organisations, Lucy McLaren's Foods, and a few others, MPs - you know, the rich."

"I thought being committed to a cause meant you gave up time and money for it. I wasn't expecting any payment for this. How much do the hunters get paid by the aristocrats?"

"They don't. The regular hunters pay a subscription membership fee to the hunt clubs, and they pay a fee on the day, as do the irregulars who turn up. Often the spectators also contribute to the cap. Here's your tenner by the way; if we're hanging around we'll have to put it into the box as it comes round. You'll get the rest later."

"So they make a profit from their hunting?"

"I wouldn't think so. Most of the money goes into keeping the hounds and horses, and they often put money into building and maintaining coverts and hedgerows."

"They do what?" Flood was puzzled at the contradictions that once more fought inside his mind like two vast weather fronts, undefined and mostly invisible yet flashing understandings and confusions. His mind was still unsteady from the previous night's wine, but Gemma's face and her arguments came back to him. They were not clear but he knew that she had won the debate, especially after Maggie had killed the spider. But that could have been a non-sequitur; he shrugged his shoulders against the confusion.

"Well," Maggie was saying, "you know, they have to keep their hunting grounds in good shape, so they spend quite a bit on conservation."

"I thought these people were out-and-out bastards who don't care for the countryside, that they just use it for killing and cruelty." He was not thoroughly sure what he believed any more. He looked down to the front of the coach. He could see Jez's legs stretched out over Rat's. His irritation increased. "You're telling me they pay for their sport and pay for the countryside's upkeep and we get commercial sponsorship from Hollywood bimbos to disrupt them?"

"Must be rich bastards to afford a horse, or even two, and then there's the tackle, saddles, Range Rover, horsebox, subscription fees. And, of course, tailor-made uniforms. They have to dress properly for the hunt." Maggie's voice had taken on a disdain towards the rich and she fairly spat out the last sentence.

"Do you think some people hate them because they are wealthy?"

Maggie started a little. "Course not. What they do is cruel. That's what's wrong. Besides, probably of lot of the hardcore antis come from well-off backgrounds. So it's not a class issue."

"What if it's a petty rebellion against rich mummy and daddy though?"

"You make it sound as if they could be spoilt brats."

"I think some are," said Flood, noting Laura who had fallen asleep with her head propped up against the cold window. "You're from a wealthy background too, aren't you?"

"Nothing to do with my beliefs," Maggie said, shifting her shoulders uneasily. "Hunting's cruel, whoever takes part in it, and it really doesn't matter if those who fight it are rich or not."

"I agree," said Flood tired. "The truth's more important than wealth or status."

"'Course it is. I'm still tired - mind if I shut my eyes?"

"Not at all, I'll probably sleep as well." He gazed at Maggie's soft features, her long eyelashes and small aquiline nose and petite lips. Her cheeks flashed yellow and grey as they passed under suburban streetlights. He watched her head become heavy with sleep and bob with the bus's motion, until she finally rested it on his shoulder. He straightened a little to support her better and promptly fell asleep resting his head on the headrest.

Flood awoke with a start. The coach had stopped outside some hall of residencel in another city. It was still dark outside. Three more bleary-eyed students got on board. Maggie still had her head on his shoulders, and he breathed in the soft fragrance from her hair. She stirred and he closed his eyes again. He felt her sit up and take stock of her situation, and then he smiled inwardly as she not only put her head back onto his shoulder but also rested her arm around his waist. He felt her become heavier as she fell back to sleep.

When the day broke, she stirred. "Sleep well?"

"Mmm," she nodded sleepily. "What time is it?"

"About seven. We have about another hour to go." He gazed out the window at a village. Smoke poured out of chimneys, reminiscent of scenes from ages past. Then they were out in the country again in which fields expanded in size and trees and hedges became rare. Great tracts of recently mown and harvested fields stretched for miles. Some had been ploughed for the winter, leaving the land fuscous, forlorn and empty of life. The landscape was the same for mile after mile, only the low hills providing some contrast to the levelled fields. Nothing broke the emptiness. Flood sought landmarks and saw several skeletons of hedges that had been diminished by constant cutting; they looked like worms that had been traversing the fields and had been caught by a drying sun. The sky had lightened under the coming dawn, but the land around was grey, a solid mass of uniform arable land supported by heavy subsidies and hence semi-nationalised, although none on the coach would so admit.

Jez's face suddenly emerged through his half-closed eyes.

"Comfortable?" she asked with a sharp edge.

"Mm, yes thanks," he replied, nonchalantly aware of Maggie's close presence.

Jez scowled and bent down to talk into his ear. He pulled away, ruining her attempt at privately scolding him. "Andy says you were with her last night. Don't expect me around tonight."

Flood expressed fake surprise. "I won't. And I wouldn't want to expect you anyway. I don't expect to see you again. You were with Dr Peterson the night before, and you'll probably be with Rat tonight. For heaven's sake, I'm worth more than that."

Jez whispered harshly, "No, I was with Andy last night, and besides you don't own me. I can do as I please."

"God, Jez, you are certainly low. Well, please yourself, you always did anyway."

She scowled at them both and headed to the bus's toilet.

Maggie, who had awoken, touched his arm. "That was brave," she said.

"Not really. Much too late. I should have extricated myself much earlier." He closed his eyes to shut the world out and to avoid any further questions. He reeled inside, and Maggie allowed him to cope with the inner turmoil she perceived him to be undergoing. He felt her head fall slowly back onto his shoulder and he fell into a shallow sleep of sporadic dreams of fire and ladders.

Finally the bus stopped and Peterson told them to get off. "We need to split up. I'll give you your instructions and goals for the day as you get off, then I have to arrange a meeting with the regulars."

They had stopped down some country lane apparently far from any village. Flood followed Maggie and took in a deep breath of the autumnal cool air. It reminded him of Bonfire Night, of huddling around the pyre when it was lit while hot drinks were served for the excited children and potatoes cooked in tin foil. The strange admixture of freshness mingling with the decay of summer foliage pervaded his nostrils and he breathed it deeply in.

The landscape around them had changed. It was more intricate and had more trees and copses; full hedgerows crossed undulating lands. Oaks guarded the smaller trees, their roots sinking deep into the earth, their trunks twisted and gnarled with age. Cedars stood prominently among the other trees. Some trees were still fully leafed and evergreens asserted their determination to wear the oncoming winter well. To the left, grassy meadows and bushy hedgerows billowed in shadows and Flood imagined dens for hidden groups of animals. Birch, poplars and ashes lined the roadside near where the bus had parked.

"This is beautiful," Flood said to Maggie as they alighted.

"So fresh," she replied taking in a deep breath. "So still and peaceful."

"Welcome to hunting country!" shouted Peterson, receiving howls of derision and expectations of triumph from the assembly.

"Right, you two," said Peterson approaching Flood and Maggie after talking to Rat and Jez. "Maggie, you are to come with Jez and myself." Flood saw Maggie's face fall. "Some of us are going to go strictly undercover today. Our mission is to mix with the spectators, making notes of names and car registrations, take photos when the opportunity arises. We have to mingle well, pretending that we're enjoying the spectacle. We're a father, daughter and cousin, named Bernard West, Jez West and Margaret Prince; that way we'll not make any slips with our forenames. You, Flood, are to head out by yourself with this," he passed over a digital camcorder, "and film the hunt from various vantage points. I'll drive you to your drop-off. Here's a map of the area." He gave Flood a hand-drawn map showing an X where the bus stopped. Another X marked the meeting point for the regular troops. A dotted path through several poorly drawn woods indicated Flood's passage to his position. "Use the woods for cover, but not the ones the hunt's heading towards, for that's where they send the hounds, and you don't want to be hunted yourself," he laughed. "Take footage of the Huntsman, we want his face for the website. The camcorder's got a good zoom, fifty times. Take care of it: it cost the club a lot of money. Right, know what you're doing?"

"I'll be by myself then?" Flood asked apprehensively.

"Yeah, for most of the day, so don't forget to take some sandwiches from the hamper over there. Oi! Andy, leave some for the others, mate. Right, yeah, when you're through filming, make your way to this road." He pointed to the second road on the map. "That'll take you the village. So, wherever you end up, head for that road or the one we're on now. We're to meet up at four; that's when the hunt will be winding down and heading for Ravens Hall. The village has a pub called the Fox and Pheasant. We will be heading there for four; bus leaves at five from here. If you miss the deadline, then don't worry. We'll be back here, same place tomorrow morning."

"You mean if I'm not here at five, you'll leave without me?"

"We can't hang around. The locals will get suspicious and after yesterday, we can't trust the hunting community. The idea is that we have been rambling and are enjoying the hunt; we meet up at the pub, but we don't know each other. We'll then go our separate ways to meet at the bus here again."

"What do you mean, our separate ways?" asked Flood growing more nervous.

"Well, there are several public footpaths that go from the village and which converge nearby. Look," Peterson said, pulling a pen out of his pocket and sketching several lines from the second road to the bus. "There's the village, and the paths that return here. If you don't reach the village by four, then head out to the bus by five. Then it goes. We're staying in a hotel - all paid for - about twenty miles from here. We'll be going out again tomorrow."

"You could have told us that earlier. I would have brought a change of clothing and a toothbrush," said Maggie.

"You don't need such luxuries in the war against cruelty. So, Flood, do you know what you're doing?" Flood nodded doubtfully. "Right, now, you two," Peterson motioned towards Maggie and Jez. "I'll be back in about half hour. I have to see to the regulars, drop Flood and Andy off and get them positioned for the sab. Wait here." He jumped into the coach. "Right, the rest of you; you all know where you're going and what you're doing. Take your positions. You need to be in place in about half an hour. Good luck, and see you this evening!" Flood and

Rat followed and took places near the driver. Peterson closed the door and the coach drove off.

Rat made some comments about the stupid countryside and how they needed some good raves and drugs around there to shake things up a bit. Flood nodded to avoid getting into an argument about his different perspective of the scenery. He watched the passing hedgerows from the window, dilapidated barns, sheep munching grass, and cows straying randomly across distant pastures.

The coach stopped and they descended. Ahead, along the road, were three coaches that had spilled out their contents, what Flood could only describe to himself as human rabble, onto the road. Peterson approached a few ringleaders and spoke with them. Several drab, uncouth entities stared at Flood. They knew Rat. He trotted over to swap some packets for cash with a few of them. Peterson pointed towards Flood, who was dressed in his Barnborough jacket, tie and sweater, cords, and boots, and who was attracting unwarranted stares and grimaces. He must have explained who Flood was, for the stares faded but the grimaces remained; then Flood realised that the grimaces were permanent features. Their owners were distracted by Rat's antics and Peterson's doling out of envelopes and maps.

Flood surveyed the assembled crowd. They looked like the dregs from the student union bars, the most unkempt buskers he had seen in town, characters from anti-drug posters, the homeless youths that often played whistles or guitars; many had brought their dogs. Several exhibited faces that were very gone on drugs and reflected an ignorance of where they were or who they were; others assisted them to stand or directed them to hedges for a piss.

"Blessed are the meek," thought Flood sarcastically, "for we have inherited them." He shrugged inwardly and turned away to enjoy an unspoiled view of rolling hills and deep verdure forests.

Peterson returned. "Right, they've got their instructions. Rat, you will be leading the pack. You will be heading along the road and then to the north over the fields to oppose the hunt as it comes out of Ravens Hall. I've got to get back to Maggie and Jez and begin our walk from the village to the meet. That'll take a while, but I don't want to be seen leaving the coach anywhere near the meet. The driver's off to Brigford, which is about fifteen miles to the west - that'll keep the vehicle out of suspicion. Now, Rat - Andy - are you paying attention? Remember, I don't want any violence. This is a reconnaissance mission. Flood, you need to keep low and if you are challenged, express your dismay at the sabbers' antics and humbly continue on your way - you're a rambler, got it? Right, off you go. Flood, you head east, across those fields, towards the forest, and then through that to the other side. You'll see a host of copses that the hunters draw their foxes from, and your job is of course to film the bastards. Got it?" Flood nodded. "Right, I'd better get back to the girls."

With that he jumped back onto the coach, which made a ten-point turn, crushing grasses and spinning mud, before heading back down the road. Rat set off on his quest without another word. The rabble began a disorganised amble along the road, obediently following him.

Flood contemplated the nearby stile. A sign indicated a public footpath leading over the meadows. He approached it and jumped over into some soft black mud that spattered his boots and trousers. He looked to the east where he was supposed to head. In front of him beckoned a silent field that stretched up a slope before evaporating on the horizon into dense wolds. He felt himself sink a little in the mud, and he began his trek.

The spongy ground cushioned his feet. It had rained a lot in the past weeks, and the water had not yet drained off the fields. In some places there lay small shallow pools and quaggy ground. Few insects bothered him, although the stagnant pools still supported hundreds of gnats. Flood trod carefully, avoiding the black muddy holes that the cows had scored into the land. The ground undulated with the furrow lines of ancient ploughing. Before entering the forest, he paused to take in the vast landscape that lay behind him. His eyes, accustomed to reading books, were not used to taking in such vast spaces. He felt overwhelmed by the expansive view. He stood staring at various objects for a few moments - a small coppice, a tractor on a distant hill, the disparate mob making their way down the country lane, the hedgerows, the path he had just taken. He could not see where the minibus had initially dropped them off, nor could he hear the bus. However, intermittent bird song kept his ears tuned to his surroundings.

Flood turned and continued following the footpath. It entered the cold forest, and he pursued the markers and telltale signs of the path over soggy fallen leaves. The wood smelled very different to the field. It was danker, with strong odours of decay, some sweet and some quite rancid. He noted various forms of fungi growing on trees and fallen branches. He stopped to examine a few of the strange fungous plates that looked as if they had been thrown like discuses into the bark.

The path ended after about half hour of walking and he came out onto a wide expanse of an idyllic rural England. A valley opened in front of him, stretching to the left and right. Old tractor tracks passed near where he stood and he could make out several other farm tracks criss-crossing the valley. In front were several small coverts, oases in the surrounding sweeping open commons. A few hedgerows crossed the valley, and he could make out wooden fences and gates sited along the hedges in places. Neither a person nor a house could he see, nor did he want anyone to interrupt the glorious and truly awesome experience that stirred in him at this moment. He focused his eyes on sheep that mottled the valley's far side; they had the entire place to themselves. He smiled at the undisturbed beauty that lay in front of him, decided upon a copse to hide in and began his descent.

Flood checked the time. It was ten-thirty; the meet was due to start at eleven. Plenty of time, he thought trudging on.

He made his way down the gradual slope to the small wood. His foot kicked a stone that caught his attention. He stopped to scrutinise the curiously-shaped object before realising he had kicked a sheep skull. He shivered for he had not seen a skull before, except in a school laboratory or museum. This one lay in its natural environment and it disturbed him greatly; it lay there as if saying, this is my resting place, why should you have any qualms about my death, it was here, in my own land, in the fields I knew. Flood bent down and peered into its deep, empty eye-sockets. A bone, the remnant of a once-living thing, now void and decaying; a sheep that once had roamed through the fields in which he stood, but whose life was now over. He saw a stick lying close by and, picking it up, turned over the skull. Its cranium had been cleaned by elements and picked clean by various animals, the bone almost shining in the dull grey light of the cloudy sky. He let it drop back to its resting place, and then could not help picking it up again and holding the sheep's head high above him, practically silhouetting it against the cloudy sky.

"Alas, poor Larry, I knew him, Horatio," Flood said out loud in a serious acting voice. "A sheep of infinite jest, of most excellent wool." He tittered at his own folly and gently replaced the sheep's skull. "There you go, Larry, I hope you are enjoying the heavenly scented pastures of Elysium." He stood for a few moments regarding the skull. "To what base uses we may return," Hamlet's words echoed through his mind.

Flood continued on his way and entered the first copse by trampling and pushing through the thickets. It was almost eleven. He had to be careful now. Supposedly, the hunt would make its way through the valley to tackle the coverts for foxes. He looked around. This did not feel right. There was a strong alien musky smell that he did not like, a strong odour that hit some instinctive reaction to leave. What if the hounds came straight to this copse? He decided to continue through and hike up the other side of the valley to hide somewhere less vulnerable. His purpose was to film the hunt, not be hunted himself, and he felt he would be safer were he to seek higher ground. Feeling a sudden urgency, he ran from the coppice and began his trek up the slight incline. He had entered the sheep's present grazing area and several turned their head to stare curiously, still chewing, wondering if he were a predator. They parted, haphazardly jogging away as he approached. He had a strong desire to go and stroke them on the head but could not get near any of them. He checked his watch, almost eleven o' clock: he took a deep breath and ran up the remaining part of the slope towards a small, spinney surrounded by low bushes. That would improve my chances, he thought, if I have to leg it from the hounds.

He took his position next to an old oak and sat down on its thick roots. He pulled the camera out of his pocket and, switching it on, peered through the lens and played with the zoom. It was indeed a powerful lens; it whirred and extended as he zoomed in on a distant object down the valley. It turned out to be ruins of a small hut. Then he heard the horns. The distant music entered the valley and his heart jumped. They were coming! The horns blasted again and Flood stood up and hid himself behind an oak. He saw a rapid movement about a mile away, heading into the valley. He zoomed in. It was a hound. Then another jumped into the viewfinder, and another, then a whole host of them running with tails high and noses to the ground. He heard the horns again and suddenly a red-coated hunter entered his view causing him to jolt a little and to look with his own eyes. In the distance he could make out about ten people on horseback following the pack. Then more came into view, fifteen, twenty - he thought maybe about forty or so men and women, children too, on smaller horses.

He put the viewfinder back to his right eye and picked out the lead horseman. He was coaxing the hounds along, his right hand holding the small horn and giving it encouraging short blasts. The man was in the traditional red jacket, white shirt, black riding hat, white breeches, and black boots. He held a whip in his left hand.

"Better start filming," Flood said out loud to himself, partly to give himself some sense of reality as well as company, and partly to an imaginary camera crew. He pressed record and followed the lead hunter for a couple of minutes and then traced the path back to the field following, alighting on three other men in the red jackets flanking the main group, one of whom suddenly cantered out to the right.

"Those must be the important ones," he said out loud. The riders picked up the pace into a faster canter and Flood shot left to film the lead hunter again, but could not find him. He stopped recording to survey the scene. The Master was leading the pack towards the woodland that Flood had first entered. "Bloody good job I left that one," he said, crouching down behind the trunk, for the entire field was now within a quarter of a mile of his hiding place.

The Master was caught up by two of the others dressed in red, who pulled out whips; they circled out around the Master and the hounds and gently ushered any straying hounds back into the main pack. Flood started filming again, closing in on the Master, who let out a different blast on the horn. The hounds responded by rushing into the thickets. Flood watched the entire strategy carefully; he found it fascinating and tried to deduce the purpose of their tactics. What would be the outcome, would they succeed, would there be a fox, would he see a kill? The rest of the field had caught up with the Master and his colleagues, but sat on their horses a respectful distance away. Suddenly he heard the hounds' howling and yelping from the copse, and the huntsmen watched every corner of the wood with a keen eye. His own adrenaline spurted in excitement.

There! A fox darted from the cover and several keener hounds were in hot pursuit. The Master blasted a tune on his horn and the pack's stragglers followed, pounding after the animal. Flood aimed the lens at the fox, who ran up the slope that he had initially come down, past the area the sheep skull lay, and then made a sharp right to follow the opposite wood in a fast sprint along the valley's edge. The hounds followed, hardly watching the fox, Flood noted through the zoom lens, but checking the ground, noses close to the grass. They stopped exactly where the fox turned and then, catching the scent, powered on with more excited barks and this time with their heads high. He looked away from the viewfinder again. The remainder of the field had not acted to intercept the fox, but had let the hounds follow first; the Master and his red-coated colleagues pursued at a quick canter, the field joining the chase.

A quiet feeling of the tradition's cultural significance disturbed Flood's thinking, but it was blurred by his excitement to follow the hunt. The fox, Flood could see, was busily sprinting away from the hounds; then the Master blew a new tune on the horn and the hounds suddenly stopped and looked around bemused. Some wanted to follow but another blast pulled them up; they circled and some were crest fallen. Flood could not understand why they had stopped hunting that fox, but the Master and his colleagues, whom Flood could now identify as Whippers-in, were attracting the hounds back to another covert.

"Perhaps that was a female," guessed Flood rightly.

There were several well-dressed ladies in black hunting jackets, and about a dozen children trotting gaily on small ponies. Most were older men and women in thick woollen tweed jackets. Their faces were ruddy and coarse. Not quite the picture of aristocrats, more like workers. Probably farmers, he again reasoned correctly.

He stopped filming to observe how the dogs entered the new wood. Then the triumphant howling began again and Flood had just pressed record and put the finder up to his eyes when a fox bolted; he caught it leaving the covert, and it was heading in his direction. The lead hounds were on its scent and the Master and Whips soon had the rest of the pack out of the copse. Flood watched in nervous excitement through the camera to see the fox sprinting its way up the slope towards where he stood. He dropped down instinctively and sought a better camouflage behind some bracken and briers; he kept on filming. The fox was getting closer and closer. The hounds' howling and barking filled the valley with their song; the horses' hoofs beat heavily on the soft ground sounding like a charge of cavalry coming at him. He crouched lower and with his free hand pulled his hood up over his head. He was caught. He could not run and would soon be held up by the hunters with grand derision and mockery. He would be lynched. His heart thumped, the camera shook in his hands, he swallowed his dry throat, and he watched the fox intently. But the fox appeared to have sensed him, for it suddenly changed its course and went back down into the valley. The lead hounds, accompanied by the Master and two Whippers-in followed;

they had sped up to a gallop, and as they past Flood's hiding hole, he saw the Master's rounded cheeks puff out a tune on the horn; the horses thundered past shaking the ground.

As he relaxed, his thinking returned to how archaic it all was. Our ancestors, he reflected, have done this kind of thing for hundreds of years - followed the beast, hunted him down, co-operated with horse, dog, and nature in the pursuit. It was a vision that engulfed him. The gallop's momentum was infectious and he felt as if it could draw him out of his cover and get him running and yelping alongside the horses in search of the fox, which he could now see heading in a straight line along the valley floor. The hounds were a hundred yards or so behind and the Master had caught up and was urging them on. The third Whipper-in passed Flood's position with a few straggling hounds, and behind him, trotted and cantered the main field. Some had urged their horses into a gallop, including several ladies, one of whom rode side-saddle, her blonde hair tightly caught in a net. Another caught his attention. Her grey-dappled horse was larger than the others' and she rode with an attractive dexterity. She was young - perhaps his age; she was slim and had a shapely figure and that rare virtue that he was beginning to recognise, dignity. Flood admired her form as she raced across the valley floor in pursuit of the lead hounds.

Without warning, Flood was aware of another presence in his midst. He put down the camera and was surprised to see a hound about three feet away. He almost fell over in surprise, but caught himself. He identified it as a male. The dog trotted over to him and sat down. It was breathing hard, but its tail was wagging a-plenty. Flood gave him a pat on the head, and the dog looked up to Flood as if to say, "well, come on then, there's hunting to be done." For a second, Flood debated taking the hound home with him, calling it a day, having liberated a hunting dog from its life of enforced hunting and artificial cruelty. He would have fulfilled a duty to the cause. But he studied the dog's eyes; they shone with a brilliance and pure vivacity that Flood had rarely seen in household dogs. At some level, he knew that this life was a proper life for the hound and that it was intensely happy in its pursuit. The dog propped a paw onto Flood's leg, sniffed at his sleeves, looked up once more, almost as if it were inquiring of Flood's station and purpose in life, and then, hearing a falsetto call of a name, its ears perked up, and off it shot from the small covert and down into the valley. Flood watched it go, sprinting blindly at first, then, as it picked up the fox's or pack's scent, following the rest of the pack, which by now had a few hundred yards' lead. The trailing Whip said something and laughed with a couple of riders as he saw the dog striving to catch up; he looked back into the copse where Flood sat hidden, searching for any other stray hounds. None discovered, he urged his horse on.

Flood watched the field gallop on after the fox. It had a good lead on the hounds. It would surely escape them, he thought with a mixed sense of relief, and, strangely, also of disappointment. The hounds, who were so alive with a vibrancy that he had not seen in people, were doing what canines were meant to do. Then he wondered what people were meant to do and drew a blank. The followers were full of life too, yet from his recent indoctrination he still deemed them the enemy, far removed from the proper humanity of his friends; they were the toffs, the barbarous cruel men and women who needed to be civilised. Then his mind conveniently produced a comparative image of Rat and the rabble he had seen earlier, and his gut twisted in confusion. He picked up the camera and zoomed in on the fox, which was running for its life, but making a very good show of it, Flood thought. Suddenly, it stopped again, and checked nervously to the left and to the right; its tail dropped, it circled and then it ran almost back along whence it came. What had caused its sudden turning?

Flood saw the cause. A mass of humanity was emerging from the woods and from the end of the valley - whither the fox was sprinting. They were shouting, running, screaming, waving placards and arms. They came from many different directions, a long line of motley sabbers, and there, Flood could see, was Rat guiding their movements. Although he wore a balaclava it could be no one else - besides, the baseball cap worn on top of the balaclava gave him away. Zooming in, he could see Slug,

Bean, Seaweed, Blossom, and Hog, the students from the party carrying their sabbing association's placards.

The fox had seen this crowd of men and women - its natural predators chanting and yelling, blowing whistles and horns. The fox realised it was not going to get to freedom that way and had turned on its tail. Flood had watched the hounds follow its scent, and it seemed as if they would pursue the scent rather than the fox, but unfortunately for the fox, its escape route ran straight into the oncoming pack. The hounds yelped at the sudden realisation that they had their prey, and Flood watched, his stomach turning slightly as a lead hound caught the fox by the neck and tumbled head-over-heels as the other hounds fell upon it. The Master caught up with the frenzied circle and blasted triumphant notes on the horn, the Whips whooped their congratulations at the hounds, almost as if they were cheering the hounds in their own language. Tails wagged excitedly and the hounds jumped and circled joyously to get their fill of the meat, breaking the dead fox apart. It was over in a second. The field caught up as the pack of hounds finished off their meal. The Master had jumped off his horse and with a swift action had pulled out one of the fox's pads and cut off its brush. The pad he gave to a young girl rider, who pocketed it as earnestly as any child who had been given chocolate, Flood thought. No blooding, he noted. The brush the Master presented to a young red-haired woman, who attached it to her saddle. Wasn't that Gemma? Flood wondered. He could not be sure.

The antis had meanwhile stopped for a few moments, completely unsure of what they had achieved. The Master trotted over to them. They stood there shouting obscenities at his apparition. Flood could barely make out their words; they fell silent for a few minutes as the Master addressed them. He rode up to Rat and a couple of the ringleaders Flood recognised from earlier. He pointed to their sudden intrusion, and Flood could make out that he was explaining why the fox had turned and why he had thus not escaped: it was their fault the fox had died; they know not what they do and should leave the field to those who lived their lives in the country. His explanation, although quite sound, as even Flood could see, was met with cries of derision and foul language. The Master shrugged his shoulders and stayed his horse, who danced nervously in response to the sudden shouting. He turned and cantered back to the hounds, who were circling the broken fox and puffing out their chests in a display of pure pride. Some still chewed on bones and Flood smiled sympathetically at their achievements.

The Master and the Whips congregated to speak for a few moments. One pointed to the other end of the valley, away from the antis, and with nods and a blast on the horn, the hounds and riders trotted away from the first kill. The antis, Flood noted, followed, jeering and jogging but increasingly behind the field. He thought it was time to move, to find a better place to film the next hunt. He stood up, stretching his tight, cold and aching muscles and departed for another wood about four hundred yards away which offered better cover.

Flood moved unseen by hunters or antis, who were both making their way down the valley. Nervous sheep darted from his presence, and he disturbed several hares, which made him jump, as he headed towards his new hiding place.

In the new copse he found a conveniently fallen tree, which provided him with an instant wooden wall to hide behind. The ground was drier on top of the gentle valley's ridge. He gathered up a bunch of sticks and branches and made a place to sit down. Aware of his hunger, he pulled out his sandwiches and devoured them. They were peanut butter and white bread, very dry, and they left him parched. He had not brought a drink. He tried to ignore his thirst as he peeked over the trunk to watch for the field. Again, he had chosen an excellent site, should the field decide to cross over into the valley over which he had an uninterrupted view.

He was not to be disappointed. Luck was with Flood as he caught sight of a fresh fox darting from the first valley and into the second. The Master led as the hounds swarmed in front. The horses got up to a gallop, and Flood witnessed a rare sight in England's culture: the entire field pounding away over flat land, gradually elongating its range between the fastest and the slowest riders. Flood was enjoying it, despite certain parts of himself that demanded political analysis and automatic condemnation. The fox ran in a straight line up the far side of the valley. Flood watched it hit a hedge, dive under, and continue its sprint for life unabated. The lead horses soon caught up to the hedge; the hounds divided, some diving under, some seeking to jump over. The Master took the fence at a good canter and was over, and he was followed by the others.

It was like watching a horse race, thought Flood, filming the jumpers over the hedge with nervous excitement. He watched a woman clear the hedge with ease, and he whistled in appreciation as the horse sailed over and landed perfectly into a canter. Then three more followed. Suddenly, a horse did not make it over; it fell sharply on the other side but got up swiftly, if a little unsteadily. However, its rider was thrown onto his shoulder, before coming to rest facedown in the grass. He got up and brushed his uniform while another rider, a woman, took his horse's reins and cautioned the following field to avoid them. Flood could see through the zoom lens the man checking his horse over and feeling its legs, then assured of its health, he sprang onto the saddle. He promptly pulled out a hip flask and took a sip of something and offered it to his friend; she laughed, took a sip and passed it back. Most of the field had now cleared the first hedge. A couple of the older riders opened the gate for the younger ones who dared not jump.

Finally the whole field was through and careering after the fox once more. Flood turned his attention to its plight, and caught sight of it dipping under a second hedge. But on the other side there lay a stream and Flood saw the fox run up the water and escape into some boscage. This should be interesting, he thought, zooming the camera onto the riders approaching the fence. The hounds pounded through where the fox had entered and instinctively crossed the stream and then checked - bewildered. Some let out a howl, others began sniffing up and down the stream to rediscover the scent, but to no avail. The Master and a Whip joined them, calling and encouraging their progress with their long whips. The rest of the field pulled up before the hedge, leaving the professionals to do their work.

Flood laughed, knowing how close the fox was. Whose wit would win out, he wondered. Then a lead hound jumped back into the water and waded upstream, smelling the grass and embankments to either side; then he was upon the fox and let out a triumphant yell that sent a sympathetic shiver down Flood's spine at one species' cunning triumph over another's. The fox leapt from his cover and ran back over to the hedge it had come through; he burst through the hedge as the lead hound and others snapped at his heels, but he got through and darted out, right into the middle of the startled field that had amassed patiently. Flood laughed as he saw the fox run right through a horse's legs.

The hounds streamed into an arrow as the pack converged on the new scent. The followers parted to allow the Master and the Whippers-in to catch up before it too turned and followed the fox on its new route. The pack and the field chased the fox up and over the valley's slope.

"Time to relocate," Flood said to himself, feeling like a wartime sniper. He checked for any sign of the sabbers and could see none.

This time he ran to the left of where the fox had turned, hoping to circle from where the hunt had been to where it was heading. He ran fast and hard, not wishing to be caught out in the open should the field turn again and come his way. His legs found the ground hard going as it became softer and muddier on the valley floor. The stream he had seen the fox use for cover trickled to the right of him, but it fell into a broader current that he could not see from his previous vantage point. In front of him it was about three feet wide, but very boggy on both sides. He had to stop running to search for a good crossing point. He tried to cross the water at various points but found himself quickly sucked into a boggy soil. Finally he found a narrower stretch, which he was able to run and jump over; he faltered on the other side and his knee sank into a deep puddle.

"God, if only I had a horse," he muttered. He stood up, looked around, and listened. He could not hear the antis, who had not followed the hunt into the second valley. He caught the sound of the hunting horn, which stirred him into reaching the slope's summit. At the top he faced a forest. To the right, the track went down into the valley he presumed the pack had entered. He took that path, listening out for the horn. He could hear its distant notes every now and again. He ran along the forest edge to catch up. This time he had missed the pack and had not anticipated its next movements correctly. A sense of urgency overcame him, and he sprinted down the tractor path he found and onto the corner of the wood.

He could hear the horn and perhaps even the hounds, but they were not in the valley he now found himself in. He imagined that they had headed to the left of his present position, and so he ran on to give himself a clearer view of the valley. No sign. He gave up on hiding and would have welcomed a stray rider, or even the whole hunting field to find him. He would bluff his way with them, as long as he could be helped back to where he should be going. Not this valley, then perhaps the next, he thought. He ran to the top of the opposing ridge and sought the field there. No one could be seen.

He pulled out his mobile phone. No signal.

Unbeknownst to Flood the hunt had headed due east of his previous position, not north as he had conjectured. They were now three valleys away, eager to shed the antis in their pursuit of fresh foxes. The previous one had escaped the hounds and was now making his way back to his den. The hounds were now seeking fresh scents about three miles from where Flood stood. He was sure that if he continued in a straight line, he would once again hear the Huntsman's horn and find his way home. He assured himself of the English countryside's smallness, and that he would soon come across a village, a road, something, and he would no longer be lost.

Stanthorpe Manor

Peter and Liz sat enjoying tea in the large library at
Stanthorpe Manor. The room supported twenty thousand titles
dating back to the collections made by family bibliophiles in
the seventeenth century. Spotlights, housed underneath a
gallery containing a second floor of books, shone golden circles
onto the middle of each section of shelving, the light catching
gold-embossed spines. In the corners Georgian busts sat
patiently gazing out at the titles as if caught in an eternal conversation with themselves and the authors. Between the walnut
shelves were hung portraits of family members. Their portraits
ran chronologically from left to right, starting with mid-seven-
teenth century men with flowing locks attired in Cromwellian
armour and plain cuirasses, through the eighteenth century
commissions of men in naval and cavalry uniforms, ladies in
rural settings, and on to the nineteenth-century canvases of
bohemian poets, Pre-Raphaelite women, young children, and
on to the starker modern portraits of the last two generations,
whose broad geometrical and fauvist patterns caught the
family resemblances but without the frivolous detail or the
paraphernalia of the earlier works.

They had just come out of a meeting with Lord Laurenten
and, while he made further telephone calls, he had invited
them to take tea and relax for an hour.

"I think we have to accept," Liz said, placing her cup on the
tray sitting on low, dark oak table. She leaned back into the
large sofa and rested her arm along its side. She surveyed the
vast array of books, the baroque painted ceiling, the Persian
rugs, the stuffed animal heads from 1920s safaris, all the traditional collections of centuries of ownership, more usually seen
in National Trust properties.

Sally, curled up on another sofa, was stroking a rather indif-
ferent, plump, fluffy tabby. "I'm up for it. I've read over the
contract they're offering me, and I'll accept this over the office
any day. I need to hand my notice in tomorrow, though.
Laurenten said he would see to the arrangements. Find that

hard to believe, somehow, but the offer's good. I mean, it's highly political, but at this juncture in my life, I could do with a change of scenery, and I do love an argument. I'm perfectly sick of schools and dealing with teachers demanding last-minute changes to plans that have been around for months." The cat jumped off her and, stretching its legs, headed off for a spot of sunlight it had espied below a large lattice window. "Ta-rah, puss."

Peter remained silent, drinking tea and eating a biscuit. He nodded appropriately as the two women spoke but remained caught in his own thoughts. Liz, sitting next to him, stroked his back.

"This does offer ... what did Laurenten just say to us?" She nudged Peter, who blinked a faint acknowledgement of her words. "This offers, he said, 'a unique opportunity in the history of this nation.' Couldn't pass that one up."

Peter nodded.

"Darling, are you concerned about what we're giving up or thinking about what we'll be doing?"

"Hm? Oh, the future. We will be very busy and very soon, by the looks of things. When you left, Laurenten told me that they have that minister holed up somewhere in Scotland."

"Good Lord," said Sally. "Mind you, if this is what we're getting involved with, we'd better get used to it." She tried to call the cat back over but to no avail.

"Things are likely to get rough," continued Peter. "The government's pulling out all the stops to get him back. They want Harrison's blood. They consider Harrison's work an act of terrorism."

"Blowing up a building is a little extreme," said Liz.

"I know. Nobody was hurt though. They won't be able to repeat that experience in a hurry. Laurenten says Scotland Yard has been called in to hunt for Harrison and his committee members. Funny, I thought the man was rather weak when I spoke to him. Too urban, perhaps."

"Perhaps he had sensed what was coming," said Liz.

"Perhaps. Well, Sally," said Peter stretching his back and twisting, "what have they asked you to do?" Sally had been given a job refitting the Assembly's rooms it owned for its parliamentary building in Northchester, and Liz was to work on possible blockades and road barriers with army regiments that were set to shift their allegiance.

A door behind them opened and in stepped Harrison.

"Mr Hickling, we meet again. Different circumstances now."

Peter rose and introduced Liz and Sally. "I read about your speech to the crowd. It was good. It was what they needed to hear."

"Thank you. Your comments helped, I must say."

Harrison looked stronger, his shoulders sloped less and his eyes had an intensity that they lacked in Northchester, Peter thought.

"Some effect," said Sally, "burning down a DEFRA building."

"I'm facing a lot of stick for that. I've gone to ground now, as you probably know. I'm getting a lot of flak from members as well as the media, but I know it was the right thing to do."

"It drives home the point harder than going topless, that's for sure," said Liz.

Harrison laughed. "True, true. And the marches. Sorry to hear about your house. Sounds as if the antis co-ordinated a lot of attacks that night. We think they may be focusing on one county at a time. Now, I'll need to speak to Laurenten with Peter alone for a while. Terry said he would come and rescue you two and take you around the house before we enjoy lunch."

"Is this an all-man thing then?" demanded Sally.

"No, not at all. We have Colonel Beatrice Major and Professor Alison Whitman from Northchester University joining us. We're meeting with the Opposition leader to discuss our next movements. We need to assess whether Michael Radcliffe's on board or not. He's in an awkward position, as you can imagine. We could do with him. We're also working on sympathetic Liberal and Labour MPs from the area who can be persuaded to join, but Radcliffe's needed more than them."

Gibbon entered and invited the women to join him. As they left, Laurenten entered the library from the other end and bade the women enjoy their tour.

"Thanks again," Harrison murmured to Peter as Laurenten approached. "You were right - I'd lost the plot and the time required decisive action."

"Vincent, good to see you," said Laurenten shaking his hand. "Well done! I'm glad you went through with it."

"Thank you, Douglas," Harrison replied. "I want to thank you for your support and especially for your advice. I had been thinking of another march. But the government's lack of response to the last one ruled that out."

"Look at these works, Vincent," said Laurenten gazing fondly upon his library. "Here are lessons indeed. So many writers have struggled to put into words their love and justification of freedom. But nobody listens to them any more - few can read what they have to say," he sighed. "No wonder we're in such a mess."

"I was one of the other opinion," Harrison declared. "I thought freedom to and freedom from were equivalents."

"We need to be consistent when discussing freedom," noted Peter. "There can only be one meaning - the freedom from aggression. No man has a right to coerce another or to use physical violence against another."

"Aye," agreed Laurenten. "You cannot have a right to some one else's life or to the product of their work. But such phrases - such ethics - have almost been lost in the din of the modern world. The individual screams for self-development, but has no self, because he has no values; and he has no values because he possesses no consistent ideas. The war of ideas is the only real war that matters. When men stop thinking and seek instead daily pleasures and comforts, then their minds are ripe for −control." He turned and walked to one section of his library. "We have lost many battles over the past century. But these men," he prodded some titles, "remind us of what we should be fighting for."

Harrison wandered over to look at the titles. "I had been worried that civil unrest was the only option."

Laurenten looked at him. "Civil unrest - but to what purpose? Without a guiding standard we'd lose immediately. We must declare our adherence to freedom unconditionally.

Not many like consistency, but without it, we are lost. You cannot justify a freedom from interference for hunting and then accept state intervention in economic or social matters. Freedom is not to be compromised at any level."

Harrison paled as implications whirred through his mind. "That will be a brutal regime, Laurenten."

"Brutal? You think being in charge of your own life and not having anyone else interfere with your decisions will be brutal?"

"We make mistakes, Laurenten."

"And we should live with them," Laurenten replied firmly. "At present, mistakes are subsidised by the productive work of others. We underprice education and then wonder why so many youths are pig-ignorant and violent. If their parents had to pay the proper price, they would respect education more. And so on, throughout the welfare state. The lessons are all here - in history. And that's why this government is so dumb-founded when people march for freedom from interference. It genuinely does not comprehend that taxes, regulations, prohibitions, directives, initiatives, subsidies and duties are all violations of a man's right to live as he sees fit rather than as some prat working in a ministry thinks."

Harrison nodded and then said, "I fear that you'll have your work set out for you."

"No more than other campaigns for freedom," replied Peter.

Laurenten shook his head. "No, Vincent's right. It will be hard work. But freedom's worth it."

The Undiscovered Country

Flood was lost.

It had been over an hour since he had last seen any of the others or even heard the hunt's horn. The valley into which he had blundered gave him no indication of his whereabouts. He attempted to work out the direction from the sun, but hidden by clouds it was none too helpful. Vertical streaks in the distant clouds suggested heavy rain. Underfoot the ground was soft and yielding, and the mud clung to his boots, making them heavier to lift with each step. A couple of times he staggered from a lack of momentum but caught himself before he fell sideways into the sodden peat. He stopped frequently to hear for any signal; from his friends, from the hunt, or from a car. Surely there must be road soon, he despaired - this is a small country.

He began a steady ascent up the hill to get a better view and to assess his direction. Water from hidden springs wallowed around his feet as they momentarily sloshed onto the land-scape. The gradient intensified and he breathed harder and rested his hands on his knees for a surer balance. A hare suddenly darted out in front of him and ran off at speed. No chance of catching that one if I were hungry, he thought, watching the animal bound off toward a distant hedge line. No chance of shooting it either, he decided, without thinking too much more about it. His attention was focused on the hill's brim, which, as he climbed, seemed to get increasingly further from his grasp.

The lip of the hill was darkening perceptibly as he climbed. He halted. No, it was not the brim; the horizon in front of him had changed from the valley's green and browns to a darker hue. He strained his watering eyes against the biting wind and recognised a tree line. Good. He hoped there would be a road nearby, or some sign, a public footpath - something. He frequently checked his phone. No signal. "Some direction," he said to himself aloud, the words echoing in his mind with various implications and nuances that he preferred not to examine.

"Okay, I am lost," he declared. "I am bloody lost."

He put his left leg forward and fell, this time without catching himself, onto the miry ground of a water channel. The damp penetrated his trousers as he sat for a moment and cursed.

"Damn you!" he shouted to the landscape. "Damn you!" Sabbing was not supposed to be this difficult. One was supposed to alight from a bus full of supporters, chant slogans, harry the hunt, wave placards, and then retire for a hot pub meal somewhere to gloat over the moral victory. That was probably what the others were now up to, he surmised. For a moment he wondered if he had been left to wander alone on purpose but could not reach a conclusion. It was his fault and he did not like facing the fact that he had chosen this path and all other paths leading to this moment in which he sat alone on a cold autumnal hillside, completely lost.

He struggled to lift himself up off the ground but got thoroughly muddy and wet in doing so. Finally standing, he felt that the distant rain had begun to catch up with him. The water formed droplets and ran off the wax, and his muddied jacket gave him a worn appearance, as if he had spent his years on tractors rather than in a suburban house with a postage-stamp garden. He pulled his hood up and through the narrowed vision looked around to assimilate his surroundings again. He saw how far he had trudged and felt proud surveying the steep slope he had conquered.

"Right, not much further," he said out loud to encourage his body in its upward movement. His lungs were seared with oxygen burn and his heart pounded from the exertion. "Not much further, I hope," he puffed on. But he could not consider where he was going- he entertained thoughts of "reaching civilisation" to keep him moving.

The steady incline appeared as if it should be about a five-minute climb, but it was twenty minutes of hard toil before he could rightfully claim that he had reached the summit. A vast forest lay ahead. No sign of a road. No sign of a sign. The world was signless. There was nothing below, nor around, only the omnipresent above. He turned to seek any landmark that might help. The rain dripped off his hood and distorted the distance but he saw nothing that could assist.

The valley below also stretched into forest at its far end. Across the valley he saw more forest spreading down the hillside. No sun, just a blanket of grey clouds and a cold breeze. He could not even tell the direction of the wind. It felt as it were coming from all directions. He wet his finger to test its direction. A pointless move in the rain, he realised.

"Which way to go?" he appealed out loud, both to himself and to his last resort, the gods. No reply from them. He pulled his hood down to listen. Silence. Not even birdsong. Nothing. Emptiness. He was totally lost; his mind separated from his body with the physical reality of disorientation. He again inspected his surroundings and took in a deep breath. The air speared his lungs with the cool, jagged sharpness of a closing day.

I need someone to show me the way, he thought, but there is nobody. It dawned on him that he had to rely on his own mind and abilities to get out of his predicament. He would originate the signs, he would forge the direction, and he would make the choices he thought fit. The responsibility of his situation was his alone.

For a moment he felt paralysed with fear, realising the enormity of the task and wishing he had his friends. But he reminded himself that no one else was around to help him. The fear subsided into a need and the need into a desire to make his own way. And if I should die, he thought, think only this of me, that I found a corner of some English field all by myself. He smirked and straightened up.

His eyes followed the sky to the horizon, the ground to the horizon, the infinite horizon. The vanishing point of all his worries. It responded with a beckoning realisation, deeply-felt, that he was alive, sentient, grasping for direction but direction did not mean anything. Life did. He could be alive or he could be dead, he was alive and knew it. For several minutes he contemplated, or rather he stood as if in contemplation but thought nothing. The liminal feeling remained, fleeting, ephemeral, an angelic touch over his whole body, a metaphysical urge from somewhere bringing tears to his eyes; no thought, no speech, a oneness with the world. He wafted with the wind. The sun appeared for a few moments and he closed his eyes to feel its fading warmth and light, enlightening, drifting but alive, rooted to the earth, of it but separate; he slowly came back from the something, or the something released him. Thoughts revoiced concerns. He hadn't eaten for a long time. He was thirsty. He was still lost. Drawing his consciousness back to the situation but still feeling ethereal, he chose to explore along the forest's edge in the hope of finding a path or a sign to a local village at some juncture.

Thickets of briers and bushes protected the forest, but he could see no blackberries or anything edible. No food presented itself, but why should it, he countered. I have to earn my way through this life, he realised.

The sky above darkened as the sun faded again, this time darker than before. He checked the sun's position. About twenty degrees above the horizon, and what ever time that was, he knew it would be getting dark soon. He shuddered and did up the remaining studs on his coat. The forest was truly uninviting, its shadows blurring its internal contents. Still no path, tractor road, or break in the thicket, and as far as he could tell there was no fence or barbed wire behind the shrubs. He inspected the ground to check for any traces of other people having come that way. None. The heavy, damp-laden grass gave no telltale indentation.

Perhaps if I use the zoom on the camera I may see something, he thought. He reached down but his pocket was empty. Then he remembered not feeling its weight for a long time. He searched helplessly and backtracked but could not see it. "Fuck! That'll cost me a bunch," he cursed and moved on.

How far he had travelled he did not know. Suddenly a rabbit darted across his view and headed into the forest about thirty feet in front of him. Perhaps he knows a path, Flood thought. He jogged over to where the rabbit had vanished and there between the sharp blackthorn and hawthorn and empty blackberry bushes was a narrow gap. A shallow channel led into the forest. Perhaps it was a path that had not been used for many years, but, he reasoned, it's the only place I've seen any entrance, so I might as well try it.

He dropped his hood and stepped into the gap, the long thorns tugged and pulled at his cords and cut his hands. A branch suddenly snapped back hitting his forehead. "Shit," he seethed, breaking through the thicket, rubbing his forehead. It was bleeding. The blood bubbled and dripped down his face onto his coat. He looked around for some natural remedy, saw some dock leaves, the only remedy he knew, and stumbled through the gorse, cutting his hands more to reach out for them. He pressed one to his cut as he sought to rediscover the rabbit's path. Never leave the path! he recalled - there children's nightmares begin. He ploughed through a morass of overlapping roots and branches until he stood in a small clearing under a canopy of trees.

The light had diminished but what lay behind him did not present anything more inviting than what lay in front. So he set off in what he hoped would be the right direction: the rabbit's direction.

"Wonder if it's a white rabbit?" He could just make out a gentle furrowing in the mud, which rambled around tree trunks. For the most part, the land was flat. He imagined he was on the top of a ridge and hoped that he would make his way through the forest to the other side, and there in front would be a warm village pub and a phone-box. He dug into his pocket to make sure he still had some change and patted his coat to make sure his wallet and mobile still sat safe.

Above him the trees' semi-denuded branches were laced into an open thatched roof. Below, the dank mud beneath his feet provided the only sense of movement as he stomped onward. Around, the trees formed a persistent, accompanying circle. The temperature was dropping. The forest felt damp and still. The sun was sinking fast and with it Flood's daylight faded. Colours withdrew to a uniform greyness. He hoped to see the rabbit again, and wished that it would be white and would stop for a conversation. "If you please, sir," he would say, interrupting the rabbit's journey to ask for directions. But no lagomorph beckoned him down a hole.

Onward, ever onward, he thought, I must persist, something is bound to happen. In the dull disorienting light he fell over fallen branches; he felt drooping brambles claw his shoulders and arms. He raised his feet higher and tentatively placed them back down. A few times he lost his balance as his foot found the edge of a hole or fallen branch. He concentrated his entire awareness on every movement and periodically stopped to review his chances and the hope for something to be out there.

Something finally happened. A smell, different from that of the undergrowth, tested his nose. Wood, burning wood, his mind told him. He wondered if the forest was on fire, but could hear no rush of flame as he had heard on telly; it was too quiet, but the smell was enticing - it was the smell of civilisation. A fire, a small fire, he reasoned. People, ah ah, maybe my pub, warm ale, pleasant conversation and a taxi-ride home. Finally, I'm free, he said to himself. Made it. Yes.

But he had to find its source, and that was not easy. He could not tell its direction, there was no wind at all in the forest, and the smell of smoke gently teased as it pervaded the air. He endeavoured to continue along the same path that he imagined he was following, but looking down he noted that the ground was as similar as the rest of the ground lying all around. The smell, disembodied from any source, became his only guide. Yet it presented no direction. Again he felt like he was floating, this time with one sense anchored to a fleeting existent. Such a faint perception; the trees dominated in their unhelpfulness. He decided to call out.

"Hello?" he shouted at the smoke. The trees remained passive in their gaze, soaking up the sound. "Hello!" he shouted again, this time louder. "Is there anybody out there?" Nothing. Again, that nothing which so irritated his, his what? Soul, his mind ventured. The soul that needs direction and needs another. "Whatever," he shrugged and called out again. "Is there anybody out there? Hello?" Nothing.

He proceeded but now the smell of smoke intensified; perhaps he was heading in the right direction. He hoped to see an inviting column of smoke but could see nothing apart from the darkening sylvan silhouettes that stood against the foreboding forest backdrop. Surely there must be someone out there. He called again but his voice sat lonely amongst the trees.

He stopped to ascertain the smoke's direction. Darkness continued to seep in around him, cutting his vision to blurry images beyond twenty feet. His world narrowed, closing in on him from all directions as the light waned. And the smell of smoke continued to torture him. Perhaps I'll see the light from the flames, he thought, but then worried about meeting gigantic spiders that live off the proverbial path not to be left. He started again and immediately tripped over some branches. He fell forward but caught himself with his left foot. He stopped now, thoroughly unsure of how to proceed.

"Hello!" he shouted again, this time at the ubiquitous black of night, which had shrouded his circle and diminished his vision to almost nothing.

"HELLO! IS THERE ANYONE OUT THERE?" he shouted desperately, straining his throat.

A voice responded. A voice responded, oh God, how beautiful. But was he sure, did he not just hear an echo of his own? He called again, "Hello?" this time with a greater sense of urgency and of doubt. Was it an angel? Was he saved? Or was it some behemoth awaiting its evening feast with trolls and wood elves?

"Hello?" came a reply. A reply. Definitely not his own voice. As he was sure of anything, it was most certainly not his own voice that came back to him. He called again and a different reply came back, "Who is out there? Are you lost?"

Am I lost? He thought, am I lost? Dare I admit it, but what the heck, I am lost. "Yes, I am lost," he called out into the dark to the disembodied voice that was reaching out a hand he could not yet see but desperately so desired to.

"Stay where you are. I shall be with you shortly."

"Okay!" he replied and then wondered how this other person could find him in the dark when he could not find his own feet. He waited and went over the voice in his mind. It was a female voice: yes, a woman's. Truly an angel. So he must be near the edge of a village, perhaps - a lady gardening near the forest edge, he thought. Oh good, she'll invite me in for tea and show me where the pub is, and I'll be safe and warm in bed tonight. It's all I want. Not much else to want really. This nature thing is too much. But the voice had now gone, leaving the forest to reimpose its silence. He stood for several minutes, not daring to move, for he gave the woman mystical powers of searching, which, were he to move, she might lose.

A breaking of twigs to the left alerted him to a sudden rushing movement through the undergrowth. His heart jumped, perhaps it was a wild boar that had got loose, the kind that gore kings to death on their hunts, or perhaps a wild puma or cat, a beast of Oakland that the press annually reported stalking lambs. The noise was definitely an animal and it was definitely coming towards him at quite a pace. He turned to face the charging beast, he automatically bent his knees in preparation for a springing bobcat or tiger or a wild, big-fanged, sharp-toothed, yellow-eyed spitting and foaming monster. It came through, bounding through the undergrowth; by the sound it made, it was massive, unidentifiable, over three - perhaps four - feet high, racing towards him: he imagined eyes glowing, teeth bared, snarling mouth, heavy muscles pounding over the last bush. Flood was about to die, this would be his death: a hound from hell goring him and chomping on his marrow.

Then it stopped right in front of him and the massive beast let out a series of barks.

WILLIAM VENATOR

Opposing

Laurenten presided over the long table in the French-style Gold Room, its fittings and decorations having been bought for a song during the French Revolution. To his right sat Vincent Harrison and Peter Hickling dealing with crucial rural and business contacts; to his left sat Colonel Beatrice Major, offering the skills from her multi-faceted past, and Professor Alison Whitman, a previous tutor of Cosima's, assisting with the propaganda aspects, as he laughingly called them. Their personalities, he thought, would suit today's meeting.

He poured coffee and passed around the silver bowl of sugar cubes. The day had proceeded well at Stanthorpe but Downing Street was fuming. Cramp, caught unawares had given an excellent stultiloquy, much to the press's amusement, on the need for "action, containment for flaunting the law, overweening disapproval, community and tolerance needed." The Spectator carried a cartoon of Harrison in tweeds 'flouting' laws with horses and hounds acting as a music-hall chorus. The top editors were up in arms but divided over the Rural Alliance's actions, with the majority accepting the justice of the act as a symbol of weariness at the government's prejudicial campaign but condemning the actual violence.

Laurenten's old friend John Stewart had kept him informed of the kidnapped minister's health. He had chuckled when John told him where he had put Jones after the Rural Alliance had handed him over. He had also received some useful calls from America and Europe from key allies and foreign sympathisers and contacts. But none from Brussels, which he thought hypocritical since they were negotiating the creation of a separate Basque state. All in all, it had been a good day. But, he thought, stirring his coffee, the next hour would be critical. If it failed, the Assembly would have to work a lot harder to attract Establishment sympathy and numbers; if it succeeded, they were looking at establishing a new republic.

He contemplated his companions. Beatrice was laughing with Harrison about a Lady Godiva incident at a protest at which a buxom daughter of a Master of Foxhounds removed her riding jacket to bare her breasts. Hickling was chatting to Whitman about the fund-raising concert they had both been to. They had not known each other then and were commenting on Cosima's playing at the concert. Laurenten smiled and noted that it had been a few months since he had last heard her. He smelled the Kenyan coffee's aroma. Good and strong to energise our minds, he thought - always need a good stimulant after lunch. He was beginning to look forward to the meeting.

Michael Radcliffe, leader of Her Majesty's Opposition was due any moment. The meeting was secret - obviously so, given the Rural Alliance's action. Radcliffe had prevaricated in last night's first Emergency Debate, called after the DEFRA building attack. In the debate back-benchers had demanded an immediate ban on all countryside sports as a punishment, the Home Secretary called for the tagging of all hunters, the Deputy Prime Minister parenthetically sought an increase in the minimum wage and a subsidy for a constituency battery-hen business, the Education Secretary called for more money for teachers to deal with the psychological strain the profession would undergo in light of the action, and the Prime Minister withstood attacks on his foreign policy and his inaction on hunting. One woman MP proposed a ban on morris dancing as an affront to urban sensitivities, another for the sequestration of hunt subscriptions for the public sector workers affected, and one ex-Communist, and voluntary ambassador and friend to Zimbabwe, suggested that, since the Prime Minister employed the collective concept frequently, farms should be taken over by the people and run for the people.

Laurenten knew Radcliffe could not go back to the Commons's second Emergency Debate at 3pm to bluff his way through what the London press and the Government were now calling a threat to British security, with back-benchers demanding Harrison's head on Tower Bridge. But there had been several key defections from the government - a couple of prominent veterans had conspicuously stayed away from the first debate and three others had stormed out, much to the chagrin of the Prime Minister, according to the Commons' commentators.

He tapped his finger softly on the table, drumming an irregular rhythm that matched his thoughts. Things were falling into place - a declaration could soon be possible. He gazed at an ancestor, the third Lord of Stanthorpe, depicted by a Tudor artist two centuries after his death. The face, sketched, he believed, from the ninth Lord's likeness, showed a firm chin and unyielding stare. The third Lord, William De Laurenten, had fought both Saracens and French, had increased the family lands and maintained the Lorraine valley vineyards despite the loss of lands to the English crown. The subject wore an ornate romanticised Tudor breastplates, but the artist had captured a strong family trait that the present Lord was accused of possessing by his son and daughter, the same family trait he had accused his father of possessing, a self-assuredness that would not deviate from truth and right. The family stare, when fixed, could be ruthless in severity and discipline. Only his wife had been able to melt it, he recalled. Her boldness matched his obstinacy at times, which left them both giggling in stalemate. He smiled at the passing memories of dinners and dances, of bedroom romances and rambles in the highlands and on the moors. I miss her, he acknowledged, but now's not the time to tread that lonely lane.

Hickling was now talking to Beatrice about the DEFRA building while Harrison discussed recent editorials in The Field with Whitman. Laurenten glanced at the papers in front of him. Until he had spoken with Radcliffe, they meant nothing. Many of the names on them would go unbeckoned if he could not get his support.

The door opened, Radcliffe marched in alone and the room fell silent. He was smaller than they'd expected, reaching just five-foot six, but was an athletically-built forty-five-year old with a strong jaw, bright blue eyes and thinning blond hair. He was wearing a sports jacket and open-necked shirt; Laurenten took his informal apparel to mean that he would listen, after voicing his own thoughts. A more formal appearance would have suggested a lost cause.

The others instinctively rose to greet the easily recognisable face. Radcliffe, however, acknowledged none but Harrison. He strutted angrily to the table, saying, as he pounded the floor, "What the fuck are you're playing at, Harrison?" The question sprang out vehemently. Radcliffe took a seat and began a barrage of words.

"Do you know what this means for us? We're connected to you - you and your bloody stupid tactics. We bloody give you parliamentary support, well most of us do," he added, looking down momentarily. He continued at a fast, fervent pace. "They're calling for your blood, they're hunting for you over the entire kingdom. For God's sake, you'll be on next month's Crimewatch, I hear. And because we're connected, on some levels at least, thank God, not all, they're just vilifying us in the press. They're having a field day down there. Look at Radcliffe, they're saying, one more nutter to oppose the squeaky-clean spinning regime, look at his friendships and alliances - not just a pro-hunt campaign, but an anti-government campaign - a terrorist campaign, for Christ's sake, a supporter of law-breakers. No word, no communication from you, just an independent action. Oh yes, while Radcliffe's in parliament, let's blow up a building and see how he reacts to the press. The bloody government's frying me. Some of my own back-benchers are clamouring for my resignation. I'm supposed to be down there right now, defending your sneaky ass. I mean, it doesn't look good." He slowed down to take in who else was sitting at the table. His anger abated when he saw the women.

Laurenten pushed a coffee his way. "Michael, good to see you too."

Radcliffe blushed. "I'm sorry. Fuck. Sorry. Look, it's been hell down in London, and hell sneaking away to find out what the fuck, oh, sorry, what the hell's going on. Harrison, you could have warned me. I've been in tight corners before, but nothing like this one. Do you know what this is costing me personally? The party is baying for blood, they all are shocked and incredibly angry at your antics. I've left my second in control, and she'll just balls things up without our party having any inkling as to what this is all about. Why the hell couldn't you have at least bloody warned me?" he asked again, looking at Harrison like a friend betrayed.

"No time," said Harrison, sitting back to allow Radcliffe to settle down.

"Michael," said Laurenten quietly and calmly, "let me introduce to you Mr Peter Hickling, Professor Alison Whitman, and Colonel Beatrice Major, whom I think you have met before, good, yes, and of course, Vincent Harrison, whom I know you know."

Radcliffe shook the three proffered hands. Harrison remained sitting back, his hands resting in his lap. Radcliffe nodded.

"Michael, I've invited you up to work this through with us."

"Well, about bloody time, Laurenten. Someone could have told me, you know, about four weeks ago or something."

"We hadn't planned it four weeks ago," said Harrison.

Radcliffe stared at him. "Well, any time before you actually did the bloody deed."

Harrison leant forward. "No way. I could not ensure the spontaneity of it."

"And what the hell have you done with the minister?"

"Under house arrest, shall we say? Somewhere pleasant - up north."

Radcliffe drank his coffee back and took in the other faces. "Laurenten, what do you want? This action could destroy the party, you know that."

"The party, for which I do not give a damn at this present time," said Laurenten firmly, "has to adapt, as it has always adapted. The country should not be expected to flock to your party. You have to go to the country. And this country is being shat on, pardon my expression, by a bunch of urban hoodlums who believe government gives them the power to make any piece of bigoted, regulative, taxing and cramping legislation they desire."

Radcliffe slammed his hands down on the table. "You're bloody undermining our democracy, you know, and you have the gall to talk about the law?"

"Government should never make law," said Laurenten quietly, not taking his eyes of Radcliffe.

"Don't preach that Whig shit to me. You know how the country works - this is what democracy is about," replied Radcliffe contemptuously.

"That's not what you used to argue," continued Laurenten, his stare causing Radcliffe to look angrily away for a moment. "Freedom and liberalism were your calling cards, I recall, when you were elected to your constituency. You've been in London, close to the centre of power, for too long. Smell the air here, Michael, it's free and clean. Remember the people who supported you before you were the party big-shot? Farmers and local business people who gave you their votes because you said you would get government off their backs. They listened to your arguments, they heard that freedom was the only option - no more grants, no more licences, no more appeasement of trespassers and hooligans; a strong message that you drove home. You spoke well - Cicero would have been proud. I was there, you recall, and I remember the buzz and excitement that your speech created. At first people were taken aback, but they listened to your reasons, and they were impressed. Impress them again, Michael. Don't sell out."

"I haven't sold out," Micahel Radcliffe answered quietly, if slightly petulantly, as Laurenten's words hit home. He shuffled in his seat. "Government's different. It cannot accept the arbitrary breaking of the law."

"You're not in government," Laurenten reminded him. "And the government should be a tool to ensure the proper running of the law, the law that pre-exists the state, and which is based on common morality and common sense." His voice hardened to get the point across. "For years, our so-called governments have made legislation that is contrary to the moral law of the land; power attracts those who would yield it, but don't you remember the lessons of history? Nobody can be trusted with power, neither me, nor you. Power is to be limited and reduced to a bare minimum to ensure the proper functioning of the law, certainly not legislation created by the whims of temporary power mongers riding an opinion poll. You know that!"

Laurenten raised his voice; he had not stopped glaring at Radcliffe who had physically buckled under the older man's stare. Radcliffe's mind was racing ahead, considering the implications of Laurenten's words.

"Think about the people who face you every day in the Commons. Do you think they are capable, disciplined, thoughtful MPs, never mind liberal, in the sense that they possess a glimmering of what freedom entails? No, they are not. Each week they pass some new restrictive legislation, because they are people who cannot occupy their minds with anything less than interfering with others' lives. They're lawyers making work for themselves when they lose their jobs as MPs, they're parasites who have never worked in their lives except in politicking. They're unintelligent little minds, who believe they are gods. Good Lord, Michael, three and half centuries ago this land was torn asunder for much less arrogance on the part of the monarch. In two hours, the Prime Minister will argue for the abolition of all country pursuits, according to the news - in return for support for his aggression in the Gulf! Now, take a serious look at the petty monarchs who have risen to positions of greater power than King Charles ever did. We have held back for too long. We should have acted sooner, in 1911 or 1973 perhaps. It was discussed, you know. But we thought we would go back after people realised how counter-productive and illiberal the interventions were. But they didn't and of course the war merely intensified the socialist and welfare movement, and hence expedited the death of liberty in the land. Michael, our Scottish Parliament is issuing Expropriation Proclamations on land owners. They've haphazardly banned hunting with hounds up there and now there are strong rumours that the UK government wants to nationalise land across the entire kingdom. What is this? Zimbabwe? The Soviet Union? When you mess with a people's land, you get an angry reaction. Consider history, Michael. When the European powers expropriated native lands around the world, they often met very fierce resistance. And bloody rightly so! We had no right to trample on their lands, their property rights, even though they had no concept of property. But we do, Michael,

- 226 -

we do. That concept goes to the heart of what this nation is about. And Westminster is not expropriating the lands of barely armed tribesmen in the bush. It's doing it to its own people, which is as close to tyranny and totalitarianism as you can get. And we will not take it lying down.

"The firing of the DEFRA building was symbolic. No one was hurt, for we are not in this to fight dirty - yet. We made our point. We can make it again, though, if we choose. Your pals in the government are too removed from morality to understand the significance. It was a shot across the bows, Michael, and none too soon. Look at them, parading around the country removing rights willy-nilly as if they were some Prussian occupational force.

"My family's dealt with such arrogant tyrants before, Michael, and we can certainly smell them from several glens away. This is the beginning of the campaign; we want you on board, not to give us legitimacy, because liberty does not need anyone's consent or patronage. We want you on board because you could make the process smoother. If you join us, the fight would not last as long. But if you throw yourself in with the government, well, you may as well and go and prepare for a long season of protracted discontent and civil war."

"You're threatening further violence?" Radcliffe deployed one last moral card against Laurenten.

"The aggression has already been committed by several governments upon this land and people. And this deplorable excuse for a government has been slowly intensifying its grip on our remaining freedoms. And we are not going to permit any more incursions."

"You're threatening further violence?" Radcliffe gazed up at the ceiling and took a deep breath.

"We're defending our liberties, Michael. Just as you promised to do twelve years ago to your constituents."

Beatrice crossed her arms and leant on the table. "Michael, the campaign is just about to take off. We have strict rules of conduct."

"You're talking secession from Westminster? A split in the country?"

"For the country," quipped Whitman.

"It's every man's right to forge his own government along with sympathetic people," explained Laurenten. "Our Assembly has sat on the sidelines for too long. Now's the time to bring it forth to reclaim and support the land's ancient traditions and liberties."

"We're building up foreign support networks to recognise the campaign," said Peter. "The UN recognised East Timor, the EU is just about to recognise the Basques. They will recognise us, in time perhaps, but they cannot ignore us."

"A politician cannot run from principles all the time," added Whitman. "You're certainly in an unenviable position. You are too close to power. It must be highly appealing. But Laurenten's right. That's not what you used to believe in. You sought freedom."

"All for the right to hunt?" Radcliffe asked rhetorically, regarding Laurenten.

Laurenten leant forward. "Michael. It's more than the bloody right to hunt - we'd continue that anyway, even if the government went ahead with a ban. They'd eventually buckle under mass disobedience."

"They'd try to license it," said Beatrice, "which means a creeping control until it's total. And that is unacceptable."

"Think about what this party - and others before it as you well know - has sought to prohibit and ban in the past twenty years. It's not only unconscionable, it's evil. The unrelenting purpose has been to advance state control into all of our affairs. You can't take a drink or drive a car without a multiple of its cost going straight to the Treasury; you can't alter your house without some anal-retentive little Hitler coming along to say you can't do it that way and that you have to comply with a list of EU laws; you can't buy unit trusts without filling in a bunch of forms to say you understand what you're doing; kids can't play many games because they may be too risky; adults can't own a TV without paying for a bloody licence..."

"Give me time. Give me time," Radcliffe interrupted rubbing his face. "I hear what you're saying, I know what's going on. But I'm tired. I was up late last night and have had to dodge a lot of people to get here. I should be back tonight for the Emergency debate part two - Cramp's revenge. However, I'll contact my aides to take care of issues and excuse myself from the debate. That may give us time, although I doubt it. Against such a huge majority, my presence at Westminster is sadly marginal. History may laugh at my absence from this debate, but then again, the way things are going for the Party, we're all a laughing stock anyway. Okay. Do you have a room for me?"

Laurenten smiled. "It has already been prepared for you, Michael. Welcome on board."

Radcliffe grimaced slightly but offered no retort to Laurenten's presumption of victory. "How many counties can you carry? I mean, that is what it is about, isn't it?"

"May I offer you some more coffee? Twelve, thirteen maybe, but by tomorrow, we're hoping for twenty. We have towns and areas not under the normal political jurisdictions offering tentative support. They're concentrated in the north, the east midlands, and the south-west."

"And Wales and Scotland?"

"Five from each as well," said Peter, who had caught up with the developments earlier.

"And Europe, what the hell will you do about Europe?"

"You know my views on Europe, Michael. We'll be declaring our independence and our free trade status at the same time."

"What about a plebiscite?"

"I agree, we could do with one, but in our haste we will have to set a guaranteed date a year from the declaration. But, you know this - we've spoken about it before - we'll support those areas that wish to remain independent. If they're the only ones to support us in a referendum, then we'll go with them."

"You know you're speaking treason?" Radcliffe said then swallowed back some coffee. The others looked at each other.

"Nonsense, man. Treason is committed against a state to which one has pledged allegiance. It was a feudal concept designed to increase the monarch's power over the independent barons - because they were independent. Besides, in this context any hint of treason is rather superseded by the government's treachery towards every civilian in the land.

Government does not exist to infringe rights and to trample on its citizens, as if we had mandated the MPs to become petty, lying and cheating Caligulas to whimsically alter the land as they see fit. Good God, Michael, don't forget your roots."

"I've not," Radcliffe glowered. "I just wasn't expecting to be working for a regime different from the one I've trained for."

"This won't be easy. At the moment we're on a knife edge. Then things will get difficult. We could do with your energy and passions on board."

"In what capacity?"

"There is a pre-established order, Michael."

"So, I won't be getting any promotion then?" Radcliffe chuckled sardonically.

"Only for your conscience."

"Hmm," said Radcliffe thrusting his hands into his trouser pockets.

Laurenten had struck home. There would be no point hounding Radcliffe to ground. He got up from his chair. Now would be an appropriate time to close the meeting. "May I suggest we retire to the drawing room for some biscuits? We dine early at six. We have another meeting at eight."

As they walked through the halls, Beatrice began talking to Radcliffe about the Duke of Wellington, which calmed his temper. Harrison, who had sat impassively while Laurenten put forward his points, now joined in. Both he and Radcliffe were experts on the Battle of Waterloo and they never missed a chance to discuss the battle or Wellington. They had known each other since they were boarders at Ballington College and had often quarrelled on matters historical and political.

Laurenten opened the twelve-foot doors into the drawing room where Terry Gibbon, Liz, Sally, Katherine Markham and Joanna Ribblesdale sat talking.

Initially Radcliffe remained quiet as Harrison tried to coax him into a different mood. Radcliffe certainly needed time to think, but all of them wanted to keep him occupied and interested at same time. He lightened considerably and began to challenge Harrison's perception of the battle. Beatrice suggested they consider how Napoleon might have enhanced his chances of success; they took the bait and within minutes were laying out the battle on the table with various implements - coasters, spoons, cruets, pens, paper, and glasses of port for the generals - were arrayed in symbolic lines to represent Napoleon's great thrust against Wellington's lines. In quarter of an hour Radcliffe was laughing and debating loudly.

Laurenten smiled as he watched an animated Radcliffe demolish Harrison's arguments for not following Blücher. Radcliffe's mind, he thought, had been taken off the more pressing subject, but Beatrice had turned his liminal attention to an analogous situation. Radcliffe would understand, thought Laurenten, but he also knew that Radcliffe's mind would be considering his values, career position and future, and this was a useful distraction. Laurenten sat down to enjoy the battle's unfolding strategies. Beatrice rejected Radcliffe's tactical errors, "Yes, but you've not considered the farmhouse; remember, it becomes central to the battle." Harrison argued against Napoleon putting so many against the farmhouse, while Radcliffe thought it was inevitable.

"Nothing's inevitable," replied Beatrice, "I merely noted that in the real battle that's where the focus lay. Now, do you wish to deploy your troops elsewhere, general?"

"Certainly. I'm not falling for that ruse. Get trapped in the battle over the farm losing men hand over fist. No, we'll go for the weaker right flank."

"And I'll keep my hidden strength on the reverse slope," murmured Harrison.

The battle continued and Laurenten smiled as he turned to talk to Joanna Ribblesdale, whom he had met for the first time that day. They spoke of neutral matters - the weather and the library of books - leaving the thoughts in the back of his mind to freewheel. He was increasingly certain that they now had Radcliffe on their side. Whitman, Hickling and his partner had turned to discuss music, although Hickling, Laurenten noted, periodically observed Radcliffe from the corner of his eye. He relaxed into his chair, enjoying more of Ribblesdale's conversation. She was a handsome woman, he thought. Well-dressed, slim figure, late forty-something, kind eyes and crows feet from what he hoped was from a life of laughter. No more could be said to Radcliffe tonight, he knew that. Radcliffe needed time to come to terms with the decision he had in effect made. Laurenten sympathised. A public figure has more at stake. Still, he thought, a free nation will be less of a burden for those in public life. Joanna, as she now asked him to call her, wore no ring. He shifted his mind to concentrate on her conversation.

"I'm sorry, I've been rather caught up in myself these past few minutes," he said straightening his tie.

"Yes, I knew you were," she said softly and smiled. "You've got much to consider. I was just chuntering about the state of the land."

Her kind words caught him off guard for a second. "Yes, yes, I do have a lot on at the moment." His face flickered as his heart opened, and she observed it. No one else noticed, but she reached over and touched his hand for a moment.

"You're doing well," she said gently.

He smiled and regarded her green eyes, framed by faint lines. She was immaculately clothed in a golden sweater and long fawn woollen skirt. Her curly dark hair had a few grey hairs, and her eyes drew him into a calm, wise world. She's experienced a lot, herself, he thought.

"You mentioned the library and the portraits. Are you an admirer of Rembrandt?" he asked.

"Yes, do you have books on him too?"

"Not books, but a few original sketches. May I be so bold as to invite you to come to see some etchings in the library?" He stood up and offered her his arm.

"I'd be honoured," she said taking his arm and rising.

The Discovered Self

"I'm coming, Cuch, I'm coming!" came a voice from the forest.

Flood nervously patted the dog's head. It came up to Flood's waist. He looked to where the voice had come from and finally he saw the flickering a torch beam.

"Ah, there you are!" came the voice of a ghostly sylvan woman, flattening bracken and bushes to reach him. Flood tried to say something.

"Yes, here I am. Uh, thanks, I was, uh ... "

"Lost by the sounds of it?" she smiled broadly as she stepped forward. Her smile saved him making any excuses. She scanned him up and down with the torchlight, and, from what Flood surmised, ascertained that he was no threat to her.

"Yeah, lost," he replied quite meekly.

"Thoroughly, I'd say. Mmm, is that blood? You've hurt yourself. I'll get that cleaned for you."

"I, er, got caught in the bushes back there."

"Not surprising - you're in the thickets. Looks painful," she sympathised, coming closer to inspect. "A small gash; I have some ointment for that. Right, Cuch, come on boy, let's get home. Good boy," she said giving the dog a pat as he returned to her side. "He has a good nose. I could not have found you so easily in the woods, but he could sniff you out. Come with us, I'll sort you out."

"What kind of dog is he?" he inquired, following the woman.

"Wolfhound. Gorgeous, isn't he?"

"Yes, he's very big."

"Still another half foot to grow yet."

"Goodness," said Flood, walking just behind his saviour.

"How long have you been lost?"

"I don't know. Since about one, perhaps."

"Four hours or so then," she said, leading them onto what he could discern as a wide bridle path.

"So here's the path!"

"You were not far from it. About twenty feet or so."

"I couldn't see a thing back there. It was so dense. How far's the village?"

"Village? There's no village for fifteen miles or so."

"Fifteen miles? Well, where do you come from? I thought you would live in a village or something nearby."

"Goodness no. You're not from round here are you? You're in the middle of Yore forest. Literally in the middle. Hardly anybody comes this way. Not even ramblers. It's easy to get lost and there are many dangerous potholes in and around the valleys. Good job you didn't fall into one."

"I didn't know," he replied relieved that he had not died in some thicket or pothole.

"If you'd have fallen into one of the holes nobody would have found you. What brings you to these parts anyway?"

Flood reverted to the stock excuse. "I was rambling."

She said nothing for a moment. "Not with a group?"

"No, by myself. I've been meaning to enjoy the countryside for a while, and I kind of got lost on my first day out."

She laughed. "Well you've certainly had a most interesting initiation. I do hope it hasn't put you off."

"No," he smiled. "Where are we going? Do you have a car parked nearby?"

"No. We've not got far to go. My house is about five minutes away."

Her house? Of course, the smell of smoke! That explained it. "I could smell smoke," he said trundling after her.

"Yes, I lit the fire about an hour ago. The night is going to be very cold," she said.

"Do you have a telephone?"

"Yes, but the wire from the village came down in storms a couple of days ago. Of course, I'm sorry - you will be wanting to call your family to let them know you are safe."

"And mobiles?"

"Out of range here," she replied. She stopped and turned to him, her pallid complexion dancing in the patchy greys of night. "You'll probably want a stiff drink, then we'll see about getting you back to civilisation." He could make out a comforting smile. "I was making a dinner. It won't take long to add a few more ingredients, unless you need to get back immediately?"

"Uh no," he said. "But you don't have to go to any trouble."

"Of course I do," she said but laughingly. "You're in the middle of nowhere and I'm the only person who lives here. But I don't mind going to some trouble to help a lost soul, you know. Do you like rabbit?"

"Uh," he pondered for a moment wondering whether to explain that he was a vegetarian, but thought against it. Here was a stranger who had rescued him from hypothermia or an isolated death, offering to make him a meal. This was not a time to be fussy. "I've never eaten rabbit," he said truthfully.

"Always a first time then. I make a good rabbit, don't I, Cuchulain?" The dog looked up as he padded along.

"What is his name?"

"Cuchulain. You know, the Irish hero of legend? Most appropriate for an Irish wolfhound, I thought. But he's such a beauty!" She gave the dog a loving pat as he trotted to her left, checking out the forest for deer and wolves.

Flood had not heard of the hero, but said that the dog was quite stunning.

"Yes, and he's such a good hunter. He caught a brace of rabbits the other day for the pot; I've skinned both and was about to cook one, but it will be easy cooking the another."

Flood had been through a lot already that day, but his thoughts continued to spin and dance. Starting the day on a crusade against hunting, he was now about to eat rabbit with a woman rabbiter. His mind swirled but his stomach grumbled more, and the overriding thought of being found and invited into a warm house with a fire was too much for any moralistic pretensions.

Ahead, he could see a couple of squares of light peeking through the branches. The house. Shelter. Home - man's ultimate point of return; he stopped himself asking his hostess if this were her house, for he thought he had made himself stupid enough by "rambling" into the most inaccessible area of England. A thought occurred to him - what if she had heard of the antis earlier activities in the area? What if she had been on the hunt? He shivered guiltily, but could not grasp which way his imperfectly balanced loyalties ought to lie - with his ideological crusade or a guest's manners.

From the forest they entered a small clearing and a walled garden, although beyond some orderly patterns he could not tell in the blackness what grew there. The house loomed ahead. The silhouette suggested many chimneys and several steep gables. The light from the two downstairs windows was not enough for him to discern much more. They approached the darkened door, which was framed by a wooden porch jutting out several feet.

"Come in," she said, "take your boots off in the hall and put your coat up on a hook." In the light he could make out the nature of his rescuer. She was dressed in a long coat and wore a bush-hat from under which cascaded long, tight, dark curls, surrounding a pale face of exquisite beauty.

Flood politely and self-consciously obeyed - he was quite unsure of himself in this sudden surrounding of domesticity in the middle of nowhere; the paradox unnerved him slightly, and the hall light blinded him temporarily. When he straightened up from undoing his boots to take off his coat, he glanced around.

The hall was about ten feet long; they had entered a porch with a stable door. A second door, which had been left open, led to the kitchen. The hall was cool. The walls were half white and of slightly cracked plaster, the bottom half consisted of dark wooden panelling with a dado rail; heavy timber eaves ran above his head at right angles to the length of the hall. Two iron chandeliers hung from the ceiling.

"Come on through," the woman beckoned.

He entered a large kitchen with a flagstone floor. From the ceiling timbers hung several bunches of herbs and dried flowers. A miscellany of dark and intricate cabinets and heavy shelves lined the walls. The woman had made her way to an ancient iron range, fired, it smelled, by wood. She was filling a kettle. A large oak table sat in the middle of the room, surrounded by eight wooden chairs - at either end stood intricately carved small thrones. Flood felt the smooth ebony-coloured oak.

"Early sixteenth century," said the woman, checking the oven's temperature.

"Uh, sorry, I didn't mean ... " he began, withdrawing his body from the antique.

"Oh, no, they're supposed to be touched and sat on. They're quite sturdy. Lasted this long, and they'll last many centuries yet. Now, you sit down and I'll just wash my hands and sort your cut out." She washed her hands and fished around in a cupboard to pull out cotton wool, antiseptic, and a bottle of hydrogen peroxide. "Let's have a look at you." She tilted his head back, washed the cut and administered the antiseptic.

"By the way, what's your name?" she asked peering at his forehead.

"Oh? Fl, uh ... Miles Thomson."

"Pleased to meet you, Fl-uh, Miles," said the woman, proffering a hand. "I'm Cosima Laurenten. Goodness, a few cuts to your hands as well. And you're soaking - you fell a few times?" He nodded. She knelt down to hold his hands and turn them over, cleaning them gently but thoroughly with a warm cloth and peroxide. "There, all better," she said smiling. "Now, let's get you a change of clothing. Why don't you take a quick shower upstairs before we eat? I'll sort you out some clothes. But first, let me get you some tea."

Flood observed her more closely. She stood in front of him, preparing a mug of tea. He thought she was an angel and not only for having rescued him from nocturnal oblivion. A long, thick cream woollen cardigan covered her hips; underneath the cardigan she wore a dark green wide scooped-neck top that showed her chest without revealing her bosom; tight tan corduroys outlined strong and supple thighs. Her wide friendly smile shone through to his soul and enlivened fiery feelings. Her eyes penetrated with a confident clarity and sparkle; their meeting had burned onto his mind an image he would often recall later. He felt at once naked and armed, vulnerable and invincible; his soul swooned to the ground and his body left it there as he hesitated to reply. He had never met anyone so fresh-looking, or with such sharp eyes. Her large brown irises set in wide orbs framed by a slightly freckled face gleamed and sparkled with life - there was no other way he could describe them.

She handed him a steaming mug and led him up to a surprisingly modern bathroom with a powerful shower, fetched him a towel and a change of clothing - cords and a heavy cotton shirt - and left him to wash. He considered himself in the mirror as the shower heated up. The cut had left a sharp thin red line above the left eyebrow. He stripped off and was astonished how muddy his legs and feet had got. He jumped into the shower and revelled in the hot cleansing flow. He scrubbed and washed himself clean, massaged aching muscles and felt the acute sting of his cuts. As he put on the dry clothes and drank his tea he reflected upon the disparate contradiction with his recent predicament but left the thoughts there as he politely hurried back down to join his hostess.

"What do you do?" she inquired, smiling at his cleaner self and then quickly looking down to her food preparation. Her intonation betrayed no dialect that he knew; her voice was clear and confident and her inflection precise.

"I'm studying, I mean, reading English Literature."

"Student? Oh good, my field too. Well that, history and music. I should show you my book collection. We should have time."

"There's no rush," he replied, suddenly feeling as if he never ever wanted to lose sight of her. Being rescued by a woman so attractive was thoroughly appealing to his sensibilities.

"Well, you might think there is. I didn't tell you yet that I don't have my car here."

"Oh? Then, how ... "

"Horseback. I left my car in the village and rode back after the hunt. We'd have to take the horses to get to the village, which means, if we leave at eight we'd get there about ten-ish in the dark. And you probably want your clothes cleaned or dried."

"Goodness, I mean, uh, well," Flood stammered again, not knowing how to respond to this suggestion of arcane transport.

"But," she added cheerily, "if there's no rush to get back, you could stay the night of course. I have five bedrooms. It's just that if there were people worrying about you..."

Flood thought quickly. No, Jez would not miss him, she'd be off with someone he was sure, and Maggie might miss him but she was not that important. And as for Andy and the others, no, he thought, his welfare probably hadn't entered their minds. "No," he said, "I'm not expected back on campus until Monday. There'll be no search party."

"Good," Cosima said, apparently relieved. "Then we'll open a bottle of wine and have a relaxed evening. I was going to do some writing tonight, but a good conversation is much more important, don't you think?"

"It feeds the mind," he replied, relaxing at the prospect of not having to hurry anywhere soon, especially on horseback in a demonic forest.

Cosima stopped and scrutinised him. She nodded slowly. "Yes. It does. I agree. Minds certainly need feeding. Did I tell you that I am a writer and musician?"

"No."

"No, of course I didn't. I do a lot of my writing here and it's perfect for practising. It's my favourite place in the world. All mine. Far away from hell, other people, you know."

"Sartre?"

"Yes, that funny Frenchman. I do enjoy some of his philosophy," she added.

"What do you write?"

"Literary histories, some fiction, poems when I'm in the mood."

"Do you have publications?"

"A couple of books on minor sixteenth-century figures and several poems. I've been working on an essay on Renaissance education for a couple of years. But it's become unwieldy. It needs severe pruning. I also write freelance articles for various magazines. I've just penned one about the hunting debate. But," she said, pulling two skinned rabbits out of a marinade of wine and herbs and placing them in a casserole dish, "I can only prune in the autumn, when I prune my fruit trees.

Springtime - I write profusely as the flowers bloom. Rather seasonal, really."

Flood laughed, "I guess so! I'd never thought of writing with the seasons. Well, I don't write much, except essays."

"I could not stand writing predetermined essay titles. I didn't have state schooling and I thought it unwise to study at the state's universities. So I didn't go." She chopped carrots for the dish, added some Dijon mustard and pepper and stretched a few rashers of thick bacon over the rabbits, which, she explained stopped "rabbit gas."

Flood raised an inquisitive eyebrow but she returned to talking about her education. She explained that she had been tutored from home by academics and specialists. Her family had an enviable library that the academics could use, and gradually they taught her the skills necessary to research in depth and to write well and precisely.

"That sounds liberating, when put like that, I guess," said Flood.

"You guess? Of course it is. But I don't think," she said, adding pepper and herbs "that many people could handle it. My kind of education does not suit everybody, just as state education doesn't suit everybody. Or anybody from my experience."

"I've never thought about it."

"Few do," she said opening the oven door and inserting the stew. "Let's get a bottle of wine and relax for a while." She went over to the cupboard and pulled out a bottle of red wine. "Grab a couple of goblets from the cupboard." She meant goblets too - he picked up two large pewter goblets from a cupboard shelf. He asked her about the electricity supply, which she explained came from a generator that exploited an underground stream.

"So you're really isolated here," Flood remarked as they left the kitchen.

"Yes - very dark and isolated, and very pleasant in the winter," she added. Cosima opened a door into a large, open living room, with comfortable sofas, chairs, and two large writing desks, one of which was covered in music manuscripts and the other in books. Books lined every spare inch of space along the walls. A couple of cellos stood on stands and their cases stood propped up in a corner.

"Oh, my goodness," stammered Flood at the extensive collection of books.

"This is the living room. It looks like a library, but the proper library is at the other house. This is my study, so I've filled it with the books I need for writing. Please, sit down," she said, motioning him to a sofa. She sat opposite him and curled one leg under the other. "Sorry about the mess. I do let the books and papers accumulate and pile up. Oh, here," she said, leaning forward to place the bottle on an intricately carved low coffee table. "You do the honours."

Flood uncorked the wine and instinctively smelled it. "Mmm," he couldn't help commenting.

"Yes, it's a particularly good one to loosen the tongue and free the soul. It's from a cousin's vineyard in France. Marie sends me a crate every few months."

Flood poured the flowing translucent scarlet liquid into the two goblets. It gurgled appreciatively. He professed to knowing nothing about wine. She flicked back some strands of hair. "Your taste buds should tell you if it's good or not. Just let them probe. Don't think now, just taste. Compare later."

He raised the glass and sipped. The sensation wrapped him up in a warm blanket of grapes and sunshine. He closed his eyes to enjoy the cool liquid drip down his throat. He looked over at the cellos. Cosima saw the direction of his gaze.

"They keep me occupied when I'm not writing. I'm a member of a quartet. My cousin Dugald's the first violin and a couple of others, children of family friends, well, they're almost my age, play second violin and viola."

"I've not heard anyone play cello; would you mind? Or is that rude?"

She laughed and put down her wine. "No, I don't mind. I was practising this morning. Always do about an hour or two a day. What would you like to hear?"

"I've no idea, I'm sorry. I'm not well versed in classical music."

"Oh, I can play jazz and modern too. Which era do you like?"

"Something, er, something Victorian? I don't know the composers."

"How about Mendelssohn, 'Song without Words'?"

"I'll defer to your choice."

She picked up one of the cellos, pulled out and adjusted the spike, tightened her bow, and sounded the first note.

Flood felt as if he were swimming amongst noble and refined values - a beautiful woman, fine books, a divine wine, and glorious music. He closed his eyes and flew onto a new plane as she made the instrument seep into his depths and move him in places hitherto untouched by any music. He sat transfixed. He had only heard friends jam on acoustic and electric guitars before. He had never heard a classical instrument played live. He swallowed more of his libation and remained aesthetically coasting on another level, listening to the melodies drench the room. He chased the notes' ephemeral and ineffable sensations around his body and tried to contain them into a specific feeling or thought, but they eluded him like ripples forever fingering the edges of a lake.

She played for about ten minutes, driving the notes from every part of the fingerboard, manipulating the emotions they created. Finally she bowed the last note, which rang around the room and was slowly absorbed by the books and furniture.

Cosima put her head back and gently stroked the neck of the cello. As the sound died she spoke quietly, "Yes, that is a particularly enjoyable piece to play."

He opened his eyes. He tried to anchor them onto something for he daydreamed that he was flying in warm, welcoming clouds; they fell onto Cosima's waist but that was intrusive. He raised his eyes to her face. Her sharp features demanded nothing less than veneration, he thought. He was overwhelmed.

"That was ... that was really good." He strove for words that sounded less plebeian. She smiled at him and he was not sure that she had seen him glance at her body. "Sublime. I'm at a bit a loss what to say."

"Thank you. Your face expresses more. I can tell you appreciated it." She put the cello gently back on its stand and picked up the goblet that she had left on the table. "Yes. Marie has a certain knack with the grape. Her family won't let anyone see the process itself, but the results are to die for. Now tell me something about yourself, where you are from, what books you like, what music you listen to. I mean - if you want to, there's no obligation to talk of course, just make yourself feel at home and do what you wish."

"Thank you," he said. He pondered over what to explain. His impulse was to pour out his life's story to her, bare his feelings, dreams, ambitions, take his skin off and show his naked soul; he wanted to fall into her dark eyes and vanish. But where should be begin? He wanted this woman to know everything, but then he felt that she knew everything anyway. Did he have a story to tell? Anxiety thrust its way up from his stomach and overwhelmed his being, leaving him a flattened, two-dimensional entity that could not possibly have anything interesting to relate.

"Uh," he started and mentally kicked himself. "Uh," he began dying before her pleasant face. He dropped his head and then decided be confident - at least to play it for now. It may rub off, he thought. He rubbed his eyes with both hands and looked up. "Oh, sorry, I'm not sure where to start. I'm from Stilton Stoneby," he began firmly.

"Ah," she sighed, "the hunting Mecca."

"Uh?" his ethics receded into a pit of despair and remained impaled on sharp points of rejection. "Yeah." Damn! My language, his mind remonstrated, needs severe improvement, as do my manners and my precision of thought. "Yes, I grew up there, went to the state schools, and moved to university a couple of years ago. I'm in my last year."

"Did you ever see or go out with the Stoneby?"

"I'm not a hunter, I mean, I've never hunted." He caught the logical ambivalence that had slipped through. He reflected upon the latter meaning and realised that he would like to try it. Or was that the wine speaking? The night before, Gemma had espoused her views on hunting and her arguments had caught him up; Maggie's parroting of pamphlets had annoyed him; the hunters on the train were ostensibly nice people. And

Artemis had rescued him. He was not sure where he now stood, but thought he'd better use his mind and even see for himself. He accepted his conclusion.

He thought her eyes expressed a flickering disappointment or was it an implicit recognition of his real purpose in the area? She took a sip of her wine and changed the subject. "Why literature?"

"Hmm? Oh, I've always read. I enjoy books immensely. I lose myself in them and live a life I could never lead in reality. Escapism I guess you'd call it. But books offered more than new worlds. They," he paused for thought, "they offered words to explore the world around me, although I'm not much good at expressing myself." He frowned and leant forward, rubbing his face with his free hand again. "I think I am on the edge of understanding things. I mean, today, I got lost, as you know. But as I walked I felt things fall into place, but what those things are and into what place they've fallen, I am not yet quite sure."

She observed him intently as he spoke. "Keep letting them fall," she replied softly. "You'll work out where they've gone."

He nodded. "I have led the wrong life. Or rather, I don't think I've led a life at all. I mean, uh, it's been kind of boring. I feel as if I should have been on a crusade or something, won medals for bravery in battle, written a symphony, composed a hundred sonnets, or fallen in love," he added. He turned away, then checking himself looked up at her face. Her eyes were kind and encouraging. He breathed in deeply and let out a sigh, releasing the day's stress. He drank the wine to encourage his philosophical thoughts.

"You're young," she said. "We both are. We have decades to define ourselves. I think, if you don't mind me saying so, that you are striving for some sort of immortality or recognition. There's nothing wrong in that. How do you intend to proceed though. Have you ever imagined yourself twenty years from now, and then you look back on how you got there?"

"No." He thought for a minute. "I'd be an author. A respected author," he added sheepishly.

"Don't be modest," she said. "If that's what you want, then you can strive for it. It's not up to the fates, it's up to you."

"I know. Or rather, I guess I should know. But what happens if I am cut down before I earn my immortality?"

"Then you die gloriously on the path of self development. Goodness, that sounds like self-help psychology." They laughed and chuckled over funny book titles designed to catch the weak-willed and lost. "But," Cosima continued, "what would be worse, I mean, is that if you died without attempting to put pen to paper, without having at least had a go. So many potential authors do not get up the courage to write, and they die without having tried. That is tragedy. Dying in the attempt is glory. The young private soldier who is killed the first time he goes over the top, that is heroic. The man who fritters away each day excusing his inactivity - that is inexcusable. And pathetic."

"I agree," Flood said. "I have started writing - privately, I mean. A few sonnets and short stories, but I don't think they're much good."

"You won't, not yet. It takes time and practice. Keep writing, whatever it is, just like an artist should keep sketching even though much of his work will end up discarded. Keep throwing the words down, then things will come that you are proud of."

Flood nodded and took a mouthful of wine. He scanned the room. The shelves were packed with leather-bound volumes.

"Feel free to browse," Cosima said, getting up while watching his gaze. "Let me show you a few of my favourites." She rose with a gracefulness Flood had not seen in a woman before, and glided quietly to the shelves. He put his goblet down and followed her and, standing next to her, imbibed her closeness as she pulled out volumes for him to savour. Her hair gave off a sweet smell that he breathed in surreptiously. He focused part of his mind on her figure, her stance, her breathing, her fragrance, as she opened one book to show him an illustration. Flood laughed. The picture depicted a rather rotund man in pinks attempting to pull his horse up a bank or over a hedge.

Flood read the accompanying words of Mr Jorrocks, "Come hup! I say - you ugly Beast!" Cosima showed him another picture. "Mr Jorrocks's Lecture on 'Unting", read Flood. "'Unting? Oh, hunting! He looks like one of my lecturers. Look at him pointing to the audience. He looks quite Dickensian."

"But better."

"Who wrote this?"

"Surtees. R.S. Surtees."

"Oh! I've heard of him. Mr Jorrocks! So that's what he looks like! The man in the country clothes store near the university. He mentioned him and said he was better than Dickens."

"I quite agree. He certainly is. Except it's not PC to read such great literature and most certainly not PC to profess enjoying it. I was allowed to read anything and everything that I could get my hands on - no limits whatsoever, and I was encouraged to think for myself at all times. I have many old friends and tutors amongst the shelves. Gentlemen and gentlewomen of letters, whom I periodically call upon for advice."

Flood expressed the same sentiments and explained how he felt on entering the university library and how sometimes he picked up random titles to dip into before returning to Surtees. "I attended a lecture the other day and the professor spoke about Surtees. I'd asked her to, actually. I'd been to buy some rambling clothes at William Jorrocks's ... "

"Mr Wakeman's?"

"Yes, you know him?" She nodded. "And then I asked the professor ... "

"A woman you said - that'd be Professor Whitman - Miranda. She was one of my tutors. She's very close to the family. A good friend of mine now."

"Sounds as if you two would agree on many things," Flood observed.

"You'd be surprised. Politically yes, but on music and aesthetics we have raging arguments. I enjoy a lot of modern music - for Miranda, music died with Wagner."

Flood felt too ignorant to follow that one. He turned to a shelf full of hunting titles.

"You hunt foxes, don't you?"

"Of course. My family have always been hunters." Cosima refrained from explaining that the local hunt was named after her family. "Unfortunately so few people are able to join in. It is expensive, I know, and I do feel strongly that the Masters or their patrons should encourage young people from the towns: could you imagine - a school outing! Thirty children all saddled up and taken for a hunt. Instead, schools concoct silly notions of the fox's human and saintly characteristics and man's barbarity as hunter. But I believe a man is not a man unless he's 'unted, and neither is a woman a woman unless she's 'unted," Cosima said, playing on Mr Jorrocks's accent.

Flood looked curiously at the woman in whom the blood of generations of hunters ran. He felt that her demeanour and words suggested she hunted frequently. She stood erect as if she controlled the lands around her. She seemed feudal, and even earlier than that. He could not fathom her and felt he had no right to until he'd been out with the hunt.

"Hunting brings out qualities of our nature that lie submerged - the best and the beast," she added, laughing suddenly. Her laugh was vivacious, soft and infectious. "You should give it a go sometime."

Flood smiled at her. Too much - oh well, go with the flow, he thought. "Perhaps I will," he affirmed, as much to himself as to her.

Cosima escorted him around the shelves, showing him a variety of books and teaching him what to look for in boards and bindings. They turned to the history section, and Flood, recalling several nationalistic emblems from the past adorning the walls in the hall, asked if Cosima was patriotic.

"Of course. I come from a family that has upheld and defended the land's traditions for many generations. Aren't you patriotic?"

"I'd not given it much thought. I mean, I don't know. I guess so."

"Well, it's up to you to find out whether this country is worthy or not. I think it is. I've lived abroad, in France, Italy, and America. They are all proud of their culture and institutions, yet we go around apologising for ours. Sometimes

WILLIAM VENATOR

I do get rather frustrated with people who damn our country pursuits and laws without any understanding of why or how they developed." Cosima pulled out a privately-bound book of John Locke's Third Treatise On Government. Flood saw a note saying that the author had annotated it. "And liberty, that cherished value our ancestors fought for over the centuries becomes a relative phrase - a kind of lifestyle choice on par with tyranny or anarchy, something to be discarded if it gets in the way of administration. People just don't understand what they are losing. It is so ironic that the great symbol of the old gentry, the fox-hunter in his red jacket, should now become the great symbol of liberty. It is curious what symbols freedom casts our way.

"Take a look at this picture," Cosima said, pulling out an art book. "This is by Munnings, a derided artist in the post-war years, but now quite collectable." She opened the book to a picture of a man on horseback facing the viewer.

The subject filled Flood's vision. The horseman gazed down on him from his great height, yet this was not a mastery over man nor beast, the horse was as noble as the rider, but the rider looked apprehensive, perhaps fearing the end of the day's hunting as his last. The rider stared at Flood and he felt a shiver. This was nobility captured and rendered in the late Impressionist style, the paint thick, and the strokes broad. The subject was not oppressive in any manner but it was awesome. Power radiated from the picture - the horse wanted to jump, the rider to gallop, and in that action their tension would be resolved. Energy was balanced between horse and man, nature and man. Flood felt a connection with what he had seen on top of the valley earlier. A simultaneous dislocation and empowerment; the rider stood for something greater, something older, and something else that Flood had never witnessed in a man. He could not grasp it, although glimmerings of comprehension dangled in his thought's recesses.

"Quite noble," whispered Cosima whose hand reached out to touch the man's face. "Quite noble. So little of it left today, and they would wish it banned too. Dignity, nobility, honour, grace,

- 248 -

all bygones. Such values had empowered our nation a couple of centuries ago, and their lack is destroying it."

Dignity! There was that word again. Dignity flowed from the man's face and from the horse. The word was familiar yet remote - atavistic even - drumming up images of Stoic philosophers, Marcus Aurelius, and the Duke of Wellington.

"It is striking, isn't it? So powerful. Any woman who sees a man like that would, well, melt. Dignity is so much sexier than brawn."

"I can see that," replied Flood, straightening his own back a little.

She put the book back. "I must go and turn the meat. Would you like another drink, Miles?"

"I would," replied Flood gazing at other titles. Some were French, some Latin. He recognised first editions of literary works. "You have quite a collection," he called as she left the room.

"I know, I'm very lucky," she shouted back from the kitchen.

He paused to pull out a volume of Boccaccio's Decameron, a book he had read a few weeks ago.

"I am lucky," said Cosima, returning to the room. "All my ancestors have been collectors. Each generation tries to add what it can to the collection, which spans over six households today. I've got a twentieth of the collection here, I would say."

"Where do you normally live?" he inquired.

She explained that her main home was at Stanthorpe Manor on the Northchestershire moors, but the family had another large house in Scotland, at Inverlochty. Her father, she added, had been verging on retirement recently while her brother, Jeremy, slowly took over managing the family's business interests. They had to maintain a diversity of interests because of high taxes and a generally unsympathetic political system that saw their wealth as something to be plundered at any opportunity. Flood took in the point and wondered why anyone would want to plunder a family of such wonderful resources.

They returned to the sofas to pour some more wine. The smell of meat and vegetables cooking made Flood's stomach ache with hunger and the wine, as he drank it, was going to his head. He relaxed substantially, more than he had ever done in his life. In Cosima's company it felt right for him to express deeply submerged ideas. They shot to the surface from the deep recesses in his mind. The wine helped their upward journey and unlocked hitherto unexplored or unconnected alleys of thought. For a moment he wondered how she might see him. Was he a worthwhile person? He did not think so, but a surge from his stomach demanded attention. Why not become worthwhile from now? Focus my life, he thought, get things done, enjoy what's of value. He looked at Cosima and wanted her to like him but realised that she could only like him if he had some value in himself. He stretched his shoulders back and took a deep breath. A new breath that would invigorate his soul, he hoped.

"Dinner should be ready in about twenty minutes," Cosima was saying as she sat down.

"Where's Cuchulain?" Flood asked, remembering the dog and wanting to find out more about Cosima.

"Oh, he's out. He stays in the garden area during the evening."

Flood asked whether she felt insecure living out in the woods. Cosima replied that he had not yet met Cuch's siblings, Caradoc and Boudicca, but that even if someone were determined to break in, she had means of defending herself. Did that mean guns, he inquired. She nodded and explained that there were four guns available in the house and two in hidden places in the outbuildings. Flood reflected for a moment and then acknowledged that he felt safer knowing she had guns. He asked whether the house was ever empty, but she said that was rare - her brother, and Marie's maternal aunt often used the lodge when she wasn't there.

"Don't you worry then when you're alone though?"

"No. No reason to. Even if a mad axe murderer wandered over this way and happened to reach my house and kill my dogs, he'd still have to face me." Cosima laughed very confidently.

Flood laughed too, for her face hinted that she could take care of herself but he was not sure how. He liked it when she laughed, for the air bubbled, and as she closed her eyes he could stare for a second or two at her exquisite features. He wanted to fall into her woollen sweater and her breasts and dream of an eternity encompassed in her arms. Her breasts were so comely, so welcoming. Her eyes opened and he raised his stare to the wall behind her. "Who's that?" He indicated a conveniently placed portrait of a huntsman between two bookshelves.

"That's my great, great, and I think another great, grandfather, who built this house as a huntsman's cottage," she said, turning her head to look at the portrait. Miles took in her hair and shape of her back. She is so intoxicating, he thought, taking another sip of wine. She turned round again and he smiled at her.

"The wine is something else," he said.

"I'm glad you enjoy it. I'll let Marie know."

"Is she your age?"

"Yes, well a bit older, she's twenty-four. I'm twenty-two. How old are you, may I ask?"

"Twenty one," he replied, "but twenty-two next month."

"Well I've just turned it, so we're the same age really," she said.

Flood inquired about the logistics of living in such an isolated place. Cosima explained that the lodge was accessible by car but that she preferred, once she was established, to ride back and forth to the nearest village. She stayed at the inn some evenings, for the family owned it, and they and several other isolated farmers kept rooms there.

"Sometimes though," she added, "I'll ride back, if the moon's bright and the wind's low. Then it's not too dangerous for the horse. We can even canter on some paths. That is fun. I feel," she said tossing her hair with a broad grin, "like a highwayman racing through the forest to rob the London to Northchester stagecoach."

"Do you ever meet anyone when you are riding to the village?"

"Nearer the village, yes, for in the summertime there are ramblers. Very, very rarely does anyone come as close as you did. Last year," she added with a small laugh, "I was trotting through the forest about a mile from here and I came across a man. He rather startled me, I can tell you, for it was late in the evening. But he was certainly much more startled than I. He looked as if he'd seen a ghost. I rode right up to him and he positively fainted," she laughed. "I jumped off the horse to see if he was alright, and when he came to, he jumped to his feet and sprinted off into the woods. I called after the silly man, but he would not turn back."

"Did you see him again?"

"No. I asked at the village. They told me a rambler had got lost in the woods and had seen a ghost of a headless horseman." They both laughed. "A headless horseman; goodness knows what I must look like in the dark."

"Very attractive, actually," ventured Flood and then blushed.

"Thank you," she held his eyes, smiled appreciatively, and then continued. "Supposedly, he came running in from the cold night into the pub, shaking like a leaf and mumbling about this ghost he had seen. I guess that rumour has put many others off from coming this way since then!" They laughed again and drank more wine.

"Well, the meal smells about ready," Cosima said.

They entered the kitchen and he took a place at the table. Cosima dished out two plates of rabbit stew and potatoes and sat opposite him.

Flood sniffed the steam from the meal. "It smells lovely," he said.

"Thanks. Quite simple fare. An old recipe too. I'm trying to teach Cuch not to eat or maul the damn things before he brings it to me. He was a good dog a couple of days back when he caught these two," she said digging into a piece of rabbit, "but then he had caught a brace earlier for himself."

Flood inspected the meat and suddenly could not help himself. He finally burst out laughing. "Oh, this is so funny!"

"What is?"

"This - all this. Is this real?"

"Yes," she replied, puzzled at his query.

"I'm sorry - this is just so different for me. I've never eaten rabbit, never mind one caught by a four-foot tall beast of a dog in the middle of nowhere! And I'm supposed to be a vegetarian!" He burst out laughing again.

"Goodness. Well that's just a symptom of modern malaise - bad philosophy, you could say," said Cosima taking a bite of meat. "I wouldn't let it ruin your life," she added smiling kindly at him.

"But it all seems so daft now," he said. "I mean, I'd never tasted rabbit, never experienced, well ... I'd never really met a hunter, and you're the first hunter I've sat down to dinner with, and what a dinner - a hunted dinner!" He laughed with embarrassment. Cosima joined in.

"You were against hunting?" she asked through her laughter.

He avoided a direct answer but decided to tread the path of honesty. "I knew nothing. I'd not been for a walk in the countryside, nor rambled through woods. I was brought up in the suburbs, even though the countryside beckoned all around. I stuck to the town's park, the fairs, and the golf courses. I joined a few clubs at the university, you know, Amnesty International, that sort of thing, and well, I was involved with some people you would not appreciate."

"Antis?"

"Antis." He had said it. He looked away for a second. But as he spoke, he was contracting a promise with himself to be honest. Cosima's entire personality, he thought, could demand no less. "But," he continued, turning to look at her again, "the more I think about them, the more I realise that they are just anti-everything."

"Anti-value?"

"Yes, anti-anything of value. I don't think ... no, I know I did not like them, or what they really stood for. They have some really extreme opinions. I kind of fell in with them through my girlfriend. Well," he caught himself, "she's not my girlfriend. I thought she was, but she has a habit of being everybody's girlfriend, you know, and mine when there's nobody else."

"Why did you put up with that?"

"I don't know. Well, yes I do. She liked my money and I needed company."

"That's rather low, don't you think? I mean, no offence, but ... "

"No, I mean, yes, I see that now. I went through this yesterday with another good friend. I know what I've done and, God, I know I've been a bit weak."

"Yes. Not surprising though. Think about the culture you come from. From what I see of it in the school and towns, there's no sense of dignity, or independence, never mind restraint and patience."

"I guess you're right. I'm not sure. I mean, yeah, you're right," Flood said, cutting a piece of meat and tasting the flesh of rabbit for the first time. He chewed the piece, allowing his mouth to salivate, drawing the subtle tastes from it. He liked it. The stew it was juicy and fresh, and the game very tender. Finishing a mouthful he added, "I feel such a fool. I mean, God - I feel as if I can say anything to you, Cosima. I've not felt like that before." He sat back and looked around for a second before looking at her. "Where I grew up you had to be guarded, untrusting, never open yourself up, never ... well, never think or feel." He paused caught in a strange emotion.

"It's the wine. I told you, it frees the tongue and opens the soul," she said.

"This meal, is, well, it is incredibly tasty. I'm not good at describing food well, or much else for that matter, but it's really good."

"Thank you. But you are explaining things well. Some things, I can tell, are difficult to express, and I'm ... honoured you can speak freely with me." Cosima took up her wine. "Tell me more."

Flood decided to describe his encounter with the violent youth on the train and they both laughed at his description of the older woman's handling of them. "She sounds like someone I know," said Cosima. "Yes, I'm sure Beatrice mentioned some trouble on the train the other day. Probably the same train. That would be an uncanny coincidence."

He expressed his guilt at his inability to assist and explained how he had just sat there and watched the entire episode unfold. It was not that he was afraid of fighting but the whole situation was so surreal. Cosima explained that if it were Beatrice Major taking care of the yobs, he had been in very capable hands indeed and there was nothing he could have done to help.

She described the behaviour she had witnessed in schools. They debated the cause and solutions of the country's ills and the general failure to appreciate knowledge and learning. Cosima argued that the country was heading towards a pathetic future and that its wealth and past achievements would not hold it up much longer. Flood expressed the view that perhaps all nations went through phases of growth and decline, but Cosima disagreed, arguing that there was nothing inevitable in a nation's future, for that future depended on present decisions and that anyone was free to make decisions. Flood thought about that and connected it to his experience of getting lost.

"I see," he agreed. "I chose paths earlier that got me lost. Do you believe this country's lost?"

"It's certainly losing the plot," Cosima replied.

"How could it return to its values - like the ones you've argued for?"

"It would need a radical overhaul," Cosima said, holding his gaze.

"A revolution?"

"Why not?" She smiled coyly.

Flood measured her response. She was holding back something, he thought. A well-connected, wealthy young woman - she knew something. He frowned and finished his wine. "It would be understandable," he finally commented.

They cleaned up together and retired to the library. Flood, sated with food and wine slumped onto the sofa. Cosima turned on a CD player and Chopin's nocturnes filled the room.

"You must be tired after your adventure," she said, "why don't you go to bed?"

Flood replied, "Not yet, I like talking." But as Cosima was dealing with the room's several curtains he nodded off.

He stirred, to find Cosima gently shaking his arm. "Come, you are tired." He followed her with leaden feet. "Your room is this one," she said, opening up a large wooden door and switching on a light to reveal a dark panelled room. In the middle of the far wall was a large four-poster bed. Heavy curtains festooned deeply-set leaded windows, while two wardrobes stood guard on either side of the room. "The cock crows at sixish, if the fox hasn't broken through the wiring, and I shall wake you at nine at the latest. You look as if you need the sleep."

He smiled thickly through his tired face. "Thank you," he said, "and good night."

"Good night, Miles."

The Westminster Bell Tolls For Thee

At 3pm that day, as Flood was trudging up the side of a valley and just beginning to feel irretrievably lost, the Prime Minister entered the House of Commons to open up the second Emergency Debate on the state of the country.

The kidnapping of Alan Jones, MP and Minister for Rural Affairs, had caught the government's attention, unlike any of Jones's previous antics. The timing was impeccable - and the prime movers within and without the government were not at a loss to capitalise on the nation's political insecurity resulting from his capture and the burning down of the DEFRA building. As the Prime Minister had mentioned on live broadcasts and in thoroughly contrived press meetings, the UK was just about to declare war in the Gulf and it could not accept any destabilising domestic issues generated by a league of old-fashioned and out-of-touch rural residents when thousands of British troops were staking their lives in the Total War Against Terrorism. It was with great reluctance, Cramp concluded, that, in the present situation of growing strife, he could see no other way forward than to prohibit all country sports and allow Thomas Waterside's bill on country sports and the use of Parliamentary time to be passed.

Commentators immediately reacted with anger and surprise: why tear the nation asunder when the nation's support was sorely needed? demanded the tabloids; what pathetic bone was this to give the back-benchers in order to secure support on foreign policy? demanded the right wing press; what was the point of the consultations? demanded the centre-left press. Cramp's supporters and biographers were quick to acknowledge that it was the biggest gamble of his career, but noted that supporting EU directives were also on the cards. The more astute noted the general direction towards land nationalisation that had taken place over the past two Parliaments and that the ban on all forms of bloodsports was thoroughly in keeping with the government's implicit animal rights policies.

Hugh Cramp, wearing a brown suit with a pink shirt and red tie, entered the Commons to great cheering and loud jeering. His back-benchers sensed victory and they were not going to let it slip from their grasp. The Opposition was leaderless. The media had picked up on Radcliffe's absence and debate raged about where he was. His HQ insisted that he had urgent family matters to attend to and that he had left his capable Deputy to deal with the Emergency session. Camera crews stood patiently outside of Radcliffe's parents' house in Yorrington - the reporters regularly told viewers that his car was there but that his parents were keeping the curtains shut.

The Opposition was leaderless and the cross-benchers divided. Hugh Cramp was going to enjoy this one.

The Speaker rushed through minor proceedings to get to the day's more important business. He called the Prime Minister to speak and the crowded House fell silent as Cramp stood and opened up his brief.

Cramp pushed back his thinning curly grey hair from his sallow face; he took hold of both sides of the Dispatch Box, put on his most serious and sincere face and prepared to speak.

"Mr Speaker, we face a grave and growing problem in this land. Against impending legislation to ban a form of savage cruelty against the animals of this land," - jeers drowned out by cheers - "against the moral and political supremacy of this chamber, a minority."

"Only on your benches," shouted an Opposition MP.

"A minority, has taken the law into its own hands and carried out what can only be described as an act of terrorism" - "a blow for freedom!" shouted someone" - "against the governing institutions of this land, as well as kidnapping a most respected MP and his assistants." Jeers and sniggers came from the Opposition benches. "The Opposition may make light of such actions - but they did not when they were in government. Do I have to remind any the more senior figures opposite of their stance on a particular occasion when a hotel was bombed? Or Downing Street targeted by terrorists? No, I don't have to, Mr Speaker."

"Not the same!' someone shouted."

"Terrorism cannot be condoned and this government believes in being tough on terrorism!" The Commons broke into uproarious applause. Government back-benchers were faithfully falling behind the Prime Minister while the Opposition MPs furiously waved their hands for the right to reply. The Tory MP for Oakland was heard shouting, "And on the cause of terrorism? Why - surely that's you, Cramp!" to much applause from his front bench.

"No, Mr Speaker. In the fair light of day, the entire House would agree," - shouts of "nonsense!" and "Hear! Hear!" - "I'm sorry, both Houses would agree that terrorism cannot go unpunished."

"So why are you letting out IRA prisoners?" one Opposition woman shouted.

'Order!' gabbled Mr Speaker.

"This country cannot be held to ransom by any form of terrorism, whether its source is foreign or domestic." The House quietened. The government's back-benchers knew the deal the PM had brokered and although it frustrated and angered several of the die-hard ideologues, the majority were content to gain one over the landed Tory gentry, as they characterised hunters. One veteran Labour MP shouted out "Judases", but few on his side understood the reference. He got up and left. Cramp shot him an angry parting look.

Cramp dropped the tone and speed of his voice. "Mr Speaker, yesterday's debate acknowledged the pressing issues of the Gulf crisis and the need for co-operative allied intervention. This morning, the Cabinet met and agreed that no more time can be lost in securing a safe peaceful new governments and that therefore, in conjunction with our American allies," - some hisses from the braver government back-benchers - "and in the light of incontrovertible evidence presented by the White House, this nation is prepared to send upwards of six thousand troops to fight in the final phase of the Total War Against Terrorism." Muted "hear-hears" from the back-benchers.

"My team will answers questions on the logistics later on, Mr Speaker. It also needs to be said that this morning's Cabinet meeting discussed several crucial pieces of legislation and manifesto promises," - great cheers from his back benchers - "and it agreed to put before the House today, firstly the Identification Card and Mandatory DNA Pooling Bill, which will act to assist the police and armed forces in the tracking and solving of all forms of crime; secondly, to push ahead with the Bills to reform the legal system - again," he raised his voice to cover the opposing jeers, "again, to assist the law enforcement officers of this country to secure peace in this land!"

"'Tyrant!" yelled one elderly Tory MP and left the building, disgusted.)

"Finally," Cramp turned to face his hungry back-benchers, "finally, Mr Speaker, in light of the Rural Alliance's inexcusable and indefeasible acts against our civilisation, the Cabinet has agreed to give time and prioritisation," - loud cheers - "to the right honourable Gentleman for Huntingthorpe's private bill on bloodsports." There was uproar in the House, which Mr Speaker permitted for several minutes. The government back-benchers were ecstatic, the Opposition furious. Radio and television stations across the country interrupted their regular programming to announce the government's intention to ban fox-hunting. The satellite networks immediately sent out camera crews to riding stables and to the Rural Alliance head-quarters to provide round-the-clock coverage and reaction.

Meanwhile eight troop carrying planes left RAF Densington, a convoy of ships headed to the Red Sea, two Harriers were shooting down four jets over Iraq, and four parties of SAS troops were working behind Iraqi lines to disable communications in preparation for a grand international assault. In the City, the FTSE fell to 2800 after heavy selling and the price of gold soared to $380 and several large manufacturers announced their intention to close, with the loss of ten thousand jobs. These items were addenda to the main news of Cramp's intention to ban hunting.

The Second Emergency Debate was followed by the government's pushing through its three bills all of which passed. The Opposition had no chance - three massive majorities secured the bills' passage to the upper Chamber, where the threat of the Parliament Act secured a similarly smooth path with the twenty Lords that remained. A half-hour's debate was given to the implied declaration of war and a full forty minutes to the IDNA Bill, as it was increasingly called, before the House divided, to the delight of the Home Secretary, Damien Blunderton. One hour to the abandoning of trial by jury and habeas corpus for a package of crimes before Division, and a full five hours to the banning of all bloodsports. The debate stretched on, Commons commentators noted, because several key Labour MPs were worried about the impact on their constituencies; word in the corridors was that the Whips had told them not to worry - the election was not for another three years and by then, things would have settled down. Opposition MPs tried every ruse on the books to deny the bill its passage, until the Speaker finally lost his patience and claimed that after several previous large votes in favour of banning hunting with dogs, ('Hounds, you bloody fool!' shouted the now raging MP for Oakland, for which he was immediately from the Commons), the Bill deserved to go to Division without further ado.

The Deputy Leader of Her Majesty's Opposition was frequently chastised for attempting to add more time to the war debate. The government back-benchers were having none of that - it was, as one State FM4 political commentator noted, too controversial for them to deal with. They wanted a ban on hunting and that was what they were going to get - so, he summarised, they would "damn the rest of the world, and damn the country" to get what they wanted.

On retiring from the House of Commons, Cramp spoke to reporters on the need "for co-operation from all factors of the land's aspects. While we speak, hundreds of UK troops are engaging actively in securing peace in and for the Middle East. They are risking their lives. The world needs peace and security. For us all to get along together. We are prepared to pay a blood price for fighting for freedom. Nothing less can be asked of us. In times of crisis we need to think and work as one. We are, after all, one people. And one people ought to live by the general will of the land. They are struggling for freedom over there and we shall help them." On the hunting bill he replied, "Look, the will of the Commons has been that it should be banned - and it will be in three months time. What is important tonight is that our troops are abroad - in action, fighting for freedom. Let us think of them rather than of a small minority that sought to disrupt this peaceful land of ours. We are moving in the right direction and, I think, you know, as an ordinary guy like you, that I cannot condone brutality in any shape or format."

The Political Situation

Earlier that evening, as Flood stumbled across Cosima's house, her father, Lord Laurenten, stood in the middle of the Great Hall at Stanthorpe Manor and called the meeting to order. Twelve people, including himself, seated themselves at a large, round, old oak table in the middle of the hall.

Around him sat Peter Hickling as public affairs assistant and portfolio for Europe and the City; Vincent Harrison, up until then the head of the Rural Alliance, and now in charge of bringing as many of the RA membership as possible over to the secession; then Assembly Member Patricia Forbes, acting assistant with portfolio for North America; then Michael Radcliffe, the gone-to-ground leader of the Opposition, now in charge of judicial and constitutional matters; Professor Miranda Whitman, full Assembly Member, a strong secessionist and prolific writer on hunting and the campaign for a free country. To Laurenten's right sat Assembly Member Colonel Arthur Stowington, head of the UK Shooting Society and now in charge of establishing the Assembly's bureaucratic requirements; next to him, Assembly Member Beatrice Major, with the defence and police portfolio; next to her, septuagenarian Bertrand Chasseur, MFH, and Assembly Member, assisting in rural policy; next to him Assembly Member Dr Sandy Morley, a free market and liberty lecturer, and writer of various political philosophy works, and now acting adviser on constitutional matters; next to him, octogenarian Alfred Castleton or Lord Selworthy, Assembly Member and assistant presiding officer to the Assembly; and finally Professor Simon Freebard, economist at the LSE, an Assembly Member and strong advocate of free market and hard currency policies.

Laurenten opened up the meeting with a long discursion on the Assembly's constitution and criteria for its convention, words written down in 1654 when seventy men thought it appropriate to make alternative arrangements for the potential failure of Cromwell's republic. The Restoration led to their persecution and temporary exile until the Glorious Revolution, but the seventy remained steadfast in keeping secret what they saw as the land's political guardianship. Liberty, they knew, was a fragile flower, needing the utmost care and tender attention, so they passed the mantle on to their descendants to maintain the vigil.

The Members agreed that the meeting was valid and accepted the presence of the three Strangers as advisers. Each Member took an oath renewing their contract to uphold the Assembly's tenets and each Stranger took an oath to present their knowledge truthfully and sincerely and to the best of their abilities.

Laurenten finished up the constitutional matters and then began the proceedings proper.

"In light of today's tragic and foolish proceedings in Westminster which we have been hearing on the news, and the impending violation of several cherished liberties as well as many already lost both in Scotland and across the entire country, I believe that the time has come to convene the Assembly and to secede from the Westminster Parliament." The Members and Strangers looked at him, Stowington and Selworthy nodding their heads. "It is of course, my duty to present the Policy of Convention and Secession, but, as the Members know, it is not wholly mine to enact. It rests with the Greater Assembly, which shall be convening in the next few days. But I am charged with preparing the brief that the Assembly shall deliberate on and vote upon. Accordingly, I invite Members and Strangers here to offer their advice."

The time passed quickly as the Members and Strangers debated the secession's timing and nature. They were all agreed that the Policy of Convention and Secession should be presented to the Greater Assembly for affirmation, and most thought that the motion would be carried. Laurenten then reminded the Members of the Assembly's policy of complete political, religious, and economic freedom.

Initially they debated the Westminster proceedings and expressed their dismay at the turn of events. Most acknowledged that it was only the timing that surprised them, which made the present Assembly's convention highly appropriate. The debate then turned on how those ancient ideals could be implemented and how the rest of the land could be attracted to secession. Freebard explained how the ten per cent flat-rate income tax and the abandonment of all other forms of taxation and regulation of business would tempt many their way. Morley and Freebard proposed the abandonment of legal tender to allow traders to choose their own currency - explaining how they thought people would converge onto the hard currencies of gold, silver, and platinum. Laurenten nodded - he needed no reminding that the Assembly should not get involved in economic issues and that the central bank was one of the Members' prime targets. "When the state controls and monopolises money," explained Freebard, in response to Harrison's questions, "it possesses the most powerful weapon against liberty. We're abolishing that privilege and giving it back to the marketplace where it morally belongs."

Whitman expressed the need to free farming from controls - restrictions and grants were just another form of welfare that were used to remove farmers' freedoms. Laurenten noted that the Assembly should also announce its intention to leave the EU and declare its free-trade status. They went on to argue and discuss foreign policy matters ("our army will not be involved in wars of intervention in foreign seas unless there is a clear threat to our land. Our jurisdiction is our jurisdiction alone," said Laurenten), before moving onto the welfare state's dissolution and the complete privatisation of all nationally and municipally owned and controlled industries.

"To think that the hunting debate caused all of this," said Chasseur. "Who would have thought it that we should convene because of an attack against hunting?"

"But it's not just hunting," said Laurenten emphatically. "Scotland's expropriating land and the executive up there is throwing its weight around, but Westminster is imposing its whims on every aspect of British life. ID cards, for heaven's sake. DNA pools for the innocent and the guilty. It's as if the spin doctors are getting their policies directly from old Prussia. More importantly though, the land's moral fabric has eroded to dangerous levels; if we allowed the decline to continue any more, the country will collapse into anarchy. We've all seen signs of it. The larger this government has become, the less stable our nation has become, and over the past few decades generations have grown up with declining moral and therefore political standards, they'll vote for anyone if they vote at all."

"You're generalising somewhat," said Morley.

"Of course I am, I have to, sometimes. But the people who have held onto their standards are more likely to be the ones who will come over to us."

"What about all those social democrat types who'd vote for using government wealth to support welfare services? What if they joined the Commonweal and swung public opinion in favour of high taxes and a welfare state?" asked Harrison.

"We're not creating a democracy - not like you're used to," replied Morley, "not one in which the majority can impose its will on anyone it chooses. No one will have the so-called right to vote his neighbour's income into someone else's pocket. Property and income will be inviolable. Taxes are nothing but theft and plunder, and once we're over the initial two-year set-up, they'll practically dwindle away. Some taxation will be required for defence and police perhaps, but we're also looking into how that could be ameliorated into voluntary schemes and lotteries and the avoidance of all but the minimum central control. The main point is that each family will have its own resources and those resources as well as their choices will be sacrosanct. Man is not born to serve the state or to be sacrificed to politicians. But to answer your question from another perspective, the social democrat types will stay with Westminster, while those who prefer to enjoy their hard-earned incomes as their own will come over to us."

"Which, of course," added Freebard, "would mean more voters demanding higher state funding at the same time as tax revenues for the Westminster regime declining, as the better economic producers shift away from the high tax and high regulatory environment of Westminster. But it will be hard to sustain when the producers leave. Look what happened in

Eastern Europe, and ask yourself, why did millions want to emigrate to the West - indeed, still do."

"By the way, what will be our immigration policy?" Patricia Forbes inquired.

"Completely open to all who establish themselves freely and peacefully within our borders," said Morley. "That is, as long as they freely purchase property within our jurisdiction, they are welcome."

"But what if we get a load of asylum-seekers?" asked Selworthy.

"It is not the Assembly's prerogative to turn a man away from the country, unless he's a criminal, of course," Whitman advised. "Don't forget we'll be neither subsidising immigration, nor hindering it with inane regulations. Those who come to us will have to find their own means of supporting themselves, and they will be subject to our laws just as any civilian will be. If they find work or can purchase property, they are welcome, as any British citizen of the Westminster state will be."

"But what is the logic of that? The world's changed since the seventeenth century, beyond all measure that could have been foreseen, even in the nineteenth," said Selworthy. "We've said earlier that any Westminster citizen will be free to join us through a mere declaration. Surely, if this secession is to succeed, we will need boundaries, a defined jurisdiction?"

Some around the table agreed. Whitman spoke up to defend the proposal. "Take a family living in the middle of Brumthorpe or somewhere like that. Let's say they wish to become members of our Commonweal, whose traditional boundaries, let's say for argument's sake, encompass the present counties of Northchestershire, Lindthorpeshire, Burgenshire, and Foxbridgeshire. I know, I know, there are others, and these counties will no doubt split somewhat - but follow the plot. Now this family must make a declaration to us and to Westminster that they are now citizens of our Commonweal. Their house and property will become part of our jurisdiction; just as a ship carries its registration flag in international waters, so too will this household fly our flag as it were. Any trespass or violation of their rights will be tried in our courts. In a sense, the household will be akin to an embassy situated on foreign soil."

Chasseur leant forward. "But won't that make life bloody awkward for them?"

"Decidedly in some respects, but in others no," Whitman replied.

"Our Assembly will have to maintain some functions that the Westminster government takes care of," said Harrison. "I mean, your idealistic secessionist family living in Brumthorpe still have to get rid of their refuse, have their children educated, and drive on roads."

"It's none of our business to get involved," said Laurenten. "Each family must see to its own refuse collection, for which the market will respond with probably less packaging and more efficient refuse services; and each family must look to the education of its own children, and not expect others to pay. The Assembly has no right to intervene in the education of anyone; education is a very private matter, although that's been somewhat forgotten in a century of socialisation. The Assembly is to be a neutral body, ensuring that the laws of the land are upheld and that the land is secure from domestic and international aggression. That's all."

"As for the roads," Freebard added, "they are presently owned by the councils. We will be privatising them completely, handing them over to the present maintenance crews who work or sub-contract to the councils. People driving into our territories will pay the local toll rates that the owners set up. There will be no free means of transportation just as there will be no free means of transport. There never used to be any government ownership of the roads - except for military purposes, as the Scots can testify. Nor will we make any stupid mistakes such as licensing companies for a limited-period franchise. Whoever owns whatever road will own it until they sell it on. Same with radio, mobile phone, and television frequencies. What is broadcast is none of our business, and whoever owns, say, 101 FM will own it as long as they wish to. There will also be complete freedom of exchange in land. If a farmer wishes to alienate a part of his land to build a house to raise some capital, he will be free to do so, and it is again, none of our business what crop he chooses to grow or what animal to raise on his farm. He has to manage his property according to the market-place of his customers, and that is all we need to know."

The Members and Strangers understood the general principle of a free republic, but Selworthy's point that things had changed since the seventeenth century generated much controversy. Other finer points were discussed and it was agreed that even more were to be presented at a later stage to the entire Assembly. The evening wore on until Laurenten finally called the meeting to an end, just as the House of Commons in Westminster was dividing for its second vote. They retired for dinner and then relaxed with the other guests at Stanthorpe in the drawing room and library until eleven.

Laurenten sought ought Joanna Ribblesdale to enjoy more of her company.

"What if it fails?" she asked him as they took a turn around the gardens, enjoying the starry night.

"It won't. It may take a long time, but we will win most people over. There are only a few people who wish to live as parasites on the rest of us. Most want to enjoy their values without infringement. They've just lost the means of express-ing freedom."

"So once you declare a free republic, you'll secure much support?"

"In theory, yes. In practice - well, that's what could take time."

"You'll need your friends." She took his arm as they walked to the small duck pond.

He nodded. "I will probably not be the most ... sensitive person though."

She stopped and turned to face him. "I understand. You could do with an understanding companion." He nodded slowly. She stroked his face and then kissed him. He pulled her close and hugged her.

"Thank you," he murmured.

WILLIAM VENATOR

Flood's Dream

Flood rolled over. He let out a long sigh, not wishing to leave the bed's warmth. He opened his eyes and blinked at a stream of sunlight.

"I thought you might not want to lie in much longer," said a voice. He retrieved his wits from sleep's slumber to follow the sound of footsteps. Cosima was going from window to window, opening the curtains. "It's eight-thirty. You've slept nine hours or so. Did you sleep well?"

"Uh, yes, thank you," said Flood, stretching his body under the sheets and trying to gather a sense of the morning. "I had some strange dreams, though."

"Not surprising after being lost yesterday; it's sure to bring back deep instinctual fears."

Flood sat up and strained hard to recollect what he had dreamed. "Yes, I recall most of it. Very strange."

Cosima sat on the edge of the bed. "Want to tell me about it?"

"Yeah, let me get my thoughts together." His eyes focused on her. She was wearing a thick white shirt with a loose russet cravat that lit up her soft pale face with echoes of a warm summer's dawn. She suggested coffee and breakfast as soon as he was ready and explained that she was going hunting later and that he was welcome to come along and that she had put some riding clothes out for him. She left the room and reluctantly he dragged himself to the bathroom. He discovered that the jodhpurs fit tightly and to his embarrassment emphasised his anatomy. He felt like a ballet dancer. He tucked in the shirt, which made everything worse, so he sought the sweater he had worn the night before to cover the focus of his embarrassment.

When he reached the kitchen he was overwhelmed with the delights of fresh coffee, bread, mushrooms and bacon. Bacon! - the vegetarian's perennial weakness! A flutter of guilt, tinged with the surrealism of his surroundings and shifting belief system, traipsed momentarily around his mind, but the vision of Cosima standing at the oven range, frying sausages and bacon in one pan, and eggs in another, evaporated any lingering disconcerted feelings. Cosima hurried around the kitchen, explaining that she'd picked some fresh mushrooms and that they needed a hearty breakfast for their long ride to the village. She checked his cut and commented that it was healing quickly.

"Fresh mushrooms? Do you know which ones are poisonous?" Flood reflected his generation's belief that unless it came vacuum-packed on a supermarket shelf, it was not to be trusted, a belief that was forcing hundreds of farmers out of business and abroad. The mushrooms looked decidedly like toadstools to Flood; their caps were yellow and black, ridged with indentations, and the stems were wrinkled and slightly mottled.

Cosima laughed. "Of course I do. I grew up learning the flowers, trees, fungi, and fauna of the woods. These are particularly good ones," she said showing him a small basket holding a dozen mushrooms. "They're morels. Quite rare in this country. Just have to fry them in a little butter, otherwise they would be quite upsetting to the system. And I found a horse mushroom. That's it over there."

As she cooked she caught sight of him pulling his sweater down. "You look good in your jodders, don't worry so much! You have really nice legs." She smiled gently at his reddening face. "Wait till you get your boots on, then you'll feel the bees knees."

Flood surveyed his plate of cooked flesh and ova. The sausages' tangy smell and the salty smell of bacon caused his mouth to salivate in expectation. He poured two coffees and gulped a mouthful down. His mind jerked up a gear as the aromatic liquid stimulated his mouth and stomach. He cut up a piece of bacon and placed the hardened salty flesh to his tongue. He chewed the long unfamiliar texture and then tucked into a sausage. As he chewed he vowed never to be a vegetarian again.

They finished breakfast and Cosima asked him to describe his dream.

"I've remembered it all, I think." Flood poured more coffee and began his story.

"There was a shallow river winding its way around a grassy embankment. The river shimmered gold. A man and woman were in a boat, they were dressed in peasant costumes from long ago. He was punting and she was sitting watching him. Three cows were strolling in front of the boat. They were all moving towards a large white house, perhaps a mill. Large trees surrounded the house. The cows trod through the water, pulling their legs slowly out of the mud, but they enjoyed the cool water. It was summer. The sky was mottled with clouds.

"But then it got cooler, and darker clouds emerged. The man who was punting looked up and said something to the woman, and he urged the cows on. Birds stopped singing and flying. They landed on branches to take cover from the impending storm. The sky turned a sickly green hue, dimming my vision. The river lost its lovely colouring, turning to the colour of, well, recycled toilet paper. A dull grey and hardly flowing. The man urged the cows up the embankment. The cows got out of the river and then steadfastly walked into the woods. They weren't supposed to. The man looked despairingly at the cows. They entered the forest and the man ran after them and came back shouting, although I could not understand his words. He was terribly distraught. The woman looked around too, confused at the colour the river had taken. She reached out and took his hand and led him to the house, but he kept desperately peering into the forest to see his cattle. She led him home and they shut the door.

"Then came the storm. I was in it. I felt the rain, I heard the thunder over my head, I saw lightning crack in front of my eyes; I ran for cover but every cover I sought crumbled around me, leaving me vulnerable and exposed. But I was not afraid. I gave up on finding cover and stood in the pouring rain, watching the storm. The grey river burst its banks and left paper and litter strewn across both riverbanks. More litter, and plastic things, bottles, and cans, drifted past. I could dimly see the man and the woman gazing out of a window. They watched the tumultuous scene, or perhaps they watched me.

"The lightning began striking trees opposite. An old, tall, twisting birch tree fell first, shattering in sparks and sending cascades of branches and wood splinters into the air. Then an oak was hit, and I felt the shards fall all around me. They pierced my skin, causing me to bleed, but I was still not afraid. I was an observer and I could not feel the pain. My hands dripped blood, and blood dripped from my head into my eyes, colouring the entire scene red. I wiped the blood away and tasted its iron on my tongue. Then an elm was hit, then a cedar. One after the other, each tree was hit by a direct bolt from the sky. The sky had now turned such a greyish-green that it sucked up light and even life. Then I saw that as the trees fell they disintegrated, leaving a barren land in their wake. Shrubs and hedges were swallowed up leaving a flat landscape. The river then turned another colour. Red. Blood red.

"My heart jumped when I saw a figure arise from the river. He stood proud and violent, his eyes burned fire, and he marched through the thick bloody stream. I sensed he had a purpose and that he would do anything to achieve it. In his wake a mass of faces followed him; they were indistinguishable. Men looked like women and children looked like adults. Their bodies were dripping red from the bloody stream. They hoisted up black flags and sounded discordant trumpets. One man tried to get free from this herd. I watched him stand for a moment. He caught my eye. He did not plead or beckon for my assistance, but I knew that he was in trouble. He was proud of his action. The atmosphere was charged with a sickening vile heat. I watched the mass turn its head in tune with its leader to look at the proud man, but then the leader shot a barbed tongue from his mouth that pierced the man's body - straight through his heart. The man crumpled in front of my eyes, but the mass of people turned their heads back to where their leader directed them. But as they marched, generation after generation, they sank further and further back into the river. Most went without a flicker of fear, or without a flicker of intelligence or understanding, but I knew they were drowning.

"Then the river was streaked with black, and sharp silver fish jumped out, pouring fire from their mouths. I saw men in black, with brilliant white faces, ooze from the morass. They too followed the same leader, who watched over them and initially they advanced in unison with the hordes of red figures. Then they rose to the river's surface and then stomped on the red crowds. Some individuals were straining to reach the surface, but none did though. The red and black army marched in unison, keeping down anyone who showed any sign of getting in the way. The red and black crowds were all the same. Some led dogs - large Alsatians - but fed them apples and cabbage leaves; the dogs did not possess teeth, and looked very effeminate, almost like poodles or lap dogs, until they saw a head of a person escaping from the river; if he had not been trampled and had managed to free his body and arms then the dogs suddenly sprouted fangs and tore the man limb from limb, feeding on his bloodied carcass. When their masters retrieved them, they lost their fangs and returned to being almost puppy-like, gazing up at their masters in awe and obedience.

"Then there was a terrible thumping, which shook the ground on which I stood. The leader opposite, who had directed the masses had vanished I noted suddenly. My heart leapt to my throat and I thought I was going to die. I felt fear for the first time. I watched the bend in the river carefully looking for the source of the sound, and from the black horizon I could see an enormous monster coming - I knew it was the leader again, but transformed. It was predominantly black although its eyes were flashing red; it was puking vomit onto the landscape, a vile acidic vomit that ate up the embankment. Huge claws ripped the ground up as it stomped towards me. But then another noise came from my right and I suddenly saw a dragon, a white dragon, spew forth from the river with a hissing steam to fight its way out of the masses. The rain splattered on the dragon's hot back, causing it to smoke. It espied the black behemoth, or whatever the foul beast was. The dragon looked at me, and communicated something in its eyes, but I am not sure what. It flashed a red tongue at me, licking its lips, and then prepared itself for a fight. The behemoth growled fiercely and sought to swipe the dragon, but the dragon took to the air and flew around the great hulking black beast.

"The beast was surrounded by the dogs I had seen before, except this time they were much larger, and were sprouting wings. Some breathed fire, others flew over the house, where I could still see the man and woman. The dogs then shat on the roof of the house, but their excrement punctured the roof and destroyed the eaves. The dragon saw the dogs and immediately sought to stop them; it was a grand fight that I saw - the dogs flying around in formations or by themselves, firing acidic vomit at the dragon or shitting on the landscape. But the dragon dodged the dogs and killed them one by one with his tail or mouth, hurling canine carcasses to the floor, where they blew up, sending forth effluence into the river. The behemoth then tried to kill the dragon, but the dragon suddenly got massive, I heard a fanfare of trumpets, a marching band even, and I saw the river turn from black to blue; the light glistened on the blue surface causing a sparkling effect; the dragon changed shape as I watched. Its wings turned to feathered birds' wings, and its feet looked like a bird of prey's; its mouth sharpened into a beak. It spurted white fire at the behemoth, and a horrific fight took place between the stolid black beast and the dodging dragon-bird. Finally the dragon-bird dealt a swift blow to the beast's head with a sharp right claw and then it fell back into the river, dead.

"The sky lightened perceptibly, and the man and the woman cheered. They came running from the house and danced in the desolated garden. But then they looked around and their spirits dropped when they saw the devastated forest. The man gestured that perhaps he would now find his cows and he ran off looking for them; the forest had certainly gone, replaced with a vast empty land. But the cows could not be found, they had gone or had been killed by the hell-hordes that had wrecked so much with the storm. Then I saw something the man and woman had not; the dragon-bird had returned to the river. It sat for a moment cleaning its wounds, then it looked at the man and the woman, and then at me. It tried again to tell me something in its eyes, but I do not know what, although I get the strong feeling I should know what it wanted. It then sank back into the river and the river's colour turned back to the drab grey of recycled paper. It was not all over yet - I could tell. The air remained tense and I wasn't surprised when the behemoth suddenly revived. In front of my eyes it changed shape. I wanted to warn the man and the woman but they could not hear my voice, which was drowned out by strong winds. They were looking different ways, and not paying attention either to me, the beast, or each other. The beast righted itself. It shed its black body to take on a smooth, grey, almost metallic skin; it put on a white lab coat, and held a clipboard and pen, and then it shrunk to a human level, put on some glasses, picked up a briefcase and sought out the man and woman.

"They did not see that it was the same beast, and I tried to warn them, but they could not hear. I jumped and waved my arms, I shouted, but to no avail; then the woman looked over and strained her eyes as if she saw me, as if she could see I was trying to contact them, but she merely shrugged her shoulders and went back to listening to what the beast-man was saying. He pointed to the house, which changed from an intricate old white building to a uniform block, with several other houses of the same style being built next to it. People hung out laundry and polished chrome boxes. Then the beast-man let loose some dogs from around his feet, they flew into the sky and I thought they were going to bomb the new houses with shit again, but this time they put aerials onto the houses. The beast-man laughed and said things into a radio he was holding and the people in their gardens rushed in to listen to his broadcasts; I knew that's what they were doing. Then the beast-man commanded roads to be built right up to the couple's old home. A shopping mall rose up and people rushed out to buy things. He then looked with concern at the remaining bushes and roses around where their old house stood, and with a spray from a can, he coated everything with a fine dust; the green vanished and the land was coated in cement. He turned and turned and sprayed and sprayed turning the entire landscape into a joyless park of cement. Spray got into my eyes, and I screamed aloud in pain, it burned so much, I fell to my knees and tried to get up, but then the beast-man's boot came down onto my face. He stamped me into the ground and I could not move. To top it off, a dog came over and urinated on my head.

"Then I felt a fresh breeze. I saw a woman coming over the horizon. She was planting flowers, and trees, and other greenery followed her path. She rode a horse and her hounds followed her. She had long green hair, a green tinge to her skin. She wore furs. In her one hand she carried a balance, in which stood on the one side, a man and woman and on the other, nature, symbolised by a host of animals and plants. All around her the landscape was coming alive, but it was no idyllic landscape in which horses talked or deer preached the gospels, it was a land where dogs hunted, foxes ate chickens, hawks killed sparrows, and man hunted animals too; it was a landscape where men and women followed in this horsewoman's wake, tending to the plants, caring for the land, milking cows, roasting chickens, riding horses across hills on hunts, shooting birds, fishing for trout. The old man and woman scanned the horizon to see the greenery and they looked at each other - there, they could see their cows again, ambling alongside the green woman on horseback. They laughed and ran towards their cows. The other people in their tightly knit houses stirred dumbfounded, unsure of both their own plight and what all the fuss was about. I remained stuck in the concrete, watching the scene.

"The beast-man was furious. He cast a net over the fleeing couple, which stopped them momentarily, and he started to reel them in, but the woman on the horse galloped over and rescued them, cutting them free from their enslavement to the beast-man. She then rode over to me, and pulled me straight out of my concrete prison. All the time, where she rode grass grew and the land was replenished. The beast-man looked at her in horror. He pulled out a calculator and numbers flew up and around everywhere, justifying his analysis. He pulled out clipboards of statistics, he even projected graphs and charts into the sky, to tell man that the future was quantitative, that concrete was good, that uniformity was easier to count, that choice was bad, for it made his plans impossible to prescribe and pursue. But the woman laughed at his smallness and rising up in her saddle, causing her horse to rear up next to me and, she threw open the clouds like curtains across the sky and down came the most brilliant sunshine and warmth, and in a single breath, as the sun hit the ground, the river turned back into its original colour, shimmering gold, and the landscape reverted to thick hedges and grassy embankments. Animals appeared, played, frolicked, hunted, gave birth, struggled, died, new generations teemed all over, butterflies fluttered around me, and flowers grew between my toes. It was beautiful, and the burst of light changing the landscape corresponds with you opening the curtains, for that's when I awoke!"

Cosima had sat taking in every word and image. Her eyes had not left his face and he blushed as he finished his story. She responded after a pause, quietly and gently.

"Certainly a lot of symbolism in that dream, and how extraordinary that you remember it in such detail." Then she added energetically, "You must commit it to paper. I can see strong symbols of history and rural issues that you may have been grappling with recently, and the three cows suggest a loss of religion. You certainly have engaged your imagination in this. You must write it down, Miles, before you forget. You will be an excellent author, you know. After breakfast, I insist. You can use my desk in the living room and I shall prompt you if you forget anything you've told me about. Will you do that? And give me a copy?"

"I never thought about writing it out, but I shall."

"It sounds as if it's historical and descriptive of the present, but you must get it written down before we begin to examine it, otherwise you'll add things that were not there, or forget things that were."

They finished breakfast swiftly and Cosima ushered Flood into the living room and gave him some paper. She left him to write up his thoughts while she cleared the breakfast away and went out to prepare the horses.

Todthorpe

When Cosima returned, she found Flood had finished writing and was staring at the Munnings portrait he had been shown the night before. He stood silently, bent over the book, his entire attention focused on the image. He heard her footfall and turned to look earnestly at her.

"Things are beginning to make sense," he said, pointing to the portrait.

"What do you mean?"

"I'm not sure, I can't put it into words; I am close to doing so, but, no ... not yet. But," he said, leaving the desk and pacing the room, "there is something not right in the world. My dream tells me that, but there's something not right in me, in my life, it's never been there." He emphasised the word with a fist into his other hand. "Something's missing. I don't know what, I'm not sure who I am, or where I'm going. I have deep concerns about my friends, but I don't see if I should drop them. I mean, I don't know. I'm not sure who I am," he repeated. He stopped. His face fractured into frustrations and yearnings, tensions and immanent resolutions.

"Miles," Cosima said, "you are who you are, when all else is taken away."

She sat down opposite him and took his hand. She held it firmly. It soothed him and he didn't want her to let go.

"I felt something there," Flood continued, "which I've never felt before, and to tell you the truth, it left me very disconcerted, confused. I don't know. That's part of it, I don't know. I realised that. I realised that I don't know, but what is it that I don't know? And in the dream too, I ... I seemed to warrant a burden in the dream. I ... took up a burden as I was observing. I tried to interact, but I couldn't. It's left me a bit shaken up," he finally said raising his face. She squeezed his hand.

"I don't know either, but it sounds as if you're dealing with some metaphysical issues at the same time as dealing with your own self. Goodness, no wonder you're in a tizzle."

"It's my being here too. I think it has something to do with you, I mean." Flood saw her look of confusion and added quickly, "I mean, our chat last night, you living here all by yourself - and not afraid. You are free here. Free and apparently very comfortable with it and with yourself. I'm coming down to land somewhere, but I'm not sure where," he laughed nervously. "Crikey, it feels strange, but it will be good for me to land somewhere soon!"

Cosima laughed and gave his hand another squeeze. "You're bright enough to sort the issues out in your dream, I'm sure. As for finding your right landing spot, that's up to you. You choose, remember."

Flood smiled. "I guess you're right. Well, I've taken up too much of your hospitality, I'm sure. And now you have to escort me back to, to, well, I was going to say civilisation, but I'm not sure it is."

"Well, let's get you on a saddle. You've not exhausted my hospitality though," Cosima said. "You are more than welcome to stay, for a week or two if you ever fancy it. I wouldn't mind your company for a while, and you could get on with some uninterrupted soul-searching, and perhaps some writing of your own. I mean that - it would be a pleasure to have you stay. You may need it as well. And you don't have to let me know ahead - just turn up."

She had spoken with such sincerity that Flood at first was too overwhelmed to reply. Finally he recalled his manners. "Thank you. That is kind of you. Have you been like this yourself? You seem to understand well."

"Yes, a few years back. It's the old story of a bright, inquisitive mind, brought up with an excellent education that begins to question everything it's been taught, often only to put it all back into place after one's own fashion. It's tough, because you have to free-fall, and you can free-fall for a long period before things fall into place. It's as if you're a jigsaw that someone else has been making, and you can not see the picture nor the puzzle's shape. You need to: your mind drives you to understand, but then you burn with the need to reshape that vision in your own image. This is where I ran to when I buckled and rebelled," Cosima said, looking around. "Of course, they all knew I was where I was, but they also knew I had to deal with myself. Alone. Not an unusual occurrence in my family, Daddy said later. I wish I could say that you are not alone in this. But, ultimately you are. Only you can find out about you." Her face lightened and she planted a soft kiss on his cheek then turned to put on her boots.

He smiled through his confusion and floated once more, unanchored except for the fading pressure of her fleeting kiss. He followed her outside to the large stables where two horses were waiting patiently. He noted a large grey in the stable. "You said you were hunting yesterday?" he asked nonchalantly.

"Yes. A fantastic ride. I rode Samiel." She went over to him and stroked his nose. "We had some trouble with antis. They are so tiresome."

Flood nodded and then explained that he had not ridden before, but he was sure he could handle it. His mind swirled even more as she helped him onto the horse. He sat there thoroughly bemused by striving to sustain his confidence. He asked her about riding skills he should know about. She jumped on her horse and pulled it closer to his.

"You've got Otto and mine's Lysander." Cosima explained how to sit and ride, what the horse, and particularly Otto, would respond to. She continued giving him encouraging instructions as they left the stable and took the path leading into the forest. The Irish wolfhounds trotted gaily alongside for a hundred yards before turning home on Cosima's command.

Flood was in another world, sitting on a living beast that possessed its own purpose, guided by him, yet retaining, he could tell, its own sense of strength and dignity. He watched Cosima, who took the lead on the narrow paths. He tried to mimic her style of riding - it seemed so natural, but Flood's brain was whirring. Cosima shouted instructions to find the beat; the bouncing concentrated his mind and he finally clicked into the trot's one-two rhythm. Just when he was settling, she got him to canter, which took more getting used to.

The trees encroached and they returned to trotting and walking through the forest. Then the woods opened up to expansive moors that tookqill Flood by surprise. There it was again, that vast expanse of nature confronting his senses. Feelings of disembodiment and elation overwhelmed him, but what it was he could not define nor capture. He jogged along, feeling increasingly more comfortable with his position and the beat underneath. The scent of gorse and heather filled his nose, augmenting his ecstasy.

They halted at the top of a ridge, to enjoy a view of three counties and vast tracts of uninhabited forest and moors. Cosima indicated where various folk lived tucked into small hamlets in hidden valleys, in which direction the nearest village Todthorpe, lay, and where the nearest town stood - although nothing could be seen of it in daylight, its glow was visible at night, she explained.

They rested silently surveying the vast rustic demesne. Flood watched rabbits popping up and chasing each other from place to place. He listened to the birdsong. The soft breeze brought with it remnants of the westerly seas. It was as if he were gazing out on the haphazard landscape forged by nature and by man, and yet he was an essential part of it, as were the horses, and as was Cosima. The moments were perfect, yet so fleeting. He sat stretching out the time yet knowing it was coming to an end, but each moment led to further procrastination that he savoured. Both he and Cosima were reluctant to move. The horses idly stretched their necks to chomp on the grass. The moment stretched further and neither wished to end it.

An hour later Flood and Cosima reached Todthorpe. The track they followed changed from long grass to a hardened mud driveway, until they reached the tarmac road. The horses' hoofs clattered on the road, disturbing the tranquillity. Familiar smells of car fumes hung in the air and he could hear children playing, and dogs barking. The first house they passed was hidden by overgrown privet hedges. From his vantage point Flood could down into a delightful garden of fruit trees, wooden benches, trellises, bowers, and a path cut through long grass. The following houses were small slate-roofed cottages that spoke of the area's industrial boom toward the end of the eighteenth century.

They clip-clopped on for a few hundred yards, passing several rows of small cottages before they came to the inn. It was very small, Flood thought. He would have ridden past it if Cosima had not halted. The only sign hung over the doorway announced the proprietor's right to sell intoxicating beverages.

"What's the name of this place?"

"The Todhunter Inn," she replied.

"Why doesn't it have a pub sign?"

"Because it's for the locals. They are a fiercely independent bunch and cherish this inn," she said tying up her horse. "It's not that they're against visitors drinking there, but they prefer to keep to themselves."

Flood managed to get off his horse without falling, although he half expected to make a fool of himself. The muscles in his legs wobbled as he led the horse over to Cosima. It bowed its head and nuzzled its nose into Flood's chest.

"He likes you and is saying thank you for riding him so considerately," she said smiling.

"I thought he was saying, 'oh you poor thing, you did try, never mind.'"

Cosima laughed. "No, you should be proud of yourself - you rode very well, considering it was your first time on a horse. Quite a natural." She tied the horses up and took Flood into the pub. Several men were enjoying a lunchtime beer. When they entered, the men greeted Cosima but stared at Flood.

"This is Miles, a friend of mine," she said to the stone-faced men.

"Greetings, young man," said the publican, going to the other side of the bar. "What drink would you like?" He began pouring Cosima a glass of port.

"I'll take a port as well," said Flood, reaching into his pocket for some money.

"No charge here," said Cosima, "this is my inn, remember. Now, let me introduce the chaps. Mr Ralph Smith - local builder and freelance writer, Thomas Metcalfe - the local butcher, John Coates - a thatcher and the local earth-stopper for the hunt, Fred Scott - general maintenance man, who can turn his hand to anything, and John Price - the publican. Gentleman, this is Miles Thomson. He's reading English at university."

"Helping 'er out with her books are you, Miles?" asked Metcalfe.

"I'd very much like to, but it would be a case of Cosima helping me." The response was warmly received by the men, who not only respected Cosima as their patron but also had a fond regard for her talents.

Smith asked Flood whether he had enjoyed the ride.

"Yes, it certainly presented some beautiful views of England. I never realised such views existed."

"Well, you're in God's country," replied Smith, "and we would like to keep it that way. It's a rare pleasure, I can tell you, to live round about."

"Well, it certainly is a most beautiful land," said Flood accepting his drink. Cosima sat down at the table and Flood joined her. The men stared at him for several moments before Cosima spoke.

"Gents, stop your stony habits. Leave that for the tourists."

The men looked sheepishly at Cosima. Coates prepared a toast, impersonating a downtrodden medieval peasant. "To Lady Cosima, her illustrious family, and of course to her indomitable ways."

"Oh, Mr Coates, do be sensible. Miles, the men often pretend to be browbeaten and feudally dependent, but they only do it to tease. Each is a freeholder in his own right. They work for themselves, something my ancestors arranged a long time ago. But they do like to tease me about the old feudal orders. What news do you have for me?"

Smith paused. "You've not heard, missy? I thought you kept up with events."

"What do you mean?"

"Well, Miss, Crap's gone and banned hunting and shooting last night. Says we have three months."

"Bloody hell!" Cosima quietly seethed. "No ... oh, my God. My phone-line's been down for a few days and I hadn't turned the radio on, since I had company. Oh ... "Her serene, confident face had fallen. A tear welled up and she swallowed hard. Price softly explained what had happened the night before in the Commons.

"The destruction of the DEFRA building's caused quite the stir," Coates added. "Harrison has gone to ground - so too has Radcliffe. He wasn't involved in last night's debate. There's a rumour that your father is also mixed up in it somehow, but that's not been reported," Coates winked.

"Have you heard from him?" she asked.

"Let's say that the old man is wanting our help," answered Smith his face giving nothing away, but Flood noticed Cosima's expression brighten considerably. She nodded. "Said he's going to make an announcement about the hunt ... and other matters." Then looking at Flood he added, "she did tell you that the local hunt is Laurenten Hunt, I presume?" Flood shook his head. "Aye, a sorry state of affairs. It was about time someone made a proper statement. All that marching and keeping camp outside of Parliament did not come to much good," said Smith.

"Funny thing is, the response from Europe," said Price. "Apparently, their President, or whatever you call him, is worried. You see, the DEFRA action has rather stirred up the fishermen too. They're threatening to board and sink Spanish trawlers following the EU's decision on new fish quotas. But they also say that the EU is pushing for new controls on animal welfare and hunting across the continent."

"Local news?" Metcalfe warmed up. "Reports of many break-ins and vandalism across the northern counties. Hunters have been targeted by antis, daubing paint on their walls and furniture. Some injuries at one farm we gather. Supposedly thirty houses and farms were hit all in Lindthorpeshire one evening. You saw the antis come through yesterday? We're expecting a repeat performance this afternoon. John here," he said pointing to Coates, "was out early, closing the dens and setts, and said he saw some massing near Garrett's Lane."

"Aye, but the Master led them astray yesterday!" laughed Coates. "Took them four miles into the Harkenskrag valleys, many miles from any road. Most became so lost that they burst into tears or started fighting with one another!" The men all laughed. Flood could not help joining in with a smile while avoiding the painful guilt, confusion, and concern mixing in his stomach.

"Did you ride yesterday?" Flood asked Scott.

"Sure did, never miss a hunt," he replied.

"You've not been on one, have ye?" asked Coates.

"No, can't say I've ever hunted."

"Then you're missing a real treat," said Smith. "Look at us, we all hunt or help. Mr Coates can't ride no more, so he's turned to earth-digging. He also trains the lads to beat the pheasants during the shoots. But there's no time like the present, if you're up to nowt. Missy can talk to the Master - he wouldn't mind you joining in. Come out with us lad - see what it's like."

Flood sat thinking about it.

"Well, now Crap's banned hunting," said Smith changing the tone, "we'll be raising the old standard."

"Hear, hear," said all the other men, "let's drink to that."

"What's the old standard?" Flood asked Cosima.

"It hangs in the church and comes out when the land is under threat. It's a fourteenth-century banner depicting a wolfhound. The hound protects the village from wolves, whether real or whether in the guise of men - anyone who comes to take away our liberties. It comes out once a year as a reminder to the community of their past fights and of their duties in the future to fight as their ancestors have done."

"Do you mean to say that you're willing to break the law?" Flood asked Smith. Wherever he turned he found people who held a low opinion of the land's laws - the old woman on the train, those who blew up the building, and now English villagers. Then he realised that he had recently been on the other side - his colleagues had broken the law and were willing to break it again. But, he thought, then he was on the side of the oppressed and the world's vulnerable species, and since they did not possess a voice, it was right for them to break the law on their behalf. Now the tables had turned and he was on the other side - of people who were adamant that they were the oppressed and who were willing to fight for their rights. He nodded as Smith continued.

"Without a doubt, young man. Our people have borne the brunt of many an injudicious law, going back centuries. We fought those laws then, and we'll fight any laws that take away our liberty to hunt," replied Smith. He took a mouthful of beer and held Flood's eye. "Make no mistake, lad. We know how to fight Normans - whether they come in the guise of Tudors, Stuarts, Hanovers, MPs, Civil Servants, men from the DEFRA, antis, or European Commissioners. I can tell you that local farmers, and probably those elsewhere, are sick of encroachments. They've lost millions with the BSE and foot-and-mouth crises and they've effectively lost all rights to their land. Do you know that a farmer cannot build a house, convert a barn, fell a wood, plant a copse, sow a field of corn, breed a calf, catch a trout, dredge his ponds, move a hedge, or drill into his own land without a bloody licence. No lad, they're right sick of government. Always have been, mind you, but they've been pushed to the brink recently."

Flood held the man's gaze for a couple of moments, taking in what he had said then sought his drink. He knocked the rest of it back.

"It doesn't look good in the kingdom, though," said Coates. "I keep hearing the news reports and I don't like what I hear. The government's threatening to arrest Harrison if he raises his head, and disband the Rural Alliance as an outlaw institution - same time as they free IRA folk, mind you. The country's losing the bloody plot. Oh yes, we're at war in the Middle East making the world safe for Cramp, but nobody's bothered about that - it's Crap's campaign to get himself into the history as something other than a twit and a loser."

"Government shall do what it likes," added Scott, "but they'll get a reaction."

Scott leant forward. "I heard at the DEFRA bonfire the local police put on flat caps to declare their allegiance to the country.

I reckon people we know, let's say, are working for a big change. And I can tell you - they'd get our full support."

"I heard the antis turned a fox yesterday," said Price, bringing the topic back to local matters.

"Aye, they did," replied Metcalfe. "Right stupid, they were too. Came running over the hills shouting obscenities, making a fearful noise. Poor fox doubled backed and almost made it, but was caught by the hounds."

"You sound sorry for the fox," said Flood confused.

"Course, he's a living thing like the hounds and men. He's a clever thing, though. Very sly. But he's a predator and is likely to get too numerous, so he needs culling or spreading about a bit."

"Why don't the farmers shoot foxes?" Flood gently felt his way into the discourse not wishing to upset the men but genuinely wanting to hear their opinions. In the back of his mind, the posters, pamphlets and propaganda still amassed pictures of foxes with their stomachs torn open and caught in snares and of hounds shot dead because they had lost their use.

Smith chuckled. "Shoot a fox? And nine times out of ten miss it with a clean shot? Even the best marksmen can rarely hit a moving fox cleanly. So then it's an injured fox, that goes off to suffer and die miserably. Perhaps not that night either; might take weeks of suffering. Hunt with the hounds and either it's is killed or gets away clean."

"Some farmers do shoot 'em of course," said Metcalfe. "But the result is rarely tidy. The hounds seek out the foxes, chase the weaker, injured, or vulnerable foxes, and kill them instantaneously. You ever seen a dog go for an animal? Straight for the neck. Dogs have strong jaws and sharp teeth for a reason. The fox has a chance to run. He uses his instincts to the full, and my God, what a bright animal he can be - why I've even seen Tod jump into the back of a moving pick-up truck once and got a clean escape!"

"Or that one that was cornered in a farm and then went to ground. The hounds looked everywhere," chuckled Coates, "until we spotted him racing along the chicken shed roof and out into freedom once more."

"Then there's the one that ran into a farmhouse," said Price. "Old John Tucker's farm, you remember him, Cosima?" She nodded. "Well, the sly fox runs into house where Mrs Tucker was. She jumped a mile, she says, but only thought it fair play, that if the fox had sought her sanctuary, that she should give it. Well, she has a stable door, and she shut the bottom half. The hounds went mad - barking and yelping at the door, scratching and pawing at it, begging her to let 'em in. But she would not give in. And if you'd a met her, you'd understand," added Price, causing the whole table to burst out in laughter with his impression of a broad shouldered gibbon. "Aye, even the Master relented and it took a good quarter of an hour to get the hounds away from the farm and onto a fresh scent."

"Aye, it would do," said Smith.

"But of course, the funny thing is," added Price, "Mr Fox, took his own liberties. First he ate up some chocolate cake she'd just baked, then stuck his snout into her apple pie, and then," he began laughing until he was red in the face, "killed her big fluffy white cat in the living room!"

The table burst out laughing again at the picture of comedy turned into tragedy.

"What did she do with the fox?" asked Flood through his laughter.

"Oh, shot the thing in the living room. Fair's fair, in Mrs Tucker's place," said Price, "but if a guest over steps the bounds of hospitality, then he's fairly dealt with. She didn't tell the Master though, not for a few months. Fact is, she was a weird one, she had both the cat and fox stuffed. They're still in the house now. Her son lives there with his wife. She did have a sense of humour though, for the fox is placed jumping onto the surprised cat!" The table laughed again.

"They say," added Price, "that her husband had to deal with her notions of fair play too."

"Aye, poor man, God bless his soul," said Coates.

"Did she shoot him too?" asked Flood.

"Aye. Came in late after one too many pints at pub and wanted, well, a bit of the old hanky-panky. He was thrown out of house with his trousers down, and as he ran for cover she shot him with her twelve bore," said Coates.

"Goodness, was she done for murder?"

"Oh no, lad. She only peppered his bottom. He died after her many years later. But it stopped him riding a horse for a year."

The table quietened and then Smith leant forward as if drawing them into a secret. "Did you hear where my Emily got her Barnborough jacket from, t'other day? From hunt saboteurs!"

"Eh?" Metcalfe looked incredulously at Smith.

"She did too. Heard about some anti-hunting meet down in the south, Beauville country I think. You know, she's studying at Spaville. Said they were giving away Barnborough jackets for those who turned up to protest. That Lucy McLaren's sponsoring them. Well, she'd had hers for quite a while and it were time for change, so she went along and got really nice jacket, she said on phone." His audience, all except Flood, knowing Emily very well, chuckled as he approached the end. "Aye, and next week she were out hunting in it!" The group burst out laughing and Flood joined in. "Topped her hat to a few of her anti friends, she said."

Price got up as the laughter diminished. "Another round, gents?" He popped behind the bar and drew four pints and poured two more glasses of port.

"I caught a mink yesterday, you know," said Coates, smiling smugly at the table.

"Bloody god, they cause so much damage," said the publican.

"I didn't know we had mink in this country," said Flood.

"Imported in the 1920s to be farmed for their fur, but being mink, they escaped. Ironically, many were helped by animal rights activists," said Cosima.

"Aye, little buggers have done much damage," said Smith.

"Yes, but explain this to antis and they rave and rant about how sweet the mink are," said Smith. "They don't understand it's a predator that's eating its way through our wildlife. It should be exterminated. Just like the grey squirrel. Hmm." The thought of the ban crossed Smith's mind and all recognised what he had recalled. They sat in silence for a while.

Price shook his head and crossed his arms.

"Hey, lad," said Metcalfe, "what's your thoughts on all of this?"

Flood turned to Cosima. "I'm just beginning to understand the depths of my ignorance," he said. Then he added, "But if Parliament has outlawed hunting with a democratically elected government, should we not accept the general will?"

"General will, my arse," retorted Smith. "I've read my Rousseau, lad. Screwed up frog, if there ever were one. People have rights, and rights are things nobody else can take away from you. If Parliament removes rights, then it has lost its privileges to determine anyone's affairs," he added with a strong measure of scorn. "So many people cry about the rights of foxes though, but what about the rights of farmers, or of hounds? Ah!" he exclaimed in disgust.

The words sank deep into Flood's conscience. He sat troubled yet sympathetically angry at their fate. It did not seem fair, he thought, but who was to decide what was fair?

Cosima turned to Flood. "This land has lost its soul and spirit over the last few generations. Think about what this nation once was, and look at it now. Spiritless, directionless, pathetic in many respects, laughed at by the Europe we once freed from tyrants, viewed as a quaint embarrassment by our American brethren, and disdained with increasing incredulity by many parts of the world who watch our football hooligans run riot. This land once supported the highest values that the world had striven for. We passed many of them to America, and they have made better sense out of them in many respects. The Europeans looked up to us as the epitome, not of culture, but of freedom and liberty. We have thrown that away in our obeisance to the new Sun-King's court in Brussels. We used to have an army respected by all, now we allow our soldiers to sue for post-battle stress, and we are more concerned with in which direction their sexuality points than whether they can fire a gun straight.

"Our schools once produced great minds, for they were free and allowed school children of all ages and abilities at least some glimpse of the streams of knowledge and truths that lie in our cultural heritage. Now teenagers have to study a national curriculum that will become increasingly dumbed down as to make the adult mind so smooth that any totalitarian could warp it to evil ends through mono-syllabic headlines and pathetic sentimentalities. Our industry was the best - it fired the Industrial Revolution - now it has to be sold to foreigners who can manage it better. Even the football team cannot find a home-grown national coach of any calibre. And what we're good at, the establishment shies away from. No mention of our shooting medals at the Games and very little of horse-riding." She paused for a moment, her passionate apology turning visibly into anger. "This land is ripe for a civil war."

"Hear, hear," they all said. "You should stand for Parliament one of these days," said Price.

Smith caught Cosima's eye. "What do you think the chance of civil war is, missy?"

"High," she said seriously.

"Why don't you come out with us this afternoon?" Metcalfe asked Flood, checking the time. "The hounds should be arriving in the next hour. It's an informal day - no black jackets required. We've a short hunt from two until five at the latest. Gets quite dark by then of course. You've got the riding gear on already. The horses will have rested by then, don't you think Cosima?"

"Those two," she replied, "would hunt all morning and all afternoon, they love it so much."

"Right, so what about it, young man?"

Flood eyed each man, and each in turn looked into his eyes not with derring-do but with a simplicity that bespoke volumes, similar to the look he had seen in the hound's eye yesterday that inquired, "Why not come out? It's fun and natural!"

"Okay, I'll do it," he said. "If it'll be alright."

"I was hoping you would," Cosima said to him

"Of course!" said Smith. "Only rule you need to know is not to let yourself overtake the Master, nor get in the way of the Master and the hounds."

"I'm sure I won't," replied Flood laughing.

"And to stay on your charger, if you can!" laughed Price.

"Well, let's get ready," said Metcalfe. "Coates, you finished out there yet?"

"I have a couple of more to do in the Harken woods. Best get going."

Flood looked at Cosima, who nodded invitingly. "You'll enjoy it, and I'll keep with you to make sure you don't get lost."

Politicking

Laurenten stormed out of his office and into the library where Hickling, Harrison, and Radcliffe were sitting with Freebard and Whitman.

"I don't bloody believe it," he said through gritted teeth. "Fifty police divisions have declined even an invitation to hear our views!" He paced over to the window and, gripping the sill, peered out at the view. The landscape usually calmed him, but now his fury lay unabated and unchallenged by the pacific countryside.

The others had stopped their conversation and sat watching him. Freebard, peering at Laurenten and examining him as he would a student, finally spoke in clipped tones.

"Are the police necessary?"

"Of course they bloody are!" Laurenten turned, fuming. "We are practically defenceless without a police force."

"How many divisions do we have?" inquired Hickling.

"Twenty," replied Laurenten sharply.

"Then we have a start," added Radcliffe. "Others may come over to us once we are up and running."

"If we ever get up and running," said Laurenten, standing over them. "We need the numbers."

"Do numbers really mean anything in the fight for freedom?" asked Freebard, maintaining the manner of a professor in a tutorial. He leant forward and somehow managed to twist his bony legs around in the manner of a corkscrew.

"In politics, numbers are everything," Radcliffe said quietly. "Any independence movement must carry some weight in the broader population to gain credence."

"I disagree," said Freebard, now folding his arms.

He disagrees, thought Laurenten, but he also knows he's entering the political realm and he's damned nervous. It was not a sight Laurenten found pleasant. "Look, we're not playing political philosophy games any more," snapped Laurenten. "We're putting ourselves on the line here. And everything we stand for. If we fail now, our ideals will be mocked and our cause will be consigned to history's dustbin. We are engaged in politicking, whether we like it or not."

"Please, do sit down," Whitman requested. Laurenten looked at her soft face and then complied. The comfortable chair relaxed him and he quietened down.

"Laurenten, I'm not evading the political situation," said Freebard gently, as he unravelled his arms and legs. He paused for a moment to consider his choice of words. "Think about what I asked. Firstly, are the police necessary? The present police force is in the pay of the Westminster government - who cares if they're on our side or not? We can form our own. Villages used to have their own constables, paid from local funds and subject to the traditional laws. With a little prompting, I'm sure the jurisdictions seceding with us will make their own law enforcement arrangements. Secondly, in referring to numbers, I want you to reconsider the need to play the democratic game. We're not interested in whether the whole country supports us. Most will not have a clue about our policies. They will react in a manner that reflects their upbringing and cultural outlook, and let's face it, most of the country favours a big government with a vast public services industry. But we're not chasing their votes. We're standing aside from them and saying, hey, if you like freedom then you'd better jolly well come with us."

"As I say, it's when we're up and running that we'll see how much support we'll attract," said Radcliffe. "Freebard's right. We're not after a given segment of the voting public. We're trying to change the entire political fabric of the land."

"And many people are sick and tired of increasing regulation and intrusions," said Hickling, emphasising his words with his hands. "They just need some direction from a strong representation. If we don't stand square and declare our intentions proudly and with confidence, then we may as well give up the fight, and let the government trample all over us."

Whitman agreed. "People are apathetic because they've lost sense of the old liberal traditions."

Laurenten patiently listened. He nodded slightly in agreement with Freebard's arguments. "I hear you all. It's just so damn frustrating speaking to the police chiefs."

"Yes, but they don't work for us," said Whitman.

"Nor do they work for the law," added Freebard. "They're politically infested." He leant back in his chair, in a pose that reminded Laurenten of the famous portrait of Wilberforce: intelligent eyes, slightly smarmy face, and a weak, floppy stature.

Whitman turned to Freebard. "I don't like that language. Once you start describing the impurity of any group, policies towards them often harden. If we do enter a full-blown civil war with Westminster, we must always remember that our enemy are people who we should try to attract over onto our side by the reasonableness of our ideas. If we characterise them as infested, or as vermin, then we dehumanise them. And in the potential chaos of a civil war, freedom and the dignity of the individual would lose out to inhumane tactics."

Freebard sat back and considered Whitman's words. "Possibly," he said sceptically and a little defensively.

"Whitman's right," said Laurenten. "I know how you see the world, Simon. Black and white. Good and evil. Freedom's good, statism's bad. But don't forget we're also talking about people. And very few people are without their contradictions and inconsistencies. Indeed, you have to give them that: that's part of what it means to be human. I recall you once said, 'people have the right to be wrong.' Don't forget that."

Freebard put his hands together. "Freedom is indivisible. You either have it, or you don't. It's like what Kierkegaard called his religious philosophy: "Either/Or". You can't have a free society with a big government."

"We know that," chimed in Radcliffe. "That's what we're struggling to explain to the rest of the country."

"But we're also interested in the uniqueness of the individual," argued Whitman. "Don't make the mistake of fighting for the abstract while forgetting the particular. Regardless whether or not a man is for or against freedom, we must respect his beliefs."

"But that's exactly what we're up against!" countered Freebard, putting his hands together in supplication. "So many people say they believe in freedom, but their view of it involves imposing their particular beliefs on the rest of us."

"Aren't you all losing the plot somewhere?" asked Harrison, who had remained hitherto quiet. "You all agree freedom's a good thing. And from what I understand, you wish to secede from Westminster and declare a free republic. Fine. What's the problem?"

"I think we'll have a big fight on our hands, and if we're to win, we need to be ruthless," said Freebard.

"Freedom demands toleration, not ruthlessness," Whitman retorted.

"Miranda, we'll be swamped by Westminster if we tolerate statism," countered Freebard. "Some people in society are not reasonable. They do not understand what it means when I say that I wish to be free from their interference. Do you not see - if we tolerate the intolerant, we may as well pack it all in now."

"History," said Laurenten to Harrison. His comment silenced Freebard and Whitman who dropped their argument to listen to him.

Laurenten rose from his chair and returned slowly to the window. He turned to face the group. "If the Assembly agrees to convene and we secede from Westminster to declare a free republic, we shall unleash forces across the land that none of us here could predict. The history of all revolutions contains surprises that the protagonists could not foresee. That's what worries me. That's what frustrates me."

He folded his arms and rested his back against the casement. "We are putting ourselves into a very dangerous situation. Simon's right to express his theoretical direction, let's call it. We need to constantly reaffirm the standard by which we shall declare our independence and, if necessary, fight. But Miranda's also right in stressing that we are not ideologues wedded to abstracts. What we do affects people. We shall be disturbing sleeping giants and waking up the slothful. Moreover, we'll be sowing a hell of a lot of confusion across the kingdom. We must be clear, yes, yes," he nodded and walking back to his chair with a tightly furrowed forehead, added, "if we're not, then we are lost."

He went to sit down but stopped. "No," he said to himself. "I need to get back on the phone. The rest of you, I want you all to devise contingency plans in case things do not go our way. Your lives will be at risk in this country, so I want you to consider where you'd want to go, if you had to. Radcliffe, I want you in my office in half an hour with a list of MPs we can contact. Harrison, a list of landowners. Whitman, professors and lecturers please. Freebard, your American lobbyists. Hickling, a list of top bankers." His words stirred them into action. They all rose from their chairs. "Keep me informed of who's for us and who's not with us - yet," he added. "We'll need a thorough political foundation to offer the Assembly."

He returned swiftly to his office and, peering down the drive, picked up the phone to call the next Chief Inspector on his list.

Eboulement

Following a quick snack of bread and cheese, Cosima went to retrieve the horses, leaving Flood to stand in the yard, contemplating the countryside. He had come to sabotage this institution, but now he had been invited to be a part of it the remaining feelings of distrust dispersed. He breathed in the cold air, enjoying the lingering taste of port in his mouth. Cosima came out, leading Otto and Lysander.

They mounted and trotted down to the meet at the end of Todthorpe. As soon as they had left the pub's yard, the children hollered and ran towards them, calling to others. Several older folk were already on their way. The children came over to the horses and patted them excitedly.

"Don't worry," Cosima said to Flood, "the horses are used to them and won't buck or rear. Here come some others."

Along the road Flood saw five riders, a couple in smart black jackets, trotting their way over like a small cavalry battalion on a reconnaissance. The complex overlapping of the one-two beats echoed around the village. About thirty villagers had now joined the children. All were talking about the government's decision to ban their tradition and about how yesterday's demonstration that had been foiled. Talk then turned to a fight that broken out somewhere last night, but Flood couldn't make out the details. Several villagers indicated to the hounds coming. He gazed along the road and there they were running alongside three horsemen dressed in red coats and riding white horses, the hounds sniffing the ground and hedges and catching up in a cascading momentum towards the meet. From the other end of the village he heard, then saw, another dozen or so riders coming.

The crowd cheered the hounds' arrival and the children ran over to pet the dogs, who jumped up and licked shy, appreciative, and giggling faces. Cosima introduced the Master, "Mr Carlton, this is Miles, a good friend of mine, on his first hunt." The Master edged his horse over and shook his hand with a warm welcoming smile. Flood recognised him from yesterday.

"Glad to have you with us. Do you ride well?"

"Well, this is my first time on a horse."

Carlton sat back and laughed. "First time on a horse and you're on a hunt! By, this man is a brave one. But you're with one of Cosima's horses I see. They will look after you well. You just keep your heels down and you'll enjoy the ride of a lifetime! Now, let me introduce you to my two Whips. First, Andrew, he's the ruddy-faced handsome chap with the blond curls. And that's Tim, the athletic-looking one. He goes out with the foot beagles once a week - runs for the county too. I can't keep up with him. Only rules on the Laurenten Hunt to be aware of are to not get between me and the hounds. But most importantly, enjoy yourself. Welcome on board, Miles."

The Master turned to Cosima to discuss the government's action. "It had to come," he was saying, "but I want to forget politics today - we're hunting." They greeted other riders as they arrived.

A horse and rider came alongside Flood. "What a surprise! I thought it was you." Flood's mouth fell: Gemma Lawrence! In a second her sharp eyes had surveyed his entire outfit, horse and face. "I thought I saw it in your eyes that you weren't sure about your beliefs. You need to see things with your own eyes, don't you?"

Flood smiled. "Yes."

She quietly inquired how he managed to be going on a hunt with the Laurenten when Maggie had said they were both going sabbing the day before. "Just curious," she added, still keenly observing him with a face that asked, "what side are you on?"

"I've learned a lot since we last met." Flood looked over at Cosima speaking to some new arrivals. "Don't laugh now, but I got lost - on the sab, you know." He briefly described his adventure. Gemma did laugh - a wonderfully clear laugh that released him from her interrogation.

"Oh, that is funny! And Miss Laurenten herself found you. Goodness, you are lucky. I've only met her a couple of times - an intelligent woman. Do you like her?" she asked.

"Venerate, I would say."

Gemma laughed. "Very appropriate, Flood, very appropriate; close to an excellent Latin pun."

He shrugged then whispered to her, "They know me as Miles here, just so as you know."

She nodded. "Will you drop your nickname then?"

"I don't know - I'm thinking about it."

A couple of villagers came over, carrying sherry for the assembled riders.

One handed the Master a drink. "Mr Carlton, I hear there was a fight last night. Any news of it?"

"Oh, by Jove there was. But I'll let Andrew tell it. After all he was there. Andrew, come and tell the folks your tale."

Andrew was beaming from ear to ear at the opportunity to relate his tale to the entire meet. He was a fresh-faced, blue-eyed, blond-haired man of twenty-something years. He smiled almost impishly as he began.

"Me and Tim were in the Wellington Arms last night having a quiet drink, when in came a few anti types. You know, scruffy, smelly, urban folk, with piercings and dyed hair. Anyway, like I said, we were sitting quietly. The pub was quite full, but these antis managed to find a table. They ordered their pints. I could see the publican eyeing them up, as did many of the drinkers, but it's a free country and they soon were ignored and left to talk amongst themselves. They were conspiring about something, when a most surly looking youth with a nasty, obnoxious face pulled out a hunting cap from his bag. It was a Master's cap he'd nicked. He put it in the middle of the table as some sort of totem, I'd imagine. Must have forgotten where they were, silly beggars. And not really the evening after what was happening in Parliament, was it? I gather that he had stolen the hat from an earlier sabbing expedition against the Hamford Hounds. Well, young James, you know, Deighton's strapping son, the one who lifts hay bales and tractors for a hobby, saw this and approached them.

"'What's this?' he asked taking up the hat. 'None of your effing business,' came the polite reply from some slime-bucket who tried to snatch it back. James looks at the hat and then replies, 'Yes, it is our business, mate,' and punches the man straight on the nose. Blood gushed everywhere and you should have seen the others' faces!"

The riders laughed at the poetic justice, but Flood felt a stab of anxiety for his former friends, for it sounded like Rat he was referring to. The feeling ebbed, however, as Andrew continued the story.

"James then turned to the publican and got him to make a couple of calls, whilst his mates, all beefy members of Young Farmers - you know the type, them that lift cows onto their backs and pull their tractors out of mud after a few pints of cider - said "Shut the doors." The antis cowered back in their corner. An older chap, who looked like a teacher or something, stood up and started raving about his rights and that he was well connected to lawyers and stuff. James replied that so was everyone in the room, and asked him what of the rights of the Master whose hat they had stolen, or the rights of country folk to go unmolested and in peace about their business, without insulting comments from their likes? The publican confirmed the hat's ownership and James placed it ceremoniously on the stuffed fox. He then offered the three or four women with them the chance to leave the pub, but they refused. Then a really tarty-looking one, spat at James's face. He ignored that but put his fist right into the teacher's jaw; he was certainly not expecting that. He went down in one punch.

"Then it was mayhem as some antis tried to fight back or get out through windows. All the lads in the bar, and some of the girlfriends, piled in to have a shot. They smashed chairs and windows, but from the corner Lord Tricester, who was having a quiet meal with his wife, shouted, 'Any damage - I'll pay for it!' which prompted a round of applause for the old man. Soon the antis had been roundly thumped and kicked up the back-sides. Some farmers' wives then pulled the antis' trousers off. They called for treacle, were given a large can of it, and proceeded to paint the antis all over. It was hilarious! Then the publican's wife brought some feathered pillows down from the rooms, opened them up, and covered the antis in feathers. They let the girls keep their clothes on, but daubed their hair in the thickest of treacle and feathers for decoration. What a sight! God, we laughed so much.

"We then bound them by their belts and other ropes. Old Farmer Johnson had his tractor and manure trailer nearby, so we pushed them onto the trailer. Many of James's friends jumped on board and Farmer Johnson drove them up the road to Cuttings' Coverts. They came back about an hour later, telling us that they'd tied them up, scared out of their wits, and dropped them in the middle of the wood, which, as we know, is particularly boggy this time of year! But they couldn't just leave them there. James and a few others jumped off the trailer and secretly surrounded the covert in the dark. Every now and again they let out a howl or a screech or a shotgun. They got back a couple of hours later, saying that the antis were too scared to move or even undo each other's ropes.

"When they got back they were all treated to free rounds. Then Sergeant Morris came by. He was told everything that had happened, including the tarring and feathering. The sergeant congratulated him and said it was something he and his men had wanted to do for a long time, but they were prevented from even cautioning those idiots, because of Home Office instructions. So he stayed and chatted after radioing his men to look out for some feathered people in the vicinity!"

The riders laughed. Their conversation was emotionally charged, for they all agreed they were being made outlaws in their own land by the London government. Then the Master called for the meet's attention.

"Today we're here to hunt. But before we put politics aside we need a toast. Bollocks to Cramp and here's to James and to more DEFRA buildings too! And here's to the freedom to hunt!"

The villagers and riders cheered and toasted "The freedom to hunt!"

Then the Master blasted a short note on the horn and he and the Whips trotted off with the hounds racing alongside. The followers' horses clattered down the narrow lane and struck right across a common, breaking into a canter once they were clear of the hedges and muddy pools around the gates.

The Huntsman placed his Whips either side of a small covert and encouraged the hounds in. There they went, and soon a fox was tally-hoed by a Whip and they were off, the Master and Whips cantering after the hounds. Flood and Cosima followed the field and he had another revelation.

Once more he felt his thoughts falling as the horse's rhythm beat under him mesmerising his mind. The horses merged into a group, and Flood felt the synergy drawing them into the same beat and direction, pulling their riders into a strong natural bond. And all that had been confused and jumbled, all that had once been tossed around in his violent mental storms, frustrations, and inquiries, all now ebbed into a calm tacit comprehension of his life and of the meaning of life around him. A concept arose in his mind - a distant temporal echo lost in the noise of modern life: oneness. There was the mysterious sense of unity a man will feel in his solitude or in a crowd, that philosophers revere and theologians enthral to, and hymns, sonnets, marches, symphonies composed upon. Things, thoughts and beliefs, had fallen into place clarifying much and overwhelming him with a gust of beatification. This was the heart of aesthetic feeling, he philosophised - the beginning and the end, alpha and omega, the everlasting comprehension encircling the world closed in on him: life! He was a part of the world as well as a being in his own right. This was a heaven on earth, he concluded.

Cosima rode next to him. He smiled at her, a full genuine smile that emanated from the core of his soul. She sensed it, for she held his gaze as they rode and smiled back. Her eyes glinted vivaciously and slightly mischievously. He felt as if he was experiencing one of life's secrets; he had never felt so calm yet so ecstatic before. To everybody's surprise he let out a joyous "barbaric yawp" - and Cosima burst into laughter. Some others also let out whoops, yells, and cathartic screams of life-embracing noise. They cantered, they galloped, they sped over fields and jumped fences, hedges, and ditches - none fell, no horses staggered or refused, no man nor woman gave in to nerves; over they went in pursuit of the fox. As is common in the annals of venery, never did a field ride so well, nor hounds pursue so excellently, nor the Masters and Whips lead and guide so expertly.

Flood was riding beyond the present into an eternal stream of life and consciousness; for a moment he pitied those who could not feel like he did now, and he pitied his prior self; but then he wondered why he had not felt that feeling before - what had stopped him?

He looked at Cosima again and wanted to ask her a million questions. But on they cantered. No time for questions or thoughts, so he enjoyed the flowing secrets tangoing in his soul finding their way to sustain his present elation.

They halted before a large covert into which the fox had bolted and again the Master sent the hounds in. It was not long before they gave their music and the fox flew from the copse's west side. Off again went the hounds with the Master, Whips, and followers in pursuit.

"Come," said Cosima, "I'll take you to a good vantage point." She encouraged her horse into a fast canter in a different direction to the pack. Flood followed in her wake. They then galloped around to the east of the woods and up a shallow hill and onto its rise. The hounds' music died away in the distance, but still they rode until they came to the ruins of an old cottage.

Cosima reined her horse to a stop and Flood drew up next to her. "Dismount, and lead your horse over here," They both jumped off and Flood followed her, leading his horse over to a fence where he tied it next to hers. She took off her hat.

She looked straight at him. "You've realised something, haven't you? On the ride, I saw it in your face. It was if you were touching a different realm."

He nodded. "I don't know if I can put it into words."

"You don't have to," she said bringing her face slowly to meet his. Her lips parted slightly as she looked straight into his eyes, her pupils scintillating mischievously. She kissed him, a lingering kiss, allowing him to taste her and for the sensations to free-fall with the other cascading feelings still dripping in his mind.

"It's a wonderful experience, isn't it?" He nodded. "Some," she said, "call it religion. I call it the essence of life. You've tasted the essence of life. Here," she said, "I want you to taste the art of venery." She took his hand and placed it on her breast as she leant forward again to kiss him. "Don't hold back," she murmured, "not from life. Not from this. Just let things be and flow."

He pulled her tight, feeling the warmth surge between their bodies. He took off his hat and laid it next to hers. He ran his fingers up her back and into her hair, letting his face fall into a forest of dark spells and enchantments. He kissed her neck and smelled her fragrance mixed with the land's fresh air; she emitted an intoxicating natural perfume and he wanted rise to heaven on the smell. He felt her hands stroke his back and his neck as he toyed with her curls and massaged her ribs under her breasts. He lowered his head to kiss her chest and felt her pulling his jacket off his shoulders and his neck. The air froze through to his skin but the liberating cold was tempered by the arousing strokes of her fingers. He shivered slightly both from his excitement and the cool wind.

She led him into the ruins. "Where you left off," she murmured, "and don't stop - don't worry - just let things be." They made love oblivious to the dank air. Nothing moved around them. Finally, he dropped his face into her soft hair. She stroked his head and back.

"There, Miles," she finally said, "the secrets of life. What do you think now?"

"I'm too gone to think," he replied, losing himself in her body's scent. Miles, he thought, I like my name.

They lay for twenty minutes, talking quietly before moving to get dressed and return to the horses.

"I never knew hunting could be so sexual," said Miles.

"Oh, yes, it's wonderfully primeval isn't it?" replied Cosima. "Surtees wrote that 'women never look so well as when one comes in wet and dirty from hunting'!" She laughed getting up.

"I can agree with Surtees on that one. You are gorgeous," said Miles.

She smiled and gave him a friendly push. "You too. I don't normally do this, you know. Just so you know," she said putting on her hat. "And I wasn't kidding about the hunt, they'll be over here soon. They always come this way."

Miles laughed. "Do we wait here?"

"No, let's head for the covert over there. From there we'll be able to work out their direction and pace and catch up with them."

"Cosima." A serious edge to his voice caught her attention. "I've never said this before to anyone ... " The sound of a horn caught his attention.

WILLIAM VENATOR

A Tender Tergiversation

Alan Jones sat on the bench contemplating the sunset. The cold south-westerly reddened his cheeks and he pulled the zip up to close the woollen jacket he had been given. It was marvellous how it kept out the wind, he thought as he watched the sun poking out of swift-moving pendulous clouds and its light refracting upon the stirred up tide. He stretched out his legs, dug his hands back into his pocket, took in a deep breath and let it go slowly. This confinement was rather pleasant, he decided.

They had been bundled into a police van and then he and his two colleagues were hooded and transferred to a lorry. They were tied to the framework and gagged by men wearing the expected balaclavas. The journey seemed endless. In the dark he could make out the forms of Steven and Clarissa, but since they could not communicate they slept on and off for the ride. He thought Steven sobbed for a while. It was pouring with rain when they were blindfolded and pulled out of the lorry and transferred to a small noisy boat, which took them for a good hour's journey on choppy seas. Their captors pulled large nylon macs over their heads, which disoriented their hearing. He heard someone deal with Clarissa whom he heard throwing up between vehement protestations. The sensory deprivation was frustrating, but they were not beaten, which he had feared.

When the boat docked with a dull shudder, their blindfolds, gags, and bindings were removed. He looked at Clarissa and saw her fearful, suspicious eyes and pale face. He reached out to hold her hand as they clambered out. He kept a hold of it as they were escorted from the dock by four men carrying shotguns. Steven quipped, "Who's going to hold my hand?" and then followed sullenly behind.

Alan had demanded explanations but was told in a thick Scottish accent that they would be given reasons later but for now to shut up. He looked around; they were ascending a path from a low-lying bay. The rain impaired his vision and they floundered often so that he had to let go of Clarissa's hand. The sound of the rain drowned out the rough sea and after a long, tiring hike around a hill and over its crest, they finally reached a substantial cottage nestled in a sheltered dell. They could only hear the rain pounding on the ground and spilling out over gutters. They were too tired to fight and their captors were polite, so they complied with their requests to take off their macs and warm themselves by a roaring fire. They stared at each other but said few words. Hot drinks were brought to them and after being shown their three small but comfortable bedrooms, they fell asleep, dazed and exhausted.

For the first time in a week Alan slept through the night and well into the next day. No noises, no horns, no traffic or yelling from protestors or street drunks. Awakening, he had opened the single curtain and to see a wide grassy expanse creeping slowly up to a pine forest bathed in sunlight. Small clouds darted overhead caught on a strong westerly wind. The rain had stopped. He opened the window and a sharp breeze woke him up to his situation.

He noticed a set of clothes had been laid out over a chair for him. His suit was gone, so he put on a pair of comfortable cords, a thick cotton shirt, thin woollen sweater and woollen socks. He saw his pair of black shoes but also hiking boots and a pair of slippers. He put the slippers on and left the room to find someone to speak to. The house was quiet, but that was because, he found out, it was large. He essayed one corridor and got nowhere, retraced his steps past his room and found a gallery overlooking a staircase. He descended and he heard voices from one room, which turned out to be the kitchen. Steven sat there sipping coffee and scowling at a burly chef who was berating Steven for his bad attitude.

"Alan! Thank God, I thought they had left me here with this Rab C Nesbit character all by myself, oh, thank God," he said jumping up and wringing his hands, though whether with joy or anguish, Alan could not make out.

"Where's Clarissa?" he demanded immediately.

"Outside," replied the chef. "Go out this door and you'll see her. She's feeding ma chicks at the moment."

"You mean, we're free to leave the house?"

"Course you are. You're on an island, you know," the chef smiled and Steven scowled at him. Alan opened the door, leaving Steven fuming at the chef's matter-of-factness, saw the thick wet grass and thought he'd better go and change his shoes.

He approached Clarissa, who was bent over, casting grain for a dozen or so hens and a cock. "Clarissa, are you alright?"

"Alan, look at these! Aren't they just adorable? Look at that one! She's so sweet! And this one keeps pinching seeds from the others, so you have to make sure the others get their fair share." He squatted next to her and watched her feeding the chickens. He joined in and for several minutes they said nothing but enjoyed the act's simplicity.

"We're on an island," he finally said.

"Yes, it is gorgeous. You should see the views from the hill over there. I was up early and have explored over there, and there too," she said indicating a forest and a nearby summit. "You can see for miles - lots of islands, and sea, and the ocean. It's wonderful. And these clothes are rather nice, they keep you really warm. Now let's look at you," she said as they stood up. "Much better. You look quite dapper, and your headache's gone, by the looks of it. You've not eaten have you? I'll show you where, come on." Clarissa grabbed his hand and almost skipped back to the large baronial-style mansion. She showed him to the dining room where cereals and bread for toasting were laid out on a sideboard. He poured them both coffees and sat down to eat.

"I'll be missed, you know."

"By your wife?"

"Oh, Christ, I'd not even thought of her. But now you mention it, no probably not, or rather, yes, she'll miss me - someone to moan to, but I won't miss her."

Clarissa's face lightened slightly. "The PM will miss you then."

"Him, good God no. I mean, no, I mean, well, to tell you the truth I wonder who will miss me."

"Well I'm glad I'm here with you. I bet the newspapers will be enjoying the story - minister kidnapped by mad Scotsmen!

That'll do your career a lot of good. Publicity, talk shows, biographies."

"I'm not sure I want all that. I don't know," he shook his head commanding back some intruding thoughts. He glanced at her and recalled the night he had made her dinner. It was very sweet. Thoughts of sexual conquest had fallen away to a seven-hour conversation on all matters. They had got to know each other and then he escorted her back to her shared flat. Her late-working roommate raised an eyebrow as they entered but dropped it quickly - their faces too innocent to suggest a night of passion. That had been a good night. He had strolled back in the London rain, anonymous and rested. He ignored his answering machine and private email account until the next day. His wife's seven emails became more persistent and angry in tone and then changed to conciliatory and then pleading. Truth was, he couldn't be bothered with them. He sent off a quick apologetic email mentioning work in the House and catching up on the hunting consultation work and falling asleep on the couch and a broken promise to call later.

"I guess I should make contact with the wife," he finally said regretting the legal intrusion into his present serenity. "Anyway," he added as a dutiful afterthought, "who's here and what do they want to do with us? Have you found out anything?"

"Nothing. The chef's a nice man, but is keeping quiet. He said that someone would be coming by later."

"Is he the only one guarding us?"

"No, there are about a dozen men on the island. They all have guns, so it's not worth thinking about rebelling."

"I wasn't going to. I could do with a holiday."

"I'm worried about Steven though. He's terribly upset."

"Well, I'm sure he'll calm down. It's no use putting up a fight."

"The hunters do, though, Alan."

"Mm? Oh, yes, them. Yes, they do."

"Would you not fight for anything? I mean, if you had to?"

The question hit straight home, where it was supposed to. He studied her sharp eyes as she sipped her coffee, waiting for his answer.

"Yes," he admitted, "I would fight." He smiled at her then added, "I'm going to have to fight."

"For what?" she insisted quietly but with meaning.

"I need a divorce. I need to get out of politics. I need to find my own life again. I'll fight for those things."

"And me?"

She was direct. He smiled and reached out to hold her hand. "Do I have to fight for you?"

She smiled back, her eyes closing slightly with relief. "I hoped you would notice. Shall we go for a walk? I'd like to show you the views."

They had spent the rest of the morning avoiding Steven as his sulking made poor company. They explored the house and met up with other taciturn Scots who lunched with them but would not commit themselves to any explanations. That afternoon a boat landed on the dock and an old man marched up to see them.

"John Stewart," he said, offering his hand, which neither took. "I've come to explain a few things." Alan had tried to be officious but it did not suit the occasion, so they walked back to the house in silence and took up their places in a large drawing room heated by a log fire. Around the room were tartan wall-hangings, stags' heads, romanticised pictures of Scottish warriors, large drinking vessels on mahogany and oak tables. The three captives sat round the fire while Stewart spoke to them.

"Firstly, you are not in any harm or danger. My men will make sure that you enjoy your captivity as best as we can make it. Secondly, you may pen a letter to people you need to get in contact with. I'll make sure that your messages get through. Thirdly, I wish to explain why we have done this." He stared at Alan and twisted his mouth. "Where to start?" he sighed.

"Well, you're not the only one we've grabbed. The Scottish Farms Minister is presently enjoying temporary accommodation on the Faeroes, and the Welsh Environment Minister has been removed to a small Greek island. Yes - quite - lucky him! Where to start though?" Stewart pointed at Alan. "You are responsible for deciding whether or not the freedom of hundreds of thousands of people should be taken away. That can never be your decision. Freedom is not something government can create, legislate, or remove from innocent people. Freedom exists by itself as an inviolable moral principle. So we've taken you away, removed your freedom as one who would encroach on the lives of a free people. You are a criminal, and we wish you to feel what it is like to have your freedom removed. Except, whereas we're making your stay comfortable, your policy would destroy traditions and jobs and annihilate a part of this country's grand heritage."

"But you're such hypocrites," Steve said suddenly. "You're imprisoning us in the name of freedom. That's so inconsistent it's not funny."

"Nobody said it would be funny," replied Stewart sternly. "People do not have a so-called freedom to attack another, and that includes people who work for governments."

"What about the police, then?" persisted Steven leaning forward, his eyes widening. He was dressed in similar clothes to Alan, but they did not suit him as much. As a gay man used to frequenting London's expensive restaurants, he sorely missed his expensive, tailor-made suits and colourful silk ties and cravats. He squirmed in his chair, periodically scratching his arms.

"The police's duty is to apprehend those who have attacked others. They have no right to aggress against innocents. And when the state begins to act like the criminals it is meant to apprehend, then civilians have a right to defend themselves."

"This is all very Lockean," said Clarissa.

"Yes, it is, in many respects," nodded Stewart. "But whereas most who read political science in our universities want to control the land, some of us believe people should be left alone to pursue life and values as they see fit. It's really a simple political philosophy: hands off and keep your noses out of our business."

"But your business is everybody's business, especially when you kidnap people."

"No. So long as I don't harm my neighbour, what I do is my business and has nothing to do with you. But, yes, we've arrested you, because, whether you know it or not, you are violators and aggressors. You may look innocent and helpless," he shot a look at Steven, "but you wield the forces of the state - often at things you don't know about, such as hunting - and thereby violate people's rights. Because they're doing something you don't wish to do, doesn't give you a right to arrest or to fine them."

"But we were democratically elected. That gives us the right," said Alan.

"No one has a right to use violence against another, regardless whether or not you have majority, mob-rule backing for it. Freedom from coercion is the essence of civilisation."

"But we're all part of a big community, and we have to abide by what the community wants from us," insisted Steven.

"Our community, as you call it, is whom we individually choose to share our time with. No one forces us to make friends. The community I belong to, I belong to voluntarily without force. What you are implying is that some people speak for the community and that they should have the right to trample on those they don't like. As a gay man, I am sure you are familiar with your movement's desire to be left alone. Well, young man, there are others who feel the same way about their lives. You should use your head a little more about your politics. You'll probably find some gaping contradictions. Anyway, you are welcome to roam the island as you please. You will be here until our government is set up and then you will be freed to go back to where you want to go."

"I'm sorry?" asked Alan. "What government are you setting up?"

Stewart turned his head and held eye contact. "Half the kingdom is seceding from Westminster to found a new republic based on simple freedom. By the month's end it should have international recognition, and if it does not, so much for international recognition. We have a right to forge our own lives and we are choosing that option."

"You'll be crushed," said Steven.

"By whom? Several army regiments are coming over to us, as are the police forces. We're offering better pay and conditions, of course, because we won't have a socialist and welfare state to fund. But most importantly, the chiefs of police recognise that with our government, they'll be policemen and soldiers, not New Labour Thought Police. Now," he said, leaning forward, smiling at them all, "taxes in our land will be ten per cent or so, no more. Businesses will not be regulated or taxed at all, there will be no initiatives of interference from government. Government has no right to get involved in commerce. There will be no state ownership, no state control, it will be a free land. Taxes will pay for the police and army but nothing beyond them. Of course, that all means we will be signing up hundreds of businesses to our jurisdiction. Westminster's resources will dry up as merchants come over to us. But, that's for the future. For now, I want you to enjoy your captivity. I mean that sincerely, because we'd like you to come and live in our lands one day - you'd be free to." Stewart stood up. "After all, your energy to violate others' lives could be put into more productive, fulfilling, and rewarding employment you know. Well, I must be off to the mainland in a couple of hours and I need to give you time to write letters. The Assembly will be convening shortly, and I have much to do. Please excuse me."

Thus had the first day transpired. By the second the three of them had relaxed into a routine of their own, Clarissa and Alan going for long walks, discovering small, hidden coves and beaches, Steven sulking around, throwing camp tantrums to gain someone's attention every now and again. They ignored him and he finally turned to helping the chef, with whom he became good friends. By the late afternoon, Alan and Clarissa found the two of them swigging back whisky and laughing at how twee the interior design was. The chef had promised to order Steven paints from the mainland and offered to help spruce up the rooms.

Alan sat on the bench, watching the sun peek beneath some heavy clouds and dip its bottom into the horizon sending golden sparkles across the waves. Content, he put his hands behind his head and stretched.

No more politics, he thought. I've had enough. I'll retire to somewhere like this. This is heaven. He had written a long letter to his wife, explaining that despite being taken against his will, he had no desire to return to his old life, to be some political pawn to be sacrificed, he wanted off the chessboard now, and he was happy. Then he turned to his marriage. It was over. He was sorry he could not express this in person but the situation precluded it. Besides, he knew she did not really care for him, but just saw in him a person with prestige and money. She could have the house and his financial assets, the London flat, and his salary until his notice was paid up. The flat would provide enough funds for his children's education, if used properly until their degrees were over. His wording was short and to the point, but each word spoke volumes. He wanted a divorce. He also had no need for his old job, so he had also penned a letter of resignation to the PM.

He smiled and felt his shoulders unburden themselves of his past. Hands shot around his eyes, causing him to jump slightly.

"Guess who?" demanded the soft voice. He laughed and drew Clarissa to the bench. She sat and rested her head against his shoulders. "It's beautiful here," she murmured.

"We could stay, you know. If whatever they're up to fails or succeeds, I don't really give a damn, but you and I could stay."

"I'd like that. Or somewhere similar. I don't want to go back into politics again. I like this," she sat up and took a deep breath, "I like this freedom."

Jus Ad Bellum

Miles and Cosima were remounting their horses. "I'd fight for you," Miles said finishing off his previous thought.

Cosima turned her head to look at him and grinned. "Thank you, I've not had anyone say that to me before, but I'd prefer it if you'd love me."

He blushed but then the emotion sprang out of him, "I do! I do!" His unsuspecting horse skipped sideways before realising there was no threat. The horn sounded again. They were close, Cosima noted. They saw the fox a good half a mile ahead of the hounds, and over the ridge came the field.

"That one will survive," said Cosima. "Check its tail. Quite straight. It's playing with the hounds and knows where to lose them. It'll head into the covert, hit the stream that you can just about see on the hill's far side and that'll confuse the hounds. But, then again, neither foxes nor hounds are always predictable."

"The hounds are circling the wood," said Miles, reaching out for her hand as they came to a stop.

"Yes, watch the Master - he's getting the Whips to spread the hounds to reduce the fox's chances of escape."

The fox ploughed straight into the hedges that surrounded the covert with several hounds in hot pursuit. Suddenly a bellow of human cries exploded from the wood causing many of the horses to shy. Fifty or so men and women emerged chanting and screaming at the hunters. Miles noted that these antis were not like the ones Rat had gone off with yesterday. These were rougher, had shaven heads and tattoos all over their faces; their skin was punctured by studs and rings.

"Jesus!" said Cosima. "Where did they come from?"

"Looks like the anti-capitalist thugs I've seen on TV," replied Miles, calming his horse down by patting its neck.

"They look positively evil."

"They are."

The riders had caught up and paused in front of the crowd. Then out of other woods nearby spilled human debris, an assorted collection of new age travellers and anarchists, hordes of Marxist thugs and eco-warriors, all menacingly wielding sticks and poles, cursing and howling their derision on the riders.

"Miles, we're surrounded."

He looked around. In every direction sabbers were emerging to trap the hunt. Behind their position they saw about thirty yobs making their way up the hill past the ruins and up to where they now stood. Miles heard a painful howl from a hound and spun his head back to the first covert where the dogs had sought their fox.

"Oh, God, they've grabbed a hound," he said, pointing to the first group.

A burly, leather-clad oaf with long dreadlocks, goatee, and tribal piercing had picked up a hound and was holding it firmly. Cosima spurred her horse on and Miles followed, to avoid the antis marching up behind them. He watched Andrew dismount and approach the miscreant. Then he recognised Maggie, Jez, and Peterson, all cheering the brute. Miles could just see that Peterson sported a black eye. They did not see him nor would they have expected to. Their attention was focused solely on the Whip.

Miles and Cosima joined the field forty yards in front of the mob. He thought the mob looked like the urban equivalent of an ancient barbarian horde; they shouted out their curses at the hunt. He felt nauseated surveying his old allies and their friends.

A slim young man next to him spoke. "Damn, no signal." He was fumbling with his mobile phone.

Smith called over to him. "Run to the top of the hill, you'll probably get a signal from there. But be quick! This could turn nasty." The man nodded, turned his horse round and galloped hard and in between two groups of converging antis wielding long branches as pikes and carrying baseball bats. He just made it through before they closed the gap.

Meanwhile Miles could hear Andrew reasoning with the Neanderthal face to face.

"Give the hound back," he was saying, "he's not yours and you'll regret it if you keep him held like that."

"Fuck off. I'm liberating this animal from human oppression. And there's nothing you can do to stop me."

It certainly looked that way to Miles. But Andrew's left hand suddenly darted up to the dog's testicles and squeezed them hard. The dog yelped and sunk his teeth into the ape's arm. He let out a pathetic yell, but the dog had fled back to the pack, which sat under Carlton's and Tim's control, patiently watching the proceedings. The simmering mob quietened for a moment.

The Master Huntsman moved forward on his horse as Andrew returned to mount. He shouted out to the mass. "You've no right to be on this land. This is private property and belongs to the local farmer, who has given us permission to hunt here."

A particularly well-dressed anti screamed back in a public-school accent, "We don't give a fuck about property! It's all theft! Scum!" Chants of "scum, scum, scum," echoed around the valley as the antis forged their circle around the riders.

Carlton remained posed on his white horse. Miles recalled the Munnings portrait that Cosima had shown him - Carlton was similarly confident, dignified, and heroic.

However, the mob's potential dissolution was not to be. As Andrew approached his horse, an anti ran out from the crowd wielding a short thick bat.

"Watch out!" screamed some riders, causing their horses to rear and buck nervously; Andrew turned in time to see the threatening swing at his head. Fortunately, Andrew managed to block the force of the blow with his forearm, but it knocked him down. The narrow eyed, slick black-haired rodential youth was about to deal a second blow, but the second Whip had ridden up and with a flick of his whip struck the man right on the face drawing a long gash.

"You fucking bastard!" screeched the man reaching up to his torn face.

"No more than you," replied Tim, diligently controlling his horse.

Andrew stumbled to his feet, his face pale. "It's bloody broken," he said clutching his left arm. "Let them fucking have it."

The Master scanned the circle of angry faces. He called for the riders' attention. "Hold still, all of you. Form up behind me. Tight. Next to - not behind one another," he shouted. The riders obeyed.

"Mr Carlton is an ex-army officer," Cosima explained to Miles as they pulled their horses close to one another. "Follow his directions. He knows how to disperse a crowd. Whatever you do, just sit tight, hold on to the horse, and his mane if you have to." Miles looked to his left. He and Cosima were close to the line's end, and to the left about thirty horsemen and women stood fast, nervous but grim-faced. He took stock of the circle.

"There must be a few hundred," he whispered to Cosima.

"Don't worry about numbers. They tend to scatter when you ride at them. Usually the men run and hide leaving the women to face the hunt, on the grounds that the hunt will not hurt the women. Not this time though. I've seen the police tied to the politicians for too long. These bastards have got away with all sorts in the past because the government refuses to give us proper protection. Once a government fails to act impartially, it loses its right to govern."

"Wholeheartedly," replied Miles. "That means the law's in our own hands."

"To uphold when others don't," she corrected, pulling her reins up slightly.

Carlton once again addressed the crowd. "You have broken the law. You have trespassed and attacked a member of my staff. You will answer for your actions. We have a man calling for the police. You are in the deep countryside - a long way from any assistance."

("Attack's the best form of defence," Cosima muttered to Miles.")

"We on the other hand have our horses and can be home much quicker than you. What you do now - is up to you. Your man," he said, pointing to the bleeding thug, "will face severe charges of assault with intent to endanger life. The rest of you may peacefully disperse."

"Fuck you!" came a chorus.

"The fucking pigs don't give a damn about you bastards," shouted one.

"No, and they're tied up with a diversion in the local towns today! No one will be here to save you," shouted Peterson. "We have our rights! And we'll have you! We're legitimate protestors and the government's on our side."

"Then so much for the government!" shouted Miles, who suddenly found a voice. Some antis stared at him with hate, his old friends not still recognising him. They saw a toff, an enemy, a cruel, twisted soul who thought hunting was just - someone to be stopped at all costs.

"I agree," said another hunter three horses to Miles's left. The field faced its moment of choice - to back off from mob rule and the personification of state power and violence, or to stand up for their morality and rights.

"Well said, Miles," whispered Cosima.

The Master steadied his horse in front of the seething mob. "Morality," he shouted, "comes before the law and you have broken moral laws, regardless of what the government says about it."

"Don't you fucking preach to us about morality, you sick scum!" shouted a corpulent woman. "Government's on our side, and there's nothing you can do about it."

The mob chanted, "Scum, Scum, Scum," in belligerent unison. Chants and curses raged from intense, screwed-up faces.

A denim-clad man pulled his penis out and urinated in the direction of the hunters. "Piss on you!" he shouted, but he pissed mainly on his own feet before drunkenly reeling away.

"Hold steady," called the Master, noting some skittish horses. "Follow my lead, we shall hold them until the police come."

"Don't you get it, you fucking toff? They're not coming, we have them working elsewhere!"

Carlton, who had seen mob dynamics in action before, was aware that its common hatred soon overwhelms any sense of restraint, especially amongst the women. He stiffened and shouted out again to hold steady. His command was met with derision from the mob, which heaved rhythmically, unknowingly echoing an ancient human battle tactic very well understood by the Master, and ironically a distant echo of ancient communal hunts. The hounds stood between Tim and Andrew's horses, their hackles up. Older hounds bared their teeth, and the younger ones circled anxiously.

A stone flew from amidst the mob and hit a hound squarely on the head. It whimpered and collapsed forward on its front legs before keeling over suddenly, shaking for a few seconds. Word went down the line that the dog had been killed. The riders looked at one another horrified, while the Whips tried to calm the other hounds. Carlton called for them all to keep their position. Another stone caught his horse; it reared for a second before he steadied it. "Hold steady!" he called once more to his field. More stones and clods of earth flew at them, hitting riders on their hats, their arms, and their horses. Another dog fell, this time only injured; it yelped and shook its head as blood poured over its nose. A stone whizzed past Cosima's head and one fell to the rear of Miles.

Miles felt no fear, although things were certainly turning nasty. He too momentarily checked the flanking hills for any sign of the police. None. Neither could he see Gemma. His head snapped back when he heard the Master shout.

"Eyes forward! Hold steady! Focus on a point behind the mob. Keep it in your mind and get there." The earnestness in Carlton's voice focused the entire hunt. Many stones now pelted down on them; a woman to Miles's left yelped and he saw blood pouring from her ear, but she steadfastly held her position. "Hold steady! And on my command!" shouted Carlton. Miles keenly mimicked Cosima's moves.

The mob moved slowly towards them throwing stones and clumps that landed on and around them. One caught Miles's arm, but he ignored the dull pain and kept his eyes rooted on the mob. He faced something he had never faced before. He had never got into a fight with anyone at school, he had avoided trouble, always dodged the obvious bad spots in town. His inaction on the train was symptomatic of his general pacifism. He had been lucky, but then he also felt that he had missed out on some defining experiences. Now he sat on a horse facing a violent mob; he was about to enter a battle. He felt like an officer at Waterloo, a French knight at Crécy, a Hussar, a Lancer; his blood pumped harder and his veins stood out on his temple, his eyes widened and his vision focused onto a specific target to ride to. His awareness of the external world intensified, his breathing increased, his heart pounded; he instinctively sat upright in his saddle, his chin up, looking down on the unruly mob with the arrogance of unclaimed officer ancestry.

He despised people for the first time in his life. An emotional flash surged through him connected to the realisation that he was fighting for liberty, for freedom, for a life with Cosima, and there in front of him, lurching maniacally towards them, was the great enemy of man's freedom - the valueless, directionless, blank-eyed nihilistic mob, spewing its curses and self-hatred into the air. Its soul rose above him, as in his dream, as the great usurper of life that desired to spit men out and swallow their souls whole leaving nothing but amoral hunks of flesh falling into mechanism and death.

He took a deep breath as the adrenaline fought its way around his body, the life force pulsating around him, energising every muscle. Up until now, he realised, his life had been empty; now he felt morally grounded. He felt invincible to the stones that pummelled them. His stature expanded visibly in his own mind, and his horse took on the spirit of his comrade-in-arms. A sense of solidarity rushed through his veins as he took a peek at Cosima, who likewise sat stone-faced, concentrating on the horde. Her eyes flashed with pride. He turned back, his ears tuned to the Master, his eyes to the threat, his soul with Cosima and his values for liberty and for a land that he was just beginning to know. Threatened by a people who derided freedom, and he knew them - he had listened enough to their conversation. Here were a people who excused their violence in the name of raging against the machine, against capitalism, against wealth, against dignity, against anything their lowly intellects could not comprehend or their indolence refused to strive for. Any sense of achievement was to be destroyed by the mob, and he knew first hand the dulling effects of their snide and sarcastic comments. There in front of him stood the condemning mob of school and life, who despised his mind and who acted to undermine his confidence with their glorification of ignorance and depravity. They, he realised, were truly the small people of the world - the average and pathetic who dragged the world down, so they could embrace the ensuing misery.

He focused on one man in particular - a sneering, drooling, barbaric mess of smells - detritus of modern life, held up as the ideal of postmodern thinking - and so nothing.

Cosima reached out and squeezed his hand. "Good luck," she said.

"You too," he replied smiling at her vibrant face.

"One more secret."

"Hold steady!" shouted the Master. Miles watched him out of the corner of his eyes. His horse had straightened its legs and paraded as if it were practising dressage. It was a beautiful sight as it marched with its head caught close to his neck. A stone hit Cosima in the chest and she wheezed.

"You alright?"

"Yes, just winded, I'll get that little shit," came the swift reply.

"On my command!" shouted Carlton. The riders stiffened at his bark, the hounds edging forward under Tim's lead.

"Charge!!" he shouted, kicking his horse into a furious canter. Its nostrils flared up and it threw its ears back. Within a moment the entire field followed suit. The horses' collective and nervous energy turned them into a directed, bolting herd. Miles was jolted back and he quickly had to regain his balance as his horse accelerated. Around him the riders spurred toward the startled mob. He could make out their fearful faces; hands dropped stones, bodies turned and their power melted away under the impending threat. The hounds pursued the horses eagerly. The mob shrieked and turned running, collapsing, breaking apart into the nothingness that had sustained them.

"Stay together!" shouted the Master as he approached the mob's vanguard. The line of horses was about to overwhelm the first yobs as the aimless dispersal continued. In the back lines, Miles could see men and women seeking shelter in the woods - jumping and flinging themselves into bushes and ditches. Carlton was upon the first of the mob and crack! his whip came down, opening a cheek to the world, and onward he pushed at a ferocious pace, followed swiftly by the broad line of horses behind him that now ploughed into men and women; some horses jumped at the human obstacles, their hoofs clipping heads and backs, sending bodies reeling into the mud. Some were knocked unconscious, some cut open, some screamed in pain, some screamed in terror.

Miles's horse hit a man who twisted away from the impact. Then Cosima rode into someone who fell into Miles's path; he rode over him but almost tripped his horse. He spied Peterson running towards the covert; but then a tattooed skinhead rose up in front of his vision, swinging a large branch. Only for an instant could he make out the twisted face of aggression snarling at him before he hit the man square on with his horse, sending him crumpling underneath. Then he spotted Jez running behind Peterson and for a split second his old self almost called her name; but she had lost all value; no - she never possessed any, and he even smiled when he saw her trip and fall into the mud.

Cosima caught up to him. "Stay with me!" she shouted, veering her horse and his to the right. "We don't want to get stuck in the woods."

A woman with dyed green and burgundy hair rose up next to Cosima and attempted to pull her off her horse, but Cosima was too quick and sent a decisive blow from her riding whip onto the woman's head, causing her to shriek as blood cascaded down. She fell silent as another horse ran her over.

The mob was reconvening and the riders were separating. "Behind the covert! Ride behind the covert!" shouted the

Master, taking some riders with him to the left as others fled to the right.

Those who had sought refuge behind the trees were now throwing stones at the riders and their straggling friends who tried to crawl back to the covert's security. Miles saw the hounds pestering dazed yobs, nipping here, jumping there, all working under the direction of Tim and Andrew who was managing steer his horse with one arm. Tim expertly whipped one man who tried to jump up at Andrew.

Miles and Cosima wheeled to the left as they rounded the wood and charged at a couple who stood flinging stones relentlessly at them. They rode over them, knocking the pair flying to either side. "Come on!" Miles shouted, encouraging those that had followed him and Cosima, the martial resonance of his voice shocking himself.

The riders were now converging on the covert's other side. "We must check on the Whips! They were left behind!" Miles shouted to the Master as they approached one another.

"Continue the circle Miles! Continue the circle, I'll meet you round the other side!" he heard the Master shout as he passed followed by several men on horses.

Several women reined in their horses. "You stay back and head for the hill top," Carlton shouted to them. "Don't get into danger. You can break through their lines over there, where there's a gap." A woman rider saw the gap and took control. Eight riders galloped towards the antis outer circle causing them to disperse quickly. But one woman was caught by a branch-wielding thug and knocked off her horse. Miles was about to gallop over to her but he saw the lead woman had turned her horse sharply and was aiming to plough her hunter straight into the man's back.

Cosima pulled up next to him as they merged into a canter around the covert's far side. Four others joined them, two women and two men. As they rounded the wood they saw that the Whips were in trouble. Andrew was just about to be knocked off his horse by two men, while Tim was working to pull the hounds back to safety. A thug smashed a branch over the head of one hound, killing it, before taking a sweep at Tim's horse, which reared as the blow came. Tim fell back and was righting himself, when the Master, who had seen the trouble, spurred his horse on to knock the brute out of the way. Miles rushed on to assist Andrew but could not reach him in time. The man had pulled Andrew off and had begun punching his face. Miles knew he could not hit the man with his horse without hitting Andrew, so, as he would with a bike, he threw his right leg over and behind his left and then he dropped off his horse as he approached, landing at a run and crashing into the heavyset man who was raising his arm. The surprise knocked him sideways, big though he was, indeed, bigger than Miles had realised from his perspective on top of the horse. The man now turned to face Miles. His face was scornful and vehement, twisted and morose, and his mouth fired curses. Andrew shouted something about his whip, but Miles did not have time to look as the man thrust forward.

Miles possessed a natural agility - he easily side-stepped the man's lunge, and, sticking out a foot, managed to trip his assailant, but the man turned swiftly, knowing the ruse well, and threw a punch that caught Miles square on the cheek causing him to fall sideways over Andrew.

"You fucking bastard, I'll kill you both!" shouted the man as he rose up above them. But not for a second longer could he hold that pose, for Gemma Lawrence reared up behind him and with a swift slash of her whip stung the man's head. He turned to see who was attacking him, only to find to the horse's heavy fore-legs descending on his shoulders, crumpling him into the ground. Miles tottered to his feet as Gemma pulled her horse sideways. The man was getting up.

Miles had never hit anyone in his life - he had never thrown an angry punch. But now, Miles pulled his arm back and let an almighty swing fly at the man's face catching him on the nose and knocking his head sideways and his body back into the ground.

"Bloody good shot!" shouted Andrew, managing to stand up.

"The Master!" shouted Cosima who had ridden over to help. Miles looked over to see the Master's red coat swamped by a sea of arms and punches from all directions. His horse was also overwhelmed and screeched, scared and confused. Carlton was pulled down and drawn into a small mob. Miles ran at them. Realising that he did not know what to do as he approached, he quickly tried to consider some strategy. He picked up a branch that had been cast down, and as he sprinted swung it above his head and brought it down on the first head he saw. It dropped under the blow. Faces turned in hatred and anguish to Miles, as he took another swing, catching a young woman on the cheek and causing her to spin into the arms of a banshee. He switched tactics to push the end of the branch quickly and rapidly into a man's face, causing him to tumble backward over the fallen horse, which was kicking and desperately trying to get up; but Miles saw that it had been cut badly - a gaping wound across its chest rhythmically spurted blood, its life slowly draining away.

The Master, bespattered and bloodied, was protecting his face from blows and kicks. Miles felt a surge of Achillean anger that spurred him on; he lashed out, cracking the nearest head, and then, swinging fast and hard, caught two others who stood over the Master kicking him. The horse fell into its last sleep with a whinny, as Miles punched his branch into the stomach of a particularly tall and skinny man with a rooster-style haircut. Suddenly, Tim was next to him, whipping the brutes away from Carlton; Gemma and Cosima rallied behind, smashing their whips down on others' heads and kicking with their feet. Carlton fought to free himself but was dealt a swift kick in the groin from a woman. Maggie, it was Maggie - Christ, what had happened?

She was screaming, "You fucking bloodthirsty cretin, you fucking scum, I hope you die!"

Miles sprang over a fallen anti to stop her. She looked up and saw his face, a momentary acknowledgement flashing in her eyes. He stopped for a second.

"What the hell are you doing?" she screamed. "You fucking toff-lover, you fucking traitor!" In her hand she held a rock, which she lifted deliberately. "I'm going to fucking kill this bastard! You stop me!" Her eyes flamed insanely and Miles stopped her with a swift, hard punch to her nose. She fell back unconscious.

"Know that one?" asked Cosima.

"I did, and I know a few others."

He had no time to explain for a shout from the wood erupted. A hail of stones fell around them, a few catching them on their hats and arms. "Bastards!" exclaimed Carlton as Tim helped him to his feet. "And the fucking government doesn't know why we bloody marched?!"

"Here they come again!" shouted Gemma behind them. She saw Maggie's collapsed form and gasped but then a stone caught her horse; it reared, and almost threw her off as it cantered fearfully away.

A dozen stick-wielding yobs came sprinting at the group to exact revenge. The injured who had fallen around them also began getting up and, gaining their bearings, turned on Miles and his company.

"Get Carlton to my horse!" Miles commanded Tim. "I'll hold them here." He picked up Andrew's whip and holding the branch in his other hand stood menacingly, facing the oncoming rush. Tim punched out a couple of antis and assisted Carlton to Miles's horse, which Smith held.

"Hurry man!" Smith shouted. "We need you on horseback!"

Cosima jumped down from her horse and stood next to Miles. "What are you doing?" he asked, surprised.

"I was going to ask you the same thing," she replied picking up a stone and branch. "Do you know what you're doing?"

"No. Making it up as I go along."

"Me too. So we can do this together."

He smiled at her. They stood next to the fallen horse, antis surrounding them, a mob running from the covert at them. "On my word," he said. "Charge them."

"Charge them?" she managed to ask before he shouted, "Charge!" She was caught up in his power, driven forward in a momentous bound. He leaned forward and sprinted toward the mob, his face snarling with anger. She followed, throwing her stone - too short, but the mob paused; individual faces looking unsure at the tenacity they faced. Miles let out a war whoop that came from his depths, as he increased his momentum, pushing his shoulders down into the run, pumping his thighs against the soft soil underfoot; Cosima at his side - a racing Amazon - letting out a fearful scream that caused a few antis to retreat.

Then Miles and Cosima were on them, swinging their clubs at heads, catching upraised arms, knocking men sideways; then they thrust down on unprotected skulls, kicking out at bodies, whipping out with their left hands at startled faces, before they broke through the melee and faced the hostile ranks in the coppice's trees and shrubs. Three riders had followed them - Tim, Smith, and Gemma - so when Cosima and Miles turned to defend their flanks, they found the mob dispersing under a rain of blows from whips and sticks.

Miles checked Cosima, standing radiant next to him - the face of battle and love, he thought. He suddenly stumbled forward as a stone deflected off her neck. He tried to support her, but she fell quickly, unconscious, onto the ground. Gemma had seen her fall and dismounted to come and help.

"I'll see to her," she told Miles, "you just look after us."

He turned to find the source, and saw a vile, skinny, vermiculous youth hurling stones at him. One narrowly missed his face. He ran, caught up in the unrelenting momentum of primitive battle, yelling his hatred at the now crouching man who was turning to run. From behind, he heard Carlton shout, "Leave him! Leave him!" but the image of Cosima falling was not to be erased from his mind; revenge seared his veins and engrossed his frame, as he fell upon the man. He threw a punch at the man's nose, causing it to spew blood, and threw a left to catch his cheek, but the man was falling backwards and Miles's momentum took him right over the man's head; he tumbled into a shallow ditch behind his victim. He tried to get out but caught sight of a boot speeding towards his face and felt its sudden, dull impact on his cheek. But his rage was not abated. He jumped back to his feet, unsteady in the ditch's bracken, nettles, and soft mire underfoot, and grabbing a fresh stick took a swipe at the boot's owner. The stick caught flesh, but as the man fell back, Miles lost his weapon - it shot out of his hand

and swirled in the air. He had lost his whip too, and there he stood weaponless against hands and faces seeking his demise. Tim suddenly rode through a hedge next to him and threw him another branch, simultaneously cracking his whip to keep the mob at bay, then hounds poured in, yelping and snapping at the antis, some jumping for outstretched arms and vulnerable hands. Smith broke through to his left and his horse knocked down a podgy, slovenly woman. Gemma followed Smith; she wielded a yard, crashing it on exposed heads and grasping arms. Their entrance gave Miles a chance to down the kicker again and a second to consider their situation. They were hemmed in, and although the hounds could keep some antis at bay for the moment the increasing numbers did not give them too much time.

But then he heard a shout followed by a series of yells, a blast of horns, and the spinney in which they stood was invaded from the far side by a motley host of strapping youths with thick arms and necks.

"Who are they?" asked Miles.

Tim laughed as he cracked his whip at some woman who was about to drop a rock on a dog. "Young Farmers. The boys Andrew was talking about! James and his friends! They do enjoy a fight!"

Into the wood they rushed, throwing punches, grappling and wrestling, their broad shoulders swinging sticks; they head-butted, punched, kicked, and thrashed their way through to Miles. The fight was bloody and intensified even though the numbers had evened up somewhat. Many hunt-saboteurs saw their situation was becoming difficult, and fled the wood. Others, the hardened, tattooed veterans of poll-tax riots, miners strikes, and anti-capitalist riots, pulled together to fight harder.

"Tally ho!" shouted Miles, throwing a punch at one man who stood in his way. He missed and felt a return blow thump into his stomach, causing him to double up and fall. Tim lashed the man's face, streaking blood across the man's forehead and nose, and helped Miles back to his feet, "Not like that! Watch how you hit!"

"I'm learning a lot today," Miles breathed out his winded lungs.

Someone pushed Tim from behind, causing him to fall forward and knock Miles over. Miles looked up to see a familiar but bruised face standing above him: Dr Peterson. "Flood! Is that you?" he asked incredulously.

"No, I'm Miles Thomson," he replied, sending a swift foot into the lecturer's groin. It found its home. Peterson in turn doubled over. Tim, having caught his balance, swung back round and gave Peterson an upper-cut, knocking him out. They caught up with some Young Farmers who were fighting in a corner with several antis; Miles plunged into them, pulling back long hair and dreadlocks to punch noses, kicking the backs of knees and following with swift blows on exposed necks and faces. Tim was doing the same and between them and the Farmers the fight shifted in their favour. Gemma and Smith stayed on their horses, whipping and striking at anyone in their way.

The Master suddenly rode into the middle of the copse, accompanied by three other men and Cosima, who looked eagerly in Miles's direction. The antis standing near them hesitated and then ran to escape. The horses brokered no resistance, providing a solid wall of muscle that intimidated the saboteurs who remained to be knocked down by the farmers.

"This is our land!" shouted Carlton, his face bruised and bloodied. "We shall always fight for it!" The farmers cheered and the remaining antis pulled back sullenly. All stopped to observe the Master.

"This is the land we have all fought for. We have fought for our rights to hunt this land from Norman aggressors, and we shall fight again to defend our rights from the likes of you and your politicians. Now get you gone! Get out off the land and don't ever come back!"

The antis instinctively feeling defeat morosely cursed their way out of the covert. The wood slowly emptied of the mob. Miles, catching his breath, sought Cosima.

Suddenly a sharp crack rent the air - a stinging crack that sounded like a branch breaking but much louder. Miles had no chance to see its source - only its result. Carlton was thrown back out of his saddle, twisting in mid air as he fell towards the earth. A gunshot! Miles swivelled to see where it came from, but saw only trees, nothing but trees. As Tim rushed to Carlton, Miles saw movement - a form in a thick hedge, readying its aim. Miles saw the barrel levelling.

"Noooooo!" he screamed as he raced at the man. The second shot went off - he could not check where it hit; he sprinted and dived into the hedge. A face turned toward him with a sullen snarl; it was Andy, crouching with a rifle poised at his shoulder, his face looming large as Miles crashed through the hedge at him. He caught Rat on the shoulder and thrust him back, hearing a distant muffled voice call his name - Cosima's - calling, warning; but beneath his body Rat was battling free of his grip, sliding sideways in an attempt to bring the barrel down; Miles pushing it up swiftly, the finger squeezing and watching the fearful, crazed, hating face, hearing a loud ripping of the air as the gun fired; Miles punching a fist into Rat's stomach then face, his hand pulling upon Rat's fingers to loosen the grip; a fist returning and blurring his vision, the barrel dropping, falling back, levelling, hands once more struggling to disarm Rat, his right hand dropping to the ground, finding something weighty, picking it up and bringing it down with preterhuman power, a crushing of cartilage, a falling of the gun, a weakness, a limpness, an ending, a head falling heavily to the side, a dropping of hands, an unloosing of fingers, a stopping of breath.

His vision cleared, his mouth tasted blood, he licked his lips, and brought into focus the form in his hand, a heavy jagged rock resting on a flattened face; pupils caught in nothingness; bloodied skin belying an encroaching whiteness. Rat was dead.

Ante-Bellum

"Drink this," said a face bending over him. A bruised face with dark eyes. Miles sat up and focused on the stolid countenance and the red coat came into view. The Hunt Master presented him with a hip flask. "Good brandy, it'll help."

Miles drank a shot gasping on its strength. "Thanks," he said pushing himself up from the ground. "Where's Cosima?"

"Right here," said Carlton.

Miles felt a couple of arms flung around him from his left and he could hear soft mutterings from his chest as she nuzzled in. "You're alright, thank God, I was so scared he'd shot you."

He stroked her shoulders and turned to Carlton. "But you were shot, are you okay?"

"Caught me in the shoulder, I've had worse."

Miles saw the tear in the jacket and the seeping blood.

"I'll have it patched soon. You saved my life, lad. Thank you."

"Where did that second shot go?"

"Unfortunately into a horse - Jenkins - Tim's colt," said the Master. "Bastard. Least he got what he deserved," he added looking contemptuously at the body.

"I knew him," Miles added. "From the university. There were others too."

"Don't worry, lad, you did what was right," added Carlton.

"Miles," said Cosima pulling away to look at him. "One of the Young Farmers has it on tape. He found a camera that had been dropped by the saboteurs yesterday; he caught what you did on the recorder. You won't be in trouble with the police."

The camera? Miles wondered if it was the same one he had lost yesterday. That would be ironic, he thought.

The Master turned to inspect the hounds that Tim had gathered around. "Good God, and it had to come to this."

"We lost five," Tim was saying, "Repton, Lancer, Mirkwood, Portia, and Penny."

"Christ."

"Miles, are you fit to ride?" Cosima inquired.

"Sure."

"Good, then I'll arrange Lysander so we can ride together. James says that the police are on their way."

He turned to her. "Cosima. I knew some of them. They were the people I was telling you about. I knew them."

She took his hand in hers. "But you did nothing wrong, Miles. Your friends wanted you dead, wanted us dead."

"I know. It's just that I feel ... " he paused.

"Guilty? For their conduct?"

"Yes, guilty."

Gemma was standing close by. She had taken her hat off and was surveying the corpse. "I knew some of them too, Cosima. That one's a particularly nasty character. I've seen him at a few of our meets." She turned to Miles. "They're responsible for their actions, Miles, as you are. You saved a few lives today by your action. They wanted us dead, remember."

Miles regarded the scene. Andrew was having a temporary splint put onto his arm by a woman; Tim was seeing to the hounds; Carlton had wandered off to speak to various riders who had gathered in the coppice. Gemma mentioned that a dozen riders or so had escaped. There were twenty left. The antis had picked up their injured and gone off to the north. After ensuring they were all safe, the Young Farmers had made their farewells and begun making their way back to the villages. A couple of men trotted around the covert watching the retreating antis. Near Miles's feet lay Andy's body. Blood poured around a crushed eye socket; the other eye was fixed open. The gun lay at a diagonal, pointing towards where the Master had first been shot.

Unlike the sheep's skull that fitted into its environment, this body did not, Miles thought. It was reminiscent of photos of the American Civil War he had seen - the young man lying next to his weapon with twisted legs and a crooked arm, his limbs sprawled out in an unexpected death in the woods far from his home. Miles had not seen a dead body before and the one staring at the canopy of trees was not the most pleasant sight. The blood coagulated and darkened. Miles felt the colour drain from his face.

"Are you okay?" Cosima asked.

"Yeah, just a little dazed."

They heard the distant hum of car engines approaching and stepped outside of the umbrage to see couple of police Range Rovers sluggishly bouncing their way over the heath.

"Here comes the cavalry," said Cosima sardonically, watching their progress. The lights flashed but there were no sirens.

Miles stood erect as his head cleared completely. "They should be on horseback," he muttered.

Smith laughed, "I agree, lad. Probably catch more criminals too."

All of a sudden the rabble reappeared from the right.

"Oh, Christ," said Cosima. About a hundred people stormed the slow-moving cars. First they threw stones that smashed a window or two, causing one car to veer sharply, then the throng ran and clambered over the cars, causing them to stop. They could see them bouncing the cars, they heard screams, shouts, a vile outburst of hatred. They saw the doors ripped open.

"Shit, where's that bloody rifle?" demanded Smith, he turned and ran back to the corpse as Cosima and Miles ran to convene with the Master.

The Master, holding his bleeding shoulder, solemnly studied the unfolding disaster. "Everyone get on their horses," he shouted, "we will charge those swine once more. Tim, Tim! Get the hounds howling and follow our lead."

Cosima brought Lysander over and helped Miles up. "Take your foot out the stirrup," she advised, "then pull me up when mine's in, ready, one, two, three!" He pulled her easily up for she had sprung up on three. She sat behind him and shuffled as far forward as she could. "You're driving," she said, "I'll give you instructions." She wrapped her hands tightly around his waist and he felt her body envelope his, her legs dangling behind his. "You put your feet in the irons, I'll hold on, don't worry, Jeremy and I used to do this all the time when we were kids. And he had fast horses."

Miles watched Carlton helped onto his horse by a couple of men. Others waited for his commands. Smith rode to Carlton and said something. Carlton nodded and Smith spurred his horse into a canter, jumping him over the bracken and into the open, galloping to the left of the mob.

"Ready!" shouted Carlton. "Follow my lead! And if I fall, follow Tim or Cosima! Charge!!" he screamed and the copse resounded with the thumping of hoofs on the dry floor and the cracking of branches as the riders broke out into the open.

Miles jumped a small shrub and once clear Cosima kicked Lysander into a gallop as they followed the riders towards the stranded police cars. Miles saw Smith racing ahead of them to the left of the police. Suddenly he pulled up straight, about a hundred yards below the cars, and aimed the gun. He fired. Miles looked to where the barrel was aimed. The bullet had already arrived at its target - a man who had been bouncing on the roof of a Range Rover in some triumphant tribal dance was forcibly thrown off into the crowd below. A spurt of blood decorated his fall.

A shriek went up and the gun cracked again. Another body fell from the edge of the mob's circle. The antis began running in all directions. The galloping horses were almost upon them, the Master once again shouting, "Charge!" brandishing a stick he had picked up, his left arm tentatively holding the reins, his weight forward, his heels deep into the irons to balance himself.

A collective realisation of impending doom washed over the congregation surrounding the cars. More ran, up the hill, away from the horses, away from Smith, away from the cars, but still some remained who were applying hands and fists into blue bodies. The gun cracked again and a man sprang into the air, arching backwards and falling into a heap. Now faces were clearer to Miles, thirty feet, twenty feet.

"Don't stop," said Cosima, "run through them, Lysander will jump though, so hold on."

He held the reins tightly and felt Cosima push him forward so the reins dropped slightly around Lysander's neck, ten feet, a thug with no hair, swinging numchucks, and Lysander left the ground, his forelegs clipping the man's shoulders spinning him down with a shout, they almost landed on a fallen policeman but Miles spun Lysander swiftly enough to avoid another impact. The other riders were to their left and right and had crashed into various bodies. Miles could see a few horses stumbling under the impact. Their riders colliding with shaven-headed louts who were too surprised to react for the moment. Gemma had fallen to his left then he lost sight of her.

"Pull up and turn," said Cosima. Miles pulled the reins and jerked them sharply to the left. Lysander responded well but dropping a shoulder as he turned almost unsaddling Cosima, who shouted at her horse. "Lysander! Behave!"

Miles glanced around - about twenty yobs were still there, some were fleeing, two policemen lay motionless - one face up, the other on his side; the other two PCs were struggling to their feet. One received a kick in the stomach from a raven-like man with long hair. Miles kicked Lysander at him, only twenty feet or so away. The thugs who had stood firm pummelled fallen riders. A yob kicked Gemma in the stomach. Miles shouted to Cosima, "You take the reins, I'll sort him out!" He stopped the horse and tried to get off but with Cosima behind him he found it difficult. They attracted the attention of a couple of heavyset men who made their way over, aggression straining and twisting their faces. Cosima suddenly slipped off. He saw Gemma fly backwards from another punch.

"Get off then," he heard Cosima say, and as he dropped she slapped Lysander hard on the rump causing the startled beast to fly forward and into the path of a ruffian, knocking him down as he tried to get away from the horse's momentum.

Cosima and Miles stood together then ran at the man attacking Gemma, who halted, surprised. He geared himself to swing a fist, but to both his and Miles's surprise, Cosima slid to the ground underneath the man's flailing arms and swiftly kicked the back of his leg, causing him to fall forward. Miles could not resist the opportunity - he swung his arm back and with great force smashed his fist into the falling man's nose, knocking him sideways. Cosima jumped up and gave another thug a swift, smart kick to the head, followed by a kick to the stomach that knocked him back. Miles was momentarily flabbergasted but had no time to enjoy the man's amazement.

Gemma got up, her nose pouring blood. She thanked them and picked up a discarded baseball bat.

The two policemen were still being beaten by several men. Miles rugby-tackled the first attacker in his sights to the ground. He felt a thump to the back of his neck but remained conscious. The man tried to scramble up but Miles fell on top of him and dealt him a hard blow on the back of the head that cut short his day. As Miles sprawled, he saw the second man swinging an iron bar and rushing at him, but then the man's head sprang from his shoulders and a gush of blood and brain showered the air. Smith rode up, still shooting - another man fell, caught in the back of the leg. Gemma calmly approached another man who was strangling a policeman and with one blow from the bat shattered his skull. Cosima and Miles ran over to help free the policeman.

In front of them, the raven-haired man flashed a blade at them. He was standing over the policeman that he had floored. With a swift stab he sent the blade into the policeman's throat. Blood rushed from his windpipe, the semi-conscious face drained and his head fell back. The man wielded his knife at Miles, grinned, and then retreated quickly. The remaining rogues fled the scene as the gun cracked again and again, this time over their heads.

Smith pulled his horse up in front of the cars and maintained an aim at the moving targets. "Everyone all right?" he shouted.

"I'm not sure," replied Cosima. Miles rubbed his head and shook it;, the stars faded somewhat but the ringing persisted. He turned to the policeman whom Gemma had tried to save. "This one's alive," he announced. "Gemma, you see to him."

"So's this one," said Cosima. She was next to the other policeman they had seen fighting to get away from the blows. He was sitting with his head in his hands, blood pouring over his face and hands mumbling in pain.

"What about the two there?"

Tim, who had brought the hounds up, jumped off his horse and checked. "'Fraid not," he reported. "One unconscious, one gone."

The Master walked his horse over; he had been checking the other riders who had fallen. "Use the radio and call for any assistance they may be able to offer," he said in an exasperated tone. "This is what happens when you give these kind of bastards free rein. How many of them are dead?"

Tim checked. "Three dead. Two critically injured. One who's just smarting. We have two unconscious. Mrs Willows has a dislocated shoulder, but the horses are fine this time."

Miles managed to revive the unconscious policeman. He covered him with a blanket he found in one of the cars and handed out other blankets to the injured.

"Any other guns in the Rovers?" inquired Tim.

Cosima checked the other. "No. None here."

"Shit."

"This one's got a pistol," said Miles.

"And you thought the government had made the country safe by banning handguns? Take it off him," said the Master. "Now, how's the radio?"

"Wires have been pulled out everywhere," Tim reported.

"Will they start?"

Tim jumped in and turned the key. Nothing. "They've pulled the ignition wires out."

"Can you fix them?"

"I'll try."

A series of howls and screams rumbled down the slope. They looked up and saw that the mob had reassembled, stretching out along the ridge.

"Try quicker," shouted the Master. "Smith, how many bullets do you have left?"

"Four. And six in the pistol"

"Don't use them unless you have to."

Smith, still aiming his rifle urged his horse away from the cars. He stopped to the side aiming his threatening weapon at the mob.

An engine turned, spluttered, and then hummed. "Gottit!" shouted Tim.

Cosima called to the other riders. "Help me get the injured into the back, then ride like hell out of the valley!" The others grabbed arms and steadied the injured, opened doors and helped them in. Tim meanwhile had moved to the other car and was fiddling with its wires. "No good here," he reported, getting out. "They've ripped out too much."

Cosima ran over to the Master. "David, as my father's daughter, I insist that you get into the car. There's room for you and Mrs Willows up front. The rest of us will get the horses and hounds clear. No arguments! You have to leave now."

The Master saw the Laurenten stare and acknowledged her logic. With a reluctant face he slid off his horse. "Mrs Willows - I may get you to change gear and I'll steer. Between the two of us, we'll drive." She was helped into the cab with the two injured policemen and the Master ran to the other side.

"You and I have our own horses now," said Cosima, turning to Miles. "You come with me. Tim, you take Mrs Willows' horse, Sebastian. The rest of you go with Tim. He'll lead you back to Todthorpe. Take a different route from the car though," she added. "Miles and I will head north away from the village. We'll probably attract a few our way to separate and confuse them."

"Will you be alright?" Tim asked.

"Of course. I know our land."

Tim, who had taken the Master's horn put it around his neck and jumped back onto Mrs Willows' horse. Andrew, who had been keeping the dogs together while Tim had worked on the car, now pulled his horse to their rear and called the other riders over to follow. Carlton revved the engine and turned the wheel. The car lurched to and fro as it turned around over the mud and made its way down the field following the tracks the cars had taken not twenty minutes before.

Tim blasted the horn and the hounds followed obediently. Andrew mustered the other riders to follow, leaving Smith, Cosima and Miles alone.

"I'll catch up with them in a minute," said Smith. He had not put the gun down, aiming its sights at the unruly rabble that shouted and cursed from a few hundred yards away.

"Do you know any Welsh hymns?" quipped Miles.

Smith laughed. "Only the ones to get us out of trouble."

Cosima helped Miles onto Otto once more and she jumped up onto Lysander. "Welsh hymns?" she asked perplexed.

"Zulu. Great film."

"Good ending, too," added Smith. "Well, we'll drink to your bravery in the pub sometime soon. It's time to go. You take the pistol, I'll be heading south for a few miles. I won't need it. You might." He passed the gun to Cosima, who tucked it away.

Smith remained motionless on his horse. "Right you two, now's the time to vamoose. I'll get the police, for what it's worth, to check up on you tomorrow. Good luck."

Miles smiled. "See you soon," he said. "Make sure you get away yourself"

"Don't worry about me, lad. If the horse falters, I have the gun, and if both falter, I have my training to fall back on."

"He'll be fine," Cosima assured Miles.

Miles surveyed the abandoned bodies and car. It was a messy scene. Corpses sprawled over the mud, blood still running from open wounds. The two policemen, surrounded by several ragged bodies, looked like symbols of the decrepitude into which the government had fallen. It had permitted years of protests and sabbing on private land, of death threats, injuries, insults, and fear mongering, by anarchists and man-haters. Now the state's officers had fallen in this small valley, unable to contain the belligerent forces it had unwittingly permitted to fester. He scanned the fearful but threatening mob that had arrayed itself in a long line, howling curses at the three of them. There was Thatcher's enemy within, he thought, not the miners who had been promised work on spurious grounds, but the voluntarily dispossessed, the hateful, rebellious, anarchic, excess of modern life that despised values, that trounced culture and barracked those who wanted to live peacefully and enjoy the fruits of their work, while living off them and their products. Parasites, he thought.

Cosima whipped Lysander into a canter and Miles followed.

The hellish calls from the temporarily vanquished pursued them. He turned to see Smith holding his position for a short while and before heading after the main field that was now traversing the distant valley.

"We need to make some distance," urged Cosima.

They galloped past the covert where he had killed Andy. She checked behind. "They're following the field or the car, from what I can make out. No, some are coming this way. Good, we've split their numbers."

"Can they follow us?"

"For part of the way they can. The light will be fading soon. They'll see the tracks, but I'll tell you what to do once we're over that slope there."

The horses slowed to a plod as they ascended a ridge. Still Miles could hear shouts and curses, although he was not sure whether they came from behind or from the blow to his head he had received.

Over the ridge they trotted. "We're going to make a large circle, ride back here, then ride off to that corner, there's a stream." Cosima pointed to an area between two coverts. "With any luck, they'll follow the tracks around and get confused."

She whipped Lysander into a fast canter and then a gallop and Otto followed suit. Miles felt the air rush past him and the horse pounded the ground to catch up with Lysander. He stood up in the saddle, balancing himself as he had seen jockeys race, leaning forward over the horse's withers, his thigh muscles taut and painful, his hands following the horse's neck as it strained, hoofs pounding the ground to catch his friend. They raced around the shallow cirque, until they made a full circle. Then, a third the way around again, Cosima indicated to the stream. They crossed and headed down into another valley where they met a shallow river.

"We go upstream," she said. "If they get this far, then they'll assume we've gone downstream to the villages. And if they do go upstream, there's a waters-meet a quarter of mile upstream that will divide their search further. But I don't think they'll press it that far."

"I hope not. Are we heading back to your house?"

"Yes, in a roundabout way. I don't want any intruders, not after this day."

They rode in silence up the shallow river, guiding the horses as best as they could. Sometimes the horses slipped and instinctively sought refuge on the bank and the riders had to pull them back. The night was coming on quickly. The clouds betrayed a hidden moon in the sky to their left. After a while they came to the confluence and took the right fork. "We'll be out of the river shortly," said Cosima, breaking the silence.

Miles rode on, concentrating on the path in front of him, but the day's images and sounds tormented him. His head throbbed and his body was bruised. He was tired but not sleepy. The cold air burned his lungs and periodically he took a deep breath to awaken his senses. The land flattened somewhat and Cosima veered right. "Marsh grasses. They're about a foot deep but keep him moving in case he gets his feet stuck. Keep using your heels to move him on."

The horse's hoofs moved sluggishly through the marshy grasses. The sky had lost all light except the hint of moonlight that seeped from one corner of the firmament. To Miles all was black in front and around. He could make out tree silhouettes but not much else. Then they reached harder ground and the horses moved on more swiftly through the grass. Cosima rode a few feet in front of Miles, guiding him over pastures and meadows and through small spinnies. "We shouldn't have to worry about them following this far," she finally said. "How you are feeling?"

"Tired, but alive. I've never felt so alive in some respects."

"Me neither. I'm looking forward to a stiff drink when I get in. Not far to go now. About another twenty minutes. We can trot soon - the horses know the paths and it'll be safe. Just keep your head down in case of low branches."

They trotted in the dank air of the boscage and woods and across arable fields and wild heaths stroked by light westerly gusts. The moon appeared and lit up their surroundings, the grass reflecting the silvery light, the trees presenting definition and intricate shapes to the riders. When the moon withdrew, the land fell back into an eye-straining blackness.

The nocturnal journey lasted ages but Miles did not care. He was alive and with Cosima. It would soon be safe to lower their guard and fall asleep, miles from the trouble.

"We're here," she said finally, halting to undo a gate. They dismounted and the horses trotted to their stables for food. The wolfhounds greeted them. They both fussed over the dogs and tried, with lots of licking and pawing from the dogs, to see to the horses. Cosima explained to Miles where to put the tack as she brushed them down and checked for injuries.

"I'll put the dogs out for the night. They'll keep a good guard." Cosima opened the door and cajoled the dogs out. "Off you go, go find some rabbits!" The dogs sadly left the house and marched over to their kennel near the horses. "How about a drink?"

"Indeed," replied Miles following her into the kitchen.

She poured them both a large whisky. They clinked their glasses together in silence. The sharp, tingling golden liquid burned his throat and prompted a cough. "Whoa," he commented, "that's strong."

"Family distillery in the Shetlands," she gasped. "Great Uncle MacIntyre's company. Good, isn't it? Drink up, you and I need to clean up and get out of these clothes."

"Will we be safe?" He took another gulp.

"Hope so. The dogs will bark if they hear anyone approaching. Besides, I have other guns as well as the pistol." She opened a kitchen cupboard. Fumbling for something on a shelf she took a set of keys and headed into the hall and unlocked what Miles had thought to be a coat cupboard. With a second key she unlocked a metal case, pulled out two shotguns and handed them to Miles who had never handled a gun before except the one he had wrestled with earlier. "We'll keep these next to us at all times. We'll also need these." She pulled the pistols out of her jacket and matched it to a box of bullets in the cupboard. "We have plenty of ammunition. Thank God, my family have always supported the right to bear arms."

"I don't think I'll sleep tonight," Miles said regarding the guns anxiously.

"Nor me. Right, let's get cleaned up." She led him back to the kitchen and opened up another door to the laundry room. They put the guns down and stripped off their outer garments to their underwear. Miles gazed at her supple, fit body as she threw the clothes into the machine. The room was cold and he shivered.

"You're beautiful," he murmured, rubbing his arms.

She turned and smiled. "So are you. Now, I'll start the machines in the morning, I don't want to make any extraneous noise. We can't light the fire either. We can have shower though, and I have an electric fire in my room. Come on, you're freezing!"

She picked up the pistols and led him upstairs. He thought it wise to close all the curtains and to have as little light as needed. They drew them all and started the shower to warm the bathroom.

"Before I jump in," she said, "I want to see your wounds. Come here, by the light."

He stood in his shorts as she inspected his back. He was too tired for modesty and stood there as if being inspected by a nurse. She ran her hands up his back and around his ribcage.

"Ohh, that's painful there."

"Again?" she pressed her hands on his ribs.

"Ahh, yes!"

"Probably a broken rib, or a pulled intercostal. Did you not notice it earlier?"

"No, my head hurt too much."

She rubbed the back of his neck. "Here?"

"Yes, there. But not as sharp as the rib."

"Bruised. Stop stretching your neck out, it won't do any good. But you have good muscles there that have protected you well. How are your legs?"

"Sore from riding."

"I'll get some ointments out for you."

"Cosima, you're fussing over me, I'll be alright. Are you okay?"

"You can check me over later," she smiled and kissed his cheek. "You listen out for the dogs. I won't be long."

Miles threw on a bathrobe and sat in a chair opposite her bed in the low lamp light. They had put the guns on her dressing table. The smooth metal on delicate wood surrounded by feminine accoutrements looked peculiar. Cosima closed the door muffling the sound of the shower. He surveyed her large room, looking at the vast bed with its carved oaken headboard, the several wardrobes, two heavy chests, and landscape paintings. His head nodded with exhaustion.

Cosima gently shook his shoulder. "Your turn, sleepy."

He pulled himself up from the chair and fumbled his way to the bathroom. She had left the water running. He dropped his robe and shorts and entered the baptismal fountain. The water stung undetected cuts and those on his hands but he ignored the pain as he cleansed his skin. His tired mind awoke under the spray and the impressions returned - Andy, the policemen, the shots ringing out, the punches, the screams, the falling horses, the faces of his old comrades, their shocked faces, the dead Andy, the gun, the bullet, the Master, Mr Smith, Cosima, making love with Cosima, breakfast, the pub, the dead Andy.

He shut the shower off, dried himself carefully, dabbing the painful bruises, put his robe back on and rejoined Cosima.

"I don't think it's a broken rib," he said, "for it would hurt when I breathe wouldn't it? I was hit once or twice in the stomach, I think. I can't remember."

"You look pale. Let me put some ointment on your neck and ribs, it'll soothe the pain. Lie down on the bed." He dropped his robe and eased himself down. He cared not for his nakedness, he was alive and he had been through hell, and with an angel at his side who was now taking care of him. He murmured his thanks as her fingers massaged cool oil into his neck and along his back. He felt a coldness penetrate the muscles and smelled a sharp, pungent odour. He felt her shift and rub the oil into his hamstrings, which ached from riding.

"Turn over," she said.

For a second he paused, having become aroused from her tender massaging of his legs.

"Not injured there!" Cosima giggled and he burst out laughing.

"Oh, that hurts to laugh!"

"Well don't laugh," she said massaging oil into his ribcage. "I won't get this near your happy and healthy problem, for it'll sting like hell!"

"I'm just happy to be with you," he murmured sleepily.

"There, all done. I'd better go and wash my hands thoroughly. Can you get the bed ready?"

She hopped in next to him and switched off the light. She cuddled close to him and laid her head on his chest, but that hurt so she snuggled into his neck. "Miles," she said.

"Yes?"

"We'll be okay. I'm glad you're with me," she slipped her leg over his and he turned to kiss her.

They fell asleep within minutes, wrapped up in each other's legs and arms.

Gemma

Miles awoke with a start. He had heard something. Cosima had her back turned to him and he had an arm underneath her head but his sudden action, a sharp breath and a tensing of his muscles stirred her.

"I heard something."

She sat upright. "Get the shotgun. What time is it?"

He looked over at the clock. "Eight in the morning."

"Eight o'clock! We slept that long! What did you hear?" They tumbled out of the bed throwing on bathrobes, and Miles grabbed a gun. He didn't know how to fire it but its heavy, cold barrels felt comforting. Cosima pulled back the thick velvet curtains that had kept the daylight out.

"It's very misty out. I don't see anything." She opened a window a crack and the cold air whistled in. A dog barked a few times.

Miles moved swiftly to Cosima. "Are they here?"

"No, I don't think so. That's Boudicca's bark. She's not unduly concerned." She leant out of the window and called. "Boudicca! Good girl. Who is it? Go fetch them!" Miles watched the animal bound over the gate and run off into the woods.

"We'd better get dressed."

They threw on their clothes and went down to greet whoever was coming. Cosima quickly showed Miles how to fire the gun and told him to take position near the one barn in case there was trouble, while she waited at the porch.

The garden air was fresh. The mist lay around the trees near the woods. Miles ran over to the small barn and waited nervously. He heard the sound of a horse pattering along the path. Boudicca returned. Caradoc and Cuchulain were bounding around in excitement, barking. The horse got nearer and finally an exhausted Gemma Lawrence dismounted from a chestnut horse at the gate. Cosima called the hounds to her side and welcomed Gemma into the lodge. Miles put the safety catch on and stepped out from his position. Both Miles and

Gemma were surprised to see each other but of greater concern were Gemma's obvious injuries.

"Gemma! Are you alright?" he cried running out to her. Cosima saw her wounds and quickly opened the gate and took her horse. Her face was bruised severely. Blood caked her chin and forehead, and her lower lip was split. She stood, faltered and almost fell. The horse was cut in several places and was covered in sweat.

"Flood - what an irony," she said and tried to laugh. "But I'm glad I caught you in. I got lost. We got separated. Attacked again. I got lost," she repeated anxiously checking her surroundings. "Smith. Killed. Bastards. I tried. All killed. He caught up." Her voice faded as she spoke. Cosima and Miles understood the gist of her words with a growing fear, but Gemma and the horse needed immediate attention. Cosima said she would look after the horse and told Miles to get Gemma a drink. Miles took Gemma's arm and escorted the weary woman into the kitchen. He helped her into a chair and took her boots off. Her body and legs were stiff from injuries and a long ride through the night. Her coat and leggings were damp from the cold morning mist. She shivered. Miles rubbed her legs and arms to warm her and called for Cosima.

Cosima returned and poured her a shot of brandy. "She's got mild hypothermia. Keep her warm while I see to the horse. He's severely dehydrated." She fired the central heating, put the kettle on and rushed out of the kitchen.

Gemma coughed from the harsh liquor but it roused her mind. "We were set upon again. This time they had guns. But they weren't sabs, I mean. Not antis." She gulped the rest of the brandy back and spluttered. "Police. Armed unit - you know, the ones that wear black armour. We thought they were going to help us." She shuddered and tears ran down her face. Cosima came back in with a heavy woollen blanket.

"We need to get her warm. I'll sort a bath out and a change of clothes. Make her some sugary tea and keep talking if you can." Cosima's voice shook. Her face was pale but she threw herself into her duties.

Miles took the blanket and put it around Gemma's shoulders. He told her not to worry and that she could rest soon. She shivered violently and rubbed her arms. "Gemma, I'll get your cuts cleaned. Tell me more about what happened." He rummaged in the cupboard that Cosima had her medical supplies and set ointments and plasters on the table.

"They're no good," Gemma laughed languidly through her shuddering. "I need a cloth for my face; get a bowl of warm water. I'm covered in dirt and grime." Miles responded quickly and prepared to clean her face. Gemma pulled the blanket around her and rested her head on the back of the chair. Her neck was bruised as if she had been strangled. Probably from the earlier melee, he deduced. But the thick lip and cuts had come later. He dabbed the wet cloth on to her wounds and she grimaced. "No, don't stop, we need to clean them. Just be gentle." Cosima re-entered the kitchen and sorted the tea out for them. "God, I must look ugly," said Gemma.

Miles examined her with a mock seriousness and then laughed. "You'll repair to your normal gorgeous self." She looked at him out of one eye and weighed his statement. She smiled and then winced in pain. "Thanks."

Cosima took her hand. "Gemma. What happened?"

"We rode over to the police. I'm not sure they were police though. Well they had uniforms and equipment but ... they didn't seem like normal police. I thought I saw someone I recognised - the man with the knife." She shook her head. "I was sceptical of them. No, not right. Then they fired on us. Six, maybe seven, down. My horse was killed under me. Then they came at us - wielding batons and shields and really laid into us. I saw Smith fire and hit two, but someone," she closed her eyes and lowered her head. "I had to fight for my life. They weren't taking prisoners. I don't think ... " she took a deep breath. Both Cosima and Miles knelt next to her, gently holding her bruised hands, but she withdrew them and tucked them under her arms.

"Did anyone else get away?" asked Cosima.

"I don't know. I don't think so. I don't think any of us was supposed to survive," she said bitterly. "I reckon they were supposed to finish off what the saboteurs started. God knows why. It's weird." She shook her head again. Cosima sought Miles's hand and squeezed it. He stroked it until her tension eased; he felt sick but remained kneeling with Cosima as Gemma related her tale.

"Some bastard took a hold of me and was about to knock my brains out. I kicked him hard in the bollocks and he let go. I picked up the baton he had dropped and clobbered him. Then I was hit in the face; by someone else, then by him. First bastard wanted to rape me. He said so. His mate held my arms while he punched me in the stomach. But then he took his riot helmet off and when he got close I fucking bit his nose so hard he squealed. I dug my heels into the other bastard's shins - you know, ran my heels down them, and he let go. I picked the baton up again and whopped them both quickly."

She smiled. "Very satisfying sounds. Then I ran. Bloody quickly. I saw a horse and sprang on him, dug my heels in and was off." She took some of the tea Cosima offered. "I could hear shots. They were shooting at me, but I hit a hedge and got through in one bound. Then we galloped. Oh fuck, did we gallop."

She paused and sipped some more. "I heard other shots too. Not at me." She turned her head and tears streamed leaving paths over her dusty and bloodied cheeks. She pulled her arms tighter and clenched her jaw. "It was a set-up. I wasn't supposed to escape. I know. But they didn't follow me. No one was supposed to know, I think. They would have followed me otherwise. They have heat-seeking equipment surely? They could have followed in helicopters. I believe that they screwed up."

Gemma turned to look at Cosima and then Miles. She went to speak but burst into tears. "It was so awful," she sobbed, "so awful."

They lifted her up and took her up to the bath. Miles left Cosima to help Gemma clean herself up and he went outside on a patrol. Gemma's horse stood resting. The land seemed quiet and the hounds contented. He stood breathing in the damp air and listening for any disturbances beyond the pale of the garden walls and fences. He walked around the old lodge and explored some of the other buildings to ease his mind. About an hour later Cosima reappeared.

"She's sleeping. She was very badly bruised. Her face took a bit of cleaning up. Oh God, Miles. Did you hear what she said? I couldn't get much more out of her upstairs. But they were old friends of mine ... " he voiced quivered and she sought his arms. He pulled her close and drew her head onto his shoulder. He held her tight but could not offer any words. She pulled her head away. Tears streamed silently down her cheeks and she began to shiver.

"Come on. I think we are safe here," he said and took her back to the kitchen. She sat down and stared at a cupboard as he made more tea. "Maybe others got away," he said but knew the words fell flat.

"She a friend of yours?" Cosima asked. She dried her eyes and tried to compose herself. Miles explained how he knew Gemma, how they had recently argued about hunting, and how he had been surprised to see her at the meet yesterday and that she knew him as Flood.

"Why did you use an alias?"

"I've thought about that a lot - while I was walking around outside. I think it's because it obviates the need for an independent ... for a human personality. It gives one strength. The pseudonym transcends the ego. One can live an abstract life rather than live a life," he laughed, but in the present situation it sounded hollow. "Cosima, this land seems to be falling apart."

"More than you realise, Miles," she replied washing her hands to prepare some food.

He studied her face and then took in what he knew of her and her connections. "You know something don't you? You're holding back something."

They heard footsteps on the stairs and turned to see a freshly washed Gemma enter. Her soft red hair was pulled back revealing a host of contusions across her face. "I napped, but I can't sleep in the daylight."

They took her to the library and got her to sit on a soft sofa while they brought food and tea. "Could we have some music?" Gemma asked. "Last night's ride was so silent. Every cracking branch frightened me." She put her head back on the sofa and closed her eyes. Cosima quickly went through her music collection and chose Bach's St Matthew Passion, as fitting the mood - quietly spiritual and invigorating. "Thanks," murmured Gemma.

"How did you get here?" Cosima asked.

"Smith. He had mentioned you had a lodge in the forest. All I knew was that it was north-west from the meet. I had to guess the direction a lot, but I knew the forest's borders from a map and after ... " she grimaced and shifted her position. "After my escape, I headed east first, before changing direction. I wanted to get as many coverts between me and those bastards as quickly as possible. It got dark quickly and we ended up in bracken. I fell off twice. How is he? I don't even know his name."

"Sebastian. He is Mrs Willows' horse. He's fine. He'll recover in a couple of days. Tim was riding him ... Oh, God. Tim. Was he? Oh, God. No. He was an old friend. We've known each other since we were children. Oh." Her head dropped and she clenched her jaw. Gemma got up and put her arms around Cosima, while Miles held her hand. "They were all good friends ..." Through sobs she asked, "David? What about the Master?"

"I don't know. We lost sight of them before we were attacked. I presume they got back safely."

"Did you see ... ?"

"I didn't see much," said Gemma softly. "There was nothing I could have done. I rode. Maybe some others got out, I don't know."

"I never thought attacking hunting could be so murderous," murmured Miles caught up in his reflections.

"That's why we march for liberty," retorted Gemma. "Banning anything means locking people up, fining them, or killing them."

"A hard bloody lesson," he scowled. "Cosima, you do know something. Please tell us."

Cosima rose and walked to a window. She peered out at the garden and forest wall surrounding her house. She sniffed. "We're on the brink of civil war. My father is involved. I don't think we're safe here. We will have to leave soon - for Stanthorpe."

"Civil war?!" spluttered Miles. "Civil war? This is England for Christ's sake. We don't have wars."

"We've had plenty," said Cosima turning. "Not for a couple of centuries I know, but we've had them. It's been in the air for a long time, and our land is rarely peaceful. But things have gone too far recently. The government's trying to nationalise the land - the right to roam, the banning of hunts, the destruction of the farming base through welfare and regulation. Goodness, a more patient Stalin would have been impressed," she seethed.

Miles watched her face. Her eyebrows sank slightly, her soft lips tightened, her shoulders tensed as she drew an unseen burden into her mind. She took a deep breath and held it for a moment, then slowly released it. She closed her eyes as she let her breath out. "I believe that Father's done it already. He's reconvening the Assembly."

"What's the Assembly?" asked Gemma.

"Its origins lie in the old Northern Assembly of mainland Britain. It hasn't sat for a few hundred years. It used to be the northern parliament until the Stuart times. Father and his friends are keepers of the tradition, and unbeknownst to most people, including most politicians, he and a few others carry an ancient right to reconvene it. It was originally a branch of the London parliament, but in the seventeenth century various families moved it towards to a strict republican or Whig constitution. They have maintained its existence over the centuries, keeping it open as a last resort, should the need ever arise."

"Does that mean that the country will split between the north and south?" Miles inquired.

"More likely rural counties will split from the cities. We have a lot of traditional support in the north, but there's the east, the south-west and potentially the Wessex counties. Most of

Scotland and Wales, outside the urban centres, should be supportive. But I think the Assembly's purpose will be to act as a symbol of the new Britain that may emerge, one that secures our rights rather then throws them to the highest bidders or tramples on freedoms in the so-called name of democracy and progress. The Assembly exists for emergencies in case London is destroyed or invaded, but also for times when Westminster has stepped beyond its remit. Father is the presiding chair, which switches amongst the families every four years."

"Sounds like a Mafia deal when you say 'families'," said Miles rising from the sofa.

She laughed laconically, "I guess it does. But the families who are appointed to the Assembly are committed to securing freedom and justice. They swear oaths to various ancient treaties for a life-long commitment to its principles."

"Are they not democratically elected?"

"Not in the sense you mean. Freedom's too fragile to be handed over to a mob, with politicians promising to feed their bellies with other peoples' food. The Assembly has a strange structure, but let's say it has severe checks and balances on demagogues."

"Excellent," said Gemma. "My kind of political philosophy."

"I know. Miranda Whitman had noted you."

Miles was puzzled, but sought to discover more about the particulars. "So who are the other families?"

"Various descendants of the old feudal orders to some extent, with new additions in the past century from those who have shown their commitment to the land's liberty."

"Are they all Peers?"

"No, some are. Others are journalists, academics, doctors, barristers, farmers. We have a couple of novelists and a smattering of businessmen and women, as well as a few full-time conservationists and hunters. About seventy in all."

"Do they just come from the north?"

"No. In the past they did, when the country was more diffi-cult to get around, but we have people from all over these days. Their ancestors may have moved or they may have lived and grown up elsewhere. Their abode is irrelevant. Their commitment to the land's heritage and freedoms are vital."

"Is your father a Peer?" asked Gemma.

"Yes. Lord of Stanthorpe. An old title, about eight centuries old. In Scotland he's aLaird of Inverlochty, our ancient Scottish title."

"Phew," whistled Gemma. "You have found one heck of a lovely and wel- connected woman, Miles."

He laughed. "She found me, Gemma. I was lost."

Cosima smiled. "And I was lucky. We need to head out soon. We'll take three of my horses and leave Sebastian to recover with Lysander."

WILLIAM VENATOR

Stanthorpe Revisited

Cosima told Gemma to relax while she and Miles saddled the horses.

"We must take the footpaths and keep off the bridle paths." She turned to him. "Miles, you're getting involved in something that's serious. You don't have to come."

He took her face in his hands and kissed her. "I want to. I said I'd fight for you. That includes going to war for you." He laughed at the proposition, which until a few days before would have seemed so preposterous. "Civil war? Count me in."

Her face relaxed. "I'm glad. I don't want to lose sight of you. You mean a lot to me." She returned the kiss and told him what to get for the horses. An hour later the three of them were moving along narrow forest paths. The woods were quiet and they felt secure.

Miles considered the past few days, from his membership of a small sabbing expedition to being a part of a general revolt - surely, "civil war" was exaggerating matters? But he had changed sides. Where did that leave his beliefs? Could they change again? And his paths had been forged by women, as well; was he so susceptible to changing his mind? He worried that he was putty for others to mould, or that he was still truly meandering from action to action, from political position to political position, as the time or the need led him. Underneath him, his horse was breathing hard. The cold air flushed his cheeks, the wind whipped over the hills and through the forest cracking against his coat, his legs ached from yesterday's riding and his ribs and neck throbbed from the bruising. But the pain and muscular strains gave him an anchor, a hook onto the real world, a sense that he was alive, pushing his body and the horse's, racing over fields and through the woods, racing through life. He watched the two women ride and felt a strong sense of camaraderie that he had not felt with Jez and her friends; Gemma's strong but feminine form that he could not but admire; and Cosima for whom he felt admiration, love, friendship and trust. They had fought together yesterday and they would fight again. He did not know whether she would be with him as a friend or lover or more, but he knew that they shared something he had never even known that he had to share. A sense of life had flourished in her calm and solid presence, and it now flowed through his veins as its own independent presence.

They rode the horses into Todthorpe and quickly found Coates, to ask him to take them to Stanthorpe Manor. He was sitting with Price, both of them staring at their half-empty glasses. They both jumped up and embraced Cosima when she entered, and shook Gemma's and Miles's hands.

"Thank God, you're alive," said Price. Both the men had given them up for lost and they were shocked to hear of Gemma's narrow escape.

Coates briefed them on the violence. He shook his head. "No missy, all were killed in the attack. It wasn't police, but it was meant to look like them. We've spoken to Sergeant Morris. He'd been sent a fax saying that an elite armoured squad would be in the area to keep hunters and antis apart. He said it appeared official, but there was no return number or any means to confirm it. The national press has so far ignored it. One paper has a small column. It said hunters and antis clashed across the country yesterday in the wake of the government's drive to ban hunting. Some fatalities. That's all." He spat on the ground. "It don't look good. I'll get you to Stanthorpe, but we have to be careful." Cosima inquired of the Master. "He's alright. He's up at the manor, getting treatment."

Gemma sat up front and Cosima and Miles sat in the back as Coates drove. She reached over and held his hand.

They left the village and drove to the nearest main road, which gently twisted over the moors. Coates took a turning onto a very narrow road that curled over a hill to give a commanding view of the moors. Miles viewed the vast emptiness punctuated by small sodden tufts of grasses, gorse bushes, and hundreds of sheep. The car came to a gate and Cosima jumped out to open it and let the car through. When she got back in Miles asked her if they were near the house.

"A few miles yet. See the rift in the moors over there, we enter that and follow it to the one end, then it's another couple of miles."

"Your family enjoys seclusion, it seems."

"We call it a love of freedom. We have flats in London, Paris, Vienna, and New York when we want crowds and the theatre, but we tend to keep to ourselves for the most part." She saw his face drop for a second, recognising the distance that wealth can create. "Money is a means, Miles, not an identity."

"But the means can create your identity," said Miles.

"Help to," she agreed, "but it's a product of work, either your own or your family's, and the values they cherish are more likely to affect you than the cash in the bank. If you don't work at keeping it, it soon goes."

"Yeah, I guess so. I'm not good with money. My mum is; she keeps a tight rein on expenditures, but dad and I are frivolous. It'll catch up with me one day, I know."

"As long as you earn what you spend, you'll learn to care for your money."

He nodded and looked ahead to another gate. This time, as the car approached, a soldier stepped out to stop them. He carried a machine gun.

"Crikey," said Gemma, "who's he?"

"Security, lass," said Coates. "He's from a local battalion. There'll be others hidden around, watching us."

"This is serious," Miles muttered feeling that he was getting into something above his level. But his level of what though? He considered his reaction again and put it down to experience. He could comprehend what was going on. It was the fact that it was new that disconcerted him slightly. But this is new for them all, he thought; we're in the same boat. He turned to Cosima as the car slowed down.

"Are you nervous at all?"

She took his hand and kissed the back of it. "Of course. It's not every day that a part of the country secedes and you happen to be involved."

Coates opened the window to announce their business to the guard. They were let through and Miles caught a glimpse of three other soldiers near the tree line a few hundred feet away.

"Told you, Western Moors Regiment," said Coates. "They're loyal to Stanthorpe. Your dad must have arranged their deployment, Cosima."

The drive from the last gate followed the rift for a mile, rose up to a ridge, and plummeted down into a valley that opened up in front of them. The land was mainly forested and the road followed a tunnel of denuded branches until it reached an ornate seventeenth-century gate that drew together two high brick walls. The walls disappeared into the woods to the right and left. Another armed sentry emerged, checked their names and faces, and let them through.

"Almost home," said Cosima.

"Quite the home, miss," said Coates. "You'll need them rhododendrons looking after before spring," he said as they passed.

The darkened driveway suddenly opened up onto a vast manicured lawn that lay before the manor. Miles watched the house loom into view. It was smaller than he had expected but older. From the gates he had expected a symmetrical Georgian manor house with long rectangular windows, Doric pillars, and a shallow roof. Instead, the house was broad, its roof punctuated with tall chimneys, with irregular brick work and deep-set windows that suggested a Jacobean heritage. The door sat in a vast porch ornamented with a miscellany of stone carvings depicting family members in the guise of knights and priests, merchants and bankers, barristers and red-coats, politicians and yachtsmen.

As the car pulled up, Cosima's father came out. Miles noted that his face was lined with years of thought and of laughter and that he moved as easily and gracefully as Cosima. He was in a dark suit with a sombre green plain tie. His arms shot around his daughter and pulled her in, driving the air from her lungs in a gasp. "Dad," Miles heard her mutter, before she was plied with kisses.

"My dear, I thought we'd lost you. I've been given all the details from Price last night. I had heard there was serious trouble in your country. I feared the worst. But, by God, you're here. I heard you were in the thick of it. Oh, so much to hear, but later, later. Now, this must be Mr Miles Thomson, am I correct? I've heard about your exploits too. Well done, lad. First time fox-hunting as well?"

Lord Laurenten gave Miles a firm handshake which put him at ease.

"Pleased to meet you, sir," Miles replied, feeling that he ought to be slightly deferential but not sure whether he ought to call him sire, milord, your worship, your grace, so he fell back on "sir". Laurenten smiled broadly and welcomed him to his home.

Cosima introduced her father to Gemma and explained that she had survived the murderous attack the night before. He touched her face and looked at the cuts and bruises. "Goodness, lass, we'll get you checked, too. David's up in the west wing. We have our own doctor here." Gemma thanked him and expressed her relief at finding Cosima's lodge. "You were lucky by the sounds of it. We must get word out to your parents though. Price told me your lines were still down, Cosi? Yes, well, I'm sure they will be worrying. Come, let's find you some refreshments. Damned awful mess that we've got ourselves into in this country. Mr Coates, thank you for driving my daughter and her friends. Are you staying? No? Shame, I'd like to hear how the otters are doing in our rivers. Well, do come back once we've sorted this mess out. Goodbye!"

Laurenten led Cosima and Miles into the large hall where they were greeted by two retrievers. Cosima dropped to her knees to fuss over the dogs. Miles looked at the panelled hall, with its large portraits of ancestors from various periods, lances, regimental flags, muskets, two full suits of armour, a glass case with an old and worn feathered cavalier hat, a vast mahogany table supporting a large silver drinking vessel, and above him a wide wood and iron chandelier with electric lights lighting the room and creating black shadows in the corners.

Between the military regalia were stuffed foxes, a couple of wolf heads, and a deer with huge antlers.

"Who did the hat belong to?"

"One of my great something great uncle's, Henry Laurenten, who fought at Naseby. He had it shot from his head. You can see the hole still." Laurenten took Miles over to the cabinet and pointed out the rip in the thick material.

"Lucky," murmured Miles.

"Oh, not lucky at all. The bullet went straight into his brain. I said his hat was knocked off, which it was. It was rescued by his brother, great something great grandfather, who wore it for the rest of the battle as a sort of talisman. It supposedly spared him his life and he had it hung up in the house to ward off fatal bullets, or some such nonsense."

Cosima chased the dogs down the stone-flagged hallway and laughed to see them skid, tumble and yelp with joy. "I'll show you to your rooms," said Laurenten. "I've put you next to Cosima's. It has a bathroom and fresh towels. Mrs Arthurs, my help, will bring you anything else you need."

"Where is dear Nennette?" Cosima asked.

"Nenette, Mr Thomson, is Cosima's name for Mrs Annette Arthurs. She's been with the family for three decades. Little Cosima could not pronounce her first name and it has stuck. It's a good job she had a sense of humour, my dear girl, I would have hated to have lost Mrs Arthurs. She's been a tremendous help to the family." Laurenten's voice hinted at a sadness that Miles could only think had something to do with Lady Laurenten, who had not yet been mentioned.

Laurenten paused for a second as Cosima calmed the dogs down and then marched up the stairs that rose to the right of the doors at the far end of the hall. "Cosima, you've got your old room, although Veronica, who is coming later, did so want to use it. She adores your view and she only accepted the Green Room on condition that she may ride the horses first thing in the morning."

"Trust Aunt Veronica," said Cosima laughing.

Laurenten showed Miles to his room, which was a square panelled room with thick beams running across the ceiling and possessed a canopied four-poster bed. A wide faded tapestry hung on the one wall. To the right an open door hinted at a bathroom. The window looked out over the lawn and the driveway and the forest they had driven through.

"You freshen up, Mr Thomson. Tea will be served in an hour." Laurenten turned swiftly to leave with Cosima, implying that he needed to speak to his daughter, whether about him or about the country's affairs Miles was not sure. Cosima turned to close the door and sent him a smile. "See you in a short while. I'll show you the rest of the house later." She closed the door and Miles was left wondering once again about his newfound position in life.

He examined the portraits and photographs. In a frame on a writing desk was a signed note from GB Shaw: "It isn't mere convention. Everyone can see that the people who hunt are the right people and the people who don't are the wrong ones. Regards, GB Shaw." That was a good place to begin, Miles thought, moving over to the window to check the view. He took a shower, then considered the capacious bed with a grin and dropped himself into its middle.

He felt swamped sinking into the soft mattress and felt protected by the four posters and canopy. Protected enough for some barriers to fall.

As he lay there the images and emotions of the past few days inevitably resurfaced. He knew they would, for he had felt himself repressing immanent surges from various recesses of his mind. Now they were free to escape as if the iron hand holding them in check had been lifted from the threnodic chorus waiting in the wings. He did not have Cosima next to him to talk to, to distract, or to be distracted by. He was alone with his conscience. The initial, tender dripping of one or two images he could handle, but then they suddenly gushed forth, leaving him physically reeling and dizzy as a result. The palpable pain from his fight with Rat struck like a torpedo into his heart. He had killed a man. The image of Rat's body arose before him, teasing and reminding him of the surprised face contorted by physical damage, the blood running and thickening, the twisted baseball cap, the slightly doubting mouth, the cramped right arm, and the strange twisting of the legs. Miles's stomach knotted and his eyes blurred with tears. He wanted to turn over to his side, to protect himself from the pain's intensity, but he also knew that that would only postpone it temporally.

He faced the guilt and immensity of his action, gazing at various images on the tapestry that bedecked the top of the four-poster. A lion, a tree, a unicorn, a hunter, trees, castles, peasants, deer; his eyes flicked from one to the other in quick succession as his brain tried to cope with the emotional overload. He could not stop a sob, and with one came two, then three. He controlled himself after several more, allowing them to come but not wanting them to take over. Although he thought that it might be beneficial, he did not want to burst out with loud sobs that would attract attention.

He took a deep breath and let the sobs subside. He forced a rhythm to his breathing and relaxed his muscles. He had been right to defend himself and the other people, and the death, the killing, he thought, preferring to use the more precise term, was necessary to avoid others' deaths. Still, the logic could not keep the wailing emotions at bay. He took another deep breath to hold them back. His hand was shaking and his breath shallow despite the forced deep breaths. The authority that had faltered in coming forth now made its presence clear and paramount.

Guilt, the culpability and self-reproach of having committed a wrong, took centre stage and cast aside the other choruses of reason and bewildering emotion. Its source was the deep echoes of the instruction he had had all of his life, the harsh comments on murderers, the facial grimaces of people reading of killings, the sadness, confusion, and pity evoked by images on the television, the commandments evoked by thousands. Up rushed the violent storm to batter against his whole body. He shut his eyes tightly and crossed an arm across his face to bear the pain better, to shut out the exterior to fight his internal audience of berating criticism, disapproving, censuring majority, and unwillingness to permit a moment's freedom.

He had permitted guilt to hook into his every fibre, now he had to manoeuvre his thinking to come to terms with it, to negotiate a peace or at least room to subsist under its harsh moralising glare. This would be hell: to live this reminder, this pain, without any slack. He rubbed his anguished forehead to ease the stress; he took control of his breathing and reasserted control over his conscience. He had to live with this death. He had to put it into context. Gemma's escape from death, the murderous intent of the saboteurs. The threats to his life and to those of Cosima's friends. The stone hitting Cosima. The death of the Master's horse. The firing of the gun.

A hand stroked his hair and he jumped, rising up and gasping as if he were rescued from deep waters.

"You okay?" It was Cosima. She was sitting next to him, gazing down with concern at his furrowed brow and scared eyes.

"Yeah," he breathed out. "I will be. I can't get over what happened. What I did, I mean."

She lay down next to him and pulled him to her chest stroking his hair. "Miles, it will never go away. These things don't. But they get smaller and less painful. You'll experience other things to balance this feeling out," she added lifting his face up to hers. "Kiss me."

He pushed himself up to meet her lips and kissed them softly. She pulled his head closer, opened her mouth wider and sought his tongue with hers. It was a passionate, emphatic kiss that did its magic, as it was supposed to. He felt his shoulders relax and his forehead unknot its tight brow, but she would not let him go. She put all of her attention into the kiss and he was caught up by it. It was loving, caring, and sexual. He felt himself arouse and his hands sought her hair and her breasts. Then she stopped kissing him, rolled him over and sat astride his hips. "There, feel better?"

He laughed, "Yes, thank you." He wanted her, he wanted more of her lips. His hands toyed with her ribs and waist. She bent down and kissed him gently. "We can't. Tea's in about twenty minutes and I wanted to show you the rest of the house."

"Are there secret passages or places we could go?" he insisted, rubbing her thighs.

"Miles, we're next door to one another and we have, if you hadn't noticed, a communicating door. Dad's quite diplomatic but also generous when he allots rooms!"

"I like your father," he laughed as she tickled his ribs. "Okay, okay, okay, I feel better, quit!" She freed him and grabbed his hand to take him around the house.

As they passed back into the large hall a maid announced that tea was served in the family room. There Laurenten welcomed him in and made comments about the house, what was being repaired and the problems he had had with the roof.

"So Miles, have you known Cosima long?"

Miles smiled at Cosima. "Only a short while," he answered truthfully. "I was lost and happened upon her, or rather she rescued me."

"Cuch found him actually," added Cosima.

Laurenten laughed. "That's quite a meeting then. Lost and found. By Cosima too, very fortunate. You help yourself to sandwiches and there's tea and coffee in the pots. We'll arrange for the stronger stuff later when the guests arrive. Please, sit down."

Miles sat on a soft broad armchair with Cosima to his right on a matching chair and Laurenten opposite him on a sofa.

"From all accounts, Mr Thomson, you were quite the warrior yesterday."

"I killed a man," said Miles flatly.

"Sometimes you have to. He had shot Mr Carlton and had fired a second shot. You were lucky not to have been killed, I understand. I hear that you ran at the man and wrestled with his weapon. Do not underestimate what good you have done. To kill a man is of course a serious business, but you must not feel guilty. You were resourceful and you did the right thing."

"Were you in the army, Lord Laurenten?"

"Yes. I did my tour of duties in Cyprus, the Falklands, and Northern Ireland. Saw my fair share of death."

"Did you ever kill?"

"Yes, I did, as a matter of fact." Laurenten glanced at Cosima with a look that said, sorry I hadn't spoken to you about it before, but now I think you're mature enough for me to admit it. "I know, it hurts, but I'm also telling you that you must not let it worry you and become a millstone around your neck. Yesterday you were in a battle, one of many fought across the country. You did not murder anyone, Mr Thomson, you killed a dangerous enemy."

Miles nodded. He felt better to have some connection with Laurenten regardless of how surreal.

"Guests will arrive from seven onward," said Laurenten, taking a sandwich. Dinner's at eight. Drinks at seven. Then we shall be having a closed meeting from nine in the library. You and Mr Thomson shall entertain the other guests. We don't know how long the Assembly will last tonight, I am hoping for a resolution to be passed that can activate the Assembly, so tomorrow we can get on with issuing the tasks. I am hoping that you will be able to offer your services, my dear."

Cosima nodded.

"And you too, Mr Thomson. We could do with men with the guts that you have."

Miles nodded, swimming in a current of insecurity about how he could possibly help. But he felt himself mature with the possibility of some effective responsibility. He felt important and strong, and he felt depended on. This cause required broad shoulders and he had shoulders to lend.

"Right, so I can count on using both of you in some enterprise? Good. Now, how is your playing going, my dear?"

"Well, very well."

"Jolly good. And I hear that you played magnificently at the fund raiser? You must play for your father. Your cousin Dugald's coming up the house tomorrow. And I hear that you are a student, Mr Thomson?"

"Yes, sir."

"What are you reading?"

"Literature."

"Any focus?"

"Well, recent events and conversations have piqued my interest in hunting literature. I may pursue something along that line in a postgraduate course."

"Before tea I heard some more news. Riots have broken out in London following farmers' protests that brought the city to a standstill. Animal rights activists started attacking the fast-food chains, and when the two met, it wasn't nice. They are sacking the capital, by the sounds of things. A few had brought their muck spreaders and some have brought carcasses to drop off in front of Downing Street. The farmers' patience has been tested too many times I think in recent years. The thing is that they are armed to the teeth, it sounds like. The animal rights hippies soon skipped it once shots were fired. The Metropolitan Police have demanded army assistance, but we have seen that there won't be any help from that quarter. The local regiments have sworn allegiance to our Assembly or to the Queen, and are presently ignoring any directives from Downing Street or Westminster. I just hope that we don't lose too many people. We need the numbers. But these things also take on a momentum of their own."

Cosima and Miles sat in silence, listening to Laurenten. Miles knew he was involved in the making of a new history for Britain, and it excited him. Cosima turned and read his excitement.

"Dad, do you think you will succeed?"

"Timing is crucial as is the publicity we'll require. We have the funds to wage a quick campaign of posters, text-messages, emails, web sites, and contacts to ensure that we have international support in what we are doing. The Assembly, if it agrees to sit, will decide on our course of action."

"Are we truly involved in a civil war?" Miles asked.

"Not yet. We have seen riots and pitched battles between various anarchist groups, with the police and hunt groups. Several police chiefs have cut themselves off from the national force so they can act independently. This can prove very dangerous so we are negotiating with as many as we can to pledge allegiance to the Assembly. We are assured of a good many army regiments. The problem lies with the large city police forces that are unlikely to come over to our side. They are thoroughly urban and pro-Westminster. Not much we can do there. Over the next few days we should see where the balance lies. By then, all going well tonight, our campaign should be up and running."

"Will it be violent?" asked Cosima.

"That depends on many things. We have to assume that it will to some extent, at least that's the line I shall be arguing tonight, and thereby we must prepare ourselves well. Well, I should go and prepare the staff and I have a few phone calls to make. I shall see you two for drinks later." Laurenten got up and shook Miles's hand and gave Cosima a kiss on the cheek.

"Let's explore the gardens," said Cosima. "I want to show you the ponds and my private orchard." She winked at him.

Masquerade

That evening, Cosima left Miles to change, saying she'd be back in a while to help with his bow tie and cufflinks. When someone knocked at the door, Miles opened it to see Mr Wakeman holding a box of shoes for him.

"Goodness, what a surprise! Now you said you were going rambling with your girlfriend and wanted to impress her parents; if I'd only have known it was Lord Laurenten's daughter! So, you are the same Mr Thomson that patronised my shop on Thursday, and who, I hear, was a hero in battle yesterday? This is a set of coincidences."

Miles was unsure of what to say so invited Wakeman in. A question occurred to him. "Cosima says you're on the delegate list. How long have you known about its existence and the duties that you may have to perform? I've only known about for a few hours."

"Ah, not until I was twenty-five. My father had to consider whether I was worthy of the privilege. Not all sons or daughters are chosen. He sat me down and asked a series of questions that I would have thought more appropriate for a job interview and that was that for a few weeks. Then he pulled me into his study, and gave me a glass of port. I shall always remember that."

Mr Wakeman took the shoes out of the box.

"He outlined the nature of the Assembly and how the privilege was to be mine once he passed on. Well I must say I was rather bemused by the conversation, but I had to swear an allegiance to the Assembly and to maintain its secrecy. My father was a prescient man. He related that when his father had told him about the Assembly they agreed that its use would probably not be required in their lifetimes. My father however, when I had made my pledge on an old book of its constitution, looked me in the eye and said, 'son, you will more than likely be called to serve.' That was in the early 1970s when it did look as if the country was about to fall apart. Indeed, my father told me that several key delegates met that year, for the first time since the 1930s, and they were very close to calling the entire Assembly."

"Why didn't they? The 1970s, from what I understand, were very divisive and the country was plagued by strikes and bankruptcies."

"Prevarication I think. Some Members thought things would blow over, but again, the Assembly was almost called in 1982 when unemployment was high and riots were threatening civic order. But a wind of change was blowing through the country and the delegates decided to watch events very closely. Do they fit? Good. Walk around a bit. My father attended that meeting and had pressed for its convening. He told me that the country was on the edge of a precipice and that if things did not change quickly the nation would have been lost. The Falklands War changed the delegates' perception, he told me. But now we have nothing on the horizon to unite the nation, and in the past five years we have come very close to seeing the dissolution of the Kingdom."

"You mean because of the Scottish Parliament and Welsh Assembly?"

"Yes, but more than that. The nation of Great Britain cannot be lost with three divergent nations, of that I am sure. But once England, Scotland, and Wales go it alone, the apparent powers they gained as independent states will be eroded by the European Union - the old divide and conquer policy. It's already on the cards, but the separate countries will quickly be assimilated into the European hegemony that the Tudors managed to pull us out of. Secession, on the other hand, will ensure our independence. We'll be seceding from Europe as much as from Westminster."

"Will you be arguing for this tonight?"

"I certainly will. Some delegates are not Euro-sceptics though, so the wording of the manifesto, if the Assembly agrees to sit, will have to be very careful."

"Is this a meeting of Tories then?" Miles straightened his shirt in the floor length mirror.

"No. Many Tories would not abide what we plan, do not know of the Assembly, and will react harshly against it anyway.

Although I do believe I caught sight of Michael Radcliffe earlier. The Assembly Members straddle the political spectrum, but all are united in their belief in the primacy of traditional rights. They all despise the sovereignty of Parliament."

"But if Parliament is not the sovereign body, who is?"

"The law. Americans call it the Constitution and the Bill of Rights. We have no such documents, for our law is conventional and customary, but it amounts to a similar process. Some things cannot be outlawed by Parliament; the law proper precedes government; its with what we judge governmental standards. Anyhow, you'll be surprised to see who comes tonight, people you might not expect."

"Is this a branch of the Masons?"

Wakeman laughed. "No, not at all. This is a sleeping parliament, if you will. It lies dormant and only is called to session if the land is on the verge of collapse. I do think that it should have sat in the 1970s though. It may be too late now to change the problems that were born during that decade and the 1960s. Well, some go back further, but that's another story. You may hear and learn much tonight."

Miles thanked Wakeman for the shoes and asked how much he owed him. "I'll do them at cost, which is sixty pounds, since you will be helping the Assembly. Pay me when you get your first month's pay."

"Pay?" Miles was confused.

"Indeed. Lord Laurenten said that you and Cosima had agreed to offer your services, and your services will be paid for."

"Where does the money come from?"

"The land interests of the Members, who agreed four hundred years ago to defray some costs of the Assembly. All Members contribute to a fund that is presently quite substantial and earns well for the Assembly. In other words, it won't be taxpayers paying you, but the Assembly from its own fund."

The adjoining door opened and Cosima swished in. She was wearing a blue silk full evening gown, off the shoulders, with a triple stringed pearl necklace adorning her neck. She wore her hair up in a multitude of twists. A few curls she had left to fall delicately around her cheeks in the Regency style.

"My dear Cosima, you look absolutely marvellous!" said Wakeman. Miles stood open-mouthed. He had never seen anyone so beautiful in his life or anyone so well dressed.

"Cosima, you look," he smiled broadly and nervously and the words stopped. Her shoulders recalled her recent nakedness and their intimacy, her hair suggested a Greek goddess, her dress, the richest of European princesses of the belle epoch, the necklace, a simple symbol of dignified wealth. Her blood-red lipstick accentuated the contrasts of her pale skin and dark hair. "You look," pretty, beautiful, no, not right. "Stunning," he finally said.

She laughed. "Thank you, gentlemen," she said giving them a twirl and sending the dress into a delightful hushing spin.

"Well, I had better return to my room to finish unpacking," said Wakeman. "Delightful," he said to Cosima, kissing her hand.

Miles stood for a few moments, not knowing what to say, then finally he thought expressing his incapacity to say the right words would help. "Cosima, I have never seen anyone so beautiful, so well-dressed, so stunning, so gorgeous." He hesitated nervously over the words. "I'm rather overwhelmed, I don't know the proper words to say, to describe how you look to me. You look fantastic, a goddess, the prettiest girl in the world."

She laughed a joyous laugh and took his face in her hands. "Miles, I could see what you felt on your face. You don't always have to plumb the depths of your vocabulary to express how you feel. I can see what you feel, and that makes me happy. But your words are beautiful and they make me feel even more radiant." She kissed him gently on the lips. "Now, you sir, look incredibly handsome, quite ... mmm ... remind me to seduce you later."

"I won't forget!" Miles laughed. "But I was planning on seducing you."

"Miles, you do that every time you look at me, don't you know?" She kissed him once more then wiped the slight mark of lipstick of his lips. "Now, we had better head down for drinks."

"Will you know many people?" he asked as they descended the staircase.

"A few. But I recognise the names of many more. There will be some famous people here tonight."

"Celebrities?"

"Good lord, no. They have nothing to offer the nation. No, I mean editors, academics, peers, barristers, writers, intellectuals, composers. We have a couple of actors you will have heard of, I'm sure; that's the closest we get to celebrities, but their privilege has been in their families for generations. Oh, you may be surprised, but after dinner, the men all go out to the lawn to water it." Miles was astonished. "I'm serious. The ladies hog the bathrooms you see. It's an old tradition, so don't feel ashamed to join in."

"What if it's raining?"

"You still go out."

He grinned. "And if it's cold?"

She laughed. "Miles, you don't need to impress the menfolk!"

They circled into the parlour where Lord Laurenten was giving Nenette some instructions. "Ah, Mr Thomson, I don't think you met Mrs Arthurs, did you?" He introduced Miles to Mrs Arthurs, a pleasant woman in her late fifties with feline eyes and a broad smile. She was stolid, plain, but her eyes sparkled a kindliness that made Miles smile broadly in return. "Now, Mrs Arthurs, you make sure you get an early night. The rest of the staff will take care of things. You've been on your feet all day as it is."

"Stop fussing after me, milord, I know when I am beat, and this is the most exciting evening. I shall remain in your service until I fall asleep at my post." She gave Cosima a wink. Mrs Arthurs was as close as family but enjoyed playing the feudal serf at times. She maintained a friendly and caring concern for Laurenten and was not averse to telling him off when he had failed to get things done or was lapsing into self-pity. Laurenten patted her arm, not patronisingly, but with a fraternal fondness for her.

"I mean it. You are always telling me to get my sleep or to eat my vegetables, I tell you Cosima, sometimes it's like living with grandma. You get yourself to bed early, Mrs Arthurs."

She turned and kissed Cosima on the cheek. "Have a good evening, sweet Cosi, and you too, Mr Thomson." And then she whispered to Cosima, "Your father's on the make!" Cosima's eyes widened and then she giggled and smiled broadly at her father, who winked back.

Laurenten introduced the other guests, who were staying at the Manor and as Miles got into conversation with some of them, he took his daughter to meet Joanna Ribblesdale. He explained to Beatrice Major that he had witnessed her triumph on the train and he apologised for not helping. She had heard of what he had since achieved and told him not to worry. He discussed Northchester University with Peter Hickling; then he recognised Miranda Whitman and approached her.

"Professor Whitman, I have another question about Surtees," he said extending his hand.

"Goodness, Miles Thomson! I saw Gemma Lawrence earlier and she said you were here. What a delightful surprise. I had no idea you were involved with Laurenten's plans." Whitman was attired in a slim emerald gown with a grey stole. Her hair fell in ringlets over her shoulders and exposed collar-bones. Miles recognised that she was a very beautiful and highly attractive woman, but no erotic fantasies intruded on his love for Cosima. He explained that he had not known either and that he had fallen in with the rebellion only very recently. She inquired of his experiences with the Laurenten Hunt and congratulated him on his fortunate escape. They were solemnly speaking of those who had been killed when a piano burst into life in the Great Hall.

Whitman tilted her head to see who was playing. "Goodness, that's Joanna Ribblesdale. I recognise the tune. Cosima, what's that wonderful piece?"

"Chopin's Mazurka in B flat major. We just chose it. Miles, I'm going to seek Gemma. She may be feeling rather reluctant to join us." She left Miles circulating and talking with Assembly Members. As Joanna generated a perfect atmosphere to the pre-dinner conversation, he continued to ply them with questions about their constitutional arrangements and how they had become members.

Cosima brought Gemma to meet the resident guests. She had found Gemma a green silk evening dress and a red shawl that covered the bruises on her arms. She had styled her hair so her facial cuts and bruising were covered, but Miles noted that Gemma was uncomfortable. He and Whitman went over to her to make her feel more comfortable as Joanna moved on to Chopin's Nocturne in B flat major, as the ensemble sipped sherry and despite the low-level mirth, the atmosphere possessed a grave undertone that was captured on the guests' faces. They smiled and chattered but their eyes belied a serious purpose to their assembling at Stanthorpe. Miles spotted the leader of the Opposition, Michael Radcliffe, conversing with someone, whom Whitman explained was Vincent Harrison, the leader of the Rural Alliance who had been in charge of setting light to the DEFRA building. The two were exchanging jokes and laughing merrily.

Laurenten brought Cosima back over to Miles.

"Right, Mr Thomson and Miss Lawrence," he said, "I would like you to assist me in welcoming the evening's guests when they arrive. Ah, you met Mr Wakeman, I gather?" he smiled at Miles's shoes. "I'm afraid the arrivals may be staggered somewhat. There's more chaos on the roads and trains tonight, so we may be missing several people."

"Will that make a difference to the reconvening of the Assembly?" Miles asked.

"There have to be ten of the twelve Members of the Inner Chamber, and fifty of the seventy delegates. I have eight here already, and in total eleven confirmations from the Inner Chamber Members, and about sixty from the Outer Chamber. But who turns up depends on the state of the roads today. Now, Cosima has promised to accompany Joanna for a piece, so you'll have to excuse her for the moment." Miles kissed Cosima's cheek as she hurried off to the piano. Her father had arranged for her cello to be brought down from her room and Miles watched her set up as he asked Laurenten about the Assembly.

"There are two chambers?"

"Yes. The Inner and Outer Chamber. Members circulate between the two." They stopped as Joanna and Cosima began playing a Schumann Fantasiestücke, "Zart und Mit Ausdruck". The rich warm tones of the cello inexorably drew their attention to Cosima's playing as Joanna provided the background; the piece could be considered at first mournful, but its intensity rose to grasp life and value. Miles allowed his mind to drift and contemplate Cosima's form and movements and immediately fell into a fantasy of being between her legs, her fingers running up and down his back as she explored the fingerboard; she was naked and he gratefully and lavishly nuzzling her breasts and teasing her nipples. She moved back and forth with the rhythms of the music as he entered her and made love to her on the chair. He stopped his reverie on feeling his body respond, but at least, he thought, not everything changes in life.

The party applauded the performers. Laurenten stood next to Miles and confided how beautiful the two looked. Miles agreed. "Aye," said Laurenten, "I think I'll be asking Joanne for her hand in marriage soon. I've spoken to Cosima and she's thrilled. But nobody else knows yet. We've other matters to deal with in the meantime." Cosima approached just as Laurenten saw a sign from one of his staff.

"Ah, here come the first guests. Dear, you played magnificently! I wish I could hear more of your playing. Now, since it is our house hosting the delegation, would you be so kind as to stand to my right and introduce yourself, that way you will get to know the names, and Mr Thomson, as an honoured guest of my daughter's, may I ask you to join her? Good. Cosima, do fetch Gemma from Mr Wakeman's clutches, I would like her to join us too. I am expecting Jeremy soon, but he has a tendency to meander before he gets anywhere. Now, I have several waiters who will, ah good, here they come, who will direct people to drinks. Right, off we go."

They could hear the guests arriving. A man and a woman entered. "Ah, good evening, Major!" Guests began to flow in and politely greet the four before moving onto the others. Laurenten became quite animated with people he knew, cracking jokes with them or flirting with their wives. Some came with partners, others came alone. Miles was introduced to several MPs, a few of whom he recognised as prominent Westminster faces. One woman he recalled as having been a Labour MP and quite a formidable one too, but who had resigned her seat in recent weeks following various machinations by Downing Street to silence her criticisms of toadyism. Another, a Tory MP, he recognised immediately as having served in a previous government and who had remained in the news. He did not recognise the other MPs, or the SMPs, or Members of the Welsh Assembly who shook his hand warmly, nor had he heard of most of the guests. He recognised one man from the paper he had seen at Peterson's party, and when he was introduced as John Carthill, he recalled Andy swearing at his photo. Carthill was a very unassuming, polite man. The contrast with Andy's murderous violence could not have been starker. He also recognised an actor, Richard Lacey, whom Cosima had mentioned; Miles had recently seen him playing in King Lear. He commended him on his performance. Lacey replied, "Thank you, Mr Thomson, we shall be opening with a new production of Richard III in February. I'll make sure you get tickets."

"Will the play still continue then?"

"My dear," replied Lacey, "the show always must go on. First rule of theatre."

Miles laughed. "Of course. Are you a delegate or a member?"

"A member," Lacey said with a melodramatic face. "But I do declare, that the role of King Lear seems particularly apt in the present situation, don't you think?"

"And so does Richard III."

"Oh, of course! Perhaps this winter of discontent will be made a glorious summer by the sun of Northchester once more. My goodness, the parallels! I hope some do not develop and we let the Welsh take over again. I'll keep that concern to myself though," Lacey said, effecting a dramatic paranoia. "Well, I must adjourn to the sherry. We may speak later."

All of a sudden Cosima called out, "Jeremy! Where have you been?"

In the door way stood a tall Byronic man, with short curly black hair and the hint of a permanent frown. He was wearing his evening jacket and a contrasting bright yellow tie and waistcoat. He stiffly approached his father and shook his hand, but Cosima would not have him rigid and frowning. She pulled him into a strong hug and ruffled his hair, "Oh, Jeremy, get that frown off your face, anyone would think that you have the world on your shoulders. Jeremy, meet my good friend, Miles Thomson, Miles, Jeremy, my brother."

"Ah, Mr Thomson," Jeremy said with a slight flatness, "Father told me on the phone about you. A pleasure to make your acquaintance. Please excuse my present scowl, I was in Paris and have had to run the gauntlet not only of getting a quick flight out of there but then the horrors of our transport system! It has taken fourteen hours to arrive here. My head's splitting."

Miles was unsure what to call Jeremy, for as heir to the title, wasn't he a Marquis? and how was that pronounced? Markiss or Markwee? He avoided it. "It sounds as if you need a good stiff drink. May I get you one?"

Jeremy's face melted. "Splendid idea! That will do the trick, I'm sure. Yes, make it a double whisky. No, don't worry, Cosi, I'm not turning into an alky, my nerves are just so fraught after the day's travelling." Miles broke away and quickly returned with the drink before any other guests arrived. Jeremy was talking with Cosima and her father and gladly accepted the drink, which he downed in one. "Bah," he said inflecting a Northchestershire accent, "that hit spot. Thank you. Now, Mr Thomson, or may I call you Miles? And you must call me Jeremy or Screw-face, that's Cosi's nickname for me. I hear that you were in a battle yesterday and saved our Huntsman's life and that of others? Well done, man. Were you in the TA? No? What prepared you for that?"

Miles nodded to Cosima. "Your sister."

"My goodness, either she's had you on some SAS-approved out-in-the-woods survival expedition or that is one emphatic declaration of love. How marvellous, either way." He punched his sister on the arm.

Miles smiled at Cosima who returned a warm, amorous look.

"Jeremy, meet Gemma Lawrence." Gemma had caught Lacey's attention about a play, and as he left to seek out the port and sherries, she turned to greet Cosima's brother. A violin struck up from the Hall. Cosima saw that Dugald had come in with some friends and had formed a sextet. Her father leant over. "I asked Dugald to provide the entertainment while we eat - I'll need you with me at the table tonight, but I hope you and he will play for us later." She nodded and waved to Dugald who grinned and nodded his head to her as he took up the violin.

"Brahms, I believe," noted Gemma.

"Number 1 in B flat," added Jeremy. "Do you play?" he inquired.

"Violin. And sometimes the fiddle," she smiled coquettishly. Jeremy intimated that he would love to hear her play sometime.

"I would love to accompany Cosima, if I may borrow a violin."

"I'd be delighted to hear you. We have a few violins lying around the house, no doubt we can sort a good one out for you."

Gemma caught his interested look and turned her head, embarrassed by her present state. "I hope you don't you think I look like this all of the time," she said quietly.

"Even if you did, I would say that you were still the most beautiful woman I'd ever cast my eyes on," he whispered to her.

The parlour was filling up and guests were spilling out into the adjoining hall and into the other rooms. The conversation remained quiet and formal, but too many voices were speaking for Miles to hear anything but the slightest of gists. The music forged the mood - intelligent without frivolity, yet lively and purposeful.

A waiter announced dinner.

"Well, we'll have quorum," said Laurenten making his way over to the hall. "I've been told that we have eleven Members and sixty-three delegates. Not bad, not bad at all. People are certainly taking this seriously."

"Daddy, good luck tonight," said Cosima taking his arm. Gemma had already promised to walk in with Wakeman, so Miles and Jeremy looked at one another and decided to take each other's arm and walk in together, much to Gemma's and Cosima's amusement.

The dinner proceeded swiftly. Conversation covered all topics except the Assembly's potential convention. The sextet played through the first movement of Brahms Number Two and then Dvorak's String Sextet, opus 48, before the Members and Delegates left their partners and the other guests to open up discussions on seceding from Westminster. Cosima, Gemma, and Miles sat discussing recent events with Harrison and Radcliffe. Both men sat tensely, impatient to be given a critical role in the new republic.

"It could be a long haul," Radcliffe was saying. "Look how long it took Eire to gain independence."

"Shall we be calling this republic, a 'free state' or something?" asked Harrison.

"Good point, we've not heard what we're going to be calling ourselves," said Radcliffe, which turned their thoughts to potential names. Arguments proceeded on whether republic sounded too French, and how a republic could maintain a monarchy and that title. Miles chipped in that he thought Free Britain sounded good. Cosima agreed, but noted the title was up to the Assembly. Initially, she said, it was going to be called the British Commonwealth, but that was in the seventeenth century before there was an Empire. Gemma liked Flood's idea. Harrison moved onto his worries concerning the effects on farmers, to which Radcliffe responded that they would survive - no subsidies, but no regulation either. They would be able to alienate land as they wished and raise capital through land sales and development. On the other hand, he thought that the releasing of productive enterprise from form-filling and grant applications would produce a downsizing in the industry in which family farms rather than industrial conglomerates would proliferate.

They refilled their glasses and joined the members of the sextet who had finished playing. Cosima made the introductions and, after much cajoling from Radcliffe and Harrison, agreed to play Mendelssohn's Piano Trio in D minor with Dugald and Joanna. The three ended up in hysterics as they initially tried their talents on the scherzo and decided to begin at the beginning. The rest of Stanthorpe's non-participating guests circled around to enjoy the private concert and applauded and cheered as they finished the piece. Midnight came and Dugald and Gemma adlibbed some Celtic fiddle tunes together. Cosima and Miles started the company reeling and they were in full swing when Laurenten appeared at the hall's end. They all fell silent as he gained their attention.

"The Assembly has unanimously agreed to convene and to declare unilateral secession from the Westminster Parliament forthwith."

The guests cheered and shook hand. Staff brought in champagne bottles and glasses and within minutes the entire hall was full of laughing and rejoicing Delegates and Members. Dugald swiftly reconvened his colleagues as Laurenten demanded the hall's attention.

"Ladies and gentlemen, we shall return to the hard work tomorrow, but for now, let us celebrate the formation of a new republic in our land. To freedom!"

"To freedom!" cried the hall and corks popped and champagne flowed.

Dugald's sextet struck up a waltz from Kachaturian's Masquerade Suite that he had transcribed for his quartet. Couples turned their enthusiasm into the energetic pounding of the dance. Harrison and Radcliffe had found some cymbals and clashed them furiously to the music; fortunately they were both musically talented enough to play appropriately, even if they were rather over-enthusiastic. Cosima and Miles swirled around, offering their congratulations to everyone they encountered. Cosima noted Jeremy had monopolised Gemma's attention and was tentatively guiding her around the dance floor; Wakeman was dancing with Katherine Markham, and her father was gently swaying with Joanna. The dancers were jubilant and ecstatic, an oppressive burden had been lifted from the Manor, and tomorrow the land would wake up to the raising of a new standard and the Assembly would make world history.

The Fifth Column

The phone rang. Bernard Peterson reached across his desk and answered. He gave his mobile number and hung up. He was sitting in his study, reading the newspapers' reactions to the announcement of a rural secession. On hearing the news he had rushed down to the newsagents to purchase all the papers. He periodically checked the internet for updates and left the radio and television on the news channels. His email box frequently beeped with incoming messages that for now he left unread. Eighty new messages. Sixty more expected. He checked that his mobile was on and awaited the call. It was five minutes before it beeped out the tones of the old Soviet anthem. Number withheld.

"We have an interesting situation," said a woman's voice.

"Are you on your mobile?"

"Of course. I'm not stupid. Are you ready to commence operations?"

"Naturally," replied Peterson. He automatically rubbed his chin and winced. The bruising from the fight was still raw.

"Numbers?"

He checked the screen. "Eighty. Eighty-one just come in. Fifty-nine to go."

"Good."

"Code name?" he asked.

"Thunderstorm"

"Hmm," he nodded. "To begin when?"

"Forthwith."

"Will we meet?" he inquired.

"No need. Not for now. I'll text you on this phone when it's safe. You'll understand the message. Usual place in the south."

Peterson smiled. "It's been a while," he said softly.

"I know. For the cause though."

"Yes, for the cause."

"We've talked enough. Good luck."

"You too." He blew a kiss into the mouthpiece but the call had ended.

WILLIAM VENATOR

He stretched his fingers and cracked them. He got up and turned off the TV and radio, made himself a coffee, returned to his desk and reviewed his email in-box. Ninety unread messages now. All impersonal webmail accounts, as was to be expected. He smiled at the fruits of capitalist technology that facilitated the running of hidden cells. The correspondents' messages contained nothing but a series of six numbers that enabled Peterson to know nothing more than the individual's political and operational status. If it began with a zero, they were temporarily unavailable to effect any operations. A one meant that they were available. The other digits gave a clue to their identity.

He began compiling them onto a spreadsheet program. By the time he had reached number seventy, all members had emailed in. He continued cutting and pasting till he had the full list in two columns. Only ten were temporarily unable to assist. It was a pleasantly low number. He had expected ten per cent. He opened a desk drawer and pulled out a small blue address book. He received a new one every six months. It used to be every month in the early '80s, when agitation was high and the possibility of his flat being bugged or searched was also high. The book listed the same numbers he had aggregated on the screen, but four of them were underlined. These were his immediate contacts the ones he would have to meet up with. They changed every two years. He found the relevant emails and sent back a coded message; the other operatives he bulk-mailed with a coded affirmation. At five in the evening he withdrew to his lounge and poured himself a whisky.

Across the country a dozen or more cells were commencing their tasks. Peterson did not know how many groups of agitators lay dormant; he had heard some speak of twenty and others of a few. He took a broad average and surmised it would be about twelve groups each comprising on average one hundred and fifty agents, which meant 1800 agents or so now working. Most members were low-level activists who would be smashing windows and cultivating local riots in areas of high unemployment. Others were placed high in unions and in the press and would have a greater but more indirect influence on

- 386 -

events. They wouldn't be dealing with an obedient and generally ignorant peasantry as Lenin had, but they were involved in what could be a protracted civil war in which anything could happen. He ran his fingers through his hair and leaned back on the couch. Turmoil and chaos always produced the opportunities for a change in power. The incumbent regime had riled him more than previous Tory governments, precisely because this government was supposed to bend towards his beliefs. Its failure to do so had become apparent in its first two years, and since then the operatives inside and outside of the party had silently manoeuvred themselves into more strategic positions. Peterson knew enough of struggles around the world not to be thoroughly optimistic now. The comrades he personally knew were diligent and patient. They had spent years reorganising their philosophy in light of the Soviet failure; they had learned to join the more popular and fashionable causes and to adapt their language for the new generations, who would, in time, learn of the origins and purpose of their direction. They wrote and spoke in the new political language, but continued to remind their audiences of old hatreds and animosities towards capitalists, land-owners, toffs, the rich, and the establishment.

He looked at the small selection of books that adorned his lounge. In his study were arrayed the textbooks of the cause. Here sat the diaries and memoirs of comrades who had given their energy and sometimes their lives in the world struggle. He caught sight of Warbler's latest work. He chuckled. Now there was one man who wouldn't last five minutes in the new order. Too much of an establishment man. Too bourgeois by half. He closed his eyes and imagined himself leading a mob of thousands along the streets of London to ransack Westminster and install a new regime. The mobile phone interrupted his ambitions.

Her voice again.

"Diane ..."

"No names, comrade."

"Sorry. Of course."

"Good news. All cells are now active. We should be approaching maximum operational levels over the next few days."

"Europe?"

"All go."

"This is a very enjoyable development," he replied.

"We should celebrate."

"I thought we had to wait."

"I don't think we need to with this amount of responses. Besides, I've found out that I have to arrange delivery of a special consignment to you ... Expect my text in a few days." She hung up.

Peterson grinned. He reached for the tv remote and turned on the six o'clock news. He caught the opening images: running street battles in several cities; a public sector union leader calling for strikes; then the face of a man he had not seen before but whose name was all over the newspapers and news sites on the web.

"Douglas Laurenten presents his conditions for a republican secession," announced the newscaster. The theme tune intervened and Peterson prepared to learn more about the competition. He watched the ten minutes of riot footage and the five minutes of an old friend, Roger Greensmith, propounding his thoughts on why his public sector union should opt to ignore "any ignorant and misplaced demands for the allegiance of Britain's working people by the so-called republican movement." Roger was a smartly dressed alleged sycophant of the government - the new acceptable face of unionism; but he was also a member of one of the oldest Communist cells in the country. In the late '70s Greensmith had intimated his membership to Peterson, although he was not under Peterson's direction. No doubt he had made contact with his cell leadership earlier in the day and was now slowly unleashing the forces at his disposal. Roger was calling for a 24-hour public sector strike and for a march in London to support the Westminster government. Clever, thought Peterson. Greensmith had left his donkey jacket behind a long time ago; he had had a political make-over to polish his accent and tidy up his hitherto scraggy hair; and slowly he had climbed the ladder of responsibility under the guise of popular respectability. He showed himself at football matches and often made charity appearances on the government television channel; he had kept his nose politically clean for a decade, and now, thought Peterson, the dividends would pay handsomely. He nodded as he caught the sub-text of Greensmith's calm rhetoric. The "working class" had been replaced by the "-working people", the class struggle by the "fight against poverty", communism and socialism by "community"; but there was also the age-old tirade against "selfishness", "profit", and "materialism". Roger was filmed with a host of supporters behind him as he was leaving his London office. Peterson studied the crowd behind him for its cohesiveness and sense of solidarity. Good, they all looked supportive. He caught a movement of someone behind the small crowd and laughed. There was Diane Taylor evading the press and making her way to her car no doubt.

Then the news turned to Laurenten. Peterson snorted as he watched the images filmed earlier of Laurenten's news conference. Goodness! Next to him sat the leader of the Opposition. This was a Tory plot after all, Peterson laughed to himself. Oh, this would be so much easier! There was Vincent Harrison as well. And the government channel had demoted the issue to the third news slot. Good, good. The newscaster was filling in the main details of Laurenten's earlier announce-ment before giving access to Laurenten's own voice.

"... the countryside is facing a protracted campaign of nationalisation. But it's not just about landowners - it's about freedom. City people are saddled by high taxes and stringent regulations and licences; that will only get worse over the coming years unless we stand up to the Westminster government and say, 'hands off'. What the Assembly is proposing is ... " The newscaster's voice then interposed to explain that the government had just rushed through legislation denying Laurenten - as a terrorist - freedom of speech on the airwaves. Laurenten continued speaking but the engineers cut his voice.

"Lord Laurenten then went on to propose a full secession from the Westminster government," concluded the newscaster. The programme then showed footage of the DEFRA building that had been torched by Laurenten's supporters before moving onto sports news.

Peterson got up and raised his glass to a picture of Karl Marx he had next to his study door. "Soon, my brother soon!" A buzzer interrupted this libation. He sighed, and put down his glass and with a heavy step left his flat. He knocked on the neighbouring door and let himself in.

"Mother? Are you alright?"

A voice from the bedroom beckoned him in. "Bernie! I've been watching the news all day. It's thrilling, isn't it?"

He approached his bed-ridden mother and sat next to her. She pressed a button on the control unit which raised her to her son's level. Her thinning curly white locks needed washing, he thought. The room's smell of urine and lavender overpowered other guests, but Peterson was used to it. The services were due in an hour and when she was in the bath, Peterson would open the windows and change the sheets for her. He would sometimes stay and read the papers or a novel to her; but tonight, he knew that their conversation would be purely political. He reached a hand over to pull her cover up. Her hand shot down and gripped his arm as it had done decades before when she was an able-bodied, determined union activist in the health service and he was a tearaway eight-year-old. The physical pressure was not painful, but the intensity of it still shocked him.

"Bernie. This is what I have lived for. A time like this. And you will see it through. We shall have our glory indeed, my son!" Her green eyes still possessed an unnatural intensity that had attracted many lovers in her life; he was the product of one such liaison.

"Have you made your contacts?"

"Of course. Most are now operative." He gently prised her fingers off his arm.

"Good! Finally! Finally! Finally!" She clapped her hands and a shimmer of her former fiery youthfulness passed across her face. "Oh, Bernie, I never thought that I would ever see this day!"

"Nor I, mother."

"I would like to be in the great march! Oh, I would love to be there with you, my son. Is it possible?"

"Of course. I shall arrange transportation and an electric wheelchair for you. You shall be at the head of the people's delegation."

"Dress me in my red shawl too! I always wore it when a strike was called. Oh, Bernie, this is a day I shall never forget. So many opportunities. I saw Roger speaking earlier. He hasn't changed, has he?"

"No, mother. A smarter PR department, that's all."

"Good, because we need people like him. Cramp will soon be ousted, and the people of Britain will finally fly the red flag!" She took his arm again and stroked it tenderly. "Oh, Bernie, keep me informed, won't you? Will David be coming?"

Her lucidity had passed. David Huxall had died three decades before. Peterson smiled and told her that he might find it difficult getting to her. He wished he could have the kind of conversation they had had when he was a teenager, when she knew the top thinkers and agitators and was in regular contact with Communist proponents and leaders from around the world. He patted her hand. "Who would you like to hear about tonight, mother? Rosa Luxemburg? Clara Zetkin?"

"Rosa, my boy, Rosa. Always Rosa. Remind David when you speak to him that I have one of his books."

"I shall, mother." He picked up the book lying on the dressing table and commenced reading.

WILLIAM VENATOR

The Ambassadors

A week later a black Range Rover pulled up outside Athington Manor in Hornshire, the chosen venue for a clandestine meeting between the Prime Minister of the Westminster government and Ambassadors Peter Hickling and John Stewart from the seceding Republican Assembly.

The usual heavy late-autumnal weather had broken, and a westerly breeze had blown the previous weeks' clouds away. The early morning mist gathered around the neo-classical park of the manor house as the escorted cavalcade entered the grounds off the quiet country road. It stopped at a check post in front of the main gate manned by six soldiers of the North Hornshire Rifles. Their cards were checked and the Prime Minister was allowed through.

"What's that mean?" asked Damien Blunderton, the thin, bald and bearded Home Secretary glimpsing the motto in the wrought-iron gates.

The driver read out the words. "'Crudellismus est libertas homo adimere.'"

"No idea," said Cramp. "Some Latin nonsense. I hated Latin at school."

"I remember," said Blunderton. "You used to write rude words on the desk, but you got the grammar wrong, so you soon got bored."

"Yes, yes. That teacher, what was his name? Mr Martin. That was him. Yes, he used to mock me for my poor grammar. No fun after that."

"It means, sir," said the driver, "'there is no greater cruelty than to take away a man's liberty.'"

Blunderton and Cramp looked at one another. "I say, did you go to public school?" asked Cramp.

"No, sir. I went to a comprehensive. We weren't allowed to take Latin, since it was deemed elitist. I've since learned that it is rather useful. I read a lot of history, sir. So I taught myself Latin."

"Good for you," remarked Blunderton. "I can't read it for toffee."

"It is elitist," cavilled Cramp's wife, Jerri. "Children should not be taught anything that will divide them in later years."

The driver glanced and her and shrugged. He pulled the car up in front of the main door. Six people emerged from the doorway to escort the ministers and their assistants. They invited them into the house, where they were greeted by Peter Hickling and John Stewart. Cramp and Blunderton had been told that their aides would be taken to the main hall for coffee; that was to be followed by meetings with several Members and Delegates of the Assembly to discuss appropriate joint policy arrangements. Cramp and Blunderton were shown to the drawing room and were seated at a small table with Stewart and Hickling.

Hickling had met neither politician before and their entrance initially unnerved him. Two of the most famous people of the land were now sitting opposite him, but he could rely on Stewart's earlier advice to treat them like a bank's clients who had surreptitiously overextended their debt through dubious accounting means. Hickling had been party to several such meetings with hitherto powerful businessmen, so he was mentally fully armed to take on the Westminster Prime Minister and his sidekick.

"Mr Cramp, and Mr Blunderton," began Stewart.

"No, please, call us Hugh and Damien. That's how we run our cabinet, isn't it Damien? First names - much more friendly, and, you know, get along with one another."

"We're not in your cabinet, Mr Cramp. We sit on neutral territory. Now, call me old-fashioned, but I believe important meetings should retain a formal air to them." Stewart had already noted that neither minister was wearing a tie, and had commented to Hickling on the presence of the Prime Minister's wife. "The man just does not understand etiquette, does he?" he had growled. Both Stewart and Hickling were clothed appropriately, and Stewart's cutting comments and his damning Presbyterian glare made Cramp and Blunderton feel awkward. The two of them felt like two undergraduates who had finally been pulled up by the principal for a series of misdemeanours and plagiarism.

"Right, whatever you say, Mr Stewart. I'll go with that. Fine by me."

"We've come to discuss this silly business," Blunderton began.

Stewart glowered. "There's nothing silly about it, Mr Blunderton. The country has lost its direction and we're seeking to put it right."

"On whose authority?" demanded Blunderton folding his arms.

"Moral authority," replied Stewart.

Cramp looked at Blunderton and then at Stewart. "But you have no legitimacy."

"Liberty does not require legitimacy," said Hickling. "It does not need any statesman or referendum to give it credence. Freedom stands by itself."

"Look, I'm Prime Minister. I was voted in by the population of this country to head Her Majesty's Government, to govern this land. I cannot broker any negotiations with renegades."

"I'm sure you wouldn't wish to," quipped Stewart. "But let's get one thing straight. We are not here to negotiate. Liberty is not negotiable."

Cramp and Blunderton stared at the other two. Through years of international negotiations with the good, the bad, and the ugly of global politics, neither of them expected to hear such confident and challenging words from a compatriot. The word "liberty" was something that the Palestinians or Central American Marxist-indoctrinated freedom fighters bandied around. They really had no conception of the word's meaning, but knew that it always bought guilt money from European states, who were also keen on knocking American foreign policy. It was a word that had become associated with so many particular interests and hence smokescreens for tribal or political gains, that both of them had learned to ignore its emotional attraction.

Hickling leant forward. "Mr Cramp, just over three hundred years ago this land produced a Bill of Rights that sought to restrain the powers of the monarchy. It's hardly taught in schools today, thanks to the gradual socialization of the school system, but that document, or rather, the set of ideas that that document epitomised must not be forgotten. This land taught the world what freedom meant. Freedom can only mean the absence of aggression against the individual. In its purest form, the corresponding political philosophy is one which restricts the activities of government to a bare minimum - looking after the law of the land, which in turn reflects the moral authority that a man's life is his own."

"What about women?" interjected Blunderton, reeling from the early playing of the sacred trump card.

Stewart considered whether he was being serious or not. "Mr Blunderton, I am sure that your excellent educational background - your attendance at top public school and Cambridge University - did not fail to explain to you the rudimentary grammar of this land's language with respect to style, collective nouns and prepositions?" He shook his head as Hickling continued.

"A man's life is his own. He belongs neither to his fellow man nor to society. He is free to choose as he sees fit, except that he may not aggress against others."

"What about the ethnic population?" demanded Blunderton. "Are they free? We're making them free - we've introduced legislation ... "

Cramp cut him short with a wave of his hand. "But you have assaulted my minister, John Jones."

"Alan Jones," whispered Blunderton.

"Alan Jones. You have kidnapped him. What kind of moral authority is that?"

Hickling explained softly. "Mr Jones is being held for his aggression against the rural peoples of this land."

"He was a viably elected official," shouted Cramp.

"But that does not give him the right to take away anyone's liberty."

"Parliament is sovereign, and that means we can make whatever laws we choose," argued Cramp.

"Nonsense," said Stewart. "You are a man, just like me or Mr Hickling here. The fact that a caucus of people voted you leader of your party, or even if a majority of the British people voted for you - which they did not - does not give you any justification to take any man's liberty away, so long as he is not guilty of transgressing against another."

"The security of individual freedom should be the proper responsibility of the Home Office," added Hickling, "not a panoply of laws that assumes the entire population is guilty."

Blunderton clenched his fists. "The police need access to information, otherwise they will not be able to apprehend criminals."

Stewart retorted, "How did they do it in the past, Mr Blunderton? Effort. They did not assume that the innocent were guilty, as your government has been doing."

"Look," said Cramp, leaning forward in a conciliatory manner. "We're all members of society. We all are the product of society and what we do is a product of society."

"Exactly! You believe that no one is responsible for his own actions, hence we're all guilty. We all possess some maniacal form of original sin, because we were born into a society. Nonsense, man. That is why this land has withered under successive governments and why it is presently falling apart." Stewart drummed his words into the table with his index finger. "And that is precisely why we are seceding. You may keep your communitarianism and the belief that none is innocent, but we are exercising our right not to belong to your regime."

"Is this because we're banning your hunting?" asked Blunderton.

"Oh! Partly," chafed Hickling, affronted by Blunderton's ignorance. "The ban is symptomatic of your general philosophy that abhors independently-minded people pursuing their own lives as they see fit. You want to have a social worker for everybody; you want each newborn child to be catalogued and filed for every moment of its waking life; you want to follow the movements of the entire population; you assume every person is some incontinent idiot who cannot understand what contracts he makes or what education is good for his children, or what programmes he ought to watch. That," Hickling said exasperated at the vision he was creating, "is what we are reacting against - and we are reacting against it in a morally proper way. By turning our backs on it and forging our own lives as we see fit."

"But you're imposing your views of liberty on other people," said Blunderton, recalling a comment he had once heard in an undergraduate tutorial.

Stewart laughed. "That is why we are leaving your government. You just don't get it. We can muster hundreds of thousands of people to wave the message in front of your face and you just don't get it!"

"Get what?" asked Cramp.

Stewart fulminated, "Freedom! It means 'piss off and mind your own business!'"

"Being free," Hickling added, "means being able to choose your own life, Mr Cramp. Freedom rejects the initiation of force in any manner and from any individual. We celebrate individualism and plurality; regardless of your sound bites, you worship uniformity and collectivism. You do not wish to permit people to choose for themselves ... "

"They are incapable of choosing for themselves," said Blunderton disdainfully.

"But you are not?" queried Stewart. "What makes you so different?"

Cramp sat back and crossed his arms. "Look, this nation's at war."

"Whose nation? We do not recognise your government, Mr Cramp," said Hickling.

"I don't give a damn about what you think," said Cramp angrily. "I'm the Prime Minister of this land, and your cessationary idiots are flaunting the laws of the land!"

"You'll find that we are secessional, and that we are not flaunting anything, except if you say that we are flaunting our right to live our own lives as each one of us sees fit," responded Stewart gravely.

"You are endangering this land," said Blunderton calmly. "We have had a week of mass disobedience and disruption to our major cities and ports by farmers, fishermen, and hunt supporters. Your way leads to chaos."

"And ours," Cramp interrupted, "is the way of peace and order."

"For whom?!" demanded Stewart slamming the table. "You're not of the generation that witnessed the war first hand, but I can tell you this land fought for and secured its freedom from tyranny. Oh yes, it was beguiled by the socialist doctrine that the poor could be made free by nationalising education and medicine and any major industry that possessed enough capital to attract envious eyes. Oh yes, the socialists described the poor as in chains, but they put the poor in chains by denying their freedom to get on with their own lives. And whenever the poor have got richer, your lot have come along and redefined them as 'rich', 'bourgeois', or 'middle class' and increased taxes on them, just to keep them down; or you've demolished their choice in education and health by undermining the private sector; you've had the children of this nation indoctrinated in state schools for generations now - but not indoctrinated in anything as useful as an ideology, oh no, you're too clever for that. You've indoctrinated them in ignorance - you have paraded a crass ignorance by deriding our land's heritage and freedoms. And when the illiterate fools become of voting age, you promise to sort their mistakes out. Well, there are enough people in this land who can see through what's been happening, even if you don't. Now we are giving a voice and a new path to those people. Your kind only want power - you used to be priests but you had to change your appearance. You play the same tunes though."

"But you're not even promising them the vote!" cried Cramp. "Democracy is built on voting, and I agree, if I had been elected by less than what it would have taken to get me elected into office, you know, like I was, then I'd be all for a referendum - a vote, you know; but the fact is I was elected and you were not."

"Election to office does not give any man, or woman," Hickling added for Blunderton, "the right to abuse that power."

"But we are reflecting the will of the people," said Cramp opening his arms wide in sincerity.

"There is no such thing as the 'will of the people'," said Hickling. "Each person has his own will, and that means there's a plurality of wills."

"But there are common grounds," said Blunderton. "Commonalties that enable us to govern the land how the majority, let's say, see fit."

"Freedom is not negotiable, Mr Blunderton," insisted Hickling. "That means it is not negotiable with you, the Prime Minister, your government, the European Commissioners, or a mob."

"End of story," added Stewart closing the meeting. "We are proclaiming our right to live in liberty, and thereby shrugging off your burdens and impositions."

Heart of Darkness

Warbler sat drinking a mocha and reading The Times in the busy chrome-infested café. He saw Mark McLaren arriving for their meeting and waved him over.

"Our work is almost done," said Warbler, stubbing out his cigarette to shake hands.

"How can you tell? It's chaos out there."

"Exactly what the professor ordered. You get no honey if you don't disturb the bees' nest. Read your history, dear Mark. Events like this take on their own momentum for a while. Clears the dead wood, you know?"

"Jones?"

"Of course. And many others like him who are too petty and small to conceive of real power."

Mark nodded. He stroked his thin goatee and called a waitress over to order a coffee.

"It's all in the ideas, you know," continued Warbler.

Mark raised a studded eyebrow. The diamond glinted in the beam from a halogen light.

"The groundwork for the new era has been done. People are too thick and too unversed in thinking to even know what's been happening. But when a crisis arises, they turn to what they know. And what they know is exactly what you and I and our friends have been telling them to think. Man's nothing. The planet's everything. But, ultimately, Mark, and this is the bit I quite enjoy, for really, your animal rights theology is mere bullshit in comparison."

The waitress arrived and Mark accepted his coffee. He stirred his coffee and frowned.

"I believe in animal rights," he remarked petulantly.

"Of course you do - you have to. You're one of the new men that people look up to and listen to. Cool, rich, fashionable, smooth, great connections, often in the media." Warbler surveyed the café. The drumming synthetic noises irritated him but he knew he had to submit to the hymns of the new age, at least in public. He rubbed his forehead and leant forward.

"Mark, I didn't say the cause was bullshit, but that it was bullshit in comparison to what we've created. I must get you to read your history and philosophy. Why don't you come and study with me? Lucy would surely be more than generous to the campus - think about that too. We could create the new intellectual headquarters for the animal rights movement. My god, you have enough money to start your own university. We could be picky from the beginning about who we hire." He pulled out another cigarette and passed one to Mark. "The world's our oyster. It's ripe, Mark. We're in the vanguard and we are just about to seize powers beyond your dreams."

"How? I mean, you're constantly harping on about achieving power. But how? I don't get it."

"Guilt! My boy! Guilt! It's the fucking secret of the philosopher's stone! If you make 'em feel guilty for living, for Christ's sake, you've got them by the nuts. I was young when the new campaign started in the '70s and it was too pathetic for words. All they needed was a little tweaking," he pinched his forefinger and thumb together and showed Mark a twisting motion. "A little tweaking and we had them over on our side almost by default. Kids! Ah. The kids, Mark. Your mother and her friends have been very generous in getting the propaganda into the west's schools."

Mark nodded. He recalled reading the books his mother had signed in bookstores and he was dragged along to the talks she had given.

"Fortunately for us," he took a long drag, "the school system killed their intellect years ago. They are ripe, Mark. They don't know what's hitting them. Once we're through this chaos, they'll recognise our language, our ideas, and hence our policies as familiar. All tied together by guilt."

"Is that because we emphasise so much about how man destroys his environment?"

"That's the mantra. That's the rosary. That's your Book of Common Prayer. But we're going deeper, Mark. Straight to the core of man's soul and we'll own it. The Soviet system failed because it permitted some elitism - in music and athletics. We'll be building a system which doesn't even give a glimmering hope for plebeian heroism. We'll be the new Spartans and we'll enjoy our domain over the pathetic helots. We've already conquered them intellectually - they're so softened up with commercialism, regulation, and sentimentality for animals, that they'll all just lie down and think of how great we rulers all are. We'll enjoy the fruits of their labour and we'll wield power as we see fit. Oh, it's intoxicating Mark. Waitress, can I order a sandwich please? Mark? Okay, let's have a gander. No one knows us here - how about two beef-and-horseradish salad sandwiches on granary bread? Okay - two of those. And more coffee, thanks, love."

Mark put his cigarette out and ran his fingers through his long hair. "Guilt. I think I'm beginning to understand. You feel guilty, you'll do anything."

"In the long run, yes. Meanwhile, guilt makes them politically manipulable, shall we say? You listen to Cramp's speeches he's giving at the present. First he introduces fear. Fear makes people sit up and listen. Think of all the fearful fairy tales Lucy read to you. That's it - opens your eyes to the incredible. It also focuses your attention on the leader, who becomes your saviour. There we have you a little. Then after the fear comes the patriotic roll call - the reminder that 'we' - not 'you' or 'me' - we are powerful if we work together. Fits in with most of what we know, doesn't it? Now he goes for the jugular, and plays the guilt card. We've got too much. We destroy so much. We are not perfect. If we don't work together, we lose everything - not just our children's education, but the whole fucking planet; if we don't make our sacrifices, we are nothing. Guilt, guilt, guilt. Most of the philosophers knew its power and very few ever stood up to it. The priests were the practitioners, the reapers of humanity's souls." The sandwiches arrived, Warbler grinned at the waitress and gave her a fiver as a tip. She thanked him and left.

"We all want some of its rewards, you see. We want to be on top of the puppet show, pulling the strings, manipulating the masses with record-breaking guilt trips. You and I don't sacrifice. No, we're above it. The people though, need us to tell them how to sacrifice. Rather convenient really."

Mark smiled. "So do we get positions in the government?"

"No, leave that to the mugs. No, we'll be manipulating the politicians - with our ideas, you see. What do we want? What do we really want, Mark? Fuck the animals - we want power. We want to say, 'give up your pets,' and people will give them up. We want to say, 'bow to the trees,' and they will bow to the bloody trees. In other words, Mark, we say, worship us. And they worship us. The fucking population is so clueless, they'd believe anything. So, we're filling that vacuum." He chortled. "Megalomaniacs just love a vacuum!"

"What about this secession?"

"Yeah - that's an issue all right. A really outdated bloody ideology that's proving a damn nuisance. Can you arrange more attacks?"

"Our hit on the Laurenten Hunt was a success, I believe," Mark whispered leaning forward. "We've done reconnaissance of Laurenten's grounds and we're ready to hit him soon. Again, it will look like Westminster anti-terrorist police action. After all, that's what Cramp keeps saying. So we're helping him a little - as you suggested. We're targeting hunters' homes again this weekend. This time, we don't care if they're in. And, following your suggestion, we'll be attacking Cramp's country house too."

"Good. Get him riled so he really lays the boot into the fucking republican movement."

"But will we get the people on our side?"

"Jeeze, yeah. Look at the press coverage of the DEFRA building burning. Now that took me by surprise, but just look at how the press has come down on the Rural Alliance. Add to that all the pictures taken of huntsmen shooting saboteurs, avoiding of course the killing of hunt supporters, and they're well on their way into our fold. It's like chess. But first you have to get the pieces to agree to be on the board. Once they're there, then they're all yours."

"And Cramp?"

"Who the fuck cares? Whoever's in power, we'll have them in our pockets. Just enough to push the legislation we want as highly paid special advisers." He grinned. "Hugh's already offering me a committee position to 'look into hunting and sexual discrimination,' with the view of retroactively fining the hunt community for past sexual discrimination, heh heh. It's becoming as priceless as American claims for past injustices. Heh, heh," he laughed, and choked on some lettuce. "Uh uh, 'scuse me. Stick with me, Mark, and you'll be special adviser on ecological matters to HM Government and then the UN, if you want it."

Mark snickered. "Yeah, that'd be fucking cool."

"All yours. You just keep the pumps primed with mum's money, and I'll do the intellectual footwork. Remember - guilt pays. Who said that recently?" He scratched his chin. "Oh, yeah, that limey arse, Peterson. Oh, how close he was, hah," he chuckled.

"How long will this process take?"

"Not long. But we are dealing with a country that knows how to fight for liberty, though it's almost forgotten it. The traditions are strong in the countryside and with the older people. But we've been destroying their base for decades. They'll crumble. Europe will be a pushover after Britain. America will be a tough nut outside of the cities, but if Britain goes our way and rids itself of vast quantities of planet-destroy-ing capital, America will follow." He twisted his lips as if he were not thoroughly secure in his optimism. "Guilt, Mark. Just keep pushing the guilt trip."

"So, the chaos we're creating will demand new leaders?"

"May do. But what'll be important is that it will produce opportunities for all of our supporters who are waiting to climb the ladders of power. You'll see - we have allies who are presently unknown. Someone will inevitably climb to the top, but we want them in our hands. D'you get it? Good, because whoever gets there will need us for direction. Oh, Mark, this will be good. Well, got to go see Hugh-boy."

Warbler got up and smirked. "Man thought he gave up the gods, Mark. He just didn't know their new names."

Amanita Virosa

It was ten days before the Assembly got round to finalising tasks and jobs for Members, Delegates and supporting institutions. Over those days the Assembly divided into committees, and Laurenten and other executive Members supervised the discussions. A new treaty was publicly announced to a bemused and then concerned country, establishing the Assembly's constitutional position and outlining its aims.

The nation, from what could be gathered from the media coverage, at first thought it was a joke, then a silly notion, but by the third day, with the country falling into more chaos with anti-capitalist rioters exploiting the disruption in the country and practically sacking the capital, they had accepted its existence with some major papers coming over to support its aims. The day that the Assembly published its proposals to form a republic and to return sovereignty to the traditional laws of the land, the powers in Westminster derided the proposal and the government controlled and influenced media ridiculed the measures. A host of organisations that called themselves independent, but that actually received most of their funding from the British and European governments, attacked the secession. However, as the United Kingdom divided, opinion polls suggested that a third of the nation's people would support the fledging republic and about half wanted to know more. Moreover, sixty per cent of the nation thought that the Westminster Prime Minister should make more appearances on the leading soap opera, and seventy per cent liked the England football captain's new hairstyle. Nonetheless, the attractiveness of flat-rate taxes swung many who were not polled and who were sick of hard-earned money being expropriated for frivolous expenditures and being thrown at failing services. The Assembly Citizenship Registration lines and web pages were overwhelmed with applications to join.

Guests at Stanthorpe watched television images of rioting and looting in the major industrial cities. Motorways were jammed by tractors and Land Rovers, most being co-ordinated by the Assembly to cause low levels of havoc. Where government had intervened most in people's lives - in the inner cities - the violence was worse. Organised groups were co-ordinating the struggle against freedom, but following the break down in local control, the fighting took on its own momentum and the police began to pull out to let people stew in their own mess.

Law and order returned swiftly to the republican lands, especially after the right to bear arms was restored and harsh penalties introduced for any criminal activity. The republican territories enforced the law properly, which surprised political commentators and bureaucrats and rather upset criminals who were used to more lenient procedures and sentences. The Westminster government criticised the initial high number of gun casualties in the republic, but its regions continued to suffer from rioting, looting, and pillaging despite the Home Secretary's initiatives and the Prime Minister's attempts at cajoling the people to be nice to one another.

On the eleventh day, Miles and Cosima drove back to Todthorpe. The lodge was going to be used as a secondary HQ, along with the manse in Scotland, until the nation settled down to its new political realities and the old Parliament building in Northchester was renovated.

A gentle wintry wind rustled the trees as they left Stanthorpe. The first snows had dusted the moors and hills. The roads were deserted except for wandering sheep, but Cosima and Miles saw evidence of army manoeuvres from the tracks left at various gates and hamlets. The villagers had placed a blockade on the road and put up signs to warn off intruders entering the village after five o'clock at night, and all visitors were advised to report to Sergeant Morris to ensure their safety. Any movements around the village after that were deemed suspicious, Mr Fowler, the armed farmer manning the post explained to them.

"Are you alone out here?" asked Miles who was driving.

"No sir, there be a couple of proper army lads right behind me. In case there's trouble, like."

Cosima leant over and asked if he had experienced any trouble yet. Fowler replied that the village had had snoopers around in the evenings, but no one had been attacked or burgled.

"All the villagers are on their guard and a dozen men and women take their turns in patrolling the streets. After what happened with your hunt, miss, we can't be taking anything for granted, least of all our peace."

They wished him luck and drove down into the village. The frosty air bit their cheeks as they left the car to seek Price and Coates in the inn. The men were sat waiting for them; both were armed with shotguns, which they had casually left on the bar next to their drinks. They exchanged greetings and Cosima asked after the lodge, which Coates and Price took turns to visit. She had been worried about the animals, but Coates, who had just returned said there was nothing to fear. They were all in good health. He had taken a vet out to Sebastian last week and he was recovering well.

"I see the standard is flying well on the church spire," said Cosima. "It looks beautiful."

"Aye, missy," replied Coates. "We've commissioned a new one off old Mrs Hume. We're thinking of keeping it out all the time now. Just as a reminder."

"Did the police ever sort out what happened with the hunt?" she asked.

"No. As far as Morris can tell, it was a mercenary group. Not related to Westminster at all," said Price.

"That's as far as we've understood as well," Cosima nodded. "There are well-funded groups out there that are capable of fighting their own wars. We have to be vigilant."

"You mean trust nobody?" asked Miles.

"No. Not for a long time. Father said this was a phoney war. Apart from the riots and banditry, the proper war has yet to start."

Price leant against the bar. "Then all hell breaks loose?"

"Let loose the dogs of war," quipped Coates.

"Probably," said Cosima. "We have to ride over to the lodge later. We shall set off at dusk. We need to avoid prying eyes. Father's employed Beatrice Major to arrange for defences and protection for the village and lodge, but they can't afford to release the resources until next week."

"You be careful, missy," said Coates. "Why don't you drive over?"

"Firstly, we may get stuck in the snow that's forecast. Secondly, I don't wish to draw attention to our movements by driving a hulking diesel-powered Range Rover through the forest. George Fowler said there had been snoopers in the village."

"Aye. And around. I saw some torch beams last night before the snowfall," noted Price.

"And I saw some the night before when I was patrolling Cuttings Coverts," added Coates.

"You'll be taking guns, I hope,"

"Of course," Cosima replied. They spent the afternoon discussing the new republic with the two men and the other villagers. All were concerned for their safety but felt that they could protect themselves should they need to. Morris dropped in to explain to the village what he had been up to and how he was preparing for their defence; after all, he explained, he was more directly employed by the village now and wanted to ensure that they thought him competent.

They prepared the horses for the evening trip and headed out as the light faded and the church bells tolled the voluntary curfew. Morris and Price escorted them for a couple of miles before turning back to do their four hour patrol around the village perimeter.

They rode in silence, their ears tuned for any artificial sounds or for heavy movements in the woods and coppices. A light snow fell as they rode up a shallow hill to the view that they had previously enjoyed in the daylight, when they had set out for the village from the lodge. The low clouds and snow reduced their vision, but far in the distance they could make out the orange glow of the local town of Burnford lighting up the clouds. In between lay a barely visible vast landscape of spinnies, hedgerows, cottages and hamlets, of heath, moor, and farmland. It was the source of the nation's original wealth and of independent characters and eccentrics throughout the ages; its productivity had enabled millions to move to the cities and to flourish there; its beauty had enabled men and women from all backgrounds to seek solace, redemption, and inspiration; its traditions interwove with the ebb and flow of human migrations; and its form changed with human technologies. But in recent decades the town had turned its back on the land. The new masses, five or more generations removed from their farming forebears, turned their backs on their history and hence on the source of their own freedom. In worshipping urban mammon, they sought to impose convoluted and distorted images of nature on the people who lived on the land; but in doing so, they did not realise that they were similarly chaining themselves to tyranny.

"When man believes he is inferior to an animal his moral and intellectual progress is doomed," said Miles quietly. Cosima nodded and reached out and squeezed his hand.

As they sat enjoying a few moments' rest, the orange glow of the town suddenly diminished and then disappeared. Laurenten had told them that various towns along the borders might be targeted. "The republic will have its say and remind the city folk that they are closer to nature than they think," he had said.

"The neon dome has gone," said Miles.

"I'm sorry?"

"Something Mr Wakeman said. He calls cities 'neon domes'."

"Good description," replied Cosima. "The civil war has begun."

Epilogue

Excerpt from an article written by Miles Thomson published in several magazines shortly after civil war broke out.

The end of the Cold War did not see the end of invasive government. On the contrary, bureaucracies proliferated, and accordingly, Britain became more regulated, taxed, licensed, and monitored than ever before ... The path we take is forged by the ideas that we subscribe to, but when people do not lift their heads from their navels, they end up being towed by the loudest voices around them. In the clamour for their minds - that is, in the clamour for their bodies, their energy, and their souls - the loud voices never fail to demand slavery. Their words change, their sincerity remains the same; their phrases adapt, their goal remains the same: to take from you that which you work for, to take from you your highest values ... They tell you that you must live for your neighbour and that you must sacrifice yourself (your money, time, energy, happiness) for your neighbour. The story is as old as the hills: feeling guilty for asserting your own identity and freedom; but wherever there is sacrificing, there is always a reaper ... that is why this republic broke away from Westminster ...

The hunt became a symbol of man's own natural and philosophical stature ... it also incidentally and swiftly became a symbol for man's liberty in the face of intrusion and violence. Whilst watching the lights of Burnford go out as forces attacked Westminster's northern stronghold, I said out loud, "When man believes he is inferior to an animal his moral and intellectual progress is doomed." It was the product of many weeks' thinking and philosophising on what I was doing and where I was going. It was the result of my own experiences of animal rights activists and their intentions for humanity. They despised man and hence they despised themselves ...

Printed in the United Kingdom
by Lightning Source UK Ltd.
9464200001B